FINDING THE LOST

THE SENTINEL WARS

SHANNON K. BUTCHER

AN ONYX BOOK

ONYX
Published by New American Library, a division of
Penguin Group (USA) Inc., 375 Hudson Street,
New York, New York 10014, USA
Penguin Group (Canada), 90 Eglinton Avenue East, Suite 700, Toronto,
Ontario M4P 2Y3, Canada (a division of Pearson Penguin Canada Inc.)
Penguin Books Ltd., 80 Strand, London WC2R 0RL, England
Penguin Ireland, 25 St. Stephen's Green, Dublin 2,
Ireland (a division of Penguin Books Ltd.)
Penguin Group (Australia), 250 Camberwell Road, Camberwell, Victoria 3124,
Australia (a division of Pearson Australia Group Pty. Ltd.)
Penguin Books India Pvt. Ltd., 11 Community Centre, Panchsheel Park,
New Delhi - 110 017, India
Penguin Group (NZ), 67 Apollo Drive, Rosedale, North Shore 0632,
New Zealand (a division of Pearson New Zealand Ltd.)
Penguin Books (South Africa) (Pty.) Ltd., 24 Sturdee Avenue,
Rosebank, Johannesburg 2196, South Africa

Penguin Books Ltd., Registered Offices:
80 Strand, London WC2R 0RL, England

First published by Onyx, an imprint of New American Library,
a division of Penguin Group (USA) Inc.

First Printing, November 2009
10 9 8 7 6 5 4 3 2 1

Copyright © Shannon K. Butcher, 2009
All rights reserved

 REGISTERED TRADEMARK—MARCA REGISTRADA

*For Sara. I'm so glad you showed up
for the meeting that day.*

Acknowledgments

The writing process can be crazy, and I know I would have gone nuts these past few months if not for my beta readers: Sara Attebury, Dyann Barr, Julie Fedynich, Sherry Foley, Liz Lafferty and Jayne Lundy. Thanks for keeping me sane, giving me honest feedback and support, and sticking by my side despite your own busy schedules. You're all awesome!

Also in the awesome category are Nephele Tempest and Cindy Hwang for their endless professional support, and Leis Pederson for putting up with way too much e-mail from me without complaint. Thanks, ladies!

Chapter 1

Omaha, Nebraska
July 14

The little boy's frightened whimpers grew weaker by the second. Andra Madison could barely hear him now, even though her ear was pressed to a crack in the brick wall of the abandoned warehouse on the outskirts of Omaha. Those muffled, mewling sobs of fear broke her heart and made her want to tear the monsters who had kidnapped Sammy apart with her bare hands. Or blow them apart with her shotgun. That worked, too.

Even at three in the morning, the July air was still hot and thick with humidity, making it hard to breathe. Then again, maybe that was just her reaction to fear talking. There were at least four monsters in there guarding Sammy—twice as many as she'd ever managed to defeat before. And that battle had been a close call. She wasn't quite sure yet how she was going to get the boy out alive. She'd have to wing it, and pray for the best.

One of the monsters let out a deep growl that sent a jolt of primal fear ripping through her system. Sweat broke out on her forehead as she fought the urge to flee. She planted her boots hard and gritted her teeth until the need to run away washed over her and started to fade. She was left shaking and dripping with sweat, but at least she'd held her ground.

Andra knew just what these creatures were capable of—had seen it with her own eyes on more than one occasion—and the sound they were making now wasn't a good sign. The monsters were getting ready to feed.

The image of Sammy's small body being ripped to shreds by claws and teeth filled her mind and made her stomach heave. She couldn't let that happen. Not this time.

Andra had officially run out of time to scout the building and plan her attack. Plan or not, she had to get little Sammy out of there right now.

She hopped up three cement stairs and twisted the knob on the old warehouse door, but it was locked. Of course. The windows were too high for her to climb through, and she wasn't about to go wasting any time trying to find another way in. There was no time left, and she'd promised Sammy's parents she'd bring their baby home alive.

Stupid, stupid, stupid.

She never should have made promises she might not be able to keep, but when faced with so much fear and panic in the pleading eyes of helpless parents—so much love—she couldn't help herself. She'd foolishly wanted to give them hope.

After all the times she'd failed to find a stolen child, or rescue them before it was too late, she should have known better than to make any empty promises.

Andra took a deep breath for courage, said a quick prayer for luck, gripped her shotgun tight, and slammed the heel of her boot against the rotting door. Chunks of splintered wood burst into the giant room where Sammy was being held prisoner. Andra crouched low, using the frame of the door for concealment as she peered into the warehouse, frantically searching for some kind of plan that would get them both out alive.

It was dark in there, with only a few streaks of grimy yellow streetlight flowing in through the broken windows set high in the walls. The building was old, and it showed every one of its years in fallen beams and cracked mortar. Graffiti covered the walls, and trash was heaped in little mounds here and there. The wooden floor was filthy where it wasn't simply missing, leaving ragged holes to whatever space lurked below.

Along the far side of the room she saw Sammy. He was tied to one of the few columns still strong enough to hold up the roof. His eyes were huge with fear, and tears streamed down his face, leaving narrow lines of clean skin in their wake. A dirty rag had been stuffed in his mouth, but Andra could hear Sammy's pitiful whimpers coming from behind the gag. He was still alive, thank God. Now all she had to do was get him out of here in the same condition, and back home where he belonged.

Piece of cake. Or it would have been, had it not been for the hungry, salivating monsters standing between her and the boy.

Andra had been hunting these things for eight years and she still had no other word for them besides *monsters*. They were the size of large dogs, with the head of a wolf and the body of a chimpanzee. They had long, sharp claws and teeth to match. Oily, matted black fur covered their bodies, and long strings of glowing yellow saliva dripped from their too-wide jaws. And for reasons Andra still had not figured out, the creatures that kept these things as pets liked to steal children.

She didn't see any of those six-foot-tall insectoid monsters around, but she knew they wouldn't be far away from their precious pets.

Her explosive entry had pulled the monsters' attention away from the little boy and placed it squarely on her—a much better place for it, as far as she was concerned.

They prowled toward her on all fours, their long claws leaving ragged scratches in the old wooden floor.

Fear threatened to make her sluggish, and once again she had to fight back the urge to flee and leave the boy to fend for himself. She wasn't frightened easily, but these things had the ability to make her blood congeal and her breath freeze in her lungs. There was something unnatural about the fear they caused. It was more than just being face-to-face with so many claws and teeth. It was more than simply fearing for her life. There was some instinctive knowledge buried deep inside her that warned her that when she faced these monsters, she was facing something bigger and darker than she was able to imagine. And after all the things she'd seen, she had a pretty vivid imagination.

Andra forced herself to even out her breathing, stay calm, and focus on getting Sammy out alive. She shut out that unnatural fear and pretended she was just facing down rabid dogs. A terrified corner of her mind giggled at the ridiculous notion, but she ignored it as best she could.

Andra prayed her hands would stop shaking long enough to get a clean shot; then she stood from her crouch and leveled the shotgun at the largest of the beasts. There was still almost a hundred feet between her and them, and anything less than a point-blank shot would just piss them off.

So she stood there, just outside the doorway, where they could come at her only one at a time, and waited for the monsters to close the distance.

"We're close," said Logan.

"How close?" asked Paul. Excitement prowled through his system, making him grip the steering wheel tighter.

He glanced at the Sanguinar as he sped through the run-down industrial area on the edge of Omaha. Logan's eyes gave off an eerie silver glow in the darkness, and he was staring into the distance at something Paul could not see. He wasn't sure Logan knew what he was doing, but he sure as hell hoped so. Paul's future—his life—hung in the balance.

If they found the woman and she was *the one*, the power that had been building inside him for decades, and the pain it caused, would finally have an outlet.

"We've been driving all over the Midwest for days," griped Madoc from the backseat. "Fucking bloodsucker doesn't know what the hell he's doing. He's just jerking you around."

"You didn't have to come with us," said Paul. He didn't care much for the loner in the backseat. He took too many chances and wouldn't have recognized a team player if one had been sitting in his lap. He was the kind of man who left body bags in his wake. His only saving grace was that usually, the bad guys needed more of those body bags than the good guys did.

"Joseph decided otherwise."

"Since when do you follow orders?" asked Paul.

"I've got my reasons," said Madoc.

"Which are?"

"None of your fucking business. And, for the record, just because I'm here doesn't mean I don't think this is a load of shit. If it was so easy for Logan to find female Theronai, then why didn't we know about this particular skill a hundred years ago, before our men started dying off?"

"What if you're wrong?" asked Paul. "What if Logan can track Helen's bloodline and find more women like her?"

In the rearview mirror, Paul saw Madoc sneering at Logan. "We've been so busy following this supposed trail we haven't killed a demon in days. My sword arm's gonna be one big marshmallow by the time you figure out Logan's full of shit. He's leading you on for your blood, man. Don't you get that?"

It might be true. Paul knew it was possible. The Sanguinar were not the most trustworthy of men. Their need for blood made them . . . unpredictable. If Paul hadn't been so desperate to find a woman like Helen, he never would have bargained with Logan.

But he *was* desperate. The pain was becoming unbearable. He wasn't sure why his body didn't explode, why the power he housed didn't just rip through skin and bone and tear him apart. He was up to three hours of meditation every day just to be able to function, to get out of bed each night. He had only a couple of leaves left clinging to his lifemark, and at the rate they'd been falling, he wasn't sure his soul would live more than another ten days. After that, things would get ugly fast.

"Go left here," whispered Logan in a strained voice. "I've found her."

A bright bubble of hope swelled up inside Paul as he gunned the engine and took a hard turn. He blasted right through a stop sign, but it was past three a.m. and no one was around in this aging industrial area. Besides, if the cops wanted to ticket him, they'd have to catch him first.

"You sure?" asked Paul. "You've really found a blooded woman?"

"You're such a fucking sucker," spat Madoc in disgust. "There is no woman. We're going to show up and he's going to give you some story about how we just missed her, just like every other night this week."

Logan didn't respond to Madoc's accusation. His face was serene as he stared off into the night. His eyes flared brighter for a moment and he sucked in a harsh breath. "Hurry, Paul. She's not alone. I sense Synestryn."

Fear of losing the woman who could save him before he even found her made Paul's gut clench. He ground the accelerator to the floorboard just as he saw movement at the end of the street. There wasn't much light, but there was enough for him to make out the shape of a woman standing in a doorway. "There she is!"

"I don't fucking believe it," said Madoc.

Neither did Paul. Logan had actually tracked down a woman who might be able to save his life. A woman with some of the same blood running through her veins as Helen, who was the first female Theronai to have been born in over two hundred years. They still had no idea where Helen had come from, but after seeing the miracle she'd been for Drake, he hardly cared.

Paul screeched to a halt outside the old warehouse, nearly running the SUV into the metal railing that bordered the parking area. His headlights shone on the remains of a wide doorway and the woman standing in it. She was tall—nearly six feet—though maybe her commanding stance and the confident grip on her shotgun made her seem taller.

Paul had already unfolded himself from the car and unsheathed his sword when he saw two Synestryn demons—sgath—charging her, and two more behind them. Shotgun or not, she was no match for that many teeth and claws. They'd slice her to pieces before she had time to pull the trigger twice.

"Get out of there!" he shouted at the woman as he raced up three cracked cement stairs toward her. He could hear the heavy footsteps of Madoc and Logan pounding behind him.

She didn't turn to look at him, or even bother to acknowledge that she'd heard him. In fact, she showed no sign of the greasy, paralyzing fear the Synestryn usually caused in humans. She appeared to be completely calm, as if she waited for demons to attack her every day.

The sgath closed in to within fifteen feet and showed no signs of slowing. He was still too far away to help her. He was going to see her die before he even had a chance to touch her and learn whether she was meant to be his, whether she could save him.

She fired her shotgun at the closest sgath. Her body rocked slightly against the force of the weapon and the deep boom echoed in the stillness of the night. She'd hit one of the demons. It flew back a couple feet, spraying black blood across the warehouse. Beneath the thick, oily drops, the wooden floor began to sizzle as the caustic blood ate away at it.

If any of that blood had hit her, it would eat away her skin just as easily.

Paul finally reached the woman. He wanted to stop and touch her, but there was no time. Another sgath was right there, only feet away. Whether or not she could save him, the fact that she faced the sgath down without fear proved she was a rare gift and had to be protected at all costs.

Paul shouldered her out of the way and charged through the doorway, sword poised and ready to strike. She hit the wall a little harder than he'd intended and let out a pained grunt, but at least she was out of harm's way.

An uninjured sgath saw Paul charge and its eyes lit with a sickly green fire of excitement and hunger. It lifted its muzzle and let out a haunting howl to the rest of its kind, likely alerting them to the food that had just arrived. There was nothing the demons liked more than to feed on the flesh and blood of a Sentinel, and Paul and his companions were a walking feast.

It took Andra a couple of seconds to recover from being slammed into the brick wall. Good thing it had been her shoulder that had hit first instead of her head. Otherwise, she'd have been out cold. When this was over, she was going to have a long talk about manners with the man who'd pushed her, but right now she had to get Sammy out of here.

By the time Andra had shaken off the impact, two of the three men who'd shown up were already inside the warehouse. She wasn't sure who they were, or why they were here, but she wasn't about to question her good fortune. Or their swords.

The monster she'd shot was still on the floor, but it

was moving sluggishly, lapping up pools of its own blood with its long, forked tongue. She knew from experience that if it got enough of its blood back inside, the thing would stand up again, all patched up and good as new.

Andra couldn't help but shudder at the sight. It was one that was going to stick with her for a lot of nights to come.

Great. Like she needed any more nightmare fuel.

Another monster was backing away from the man who'd pushed her. He had dark blond hair and stark, angular features. He wielded a sword a little shorter than his arm, and from the muscular width of his shoulders and the ease with which he moved the weapon, it was obvious that he'd had plenty of practice with it. Thank God he was apparently on her side.

The monster crouched, then sprang up unnaturally fast, but the man was ready for the attack. He ducked below the monster's leap and swung the sword in a powerful arc that sliced open its belly. The man leapt aside gracefully, dodging the spray of filth and gore that spilled from the monster.

The thing landed with a wet, squishy sound and let out a roar of defiance as it tried to regain its footing. The man moved in what appeared to be an almost lazy circle, and his sword gleamed in a dim yellow arc of light. When he came to a stop, the head of the monster lay ten feet away from its body.

Black smoke rose up from where the thing's blood pooled on the wooden floor, burning it. The smoke created a stench so violent that Andra had to fight back the urge to puke.

"How we doing, Madoc?" asked the man, never moving his eyes from the remaining threat.

On the far side of the warehouse, Andra watched the second man—an angry-looking guy with blunt features and thick black hair—as he cut down another one of the monsters. He wasn't even breathing hard.

"One down, one to go," he said as he prowled closer
to the last monster standing. The thing had backed itself
into a corner, and Andra was pretty sure that it wasn't
going to make it back out alive.

"I smell more closing in," said a deep voice from behind her. Too close.

Andra jumped in surprise and whirled around, point-
ing her shotgun at the third man in the group. As she
laid eyes on him, her brain leaked out her ears and she
stood there, staring, unable to do anything else.

He was beautiful. Heart-stopping, seizure-inducing
beautiful, with dark hair, bright silvery eyes and a cover-
model face. He was a little thin for her taste, but he
made it work well enough that she changed her mind
right then and there.

He gave her a knowing smile full of bright white
teeth and said, "I'm Logan. My friends and I have been
looking for you."

Andra gave herself a mental shake and blinked so she
could stop staring at him. "I'm not taking on any new
cases right now. Kinda got my hands full with Sammy
here."

He frowned slightly in confusion and waved an elegant hand. "We'll talk later. Right now, we need to get
inside before the rest of the Synestryn show up."

Just then, Andra looked over his shoulder into the
surrounding darkness and saw the faint glowing green
eyes of more monsters closing in. "Right. Inside."

Andra peered through the door into the warehouse
and saw both men slicing and dicing the remaining monsters. They had their hands full at the moment, and Logan didn't look like he'd be much good in a fight as thin
as he was. In fact, he looked downright breakable, which
revved up her protective instincts.

Andra grabbed Logan and hauled him through the
door with her. She picked up the biggest part of the door
she'd wrecked and propped it across the open doorway.

Thank goodness she'd been hitting the weights lately or she never would have been able to lift the solid oak slab.

"Start shoving these old pallets in the way to slow those things down," she ordered Logan. "I'm going to get Sammy."

She sprinted across the floor, leaping over a gaping hole in the wood. They had only a few seconds before those new monsters arrived, and with any luck, they could free Sammy and find a back door out of this place before the nasties broke through the barricade.

She reached Sammy, but he was silent and staring off into space, which wasn't a good sign. His eyes were wide with shock and fear, and he cringed away from her as she approached. Tears still overflowed his eyes, and were so abundant they wet the collar of his pajama shirt.

Andra was wasting precious seconds, but she couldn't stand the thought of adding to his fear. She found a smile somewhere and forced herself to wear it. "It's okay, Sammy. Your mom and dad sent me. I'm here to take you home."

As gently as she could, she removed the dirty rag from his mouth and sliced through the ropes that bound him. It took only seconds, but by the time she was finished, the blond sword-wielding man was standing a few feet away, guarding her back.

The monster she'd shot and barely damaged was now lying in several sloppy pieces strewn across the warehouse floor. He'd done that for her, and from the black blood leaking out of the rest of the monsters, he'd done more as well.

"Are you hurt?" he asked her.

"No, but Sammy doesn't look good."

The man nodded once, as if he understood exactly what she meant. Then again, he seemed prepared for a fight like this. Maybe he did know what was going on here.

"I'm Paul. I'm going to get both you and the boy out of here alive."

It didn't sound like an empty boast. His words were solid and heavy with confidence.

"So, you've done this before, Paul?" she asked him in a conversational tone.

He turned and gave her a wink. "Once or twice. Stay well behind me. Their blood is caustic."

"I'm going to take Sammy and look for a back door."

"No. Stay where I can see you. There may be more hiding out in the building."

Andra thought about arguing and realized he could be right. She wasn't willing to risk it, especially since Sammy would be with her.

The first monster hit the barricade. The broken door and rotting pallets shifted easily.

Paul moved toward the barricade. The angry-looking man stepped up beside Paul, facing the threat. They both lifted their swords like they knew how to use them. Then again, there was proof of that fact scattered all over the warehouse floor.

The beautiful Logan moved to the back of the warehouse near Andra. "I'm going to go locate another exit. Paul and Madoc have handled worse than this before, but it pays to be prepared."

"Didn't you hear what Paul said? There may be more hiding in here."

"If so, I'll be able to smell them coming. Don't worry. I'm not one to risk my life needlessly." He smiled at her again, only this time she was pretty sure she'd seen fangs. Lovely.

Andra picked Sammy up and backed away until they were against the far wall. Whoever these men were, they weren't normal. Until she found out more, she wasn't going to let Sammy get close to any of them.

He let out a soft, hopeless whimper. Andra looked

down and he was staring back at her with unseeing eyes. She'd seen that exact look before on a night much like this one, and every week since, for the past eight years.

She was too late. Even if she got him out alive, Sammy was lost forever.

The monsters crashed through the barricade—two more of the wolf-chimpanzee things and two of the larger, roachlike monsters that kept them as pets. They were easily six feet tall and walked upright on short, spiny legs. Their tiny heads held four beady black eyes that zeroed right in on Sammy.

One of them let out a metallic hiss that sounded like the word *child*, then pointed toward Sammy and Andra. The other nodded, let go of the leash it held, and unfurled a wide pair of wings. It leaped up into the air and landed clinging to one of the warehouse support beams.

The furry monsters charged the pair of men while the second roach thing held back.

Andra set Sammy safely behind her and aimed her shotgun at the roach thing on the beam. She fired and her shot took a big chunk out of where the monster had been. Unfortunately, it had jumped out of the way, avoiding her blast. She scanned the ceiling as she reloaded, looking for it, but it was nowhere in sight. She heard a buzzing noise behind her and whirled around to find the roach thing flying right toward her and the boy.

She didn't have time to finish reloading and get off another shot. She grabbed the barrel of the shotgun and leveled it in front of her face to keep those snapping insect jaws away.

It slammed into her. She heard something crack and pain screamed up her arm. She screamed right back at it, unable to hold in her cry of agony. The weapon clattered to the ground, and Andra tried to bring her hands up to grab ahold of the roach's neck, but her left arm didn't respond. It hung uselessly at her side, burning with bone-deep pain that made her stomach spin.

She managed to get one hand against the roach's chest, but it was strong. It pushed her back easily, making her boots slide over the wooden floor. Sammy was being pushed back with her, his little body limp and rolling along behind her.

Andra took a quick look over her shoulder and saw that they were speeding toward one of those gaping holes in the floor. Sammy was going to fall first if she didn't do something.

Unfortunately, nothing came to mind.

A roar of outrage billowed up from somewhere in the room, but she couldn't figure out where it had come from, or what it meant. It was all she could do to stand upright and try to slow the thing down.

From the corner of her eye, she saw a metallic gleam flash past her; the roach thing's head flew off and its body started to fall forward.

Every beat of her heart made her arm throb, but she ignored it and put the last of her strength into shoving the roach thing to one side. It toppled over and hit the floor in a dry rattle.

"You okay?" asked Paul. His sword was coated in slime and the roach's head was rolling around near his feet.

She did a quick survey of the warehouse and saw only corpses. All of the monsters were dead, thanks to these men. She never would have survived tonight without them.

Andra nodded. "My arm's broken, but I'll live."

Now, if she could just stay upright and not crumple at his feet, that would be great. Very professional.

She focused on Paul in an effort to not think about the pain. His hair had the look of being perpetually mussed. He was several inches taller than Andra, which was no small feat, as she was five-ten barefooted. She could tell, even under his clothes, that he was muscular, but not so bulky that it hindered his movements. She'd seen his grace firsthand and had to admire anyone who could move that fast, that smoothly, while still looking like he was using no more effort than he did to walk down the street.

But more than any of that, it was his face that held her interest. He wasn't model beautiful like Logan. She wasn't even sure she'd call him handsome, but there was something in his face that intrigued her—drew her in. Weary lines framed his mouth as if he'd been through hell, but his stance was strong and steady. He might have suffered, but he hadn't been defeated.

Andra had nothing but respect for a man like that, which was foolish, because she knew nothing about him. The notion that she could read him by looking at his face was just plain stupid. Then again, stupid was the theme for the night.

Whoever he was, he'd saved her life tonight, and for that she was grateful.

"Thank you," she told him.

Paul reached toward her as if he were going to touch her face. "It's my pleasure."

"Don't," shouted Logan. "Not here. It's too dangerous. You know what happened to Drake once he touched Helen."

Paul's hand closed into a fist and he let it fall back to his side.

Maybe it had been her imagination, but the closer his hand got to her, the less her arm hurt. Now that he was backing away, the pain flared up again and she locked her knees to stay upright.

"It's bad, isn't it?" he asked her.

"It's not great," she admitted.

"I can help you," offered Logan. "Mend your arm and take the pain away."

"Touch her blood and you're a dead man," said Paul, his voice rough with menace.

Andra glanced at her arm, panicked that she might be bleeding. The monsters seemed to be able to smell her blood and it sometimes drew them to her. "What blood?"

"That's not what he meant," said Logan. "He's simply being a bit possessive."

"Drake warned us all about what you did to Helen. You're not going to do that to her."

Andra had no idea what they were talking about, but right now, she really didn't give a damn. She wanted to get Sammy out of here and get her arm set so that maybe it would stop making her sick with every throbbing heartbeat. "I really appreciate the fact that all of you were here tonight, and I hate to ask for more help, but there's no way I can drive. Can one of you guys drive my truck to the hospital and drop us off?"

"A hospital won't help the boy," said Logan. "But I can."

Andra didn't trust him. No one that pretty was human. As far as she knew, he was one of *them*.

She stepped in front of Sammy and gave Logan a level stare. "Stay away from him. He's my responsibility and you're not touching him."

"She's got good instincts. I'll give her that," said the angry-looking man.

Logan's voice dropped to a warning tone. "Stay out of this, Madoc. It doesn't concern you."

"It doesn't concern you anymore, either," said Paul. "Your job was to help me find her. Now you have."

"We have a bargain," said Logan.

"And I will uphold my end."

"I know. But what if she isn't the one? You haven't touched her yet."

Andra was hurting too much to keep up with their conversation. She knew she was at the center of it, but she had no idea why. And frankly, she couldn't bring herself to care right now. "Can we please get Sammy to the hospital?"

Logan looked like he was going to say something, but Paul spoke over whatever it was. "Absolutely." He knelt in front of the boy, but was still looking at her. "What's your name?"

"Andra."

"Andra what?" demanded the man they'd called Madoc. He had blunt features that looked like they'd crack if he tried to smile.

A wave of pain rushed over her and she had to grit her teeth to stay upright. Already, she could feel the skin below her shoulder starting to swell. "Madison," she grated out. "And just so we're clear, don't even bother asking for my phone number. I don't date guys who carry swords."

Truth was, she didn't date, period. She never had time, not with the recent increase in the disappearances of children across the Midwest. She was lucky if she found time to sleep and eat. More children disappeared every month and she needed to be available to find them.

Not that her efforts had done Sammy any good. Poor little guy was lost now—locked inside the terror that he'd seen tonight. At least she could tell his parents which facilities would care for him best. She'd researched them all.

"Logan," said Paul. "Fix her arm."

"Are you a doctor?" asked Andra.

"Not exactly," said Logan.

"Then you're not touching me. All I need is a lift out of here and we'll be on our way."

"I can mend the bone," said Logan. "It's a simple enough task so soon after a break."

As bizarre as that news was, as leery as she was of taking any more help from these not-quite-human strangers, Andra was tempted to accept their offer. Being in a cast for six weeks didn't sound like a lot of fun to her at all. Taking that much time off work wasn't going to be good for all the missing children, either. "How?"

"I'd simply reach inside you with my mind and put the pieces back together."

Andra was stunned silent for a moment. He sounded serious, a fact that creeped her out even more. "Right. I think I'm ready for that ride now."

"I wouldn't let him touch you if it wasn't safe," said Paul.

She breathed in too deeply and another sharp pain stabbed through her arm. "I don't know who or what all of you are, but I'm not sure I want to know more. As far as I'm concerned, this planet is already messed up enough as it is."

"She's not ready to accept us yet, Paul," said Logan. "Give her some time. Once the pain is too much, she'll give in."

Not likely, but then again, they didn't know her very well, so she could forgive his ignorance.

"If you change your mind," said Paul, "let me know."

"I won't. Just load Sammy into my truck, please."

Paul looked down at the boy with such compassion it made her chest ache. Clearly, he didn't know it was too late. *She* had been too late. She'd failed. Again. That failure raked through her, hurting worse than any broken bone ever could.

Maybe it was time to hang up her shotgun. Stop using her ability to find lost children for good this time. She tried to be stoic, but at times like this, it was hard. She wanted so badly to save them all.

"Hey, little guy," Paul said in a deep, soothing voice. One wide, battle-scarred hand ran over the boy's limbs as if checking for injury. On the man's left hand was a strange ring—a simple band that pulsed with color, swirling in an iridescent mix of baby rainbows. Andra had a hard time not staring at it.

"I'm Paul, and I just want you to know that you're

safe now. Nothing is going to hurt you. Not while I'm around."

And even as cynical as Andra was—even knowing the things she knew about just how many monsters roamed the night—she believed Paul was telling the truth. That alone was more incredible than the fact that real monsters existed.

Logan pulled in a deep breath through his nose. "We need to hurry with the child. He's pulling away fast." He turned and looked at Madoc. "You should do it."

"No fucking way, leech. I don't mess with kids' minds. They're too easy to scramble."

"Scramble?" asked Andra, shifting her body between Madoc and Sammy. "That doesn't sound so good."

"It's not," said Paul; then he turned his attention to Logan. "If Madoc isn't up to it, I'll take care of the boy."

"You're too weak," said Logan. "I took too much blood from you earlier. Madoc needs to do this."

Madoc shook his head. "I don't have that kind of finesse and you know it. You want me to kill something, I'm your man, but I don't go patching people up. That's your job."

Logan pinned Madoc with a bright stare. "Are you offering to supply the power I need to heal the boy's mind?"

Madoc's face twisted in a snarl and he bared his teeth. "You're not touching my blood. Ever."

Andra looked between the two men, trying to sort out what was going on. If she'd been able to drive she might have tried to slip out of here with Sammy while they argued. But she couldn't even lift the boy, much less drive, and if she tried, chances were she'd be more likely to kill Sammy than to get him home to his parents. "You can really help Sammy?" she asked Logan. "If all you need is blood, I'll give you some of mine."

"No!" shouted both Paul and Madoc at the same time.

Logan fixed her with a stare that made her feel trapped. Deer-in-the-headlights, doom-speeding-her-way trapped. "As tempting as that offer is, I fear these men would cut me down if I so much as plucked a hair from your head. Maybe another time."

She wasn't about to let a couple of brawny guys stand in the way of Sammy's future. Not while there was still a shotgun lying a few feet away. She took a tentative step toward it. She wasn't sure how she was going to finish reloading with only one good arm, but she'd manage somehow. "I want you to help Sammy," she told Logan. "Whatever it takes." If there was hope for him, maybe there was hope for Nika.

Andra crushed that thought flat before it could blossom. She had no room in her life for false hope. She knew just how bleak things really were, and it was best if she stayed a realist, just like she'd always been.

"Don't you dare touch her blood," growled Paul in a tone that made the fine hairs on her neck stand up. "I'll help the boy."

"Are you sure?" asked Logan. "I took a lot from you tonight so I could find her."

Paul's eyes flicked to Andra so briefly she wasn't sure it had happened. "It was worth it. I'm sure I'm strong enough for this."

"And if you're not?" asked Madoc.

Paul pressed his hand against his chest as if it hurt, then handed Madoc his sword. "Then you know what to do."

Chapter 2

Paul carried Sammy outside into the night and found a patch of rich earth that would aid him in healing the boy.

Andra and Logan trailed behind him, while Madoc kept watch over the area, ensuring that they'd know if company arrived.

Paul wanted nothing more than to touch Andra and find out whether she was the woman he'd been looking for for decades. The only thing holding him back was her safety, as well as Sammy's. He couldn't do anything to mess up this time. This was his last chance. If he did touch her, and he went through that same incapacitating pain Drake had suffered with Helen, there was no way he'd be able to protect them if more Synestryn came.

And they would come; it was just a question of how long they had before it happened and whether or not they would still be here.

The sooner Sammy's mind was cleaned, the faster Paul could get Logan to fix her arm. He knew she had to be in pain. All the color had leached from her face and she was holding herself at an odd angle. Already, the leather sleeve of her jacket was stretching tight over her broken arm.

"You'd better get out of that jacket before you can't," he told her. "The swelling's getting worse."

She gave it a gentle tug, winced, and asked, "Any of you boys have a knife?"

"Allow me," said Logan. A sharp claw extended from the end of his finger, replacing his manicured fingernail.

Andra flinched at the sight, and hissed in pain as the motion jarred her broken bone. "Holy shit! What the hell are you?"

"Hold still. I won't damage you."

"You'd better not," said Paul as he resisted the urge to go to her and reassure her. Keeping his distance was the most maddening form of torture possible. Moments ago, another leaf had fallen from his lifemark, leaving one, and he still wasn't sure whether she was the woman who could save him.

He'd been given two chances before. Even wishing for a third seemed like some kind of sacrilege. Too bad it didn't stop him from wishing anyway.

Andra stripped out of her destroyed leather jacket with a little help from Logan. Although her left arm was puffy and distorted, the rest of her was all sleek muscles and strong, feminine lines. Her clingy shirt showed off small, perfect breasts and muscular abs. He wondered how much time and effort a body like that had cost her and whether or not the man in her life was appropriately appreciative.

He certainly would be, given the chance.

Paul pulled his gaze away from her and focused on Sammy. The child's eyes were open, unblinking. Drool leaked from one corner of his mouth and Paul gently wiped it away with the hem of his shirt. "I'm going to help you sleep now, Sammy. But I promise that you won't have any bad dreams. I'm going to take them all away, okay?"

Paul didn't expect an answer; the child was too far gone. He closed the boy's eyes and held his hand there to keep them closed. He focused on the ground under him—warm, seemingly dead after long weeks of drought. He felt the soil and the rocks beneath, felt the roots of nearby trees seeking out nourishment and the tiny, hidden seeds that waited for rain to spark them to life. The earth beneath him was calm, patient, accepting of whatever came. There was power in that acceptance and Paul pulled some of that power into himself.

Instantly, the pain he lived with daily increased, bearing down on him, grinding at his bones, and he had to clench his teeth against it to keep from crying out. His heart pounded and his head throbbed until he was blind from the sheer force of the pressure of so much more power. His body already held too much energy, but it was energy he couldn't use—only store for someone else's use. Maybe Andra's.

He prayed it was so. He wasn't going to live long enough for another search. It had taken two weeks to find her, and he didn't think he had even one week left.

Paul's skin grew tight and burned, and his eyes felt like they would fly out of his head if he opened his eyelids. He could hear his breath rasping in and out too quickly as his lungs labored against the pain.

Logan was right. He was too weak for this, but it was too late now. He'd pulled in enough power to reach out to Sammy and enter his mind. He was trapped inside the child until he'd done what he'd come here to do—take away his fear, his memories.

The images inside Sammy were a chaotic swirl of teeth and claws, growls and screams. The boy was barely six, and had no way of making sense of what he'd seen. His child's mind had taken the sensory input, mixed it with his terror, and created an array of images even more terrible than reality. Somewhere deep inside Sammy's mind, he felt the little boy cowering in fear, whimpering, chanting, "No, no, no."

Paul felt his physical body weaken against the strain of his connection with the boy. He wasn't very good at this, but he knew enough to know that if he died while in the boy's mind, it would kill Sammy as well.

Spurred on by that thought, Paul pushed his way through those nightmares until he found the boy's mental hiding place. It was a cardboard box with crooked windows drawn on with brightly colored crayon. One side of the box had been cut open to make a door big enough for Sammy to crawl through.

Paul crouched and peered in the cardboard doorway. "You're going to be okay now. Stay here until you hear me call your name, and when you come out, all the monsters will be gone."

The boy cringed in the corner of the box with his hands over his ears and his eyes squeezed shut, but somehow, Paul felt that he'd been heard.

He rose up and faced all the images that Sammy had created, each one horrific enough to drive the boy mad. They all had to go. Paul captured the first monster in his gaze—much like a sgath, but with larger teeth and two wolflike heads. Normally, it wouldn't have frightened him, because he knew it wasn't real. But Sammy thought it was real and because of that, it had power.

Paul let himself be afraid—imagined what it must be like for Sammy, so small and helpless. He imagined what it felt like to be ripped away from the safety of his home and parents and tossed into a living nightmare. He let the fear grow inside him until his hands shook and his jaw ached from fighting the need to scream. He accepted Sammy's horror as his own, absorbing it until he'd taken it all into himself, then ruthlessly shoved it into the accepting earth. Burying it deep where it couldn't hurt anyone.

Slowly, the monster disappeared.

Paul was left feeling weak and dizzy, barely able to stand upright within the ethereal context of the boy's mind. He could no longer move, so he pulled in more power—more pain—and forced himself to take just one

more step toward the next nightmare. It left him sweating and shaking and made his stomach clench in protest,
but he had no choice. The child could not live with these
images in his head.

Andra's arm was swiftly becoming a problem. Every
breath shifted her frame enough to send searing jolts of
pain through her body. And she was losing feeling in her
fingers, which couldn't be good. But none of that really
bothered her. What really bothered her was the fact that
she was basically helpless. She didn't trust these men,
no matter how helpful they seemed. What if they tried
to take Sammy away? How would she stop them in a
three-against-one fight, with a broken arm and an empty
shotgun?

Paul was deep in concentration and Madoc was keeping watch out into the darkness. Logan and his freaky-
sharp fingernails hovered nearby, lurking in the shadows.
There was something unsettling about his stillness—his
unnatural beauty.

"We're not going to hurt you," he said as if reading
her thoughts. Then again, she kept looking at her shotgun lying a few feet away, so maybe, rather than being
psychic, he simply wasn't an idiot.

"Forgive me if I'm not all cheerful and trusting," she
replied.

"You're feeling helpless, no doubt. I can mend your
arm if you like."

"How are you going to do that?"

"Magic. Want to see?"

"Not particularly. I've seen enough weirdness for one
night, thanks."

Logan shrugged. "Suit yourself. The offer is—" He
sniffed the air and she thought she saw his eyes actually put off a silvery glow. He turned to Madoc and said,
"We've got company."

Company. That didn't sound good.

"How much time?" demanded Madoc.

"Two minutes. Maybe three."

"There are more of those monsters coming?" she asked Logan.

He nodded.

Shit! She was no good in a fight like this. "How long will it take to fix my arm?"

This time she was sure she saw his eyes glow just a bit—a cold, hungry glow that made her feel like prey. "Only a moment, if you're willing."

"I am. Do it."

"Paul's going to kill you if you take her blood," said Madoc.

"Paul has no say in what happens to me," said Andra. "Get on with it."

"I'll need your blood to regain my strength once we are safely away from here."

"There's going to be plenty of it all over the grass if you don't hurry." She was pretty sure she knew just how he planned on taking her blood. The word *vampire* echoed around in her head, giving her the creeps. Still, if she lived long enough to bleed a little, that was fine with her. She'd make more blood.

Logan spread an elegant, slim hand around the base of her neck and closed his eyes. Heat soaked into her skin, making her shiver. As the heat grew, she started to worry. His skin was too hot. He was going to burn her. She had to pull away.

Just as she thought about moving, she felt his other arm clamp around her waist, pressing her hard against his frame. He was stronger than he looked. Much stronger. And she'd been wrong about his being merely thin—he was practically a skeleton under his clothing, all sharp angles and jagged bones.

"I don't have time or the strength to be gentle," he whispered in a strained voice. "I'm sorry."

Andra wasn't sure what he meant until she felt the bone

in her arm shift and pain became her whole world. It slid through her veins and blistered her from the inside out. A scream bubbled up out of her against her will. Searing heat burned inside her as if welding the bone together. The burning went on and on until she was out of breath from screaming and sweat had soaked her clothing.

Finally, it ended. She felt his arm loosen, and she shoved herself away from him. He stumbled backward. His eyes rolled back in his head as if he'd passed out, and she scrambled to catch him before his head hit the concrete.

His limp weight was hard to handle, but she managed to ease him to the ground. Her left arm twinged, but it worked, and that was what really mattered.

Andra didn't waste any time checking to see if he was okay. There was nothing she could do for him now except keep the monsters off of him until they could all get the hell out of here.

She fetched her shotgun, reloaded it, and stood guard over the group.

"You really think that's gonna help, little girl?" asked Madoc, eyeing her weapon.

"It sure as hell doesn't hurt."

"Swords work better."

"Maybe, but only if you know how to use one. I'll stick with what I know."

"As much as I'd love to stay and fight, we need to get out of here," said Madoc.

"I couldn't agree more. Any ideas?"

"Can you drive?"

In the distance, she saw a faint pair of glowing green eyes. "I can now."

"Do you think you can drag Logan? Get him into the car?"

"If that's what I need to do. Sure."

"Do it. I'll load Paul and the kid as soon as he's done here and we'll all get the hell out of Dodge."

*   *   *

It seemed to take an eternity, but one by one, Paul drove each of Sammy's nightmares into the earth. Not even the acidic power of fear was strong enough to bother the stones beneath him.

Paul pulled out of the child's mind, gasping for air. He slumped with fatigue, but strong arms supported him. He was too tired to open his eyes and see who was there.

"Can you stand?" asked Madoc. His voice was close. He was the one keeping Paul from falling to the ground.

"Not yet. Give me a minute." He was panting and his weakness grated against his nerves. He didn't want to show even the slightest hint of weakness to Andra or give her any other reason to shun him. He had to be strong and prove to her he was worthy of her.

"Is Sammy going to be okay?" Andra asked. Her voice flowed over him like cool, clean water, restoring some of the strength his efforts had drained. He wanted to reach for her and feel her skin beneath his fingertips, but his arms weren't listening and they stayed locked around Sammy's body.

Paul nodded in response to her question, but even that small motion was draining. His body felt bruised from the inside out, and he wasn't sure whether he was strong enough to stand. Removing Sam's nightmares had taken its toll on his body, and he didn't know how long it would take him to recover. "He's sleeping now," rasped Paul. "But he'll wake up soon, and when he does, he needs his parents to be there." Only the soothing touch of a mother and the protective embrace of a father were going to finish the healing process Paul had begun.

"No time to chat," said Madoc. "We need to get moving."

A deep sgath howl split the predawn silence. It was close, and Paul was in no shape to fight.

"Help me up and I'll recover in the car." Paul forced

his eyes open, hoping it would settle his churning stomach. He didn't think puking all over Andra's boots was going to win him any points.

"Let me have Sammy," said Andra. Her short brown hair reflected the light from the lamp overhead. Her stance was rigid, her blue eyes mistrustful. "I don't want you to drop him."

Great. Now she thought he couldn't even carry a small child. Fantastic. He almost told her he'd never do that, but his arms were shaking and weak enough that he didn't want to take a chance. Even if he did look like a wimp, at least the boy would be safe.

She took the limp weight of the child in her arms just as two more sgath broke through a distant line of trees.

"Time's up," said Madoc, and hauled Paul across the parking lot to the SUV he'd left running.

Paul's legs had just started to cooperate when Madoc shoved him in the back door. He scooted over to the far seat, making room for Andra to join them.

She didn't. In fact, she wasn't even behind him. She was already in her own vehicle—a beat-up Ford that looked like it had been on the losing end of a fight or two already—headed down the street away from the oncoming Synestryn demons.

"She's leaving!" shouted Paul.

"We're right behind her. Chill." Madoc slammed the SUV in gear, and the tires screamed as he sped down the street after her. Or at least she should have been there, but wasn't.

Paul scanned the streets and saw nothing. "Where did she go?"

"How should I know? There are a ton of side streets around here. She probably took one of them."

"Find her, damn it." Desperation made his words sharp and angry.

"We've got a couple of sgath on our tail, so maybe finding her and the kid isn't the best thing right now. At least if the Synestryn are following us, they're not following her."

Paul looked over his shoulder, and sure enough, there were two demons on their bumper, keeping pace with the SUV as easily as if it were sitting still. No way could they lead those things to Andra and Sammy. "Veer off. We'll find a place to take them out and then go after her. Logan found her once. He can find her again."

Paul hoped it wasn't just wishful thinking.

The Sanguinar was slumped in the front seat, his head lolling around like a rag doll's as Madoc took a hard right. "If he regains consciousness before dawn, you mean."

The SUV sped up, and the sgath started to fall back, unable to keep pace.

Madoc spun into a turn and brought the SUV to a rocking stop. He shot Paul a grimace via the rearview mirror. "There's good news and bad news. Which do you want first?"

Paul still felt like hell—weak and shaky—but at least his legs were stronger. Madoc leaped from the vehicle while Paul kind of spilled out; then he and Madoc took a stand in a recently plowed field.

The sgath saw them there and charged. "Good news would be nice right about now."

"Logan will be able to find Andra no matter what, so you don't have to worry about that."

That was more than good news; it was great news. He wasn't going to lose her. "So, what's the bad news?"

Paul lifted his blade and prepared for the demons' charge. Madoc did the same.

"Logan can find her because he healed her busted arm. She owes him blood."

He'd have to pay the debt for her. No way was he going to let Logan get his fangs on her pretty neck—or anywhere else. "Over my dead body," said Paul.

Madoc gave him a sneering once-over. "If you feel as

shitty as you look, that may very well be the case. Get that fucking sword up, man."

The closest sgath leaped into the air.

Paul sliced at the demon, but his arms were weak, putting his aim off the mark, and instead of hitting anything vital, he only managed to lop off a leg. The thing landed hard, howled in pain, and scrambled awkwardly back onto its feet.

His sword felt heavy, which was proof he wasn't fully recovered from healing Sammy's mind. But heavy or not, he'd been fighting these things for centuries and knew what to do. His body followed his commands and he feinted right, fooling the sgath into thinking he'd left his flank unprotected. Its teeth flashed a sickly yellow as it went for the opening. Paul shifted his weight at the last second and drove his sword down through the sgath's skull before its teeth could connect.

It wriggled there, still clinging to life, slashing at him with its front claws. Paul twisted his blade and finally the sgath went limp.

Paul had killed the thing, but he was breathing too hard and barely able to retrieve his sword. Madoc watched him, standing over his own kill, which was sliced neatly in two—or not so neatly, considering what was leaking out of the sgath's gut. "Took you long enough."

"You could have lent a hand."

Madoc shrugged. "What fun would that have been?"

Paul wiped his blade on the grass to clean the oily black blood from it. His hands were shaking enough to piss him off. He couldn't afford to be weak right now—not with Andra out there, owing a blood debt to one of the Sanguinar.

"Is Logan up yet?" asked Paul.

Madoc checked the front seat. "Nope. Still out cold."

"Great. Now how are we going to find her?"

"You could look up her license plate number."

"I could if I had it."

Madoc rattled off the number.

"How do you know that?"

"I saw it when I was tearing out after her."

"So did I, but I didn't remember it."

Madoc shrugged. "It's no big deal. I remember numbers and shit like that when I see them."

Paul clapped Madoc on the shoulder, enjoying the way the physical contact made him squirm uncomfortably. "You're like some kind of genius, man."

"Yeah, the kind who's going to beat the hell out of you if you don't shut up about it and get your hands off me."

Paul held up his hands in surrender, but he couldn't hide his grin. "I'm just saying that it's a pretty cool trick you've got there, egghead."

"Fuck off."

Paul didn't know Madoc well. He tended to hang out alone most of the time, keeping his distance from the rest of the Theronai. Paul had been pretty sure he wasn't going to like the loner, but time was proving him wrong. Madoc was growing on him. And he was useful as hell.

"I'm going to call Nicholas and track her plates. You mind keeping a lookout?"

"Whatever."

Paul sat down on the ground by the SUV to let his body recover, pulled out his cell phone, and dialed the compound's head of security.

"This had better be good," was how Nicholas answered the phone, his voice gritty, as if he hadn't used it in days. Maybe he hadn't. Nicholas was a bit of a recluse, choosing to stay in his techno-lair more often than not.

"I, uh, met someone tonight. I need you to do a background check on her."

"What, did she borrow money from you or something?"

"Not that kind of background," said Paul. "She helped

us save a boy from some Synestryn tonight. I need you to find out if she's hit anyone's radar."

"Just our radar or the Sanguinar's and Slayers' radar, too?"

Paul glanced at Logan. As far as he could tell, the Sanguinar was still unconscious. Good. "Anyone's."

"You think she's a Dorjan?" asked Nicholas, using the term for a human who worked for the Synestryn in exchange for money or power.

"No, but she faced down several Synestryn armed with only a shotgun." Paul still remembered the way she'd stood there, her feet braced apart in a battle stance. He wasn't sure if he was more impressed by her courage or frightened by her ignorance. She could have been killed, and if she was what he thought she was, she was way too important for him to let her take such a chance ever again. Her life was too precious to risk.

"No shit." Nicholas let out an impressed grunt. "She's probably just some gutsy human with more courage than brains. You said there was a boy involved. A lot of people can do amazing things when there's a child at stake."

"Maybe, but something tells me there's more to it than that." He wasn't about to tell Nicholas that he'd bargained with Logan to hunt her down, and that he knew she was blooded, at the very least. Most of the Theronai were suspicious of the Sanguinar, even though their races were currently at peace with each other. His bargain was binding and not the kind of thing that would go over well with the other men at the compound. It tied him to the Sanguinar and made him a liability if that peace didn't hold.

"More? Like what?" asked Nicholas. "We'd know if she was one of ours. She'd have been wearing the ring of the Gerai. Did you see one?"

"Maybe she forgot to put it on, or maybe it was out

being resized." The excuses sounded ridiculous even to his own ears.

"Or maybe she just did one hell of a snow job on you and she really is a Dorjan. Tell me you didn't let her get away before you could question her or at least put a bloodmark on her."

"She had to get the boy to a hospital. Madoc got her license plate number. She won't get far."

"What's her name?"

"Andra Madison. Nebraska plates." He gave Nicholas her plate number.

Paul heard a quick series of keystrokes and waited for Nicholas to do his magic. He had access to more information—both human and Sentinel—than any other man alive.

A few seconds later, Nicholas let out a soft whistle. "She's not hard to find, that's for sure. The woman's name is plastered all over the newspapers. She's a finder of lost children—one of those people that parents hire when their kid goes missing and the police and FBI can't help. Apparently, she's pretty good at it, too. So good that the police have a tag on her name to keep an eye out for her. It looks like they think she might actually be behind some of the kidnappings."

"Because they can't find the kids, but she can," guessed Paul.

"Sounds about right. Says here that she only takes certain cases."

"Can you get a sense for what kind of cases she takes?" asked Paul.

A few more quick keystrokes and a moment of silence followed before Nicholas said, "Paul, my man, I think we've got a problem."

"What?"

"You've found yourself a bona fide Synestryn hunter. A human one with no connections to or support from any of the Sentinels as far as I can tell. Which means—"

"Which means I'd better get to her fast or she's going to walk into a situation that might get her killed." Paul had no more time to waste. He forced himself to his feet.

"We can't have that now, can we?" said Nicholas. Paul heard someone talking in the background; then Nicholas lowered his voice so Paul could barely hear it. "You're not going to believe who just walked in."

"Who?"

"Hold on a sec. She wants to talk to you. I'll text you that address."

There was a scratching sound as Nicholas handed the phone to someone; then a voice came on the line. It was high and childlike but imbued with an unmistakable air of command. Sibyl. The only one among his people gifted with the ability to see into the future. When she spoke, everyone listened.

"Theronai," said Sibyl. "We must speak."

Paul barely hid his shock. She'd spoken to him twice in the past century, including now, and both of those times had been within the last month. Surely so much attention from her couldn't be a good thing. "Yes, my lady."

"You've found her." It wasn't a question.

"Her? Do you mean Andra?"

"Andra," she said slowly, as if suddenly recognizing the name. "Yes. Andra. Bring her to me."

Paul debated whether or not to let Sibyl know that although he'd found her, he'd lost her once again. He'd definitely find her, but it might take a little time. He hedged, saying, "I'm not sure she's going to want to go along with me."

"Then bind her. Render her unconscious. Do what you must, but bring her to me."

"May I ask why?"

"I ... need her."

"For what?" asked Paul. As much as he respected

Sibyl and her gift, he wasn't about to lead Andra into something ugly.

"Do as you are told, Theronai." Her pure child's voice rang with an odd kind of power that made the hair on his nape stand on end.

"I can't right now. She's not with me."

"Where is she?"

"I don't know."

"Find her. Bring her. Today. Should you fail, the repercussions shall be . . . unfortunate."

That didn't sound good. "I'll do what I can," he promised. The power of that promise wrapped around him as he was bound to his word, making it hard to breathe for a moment.

"See that you do. Her presence is vital. For both of us."

The line went dead and Paul shoved his phone into his pocket.

"Good news, I take it," said Madoc.

"Same ol', same ol'. Can you drive?"

"Always. Where are we going?"

"To find Andra and bring her back to Sibyl."

"No shit? Sibyl?"

"Yep."

Madoc shook his head. "Great. If that moppet is getting involved, things can't be good."

Chapter 3

It took Andra more than three hours to get Sammy re-united with his parents and convince the authorities that whoever had taken him was long gone by the time she found him. She gave them the only story she could: She had no clue who the kidnapper was, and if she remembered anything new, she'd be sure to let them know.

She hated lying to the police, but it was better than being locked up in a seventy-two-hour psych hold. Again. Crazy did run in families. Thank God no one knew about Nika.

She gave the police the address of the warehouse, knowing that by the time they got there, the sun would have done a thorough job of burning away the remains of the monsters they had killed. Other than scorch marks in the floor, there would be no evidence left that the boy had been stolen by furry, clawed monsters.

Synestryn demons. That was what those men had called them.

Usually putting a name to something made it less frightening, but not in this case. Just knowing that the things were so common they had a name was enough to scare the spit out of her. She didn't let herself think about it, because no matter how tired she was, something like that would roll around in her head, making sleep impossible.

And right now, she needed sleep more than anything. Her body was on the verge of going on strike. Everything ached, and her head felt like she'd had a fog machine shoved into one of her ears. If she didn't get some sleep soon, her legs would just give out and refuse to propel her forward anymore. She'd been to that not-even-one-more-step point before and it wasn't pleasant. She had maybe another few minutes before she reached it again. At that point, wherever she was, that was where she'd sleep.

Maybe her dreams would be nice for a change—filled with manly, sword-wielding warriors and their pretty-boy vampire buddy. She could work with that imagery. And she was a sucker for a man who liked kids. Paul had put serious effort into saving Sammy from a life of screaming lunacy, and whatever he'd done had worked. Sammy was all smiles and hugs by the time she handed him into the loving arms of his mother. It was as if nothing had happened to him.

Maybe Paul could somehow help Nika, too.

Then again, maybe she was just fooling herself. When she got this tired, her instincts weren't trustworthy, so it wouldn't have surprised her to learn that, even though Paul had seemed like a decent guy, he was really some sort of self-proclaimed faith healer. Who carried a sword. Nice combo.

Andra pulled her truck into the garage of her apartment complex, praying she'd stay awake long enough to brush her teeth before she collapsed into bed.

She threw her purse on the kitchen counter, ignoring the sink full of dirty dishes and the stacks of unopened mail. None of it mattered as much as getting onto her mattress.

"Hi," said Paul from her couch, making Andra jump and her system flood with a whole new pile of adrenaline.

He'd kicked off his shoes and was lounging there

as if he had every right to be in her home. "Hope you don't mind that I let myself in. You left the balcony door unlocked."

Andra stopped dead in her tracks, though her foggy brain had some trouble making sense out of what she was seeing. It took her a few seconds to find her tongue through all the shock. "I never leave my door unlocked," she said, as if that were the most important thing to point out, rather than the fact that he was inside her home without her permission. "And we're three stories up."

"How else would I have gotten in?" he asked, daring to give her a charming grin that made his brown eyes glitter.

It was such a logical question, and she was so damned tired she just couldn't figure out any sort of intelligent response. "What are you doing here?"

"Waiting for you," he said, as if she should have known.

"How did you find me?"

"Your truck's license plate. I've got a friend at the DMV."

"A friend who is at work this early in the morning? It's not even eight yet."

Paul shrugged. "You look beat."

"I am. See, the problem is that I don't tend to go to bed when there's a stranger in my living room."

That charming grin widened into a smile. "We're not strangers. I know all about you."

That sounded a little creepy, making her wish she hadn't left her shotgun in her truck. "Listen. I don't know how you got in and I really don't care right now. All I want is for you to leave so that I can get some sleep." She couldn't even remember what day it was. That was a bad sign.

Paul got up and came to stand right in front of her. He was a couple inches taller than she was in her boots, and from this distance, she could see warm splinters of firelight gold in his brown eyes. His beard hadn't been shaved today, giving his jaw additional shadows to accentuate the sharp angles of his face. A small scar above his left eyebrow was stark against the deeper tan of his skin, and if the circles under his eyes were any indication, he was just as tired as she was. "I can't leave without you. I'm sorry."

"I'm not going anywhere," she said.

"Fine, then can we just sit down and talk for a few minutes?" Something about the way he said it told her that it wasn't even close to what he really wanted to say.

"Whatever it is, we can talk about it in a few hours. I'll meet you at the coffee shop on the corner at six, okay?"

His mouth tightened. "This can't wait."

"It's gonna have to." She turned to walk away and opened the door for him, hoping he'd take the hint and get out.

"I'm sorry. I have to know."

Paul put his hand on her shoulder and stopped her in her tracks. His palm was warm, even through the fabric of her shirt. Her head spun for a moment, and his touch brought about the strangest feeling of déjà vu. Maybe she'd met him somewhere before? She didn't think so, considering the fact that she was pretty sure she'd remember a man like him—an alarming mixture of masculine appeal and confidence with the competence to back it up. Not to mention the whole part where he carried a sword.

She turned to look at him, hoping that would help her remember who he was. He was staring down at his hand with an odd jumble of hope and confusion flashing in his brown eyes. After a second, he cleared his throat. "Did you feel anything?"

Oh, yeah, but she was going to play it cool. This stuff was all too weird for her. "Like what?"

He shrugged, distracting her for a second with the impressive width of his shoulders. "I'm not sure. Maybe it only works if I touch bare skin."

Andra had heard a lot of lines designed to get her naked before, but this one was by far the strangest. "What only works if you touch bare skin?"

He slid his hand down her arm until just the tips of his fingers contacted the skin below her sleeve. Heat seeped into her, along with something else. Something odd, like a jolt of static electricity, but one that didn't hurt. In fact, it felt pretty good and was feeling better by the second.

Strength roared through her system, making the need for sleep vanish. Her body came alive, soaring with a heady rush of pleasure that made her sure she could float. Her fatigue drained away, leaving behind a faint, humming energy in its wake.

She looked up at Paul, shocked at what he was doing to her, but the sudden motion made her dizzy and she lost her balance and instinctively grabbed him to steady herself.

He pulled her close, and she went without a fight, unable to do anything else in the midst of her vertigo.

"Easy, now," he said in a low voice. "I've got you."

As his words slid inside her, Andra's world ground to a halt. Her nose was pressed against his throat and she could smell the heat of his skin, see the throbbing of his pulse along the thick column of his neck. A pale, luminescent band shimmered only inches from her eyes, and she had the irresistible urge to reach out and pull it from him. She wanted it. Needed it. That choker was hers and always had been.

He was hers. All of him. From the bottom of his wide, booted feet to the top of his mussed hair and all of the lovely, hard places in between.

She breathed in deeply, pulling in his scent. A low hum of arousal swirled inside her, pushing away the grating fatigue that had ruled her only moments before. She still wanted to get into bed, but not for sleep. She wanted Paul there with her, naked and laid out for her pleasure. She was going to take her time getting to know what he liked. Lots and lots of time.

But the bed was too far away for her to wait. She needed to touch him. Taste him. Her hands went to the hem of his knit shirt and snaked beneath it. Warm, firm skin tempted her fingers to explore him further, while she pressed her open mouth against the side of his neck.

She heard him make an incoherent sound of surprise, but he didn't seem to mind what she was doing. In fact, he tilted his head to one side to give her room to slide her tongue over his salty skin.

"What the hell is happening?" he said in a rough voice.

"If you don't know, I'm going to have a heck of a good time showing you."

This was madness, but she couldn't seem to stop herself, nor did she care that she couldn't. She shoved his shirt off over his head to get to more skin, needing to feel more of him beneath her hands. He was heavily inked, sporting a large tattoo of some kind of tree that stretched from his shoulder and upper arm all the way down below his belt. She was dying to see just how far down it went.

The limbs of his tattoo were highly detailed, mostly bare except for one single leaf, and she was pretty sure it was some kind of metaphor for life or some crap like that. Not that she cared. He could be as philosophical as he wanted as long as he did it naked.

She ran one finger along a branch, down the trunk of the tree to where it hit the low-slung waist of his jeans. His abs clenched as if he'd been hit, making ridges of muscle stand out for her enjoyment.

Paul shuddered at her touch, but when she moved to

pop the button on his fly, he grabbed her hands and held them locked inside a strong grip.

"We should stop," he told her.

She looked into his eyes, which were dark with need—all those golden slivers were gone now, eaten up by his pupils. His cheeks were flushed and a fine sweat had beaded up along his hairline. "Don't you want me?" she asked.

"God, yes. Can't you feel me shaking?"

She could, and it made her smile with a sense of victory. "My bedroom is right through that door."

Paul groaned and closed his eyes. "This isn't you, though I wish like hell it were."

"What isn't me?"

"This . . . thing we're feeling."

He was right. She didn't normally undress strangers who broke into her house. Something was off here.

Andra shook her head, trying to clear it or make some sense out of the jumble of thoughts and feelings going through her brain.

While she was distracted, Paul let go of her and stepped back. His posture said he thought she might hit him or something, because he was all tensed up like he was expecting to take a punch.

She didn't hit him, of course, but the need to get him naked was also fading. He was still hot, especially with all those muscles in his chest and abs on display, but at least now she could keep her tongue to herself.

She wasn't sure if that was an improvement or not.

Andra's hands were shaking, so she shoved them into her jeans pockets. Her bone-deep weariness was coming back fast, as if it had never been gone at all. "What the hell was that?" she asked him.

"Not sure." His tone was hard, his words curt.

"Did I hurt you?"

"No."

"Why do you make that sound like it's a bad thing?"

He held up his hand—the one with the iridescent band—and stared at it as if his life depended on it. The baby rainbows trapped in it were dancing up a storm, swirling around as if kicked up by some invisible wind. "Do you see color?" he asked.

"Yeah, all of them. Where did you get that thing?"

"Long story. Look harder. Do you see any one color more than the others?"

Andra stared at the band, loving the flow of rainbows over the surface. It was hypnotic. Mesmerizing. Beautiful. But she didn't see any dominant color. "No. Not really."

"Shit," he growled.

"What's wrong?"

"I just mistook you for someone else. That's all. I'm sorry."

It didn't hurt when Paul stopped touching Andra. That was the thought that kept echoing in Paul's brain, making him crazy. It was supposed to hurt. He'd needed it to hurt.

He'd wanted Andra to be the one for him so badly that he'd begun to believe it was true.

What a fool he was to think he deserved another chance. Drake had found Helen first, so he'd failed there, and he'd never been able to make Kate happy, though heaven knew he'd tried his best. She'd been dead for two hundred years and he still couldn't figure out why she couldn't love him—what more he could have given her to make her happy.

Paul refused to dwell on it. Even if Andra wasn't his lady, she might be able to save one of his brothers. Clearly she was blooded. In fact, based on the way his luceria reacted, she was probably a Theronai. Just not his.

Paul looked down at his chest. The last leaf on his life-mark swayed in time with the summer breeze outside. It

looked a little more brown than green today. He really
didn't have much time left, and he still had one more job
to do: get Andra to Dabyr, just as Sibyl commanded.

"We should get moving," he told Andra.

"I'm not going anywhere until I've had about ten
hours of sleep. Besides, what makes you think I'd go
anywhere with you, period?"

Paul didn't have the patience for this. Too much was
at stake here. Even if he hadn't been bound by his vow
to Sibyl to bring Andra home, he needed to get her back
so they could see if she would be compatible with any
of the other men there. They were all dying—just not
as soon as he was. She might be able to save one of his
brothers in arms. Bringing her to Dabyr was the one last
thing he could do for his people before he went to his
death.

He grabbed her by the shoulders and backed her
up against a wall. She felt good under his hands, which
pissed him off. Why would she feel so good if she wasn't
his?

"We're leaving. You're coming with us. You can walk,
or I'll carry you. Your call."

To her credit, she didn't cower or back down, even
when faced with an armed man of his size. Her blue eyes
brightened at the challenge and she tipped her chin up
to meet his gaze. "You think you can push me around?"
she asked.

"Push, pull, drag. Whatever it takes."

"I have responsibilities. People who need me. I'm not
going to let you decide where I go. Sorry to burst your
macho bubble."

Paul figured he had a couple of choices. He could
make good on his threats and drag her out of here kicking and screaming, which would no doubt get her neighbors' attention, or he could use a little finesse.

Finesse wasn't his strong suit, but he'd do what it took
to get her back to Sibyl and the men.

He let out a long, slow breath and removed his hands from her body, hoping it would help him stay level. "What responsibilities?" Maybe he could take care of them, leaving her free to go back with him.

"I have a job to do. Kids are being taken from their homes all the time. I need to be here to find them."

"I've heard about your talent. Just how is it that you're able to find them when no one else can?" he asked.

She pushed away from the wall, and he noticed her balance was a little unsteady. Maybe she was more exhausted than he thought.

Paul reached out to help her, but she swatted his hands away and sank onto the couch as if standing were no longer an option. "I'm good at what I do. That's why they pay me the big bucks."

"I really doubt that's the whole story, but if it's money you're after, I can pay. I've got plenty, and I'll give you whatever you want if you come with me."

He saw a hint of victory flare in Andra's eyes, and he knew he'd found the right lever to use with her. Money.

She got up, rummaged through some papers on the kitchen counter, and scribbled down something on a notepad. She ripped off the top sheet and handed it to him. "This is the account number where I want the money sent. Put half a million in there today and I'll go wherever you want. Deal?"

Paul took the paper, and something in him shriveled. He'd pictured her as some great heroine who did whatever it took to find the children, no matter how much money she made. He'd thought she was one of the good guys, like him. He'd been wrong. She was just another person trying to make a buck off of the pain and suffering of others.

How could he have been so wrong? His instincts were usually better than that.

Paul couldn't look her in the eye. He couldn't bear to see the greed he knew would be lurking there. "Deal," he said, but he couldn't bring himself to shake her hand.

"I'm going to grab a quick shower," she said. "If the money is in there when I get out, we can leave."

Andra nearly wept with relief when Paul agreed to her terms. He was already on his cell phone making the transfer of funds into her account when she went to shower. She couldn't believe how easy it had been.

Finally, Andra could be sure that Nika was always going to have a place to live. Between the half million Paul was giving her, and Andra's large life insurance policy, if anything happened to Andra, Nika would always be cared for. She'd be safe.

Andra made quick work of washing off the sweat of pain and fear from last night, and threw on the first mostly clean pair of jeans she could find. Her laundry was becoming a problem—one she'd have to deal with when she got back, but not now. Now she had to hit the road with a man she barely knew. A man who made her go mushy with just a single touch.

Andra was going to have to be really careful that she didn't let him touch her anymore.

She went into the living room, presentable but by no means glamorous. Her hair was still wet and she hadn't bothered to take time for makeup. She was just too damn tired to care what she looked like.

"It's done," said Paul, his tone bleak. The warmth in his eyes had disappeared, making him look less human. More deadly. She'd seen him in a fight and knew that the man was a formidable opponent, but she'd never worried that she'd be on the receiving end of his sword.

Until now.

The money had changed the way he looked at her, and no matter how much she told herself it didn't matter, she knew it was a lie. She wanted him to like her. Respect her. She had no idea why it mattered. It never had before. She'd pissed off more than just a few people in her determination to find a missing child, but with Paul it was different. That slight disdain lifting his lip when he looked at her hurt.

Andra couldn't make herself not care about what he thought, so she refused to think about it. They had a deal. Nika would be safe. Time to move on. "Where are we going?"

"Missouri."

Andra nearly groaned. She was too tired to drive that far. She knew she was. She'd never make it there alive. Then again, if she didn't survive, Nika would get all that money from her life insurance.

She decided to put this situation under the win-win heading.

Something in her thoughts must have come through on her face, because Paul said, "I'm driving. I wouldn't want you to crash your truck before you finished giving me my money's worth."

Andra nodded. "Fine."

"Pack for a couple days, but be quick."

Andra picked up one of two overnight bags she kept packed and ready to go at all times in case she got a call from desperate parents. "I'm ready."

She thought she saw a glimmer of respect cross his hard features, but she couldn't be sure.

There was a loud pounding on her front door, as if someone were trying to kick it in.

Paul slid a sword out from nowhere—which was the coolest trick ever—and brought a finger to his lips for silence.

"It's probably my newspaper boy wanting payment. Would you back the hell off?" She stepped forward to go peek through the hole, but Paul held her back with a thick, muscular arm.

He'd just grazed the skin of her arm, but it was enough to make Andra clamp her lips shut over a groan of pleasure. A tingling warmth spread out from the point of contact and invaded her limbs, making them feel heavy and languid. She wanted to rub herself up against him like a cat, and she wished he hadn't put his shirt back on while she was in the shower. It would have felt so good to splay her fingers across his back and get to know all of the rigid muscles lying beneath his flesh.

Her skin heated until she was sure she was bright red. An aching, needy emptiness gnawed at her, and she pressed her thighs together in an effort to ease the ache. It didn't work. She needed Paul to lay her down and fill her up—to slide inside her over and over until the world fell away and nothing but the two of them existed. No worries. No fears. No monsters. Only Paul and the touch of his skin on hers.

He stepped away from her, leaving her reeling, nearly swaying with the potent force of her need. She gripped the wall for support, but it did little good. She ended up sitting on her ass, shaking like she'd just spent the last week throwing up.

Through the door came, "It's Madoc. Open the fuck up."

Dimly, she was aware of Paul letting the surly giant inside her home. He was carrying something big and heavy and wrapped in a sheet. Booted feet stuck out of one end.

Holy shit. He'd brought a corpse into her apartment.

"He's bad," said Madoc.

"How bad?" asked Paul. Concern roughened the edges of his words.

"He started seizing a couple minutes ago. Thought the sun might make it worse, so I brought him in."

"You didn't let any light touch him, did you?" asked Paul. "We don't need that kind of trouble right now."

Madoc laid his burden down on her couch and started closing the blinds over Andra's windows. "Do I look like a fucking idiot? I was careful—had him wrapped up nice and tight. We don't need any more surprises."

Andra pushed herself up. "What is going on? Is that Logan?"

Paul didn't even spare her a glance. He was too busy unwrapping the cocoon of sheets from around Logan's body. When he finished, he eased Logan back onto her couch. He'd somehow lost more weight and was now a skeleton draped in skin. That skin was pale—almost blue—and he was completely still.

"Is he dead?" asked Andra.

"Nearly." Paul shot Madoc an accusing glare. "Why the hell didn't you feed him?"

"I've gone centuries without letting one of those leeches touch me. I'm not about to start now."

She thought she heard Paul mutter something like, "Selfish bastard," under his breath. "Whether or not you like him, we still need him."

"Speak for yourself," said Madoc. "I don't need shit."

Logan's body started to shake as if he were having a seizure.

Paul pressed his upper body over Logan's to hold him down. He held out his arm to Andra and nodded his head toward his sword lying on the floor by the couch. "Cut my wrist; then hold his mouth open," he told her.

Vampire. There it was again—that word tugging at the frightened corners of her mind. She'd seen enough things to know that monsters were real, but she didn't like knowing that this particular one existed. It was too eerie.

Or maybe it was the fact that one was in her house that bothered her.

"Come on, Andra. Hurry. He's dying."

And she'd promised to give him her blood. Paul had already given him too much. Logan said that earlier. She couldn't risk letting him hurt himself over something she had promised to do. "How much blood does he need?"

"I don't know, but it won't be enough to kill me."

Good. Then it wouldn't kill her, either. Andra took his sword just as Logan's body arched up off the couch in a particularly vicious seizure. Before Paul could stop her, she used his sword to cut open her wrist, pried Logan's lips open, and bled into his mouth.

Paul realized what she'd done and he shouted, "Andra, no!"

The seizure stopped instantly. Logan's eerie silvery eyes opened wide and he grabbed her wrist with both hands, holding her arm against his sucking mouth in an unbreakable grip.

She figured it would hurt, but it didn't. She hadn't even felt the sword cut her arm, it was so sharp. All she could feel now was an almost gentle tugging motion against her skin, and a kind of weightlessness—as if she were being filled with helium. It was strange, but not unpleasant.

In the distance, she could hear Paul shouting and see Madoc physically holding him away from Logan. But none of that mattered.

She felt an outside presence touch her mind like a warm caress. Logan. He wanted to know more about her. Who she was. Where she'd come from.

Andra let him in. Having him in her head felt good, and she was too weak to fight something as strong as he was anyway. Too tired.

He wanted her to sleep. Rest. She wanted that, too.

For a moment, she worried that she'd forgotten to do something. Turn off the oven? Brush her teeth? She couldn't remember what it was, and soon, it didn't seem to matter anymore. Whatever it was, it was unimportant.

Andra let go and drifted away, her weightless body floating into sleep.

Andra went limp, and a sickening flood of panic rose up Paul's throat. He thrashed against Madoc's hold, trying to get to her. "What the fuck did you do to her, bloodsucker?"

Logan licked her wrist, leaving behind no trace of her wound. He was no longer bone-thin and pale. His body had filled out and a healthy glow suffused his skin. In a calm tone, he explained, "Poor child hasn't slept in three days. She was pushing herself too hard, so I put her to sleep."

Paul managed to break Madoc's hold and shoved Logan away from her. Her body slumped on the floor beside the couch, boneless and limp. He checked for a pulse and found hers strong and steady.

Relief dragged a breath from his body, and he bowed his head over hers in thanks. The scent of her skin calmed him, and he couldn't stop himself from smoothing her hair back from her face. She was going to be okay.

Paul gathered her long body in his arms and carried her into her bedroom. The place was a mess, with clothes strewn everywhere. The covers were rumpled, showing signs of where she'd last slept.

Three days ago.

Paul should have been more aware of her fatigue. He should have insisted she rest. It wasn't like him to be blind to the weakness in the people around him. That could get a lot of people killed in the war against the Synestryn.

"She hid it well," said Logan from the doorway, as if reading his thoughts. Then again, their blood oath made it possible for him to do a lot of things Paul didn't enjoy.

Paul still wanted to hit the Sanguinar, but he didn't want to take his eyes off Andra, no matter how good it would have felt to lay Logan out.

"I should have known, anyway. If she'd been my lady, I would have." Disappointment left a bitter taste in his mouth.

He put Andra on the bed, took her shoes off, and pulled the sheets up over her slim body. She was helpless like this, and it made his protective instincts roar to life. Nothing was going to get near her until she'd had time to recover. Sibyl would just have to wait.

"Not necessarily," said Logan. "It's been a long time since the Theronai found partnerships. We know so little about these women. Things may be different now. The signs may be different."

Paul stalked to the door where Logan lounged, and the Sanguinar backed up. Smart man.

"I'm not in the mood for another disappointment, so forgive me if I don't buy into the shit you're selling. She's not mine." Saying the words aloud made his chest burn.

Logan merely smiled. "I think you may be wrong."

"I'm not." Paul refused to let himself feel even the slightest stirring of hope. He was out of time and he was going to be a good sport and take his defeat like a man. He'd had more chances than most.

Paul shut Andra's door and went in search of some food, herding Logan along with him so he wouldn't be tempted to go into Andra's room.

Her apartment was small, with the kitchen, living, and dining areas crammed on top of one another. The place looked like it hadn't been dusted in months, except for the gleam of the heavy-duty weight bench that filled what should have been the dining room.

The open layout gave him a clear view of the whole space, including the kitchen, which needed a thorough scrubbing.

Madoc had beaten him to the hunt for food, and was already rummaging through her cabinets and fridge. From the meager offerings on the counter—a couple cans of soup and some questionable lunch meat—he hadn't found much.

Logan was still lurking behind him. Paul saw his

sword, still stained with Andra's blood, and picked it up.

"She's almost certainly a Theronai," said Logan.

"I kinda guessed that part."

Paul wet a paper towel and cleaned his sword, then flushed the towel down the toilet, where the scent of blood couldn't draw any trouble. They were fairly safe during the day, but he wasn't taking any chances with Andra asleep in the next room.

Logan was right on his heels. "What makes you think she isn't yours?"

"My ring doesn't respond to her like it should. No color."

"Yet."

Paul sheathed his weapon before he decided to use it on Logan, and spun around. They stood eye-to-eye, but there was something different about him now. Something Paul couldn't place. It was like Logan knew a secret he wasn't willing to share.

"Stop already and back the hell off. I'm out of time, and that's that."

"You want to go find a nest tonight?" asked Madoc, completely serious. "I'll stand witness for you."

Witness to Paul's last heroic act. It was a dangerous offer for Madoc to make—one that might get him killed. Paul would wade into a nest of Synestryn, knowing it would be the last thing he did, and Madoc would stand by close to the action, Paul's sword safely in his keeping to take back to the Hall of the Fallen.

Paul wasn't going to like using a different sword, but he couldn't afford to let his be taken, and it wasn't as if he were ever going to make it out alive, anyway. The point was to take out as many demons as he could before they took him down.

"Thanks, man. I'm going to take you up on that offer, but I have to get Andra back to Sibyl first. I promised."

Madoc nodded and started pawing through Andra's freezer, unfazed by the talk of suicide.

"Go kill yourself if you like," said Logan, "but I'm telling you you're wrong about her."

Paul was going to regret asking, but he did anyway. "What makes you think that?"

"She felt something when you touched her."

A spark of hope lit inside him, so fragile and faint he could barely feel it. "She did?"

"Yes."

"But I didn't. There was no pain. No ... nothing."

Logan shrugged. "I've been trying to tell you that your experience may be different from Drake's. We don't even know how these women exist. There's no way we can predict what kind of reaction they'll cause—not after so many years of waiting."

"But I thought you Sanguinar all got together after Drake found Helen and decided that his pain was due to the time he's had to carry his power. I've been hauling mine around for just as long, but it didn't hurt when she broke contact."

"It hurt her. In a way."

Paul felt a sickening twist of guilt in his gut. "I hurt her?"

"Not exactly. Let's just say she felt a lot better when you were touching her."

He'd turned her on. That much was clear. She'd been ready to let him take her. Maybe that was what Logan meant.

"Now you're catching on," said Logan.

"What else did you see?" Paul demanded. That flicker of hope was growing, and as foolish as it was, he was letting it. He wanted to know everything about her so that maybe this time things would be different. Not like Kate.

"Not much. She was too weak for me to spend much

time inside her mind. I sensed that she's not entirely what she seems. She's been through tragedy."

Never again. He didn't want tragedy to ever touch her life again. "What kind?"

Logan shrugged. "The same as all of us. She's lost those she loved. Her mother is gone, which is a shame. I'd hoped we'd find a way to question her and see if Andra's father had any connection to Helen's."

"Could they be sisters?" Paul couldn't see any similarities between Helen's lush, curvy body and Andra's sleeker, muscular build. Their hair color was similar, but that was about it.

"No. I don't think so. Their blood wasn't close enough."

"Did you learn anything else?"

"Only that she works too hard. Doesn't eat well or sleep enough most of the time."

"You got that right," grumbled Madoc from the kitchen. "There's not much here that's edible, and it's too damn early to order takeout. No one's open. I'm making a food run. Any requests?"

"No," said Paul. "Just be quick. As soon as she wakes up, we're hitting the road."

"That's going to take a while," said Logan. "You might as well get comfortable and take your own rest."

"Not going to happen. Not while she's vulnerable."

Logan smiled in satisfaction. "Speaking like a bonded man already."

Paul stared at his ring. It looked like it had for the last two centuries, only faded with time. He wanted to believe, but what if Logan was wrong?

Madoc shut the door on his way out.

"What if I'm *not* wrong?" asked Logan.

"Stay out of my head," warned Paul. "I'm a long way from being over you bleeding Andra."

"She offered."

"Next time, don't listen to any offers she makes."

"If I hadn't fed from her, you'd still be thinking your days were at an end. Certainly that hope is worth something."

"Yeah, it's worth a beating if you're wrong."

Logan just laughed. "Go guard your woman. It will make you less grumpy."

Whether or not Andra could be his, being near her still sounded like a good idea, so he took the Sanguinar's advice and went to her.

Chapter 4

Zillah hated being summoned by a child, but he played along because it suited him. "My lady," he greeted Maura, bowing low enough to appease her ego. "How may I serve you?"

Maura's pale hair blazed in contrast with the rest of her surroundings. Everything in her personal chambers was a deep, rich red—the color of fresh blood. Velvet drapes lined the chamber, and a thick, soft rug on the floor helped mute the sounds of his voice so it didn't echo off the cave walls. He felt claustrophobic in here, though none of the smaller rooms seemed to have that effect on him. Odd.

Perhaps it was the company that he found so stifling.

Her small, round face sneered up at him in anger. "She's done it again," said Maura.

Zillah resisted the urge to shake the girl. They needed her too much for him to kill her just now. Soon, but not yet.

"Who has done what?" he asked in a patient voice, as if he didn't have a hundred more pressing matters demanding his attention.

Her ringlets bobbed furiously as she spun on her heel. "Andra Madison. She stole the child I wanted before we even had the chance to bring him here and find out if he was suitable."

"We'll find another," soothed Zillah. "You mustn't upset yourself."

"Upset myself?" she asked in a deceptively quiet voice.

Maura stalked toward him, and even though she weighed only about as much as his leg, she still frightened him. There was something inside those black eyes of hers that made him feel cold. Afraid. It didn't matter that he commanded an army of thousands. It didn't matter that he wielded more power than all of the unbound Theronai combined. It didn't even matter that she was a tiny thing he could break with a careless sweep of his hand.

Maura was powerful in a way he couldn't begin to understand. She knew . . . things. She could destroy him with as much effort as it took her to blow her dainty nose, and he wouldn't even see it coming.

For all he knew, she'd already sealed his fate.

"I didn't mean to make light of your suffering, my lady. I meant only that all will be well. We will find another child."

"Not with his bloodline. There hasn't been a human child as strong as him born in two centuries. We need that strength if we are to succeed."

"There is still time. The girl is only fourteen."

"Which is why I wanted the boy now. We still have time to alter him to suit her," she said as if *he* were the child.

Zillah resisted the urge to slap her, and kept his voice steady. "Shall I send another unit to retrieve him?"

"No. This woman is the one we must stop. Andra. She is the one who keeps stealing my toys. I want her killed."

"Of course, my lady. It shall be as you wish. I will dispatch troops immediately." Zillah bowed low, dismissing himself, beyond ready to be out of her company.

His ploy to leave didn't work. Maura's eyes got that glazed look he knew meant she was having a vision.

The timing was inconvenient, but he had no choice but to stay and learn what she'd seen. These visions were the only reason he put up with her petulance. The only reason he hadn't fed her to his pets.

She crumpled to the floor, but Zillah didn't dare help her. No one touched Maura. Ever.

She pushed herself up, panting and shaking all over. If he'd had any parental instincts, they would have been blaring in his ear at this moment. But he didn't. He'd sooner watch her die than give her aid. Since she'd come here, every creature who had touched her died within days, screaming in agony.

If she hadn't been so frail, she would have been a formidable weapon against the Sentinels. Send her in, let her play the role of child and hug them all. An entire compound could be destroyed within days.

"What did you see?" he asked, eager to know and be gone from her presence.

Maura was pale, and if he hadn't known she was incapable of it, he would have thought she looked afraid. "Forget the boy. There's another we must find and bring here."

"Another? Who?"

"Not who. What."

"What, then?"

She smoothed the curls away from her doll-like face. "Bait. Irresistible bait."

"I don't understand," he said.

"I know," replied Maura with contempt heavy and discordant in her child's voice. "You never have."

As soon as Logan was sure Paul was occupied with Andra, Logan dialed Tynan, the leader of the Sanguinar.

"Yes," answered Tynan.

"Can you speak?"

"Yes."

"Sammy McMullins was abducted by the Synestryn last night."

"I'm sorry, Logan. I know he was one of your more recent successes. You must be desolate. Did you find the body?"

"We got him back alive."

A shocked silence filled the line. "How?"

"A woman named Andra Madison. She hunts down lost children. She found him."

"Where is he now?"

"With his parents."

"And the woman?" asked Tynan.

"I'm in her apartment. With Paul. I believe she's his lady."

"Another woman?" said Tynan in awe. "Where did she come from?"

"I'm still working on that. Her upbringing was fairly normal, but she's strong. Maybe even as strong as Helen."

"Can you locate her parents?"

"Her mother is dead. I don't think she knows much about her father. I wasn't able to search her mind too deeply with two Theronai standing guard over her. Maybe if I can get her alone."

"Can you bring her to Dabyr?"

"Yes. Tonight. Sibyl has ordered Paul to present her."

"Good," said Tynan. "In the meantime, find out what you can about Sammy. I'm going to visit his parents and console them. We don't want them to worry that this will happen with the child they're expecting."

"She's pregnant again?"

"Yes, but she doesn't know it yet. We'll let them find out on their own. Our interference will be less obvious that way."

Another success. Logan could hardly believe their plan was working. Maybe it was worth all the suffering and hunger they'd been through. "They'll need to relocate, just to be safe."

"I'll take care of it. I'll see if I can convince any of the Slayers to keep watch over the family, too."

That notion made Logan's chest tighten. "Why? Do you think the Slayers would agree?"

There was a long pause, as though Tynan were deciding what to say. Or whether to say anything. "Perhaps. I've been . . . negotiating with them. It's going well."

Shock stilled Logan's body. None of his kind had had dealings with the Slayers since the Theronai declared war upon them. They were a violent, proud, and deadly race of shapeshifters who had long ago turned their backs on humans. They protected their own and kept to themselves. "What if the Theronai find out we're dealing with the Slayers? They won't like us allying ourselves with their enemies."

"That's why they'll never find out. This war is ridiculous, anyway. I refuse to choose sides."

"We already did. We chose the Theronai's side."

"Only because their blood was purer. Not because they were right."

Something in what Tynan said set off a warning in Logan's mind. "You said the negotiations were going well. What could you possibly have to offer the Slayers?"

"They want to become involved in Project Lullaby."

"You *told* them about it? Are you mad?"

"They won't tell the Theronai. It's in their best interest to keep our secrets. They need the bloodlines strengthened as badly as we do. Their powers have all but faded."

"I thought that's what they wanted. To stop fighting the Synestryn and settle down to life like the humans."

"There's been a shift in power among them. Andreas Phelan has risen to power and has demanded his people return to the old ways or leave the pack."

"He was only a child when I last saw him."

"Things have changed. For the better."

Logan wasn't so sure, but he had no choice other than to trust Tynan's leadership until he could learn the truth himself. Besides, it was too late. The Slayers already knew too much, and they were not easy to kill.

"Be careful," warned Logan. "There's too much at stake to risk so many years of effort."

"I'm always careful." Tynan sounded tired. Weak.

"I'll have blood to share when I return," said Logan. He'd rather keep all of the strength Andra had given him to himself, but he couldn't be that selfish. Survival of his race demanded that he wasn't. Things would change soon for their people. Project Lullaby would see to that.

"Thank you, brother. It's sorely needed."

Logan heard Madoc's heavy step coming down the hall toward Andra's apartment. "I must go."

He hung up the phone just before Madoc came in bearing two big sacks of food. He gave Logan a suspicious look, as if he knew about the conversation that had just taken place. Then again, Madoc always looked suspicious.

"What have you been up to, leech?"

Logan hated the derogatory term, but he refused to let it show. "Just resting. I always feel weak when the sun is up."

"Yeah, right. I believe that one."

"What did you bring?"

"Breakfast. Lots of it. Hope you're hungry."

"Always," said Logan.

Madoc wasn't sure how much longer he could wait for the woman to show. It had taken Logan fucking forever to fall asleep, and Madoc didn't want the bloodsucker knowing just how bad off he was. No one could know.

He leaned against the front door of Andra's apartment, where he'd been waiting for the past twenty minutes. The cool wood eased the burning in his skin, but it did nothing for the rest of him. Pain pulsed inside him, swelling bigger with every beat of his heart.

Sparks of energy in the air found him and bombarded

him, making him want to scream. He couldn't take any more power. He had to bleed some off. Right. Now.

Madoc was pretty sure today was the day he was going to die. And if it wasn't, he was totally sure he didn't want to know just how much worse he could hurt.

If only he'd been able to get more fighting in over the past few days, he would have bled off some of his power that way. Or at least not added to the giant pool of energy threatening to shatter him into a bloody mess. But he hadn't been able to fight until last night. They'd spent too many days driving around looking for Andra so Paul could feel better.

Fucking pansy.

Of course, if Andra had been Madoc's woman, it would have been worth it. He assumed that when his soul started to die, he wouldn't feel hope anymore. Funny how wrong he'd been. He wasn't sure if he could still be saved now or not, but he knew that was what he wanted—to end his suffering one way or another.

In the back of Madoc's mind, he was still grieving over the fact that he felt no connection to Andra whatsoever.

Then again, his soul had started dying months ago, and it was getting harder and harder to feel anything. He was one of the Band of the Barren—the secret group of Theronai who no longer bore any leaves on their lifemarks. Their souls were dead, but they helped one another hide it from the other Sentinels, pretending to be normal. If any of the other Sentinels knew, they'd be outcast. Or worse—sent to the Slayers.

Madoc pressed his palm to his chest where the pressure was the worst. The Band was an invitation-only kind of group, but one of the brothers had recruited him in time to slow the falling of his last leaf. It now hung on his skin midfall, moving too slowly for the eye to see. The other men said that slowing the fall would help him cling to his morals. Or at least pretend well enough to fool the rest of the Sentinels.

Madoc wasn't convinced it was working. He was still getting worse by the day.

Another wave of pressure exploded inside him, nearly ripping him apart. He slid to the ground and pulled himself into a tight ball, hoping that would keep his guts from spewing out his navel. A scream of pain built inside him, but he'd learned long ago not to make a sound. No one outside of the Band of the Barren could know he was lost—no longer one of them.

A soft knock on the door echoed like salvation in his ears. She was finally here.

Madoc found the strength to push himself to his feet and open the door. The woman on the other side looked to be in her forties, but was probably a decade younger. She had frizzy blond hair, and last night's makeup still ringed her dull brown eyes. She wasn't pretty, but she had on a short skirt and that was enough for him.

"I'm Candi," she said with a fake smile.

Madoc pulled her into the apartment and shut the door. "Don't care," he ground out. His voice was rough with pain, but he didn't care about that, either.

There was no real privacy in the small apartment, so he led Candi to the kitchen, which was as good as he could do. Logan was asleep on the couch not far away, but Sanguinar normally slept like the dead during the day.

"Well, aren't you the sweet talker?" said Candi.

"How much?" he demanded.

"Depends on what you want."

"To fuck you. How much?"

"Hundred for the straight-up stuff. Kink will cost you extra."

Madoc pulled some bills from his wallet and thrust them at her. He wasn't sure how much it was, but it was more than enough, based on the way her dull eyes lit up.

"I'm going to take good care of you, honey," she purred.

Madoc couldn't wait any longer. He had to have some kind of release for all the pressure grinding inside him. Sex worked better than anything other than hard-core demon slaying.

He grabbed her hips and turned her around, facing away from him. He really didn't want to look at her while he used her, though he wasn't sure why it mattered.

She grabbed the counter to steady herself, telling him he was being a little rough. So fucking what. She was a professional. She could take it.

Madoc shoved her short skirt up and her panties down with one hand while he freed his cock with the other. She smelled like drugs and desperation, which would have bothered him at one point in his life. Not anymore. Now, he just didn't fucking care.

"Slow down there, big boy. You gotta glove up first." Candi held a condom over her shoulder.

Madoc despised the interruption. Pain was pounding on him to fuck her hard and fast, but he knew from experience that putting the thing on was the fastest way to get him what he wanted. He didn't want her screaming and waking up Logan or Paul.

He covered himself and used one hand to force her shoulders down to the kitchen counter. She gave a little grunt, but didn't complain. Madoc shoved his dick inside her and went to work. She started to make sounds as if she were enjoying it.

"Shut the fuck up," he growled at her.

Candi did.

Madoc didn't take long. Maybe forty-five seconds. He shot his wad without making a sound, but Candi was a professional and she knew when a man was finished.

She straightened, but Madoc pushed her back down. "I'm not done yet."

"Hate to argue, but I felt you—"

"Give me another rubber or I'm going in bareback."

Candi snagged another condom out of her bra and

handed it to him. Madoc pulled off the used one and tossed it in the trash before rolling the clean one on.

The whore tried to move, but Madoc's hips kept her pinned. He was still hard, throbbing as if he hadn't had a woman in a year. The orgasm hadn't done much, but at least he didn't feel like his body was going to rip apart anymore.

Maybe the next three or four times would make him feel normal again. At least for a while.

Chapter 5

Andra felt like she'd just fallen asleep, but glancing at the clock told her she'd been out for almost twelve hours. At least she was feeling better. Stronger and able to take on all the things that waited for her. Like the child who would no doubt be taken tonight. And if not tonight, then soon. The abductions never stopped.

It was just starting to get dark outside. The monsters were probably gearing up, planning where to attack.

Time to get to work.

She sat up slowly, feeling a bit woozy. She wasn't sure how much blood Logan had taken, but she hadn't eaten since, and she was pretty sure that wasn't great for her blood volume recovery. She eased her legs over the side of the bed and nearly kicked Paul. He knelt on the floor between piles of dirty laundry, beautifully bare chested with his sword in front of him. His eyes were closed, but she sensed he wasn't asleep. His breathing was too deep and controlled for sleep. He looked like he might be meditating.

Not wanting to disturb him, she carefully stepped around him on her way to the bathroom, trying to be quiet. She was in the bathroom a few minutes, and when she came out, he still hadn't moved.

She'd almost made it to the door when Paul's fingers latched onto her bare ankle, just above her sock. That tingling hum slid up her leg and warmed the insides of her thighs. She let out a rough moan, unable to keep the telling sound from slipping from her.

God, his touch felt good. She stood there soaking it in, letting it sink into her flesh and bones and become a part of her. It was more than merely a physical kind of pleasure, though it was that. It was also a sense of contentment—of rightness. When he touched her all the bad things in her life slipped away for just a while, leaving her feeling clean and content. None of her mistakes haunted her here. None of her fears. None of her grief. She was free. Happy.

His long fingers rubbed over her ankle, sliding a few inches under the hem of her jeans. Another sound of contentment poured from her, and she wished he'd keep creeping those fingers up all the way. If he could make her feel this good by touching her ankle, she could only imagine how much better it would be if he focused on her more sensitive spots.

She really wanted to find out.

"Logan was right," said Paul in a quiet, almost reverent voice. "You do feel something, don't you?"

"Yes." The word hissed out of her. Maybe she shouldn't have let him know the kind of power he held over her, but she didn't care. Not now. She was willing to give him almost anything, and the truth was easy to give.

He took her hand and rose from his kneeling position. She missed his touch at her ankle, but she forgave him as soon as his fingers traced a gentle line over her cheek.

Andra shivered, and it made Paul's brown eyes darken with satisfaction. She leaned into his touch, unable to stop herself. "What are you doing to me?"

"Do you like it?" he asked, sounding pleased, as if he already knew the answer.

She watched his mouth move. It was a nice mouth—soft-looking, with a full bottom lip that made her want to nibble at it. "You know I do."

"Then I won't stop. The closer we are, the easier it will be for you."

Andra didn't know what he meant by that. She was too busy deciding that she was going to kiss him. Sure, she didn't really know him, and yes, he carried a sword and killed monsters, but that wasn't part of the whole deciding-to-kiss-him equation. It was simply a matter of needing to see if he tasted as good as he felt.

She threaded her hands into his soft, mussed hair and went up on tiptoe. He didn't try to stop her. In fact, he met her halfway.

Her lips touched his and the rest of the world ceased to exist. His mouth was smooth and firm. Perfect. He didn't try to rush her or shove his tongue into her mouth like so many men did. Instead, he let her take her time while she learned the feel of him. She flicked her tongue out and tasted just the corner of his mouth.

Paul let out a low rumble of appreciation and pulled her body hard against his own. She could feel the muscles of his chest and abs, so beautifully defined. But even more distracting, she could feel his erection through their jeans, big and hard and ready for her.

"This can't be happening," she breathed. "Nothing this good is real."

His fingers slid under her shirt and splayed across her bare back. "Feels pretty real to me."

She kissed him again, sucking his full lower lip into her mouth. His fingers clenched against her back, telling her just how much he liked it.

Good, because she wasn't anywhere close to being through with him. There was a bed only two feet away and it was already a wreck anyway. Might as well make good use of it.

Andra maneuvered him back until his legs hit the side of her bed, but he didn't go down, as she'd hoped. He was too strong and solid for her to push around unless he allowed it, and right now, he wasn't.

She lifted her mouth from his and looked at him. "You're not interested." Just saying the words nearly made her scream. Her body was primed, slick, and ready to take him on.

"I'm more than just interested. I'm just not sure this is smart."

"Of course it's not smart. I don't even know you. I don't normally screw strangers."

"Exactly. This isn't like you."

He was right. Whoever was in the driver's seat of her body, it wasn't her. Something else was going on here. Something freaky.

Still, her body was humming and hot for him, and she didn't think she was strong enough to pull away. Not when she knew bleak reality was out there waiting for her. This was so much better.

She kissed him again, tasting him, allowing him to do the same. Their tongues mingled, making her dizzy. She sagged against him, but Paul held her up, taking her weight easily.

When he pulled his mouth away he was breathing hard. "I'm stopping this now. Before I can't. I don't want to scare you away." He set her on the bed, but didn't go far, as if he were afraid she might pass out or something.

When another wave of dizziness washed over her, she didn't think that was such a bad idea. That needy haze was fading, but this time it didn't disappear. Not entirely. She was right on eye level with the impressive bulge in his jeans, and there wasn't a red-blooded woman out there who wouldn't have been a little awed by a sight like that.

He wanted her, and the proof of it thrilled her down to her toes.

Andra had to stop staring. She flopped back onto the bed and covered her eyes with her forearm. The sudden motion spun her head around until she thought she might throw up.

Wouldn't that turn him on?

Now that she was no longer touching him, she wasn't feeling so hot. In fact, she felt more than just a little ill. Her joints ached and her eyes burned like she had a fever.

Too bad. There wasn't time to be sick. "I've got to get some water or something. I think Logan might have taken a little more than a pint."

She couldn't see him, but she could practically feel the vibration of his anger filling the room. "It won't happen again."

Andra waved her hand. "I'll be fine. Just need some juice and cookies."

"Madoc ordered some pizza. You interested?"

The idea of food turned her stomach, but she knew she'd feel better if she managed to choke something down. "Pizza works as well as anything. Give me a sec and I'll be right out."

She didn't take Paul's hand when he offered to help her off the bed. He scowled, but he could just keep on scowling. As much as she enjoyed the way he made her feel, she had more important things to worry about. So did he.

Night was coming.

Andra's phone rang and she thanked it for the distraction. She pushed herself from the bed without any help, thank you, and scooped it up. "Hello."

"Andra, this is Melanie at Twin Oaks Hospital. I think you should come over here immediately." The woman's voice was high-pitched, nearly frantic. Something terrible had happened.

Andra locked her knees to keep from sinking to the floor in fear. So many horrible things flashed through her mind. Nika was so fragile. She could be hurt so easily. "What's wrong, Melanie?"

"The doctor said not to bother you, that she'd deal with it, but I knew you'd want to know."

"Know what?" *Please, God, let Nika be okay*. Andra didn't think she could bear to lose another sister.

"Nika's gotten worse. Much worse."

Part of Andra was relieved that she was still alive, while the rest of her was seething with rage. Why hadn't they called sooner? "Did something happen?"

"I don't know. Her deterioration seems way too sudden," said Melanie. "I really think you should come. She needs you."

Paul watched Andra's face drain of blood. Whoever was on that phone had scared her more than demons charging her with claws extended and teeth bared. He couldn't hear what was being said on the other end, but he didn't have to hear it to know it was bad.

He crossed the distance between them, making sure he was close enough to catch her if she passed out or something. She looked as if she were on the verge of doing just that.

"Okay," she said. "I'll be there in twenty minutes."

The phone fell from Andra's fingers. She looked vulnerable. Afraid.

Paul moved to put his arm around her, but she flinched away from his touch.

Just like Kate had done so many times.

It wasn't going to happen again. Not with Andra.

She headed out of the bedroom and he was right on her heels, refusing to let her get away from him.

"Tell me what's going on," he urged.

Logan was sleeping on the couch and woke at the noise. Madoc was watching professional wrestling and pumping iron on Andra's impressive weight bench. He shot Paul a questioning look and Paul gave him a hell-if-I-know shrug.

Andra stopped in the kitchen and started rummaging through stacks of papers and mail. A bright sheen of tears filled her eyes, but she blinked several times to clear it. "I, uh, need to go. It's an emergency."

"What emergency?"

Her movements grew more frantic and she started throwing mail to the floor as she searched for something. "I just have to go," she said. "Lock up when you leave."

She was trembling. Pale. That stone-hard confidence he'd seen earlier was gone now, leaving her looking shattered and afraid. Paul wanted to drag her into his arms, but he didn't dare touch her. He had to remember that she was only cooperating with him because he'd offered to pay her.

"I'm not leaving you," he told her. He didn't think she was in any shape to drive safely. Besides, whatever this was, he wanted to be there for her. Just in case she needed help. *He* worked for free. "Let me drive you."

"No, thanks. You can stay here if you want. I don't care. I'll be back as soon as I can." She yanked a paper towel off the roll and scrubbed at her wet eyes.

"Anything I can do?" asked Madoc, looking a little too hopeful for Paul's peace of mind.

"Have you seen my keys?"

"Sorry."

Without anything else to do to help her, Paul started looking for her keys, too. "Tell me what's going on. Maybe I can help."

"I appreciate the thought, but there's nothing you can do but get out of my way so I can find my damn keys." Her voice caught on a sob, which she tried, and failed, to hide.

Paul couldn't stand it any longer. He had to comfort her. Help her. Something.

He took her by the arm to turn her around, and the second his palm touched her skin he was swamped with feelings of physical pleasure. He sucked in his breath against the force of it. His body tingled. Sang with joy. Every cell inside him was doing a happy little dance that made him want to bust out in laughter. So much of his life had been spent in pain that he'd forgotten what it was like to live without it.

Andra's blue eyes widened and she stared at him in shock. Her pupils dilated and her gaze lowered to his mouth.

And then it hit him—a surge of lust that crashed into him and swept him along for the ride. His body hardened so fast it hurt, but even that hurt was a kind of pleasure. His skin grew warm and his blood swelled in his veins. His mouth watered for a taste of her, and his fingers tightened against her skin, seeking closer contact.

Her lips parted as she drew in a startled breath, and he knew he had to kiss her. He was going to force her to open her mouth and let him taste her, and he wasn't going to stop there. He was going to lay her out on the floor and taste every swath of smooth skin, every sweet hollow and curve. He was going to strip her bare and make her his in the most basic, primitive way he knew.

Mine, his soul screamed, and he knew that if he moved even one inch toward her lips, he'd be lost—unable to stop no matter what she wanted, no matter what emergency she had to deal with. Nothing else in her life could possibly be more important than his need for her.

And that truth poured over him like icy water, dousing his lust until it was only a smoldering pile of longing.

With careful motions, Paul loosened his grasp on Andra and moved his hand away. Losing contact with her left him burning and stinging all over, but he rejoiced in that pain. It meant there was hope—hope that Andra was the woman who could save him.

Now Paul was the one who was shaking.

Andra rubbed her hands over the place where he'd held her shoulders and looked at him with a mix of confusion and fear. "Never again," she told him. "Don't ever touch me again."

Not fucking likely, but he kept his mouth prudently shut and continued his search for her keys. He found them hiding under the lid of an open pizza box and dangled them in front of her. "You're in no shape to drive. At least let me take you wherever you're going."

She hesitated and he could sense her indecision, so he went in for the kill. "Whatever it is, you can't fix it if you crash on the way there."

When her shoulders slumped, he knew he'd won. "Fine," she said. "But if you don't drive fast enough, I'm throwing you out of my truck."

Chapter 6

Andra leaped out of the truck as soon as they reached the psychiatric hospital, leaving Paul to find a place to park. The staff at the front desk must have known she was on her way, because they were waiting for her with a visitor badge as soon as she slammed through the front door.

The smells of disinfectant and sorrow clung to the walls of this place, but it was better than the rest of the mental hospitals she'd seen. They charged an arm and a leg for Nika to stay here, but at least they took good care of her. Andra showed up randomly every couple of weeks in addition to her normal weekly visits, and never once in eight years had she seen any signs of mistreatment of the patients. They were clean and resting as calmly as they were able, considering.

Melanie met Andra in the hall outside Nika's room. She was somewhere in her late forties with smooth, dark skin and huge eyes. The woman never smiled, but she conveyed comfort with the smallest touch of her pudgy hand.

"I didn't know what else to do but call you," said Melanie. "My last shift was only two days ago, but I swear she wasn't so thin then. And no one else seems to see it. None of the doctors listen when I tell them she needs to be put on a feeding tube. It's like they don't even see that she's wasting away."

Andra knew that Nika had a tendency to go days without eating, but it never lasted. The doctors said it would be more harmful to force her than to let her get hungry enough that her body's needs overcame her mind's imaginary fears.

Andra reached for the door, but Melanie stopped her. "We had to restrain her today. She hasn't had enough to drink, and we had to give her an IV to keep her hydrated. She kept pulling it out."

"She hates to be restrained," said Andra. Anger burned in her chest, a welcome relief from the constant grief she felt for her sister.

"I know, honey, but it was for her own good. She kept hurting herself, tearing open her veins. We got the bleeding stopped, but we can't take any more chances. She's already so weak. I'm not sure she'd be able to fight off an infection right now."

Melanie was right. Poor Nika was so delusional that they had to do whatever was necessary to protect her. Keep her safe.

In the back of Andra's mind, she wondered if keeping Nika alive wasn't just a cruel form of torture. Maybe it would be kinder to let her go. Let her slip away from the fear and misery that were her life.

If Andra had been a stronger person, maybe she would have done just that. But she wasn't. She was weak and selfish. She'd already let one sister die. She couldn't let that happen to the other one. She needed Nika to live.

Andra put her hand on the door and prayed for strength.

Melanie gave Andra a quick hug. "You need to know that there's some blood on her gown. We normally would have changed her, but it caused her so much distress that we just let her be. Fresh clothes can wait for a few hours."

Andra nodded and opened the door to Nika's room.

She'd seen Nika in distress before, but nothing could have prepared her for the wild look of fear in her sister's eyes. She was fighting against the restraints that held her in the hospital bed. Angry purple bruises marred her arms where the IVs had been ripped out. Her white nightgown was splattered with drops of blood, and the woman beneath the gown had become dangerously thinner than she'd been only four days ago. Her face was gaunt, her pale blue eyes sunken and fever-bright with terror. She cried fat tears that soaked the white hair at her temples.

Andra bit back a wail of grief. Poor Nika. So lost in her own world of nightmares. Nothing Andra had done had ever helped.

Andra swallowed her tears and went to her sister.

Paul saw Logan and Madoc pull into the parking lot behind him. Madoc was driving, and Paul went to his window. "You coming in?"

Logan was in the back, covered up to prevent the last few rays of sunlight from touching his skin. "Where are we?" he asked.

"Twin Oaks Hospital."

"That's a psychiatric facility," said Logan.

"Great. Andra's in there with a bunch of crazies." Paul really didn't care for the notion, and itched to get back to her side, where he could keep her safe.

"Any idea why we're here?" asked Madoc.

"None. She wouldn't say a thing on the drive over. Except to tell me to drive faster."

"I think I'll leave this to you, man. I'm more likely to scare the people in there than anything."

"Okay. Sit tight. I'll call you when I know what's going on."

It took a little fast-talking to convince the woman at the front desk to let him enter the mental hospital, but Paul managed to win his way inside. A burly orderly es-

corted him to the room where Andra had gone, and he
silently slipped inside.

Andra sat beside the bed holding the hand of a frail
young woman with striking white hair. The woman
thrashed on the bed, fighting the restraints that held her
in place. A series of pitiful moans filled the room, echoing off the stark walls.

"It's okay, Nika," soothed Andra, stroking the woman's pale hair back from her forehead. "I'm here now.
You're going to be okay."

Slowly, Nika began to calm down, though whether it
was from Andra's words or sheer exhaustion, Paul had
no idea.

As soon as Nika relaxed and saw Andra was there,
the glazed look of fear faded from the woman's delicate
features. She was maybe twenty, and though her hair was
white where Andra's was brown, there was no mistaking
the family resemblance in their faces. They had the same
full lips, high cheekbones, and bright blue eyes—like a
clear winter sky. Nika was much thinner than Andra,
even to the point of being gaunt, and it gave her a fragile, ethereal appearance that contrasted harshly with
Andra's healthy strength.

Paul itched to know the relationship between them,
but didn't dare ask. He felt desperation in the room—a
subtle thrumming of frantic energy that did not dissipate. It was coming from Nika, almost as if she had
fought her way through her insanity because Andra was
here. He wouldn't do anything to jeopardize that.

"Andra?" asked the younger woman. Her voice was
raw from screaming and faint with fatigue.

"I'm here, Nika. Right here."

Nika's body went limp, and she stopped trying to fight
the restraints. "Please make them let me go. I can't stand
being chained down."

"You're not chained down, honey. They put these restraints on you to keep you from pulling out the IV."

"I won't pull it out. I promise." Tears welled in Nika's eyes as they pleaded for freedom.

Andra looked at the nurse who was standing unobtrusively in the corner of the room. "I'm letting her up," she told the nurse.

"It's not a good idea," said the nurse.

Andra ignored the advice and started to unfasten the restraints around Nika's arms. "She's not fighting anymore, and I can't stand to see her like this."

As soon as Nika was free, she sat up and grabbed Andra around the neck in a fierce hug. She looked small next to Andra. Almost childlike. "I'm so glad you're here. I tried to call out to you, but you couldn't hear me," said Nika.

Paul felt Andra tense more than he saw it. "All you have to do is use the phone or have one of the nurses call. I'll always come."

"There were no phones where I was, Andra. I swear it. I'm not making it up."

Andra smoothed Nika's white hair away from her face and wiped the tears from her cheeks. "I know you're not lying. It's all right." She helped Nika lie back down and climbed into the bed beside her, pulling the frail woman into her arms. "They told me you aren't eating," said Andra without accusation.

Nika swallowed. "I try, but I can't. All she gets to eat is black blood. It burns like acid. How can I eat food when all she gets is blood?"

Paul had no idea who "she" was, but apparently Andra did. "No one is feeding her blood, Nika. It's just a trick of your mind. You have to eat."

Nika shook her head. "I try, but all I taste is the blood and it makes me sick."

Andra was quiet for a while, just running a soothing hand over the woman's hair. "Do you want them to find another way to feed you? Maybe put a tube into your stomach so you won't feel sick?"

"No!" Nika tried to lurch up, but Andra's stronger body easily held her down. "No, no, no. No tubes!"

"Okay," said Andra in a placating tone. "No tubes. But you have to eat. Will you at least try?"

"But the blood—"

"Is not real. It's a trick." Andra looked over at the nurse as if deciding whether or not to trust her.

The astute nurse saw the look and said, "I'll go get a tray." Then she left, eyeing Paul curiously as she passed him.

Once the nurse was gone, Andra said, "We've talked about this before. The monsters like to play tricks on you. They make you think things are real. No one is going to feed blood to anyone here. You're safe."

Nika grabbed Andra's hand and squeezed hard with skeletal fingers. "I'm safe, but Tori isn't. They keep hurting her. Putting things inside her. Changing her. She's so afraid, Andra."

Andra's chin trembled for a moment before she controlled it. Only the brightness of her eyes gave away her grief. "Tori is not afraid anymore. She's dead, Nika. Up in heaven with Mom."

"No, she's not! The monsters have her. They're doing something to her to make her . . . different. We have to find her soon or it will be too late."

Paul saw anguish tighten Andra's body, though her expression remained calm. No doubt for Nika's sake. "Please, honey, try not to worry about Tori. Nothing can ever hurt her again."

The nurse returned with a tray of food and placed it on the table beside the bed. "I'll come back in a few minutes. Do you need anything else?"

"No, we'll be fine, Melanie. Thanks."

The nurse left and Andra pulled the metal cover off the tray of food. "Looks like some chicken soup and runny mashed potatoes. Which sounds better?"

"Not the potatoes. Too thick. Too much like . . ."

"Get that thought out of your mind. Focus on me. Tell me what you've been drawing lately." Andra tested the temperature of the soup on her own lips before holding the spoon to Nika's mouth.

Nika closed her eyes, took a deep breath, and opened her mouth. Andra poured a tiny portion of soup over her tongue, and immediately Nika began to shake. Her body quivered and tears streamed down her face. Paul could see the effort she was making to swallow the soup, but it wasn't working. The poor girl's mind was too damaged, and she couldn't separate real food from the black blood of her delusions.

Nika grabbed the napkin and spit out the soup. "I'm sorry, Andra. I'm sorry."

Andra pushed the table away and wrapped her arms around Nika. "It's okay. You tried. We'll try again in a few minutes."

Andra turned her attention to Paul. He expected her to look at him with anger for spying on them, but instead, her eyes were imploring. "Can you help her like you did Sammy?" she asked him.

Paul stepped forward slowly so he wouldn't frighten Nika. "How long has she been this way?"

"Eight years."

Paul had no idea how she'd survived so long. Most people didn't last a year after being touched by the Synestryn. "It's been too long. I don't think I can help, but I might be able to help you to get her to eat. But it won't be easy."

"What do I do?"

Paul looked at Nika, who was watching him with wide, frightened eyes. "Can I come closer?" he asked her.

Nika looked to Andra, who said, "He's a friend."

Nika nodded and Paul moved slowly to Andra's side. "Give me your hand," he told Andra, holding out his left hand, which pulsed with the iridescent ring of the Theronai.

Andra obeyed and he felt her tense right before that wave of pleasure rolled through them both at the contact. He saw her eyes dilate and her nipples bead up under the thin fabric of her shirt. He had to fight to keep from pulling her up against him, or better yet, throwing her down on the bed, where he could stretch her out and spend his time tasting her.

Then he remembered Nika was on that bed and she needed them both to focus. Paul shoved down all those inappropriately lustful feelings and cleared his throat.

"What do I do?" asked Andra.

"Just hang on to me. Put your hand on Nika's head. Concentrate on the skin that links us. Open yourself up and don't fight what happens. I'll do the rest."

Paul had no access to the earth, so he focused on the air. He pulled from it tiny sparks of power no larger than motes of dust. He'd pushed himself hard recently, and hadn't meditated nearly long enough. His body tried to reject the power—to push it away so that he wouldn't have to suffer. Paul took control of his self-preservation instincts and forced them to yield. To accept the pain. He knew he didn't have much strength, and even less time, but he prayed it would be enough to give Nika a chance.

Rather than trying to make a connection with Nika, he used the connection that Andra already had. They knew each other. Trusted each other. Nothing he could say would ever outdo that trust. He let his energy flow through her hand, into her arm, across her chest, down her other arm, and into Nika.

Andra tensed and hissed in a pained breath. "You okay?" he asked, struggling against his own pain.

"Just hurry," she said.

Paul did. He gave up on finesse and forced his power through their skin-on-skin connection until he touched Nika's mind. As soon as he did, he jerked back, reeling from the dark agony the woman suffered. He'd never seen anything like it, and he hoped he never would again. She was human on the outside, but inside, she was a writhing mass of Synestryn-inflicted torment. He had no idea how she could stand the suffering. It was no wonder the poor thing couldn't eat. He wasn't sure that he would even be able to stay conscious if he had to live with that level of torment. And Paul knew torment.

There was no way he was going to be able to wade into her mind with his limited ability. He feared doing even greater damage. All he could hope for was to shut down the horror long enough to get some food into the woman. So that was what he did. He willed her mind to sleep while her body stayed awake. He shut down her consciousness with harsh, unyielding commands.

Paul pulled away from Nika as quickly as possible. His body was covered in a layer of cold sweat and he was shaking. Even with Andra's touch, that had been torture.

Nika was broken. Irrevocably.

"Oh, God," cried Andra. "How can she live with that?"

Paul forced his weary neck to lift his head. "You saw inside her mind?" It wasn't possible.

"No, I felt your horror. Your pity for her."

"I'm sorry. I didn't realize you'd be able to do that. If I'd known—"

"I'll survive," said Andra, her tone bleak and accepting. "Did it work?"

"I think so. Try to feed her now, but go slow. Her mind is asleep, so she won't be able to pay attention to what you're doing. She'll choke if you go too fast."

Andra lifted the spoon again, and this time Nika swallowed the soup. "It's working," she said, giving him a relieved smile.

Paul's gut tightened in reaction. It was the first time he'd seen her smile, and he couldn't remember ever seeing anything more beautiful. He'd spend eternity trying to make her smile again, given the chance.

Paul's cell phone buzzed—a timely warning against his train of thought. "I'll take this in the hall," he told her.

He stepped outside and answered the phone. "Yes?"

"Found something you should know," said Nicholas.

"Go ahead."

"That account you had me transfer funds into? Turns out it's part of a trust of some kind set up to pay the medical bills for a woman named Nika Madison. Does that make any sense?"

Paul looked back toward the door to Nika's room. A private room in a place like this couldn't be cheap. It was nice here. Quiet, upscale, well managed. Oh, yeah, this place would definitely cost a fortune.

An odd sort of relief washed through him at the news. Andra was not the money-hungry woman he'd feared. She was protecting Nika.

"Yes," Paul said into the phone. "It makes perfect sense."

Chapter 7

Andra got nearly all the food into Nika before she just lay down and closed her eyes.

She breathed out a relieved sigh and wiped a smudge of mashed potatoes from the corner of Nika's mouth. She'd never seen anything like this before, but then again, she was beginning to think there were a whole lot of things she'd never seen. Paul and his friends topped that list.

Melanie slipped into the room and eyed the empty containers. "You got her to eat."

"Paul helped," she said, just as he stepped back into the room.

"Your fiancé is a nice guy *and* a hunk? You really lucked out to find a man like that to marry. Shame on you for not telling me you're engaged. I didn't even know you were dating seriously."

Fiancé? She opened her mouth to refute it, but before she could, Paul said, "We only met recently, but when it's true love, why wait around?"

Melanie watched Andra carefully, as if waiting for her side of the story. After what he'd done for Nika, she wasn't about to go calling him a liar in front of Melanie. In fact, she wanted to throw herself at him in thanks for what he'd done. Instead, she reached out and took Paul's hand. Warm, tingling pleasure swamped her limbs and she had to work to stifle a shiver.

Her reaction must have been enough to convince Melanie, because she just grinned, congratulated the two of them on their impending marriage, and left the room with the empty tray.

Andra tried to pull her hand away so she could think straight, but Paul didn't let go.

"Fiancé?" she asked him.

"I had to get past the front desk somehow." He grinned and she was glad to see it. Ever since she'd asked him for the money, he'd looked at her like she'd committed some heinous crime, and until now, she hadn't realized how much his bad opinion had bothered her.

"Thanks," she said. "I seem to be telling you that a lot lately."

"My pleasure." He looked to where Nika was sleeping. "Do you mind telling me who she is?"

Andra hesitated. She didn't know this man, and yet he'd just finished suffering in order to help the only person on this earth Andra loved. She owed him more than she could ever repay. "My sister."

Paul's eyes widened with a desperate kind of hope. "Forgive me if this is rude, but do you share both of the same parents?"

Andra was so shocked by the odd question that she didn't even consider whether or not she should answer. "I think so. Mom had a boyfriend who would come visit her every few years. We never met him, but she loved him. She said he was in the military and that's why we never got to see him."

"In the military?"

Andra shrugged, refusing to let the hurt of her childhood rule her life now. "I think it was a cover story Mom made up so we wouldn't hate him. I believed it for a few years, but eventually I started to resent him. What the hell kind of father couldn't even send a birthday card or call on the phone once in a while? I think he was just some deadbeat who got Mom pregnant and left her to deal with things on her own."

"Sounds like a real winner," said Paul, but there was no fire in his tone, only speculation.

"I figure my life was better without him in it, you know?"

"I'm sure you're right," he said, but it didn't sound like he believed it for a minute.

"Do you know something you're not telling me?" she asked.

"About your father? I don't think so."

Nika let out a whimper in her sleep and Andra went to her side. "Shh, baby. Sleep."

"They're coming," mumbled Nika. "The monsters are coming."

Andra's heart broke open and wept for her sister. "You're safe here. I won't let anything hurt you."

The door to the room opened and Logan and Madoc walked in as if they owned the place. Andra was starting to question the security here. "How did you two get in?"

Logan ignored her question. He was too busy sniffing the air for something. Madoc shrugged his huge shoulders and said, "Once the sun set, Logan pulled his Invisible Man routine and we walked right in. No sweat."

"He actually went invisible?" asked Andra.

"Not exactly," said Logan. "It's more of a trick of the mind."

"Who's the kid?" asked Madoc. He stared at Nika with way too much interest for Andra's comfort.

Andra took a step to the side to block his line of sight. "I think you all should leave."

Logan's pale eyes brightened and he moved toward Nika as if he were floating. "You never said you had a sister." He pulled in a deep breath through his nose. "Her blood is as pure as yours. I can smell it."

Andra saw the dark spots of blood on Nika's gown.

"You can *smell* that we're sisters?" That was too freaky for words.

"Logan," said Paul in a warning tone. "Back the hell off."

"She's in so much pain. I mean only to ease her mind." He reached toward Nika.

The metallic ring of metal on metal filled the air as both Paul and Madoc drew their swords, seemingly from thin air. Paul's sword went to Logan's throat, Madoc's to Logan's crotch.

"Touch her and die the hard way," growled Madoc.

Logan lifted his elegant hands into the air and the unnatural light in his eyes dimmed. "The child is suffering. I can help."

Andra wasn't sure what was going on. "Can he really help her?" Andra asked Paul.

Paul spared Andra a quick glance. "He'd want to drink her blood."

"It's the only way to diagnose her—to find the true cause of her mental breakdown," explained Logan.

"Don't fall for it, Andra," said Madoc. "You saw the way he looked at her. He wants her blood, and he's using the excuse of helping her as a way to get it."

"That's not entirely true. I do want her blood, but I also want to help her. Just let me near her to see if I can give her any comfort."

Andra had given the vampire her blood and it hadn't hurt her, other than a case of the woozies. He'd mended her broken arm, too. If he could help Nika, she was willing to take a risk and let him near her. "You can look at her, but you can't do anything else."

"As you wish," agreed Logan.

Madoc didn't want to put his sword away. He was probably going to need it any second now anyway. Logan was a fucking predator, and he seemed to be the only one who saw that.

Madoc didn't like the idea of Logan getting anywhere near the child. He couldn't see her face from here, but she barely made a bump in the bed, she was so thin. Only the bones in her knees and her toes stuck out enough to tent the blanket.

Logan glided forward and Andra stepped aside to make room for him by the bed. Madoc got a glimpse at the girl's face and realized that this was no child. She was a young woman, much older than the ten or twelve he would have guessed from her scrawny frame.

The woman stirred and Andra laid a hand on her arm. "It's okay, Nika. He's here to help."

Madoc snorted in disgust. He couldn't help it. "The only person Logan is going to help is Logan."

"Back off, Madoc," said Paul. "He's not going to hurt her by looking at her."

Logan placed his hand on Nika's head. Just as he did, Nika opened her eyes as if someone had flipped a switch. Her skin was deathly pale, nearly as white as her hair. Her eyes were wide with fear, and a pure, brilliant blue like the winter sky. And there was so much blue, too. Her pupils had shrunk down to pinpoints.

She swatted Logan's hand away and scrambled away from him, huddling into a small space against the far railing of the bed. The IV bag swayed on the stand as her flailing swung the tube around.

"He wants my blood," she whispered, staring at Logan in terror. "He wants my blood, he wants my blood, he wants my blood." Over and over again, her words getting higher and more strained each time.

Andra rushed around the bed to soothe her sister. Madoc decided Logan's time with the woman was at an end. He grabbed the Sanguinar's thin body around the middle with one arm and hauled him across the room. He shoved him into the bathroom, shut the door, and held the knob so Logan couldn't come out until he let him.

The door rattled as Logan pulled against Madoc's hold, but it didn't budge. Logan was no wimp, but Madoc was a whole hell of a lot stronger.

"This isn't helping," he said from the other side of the door.

As a matter of fact, it was. Nika had quieted, and was now clinging to Andra's neck, sobbing. Madoc didn't care much for the tears, but they beat the hell out of that frightened look on her face—the one that made him want to kill something to make it stop.

Paul shot Madoc a sour look. "He's right, you know. He can't help her at all from there."

"Girl didn't want his help," said Madoc. "Just ask her."

Paul crossed to Madoc and spoke in a near whisper. "She's not sane. Logan scared her. That's all."

"She didn't want him to take her blood. Far as I'm concerned, that makes her the sanest person in this room."

Paul shook his head and turned around. "What do you want to do, Andra?"

She looked up from their hug. Tears were running down her face, and her eyes—so much like Nika's—were filled with sorrow.

Something about seeing that pulled at Madoc. He would have thought it was sympathy, but surely he had none left.

"I can't stand to see her upset like that. It's going to make her sick after we finally got her to eat something."

"Okay," said Paul. "How about we wait until she calms down and tell her what's going on. Maybe if she knows who Logan is, she won't be so afraid of him. She wasn't afraid of me."

"Because you didn't want to drink her blood, idiot," said Madoc.

Andra sniffed and nodded, ignoring him altogether. "It's worth a shot."

"The monsters are coming," said Nika. Her voice broke as she spoke, and Madoc had the nearly uncontrollable urge to go visit Logan in the bathroom and pound on him for a while.

"Shh, baby. No monsters can get you here," said Andra.

Nika lifted her tearstained face. Her cheekbones stood out under her skin. "They know where I am now. They see me. And you."

"No, they don't. You're safe here."

"I'm not crazy, Andra. They're coming."

Chick didn't sound crazy. Sad, afraid, tired, sure. But not crazy.

Madoc looked out the window onto the green lawn below. It was well lit down there, and he didn't see anything, but that didn't mean shit. "There's blood on her gown," he said. "If she is one of us, they might be able to smell it."

Nika turned her head and looked at him for the first time. When her eyes met his, he felt like he'd been hit in the gut with a battering ram. He grabbed the doorframe to steady himself.

Whoever she was, she had power. He could almost see it flowing through her.

Killing her.

He wasn't sure how he knew that was the case, but he knew it, deep down. Bone deep. The same way he knew his soul was shriveling up into a heap of ash more and more as each day passed, and there wasn't a fucking thing he could do about it.

Logan opened the door behind him. Madoc moved so Nika couldn't see the bloodsucker.

"Her natural protection should mask the scent of her blood from the Synestryn," said Paul.

"Not if she knows about them."

Paul asked Andra, "Does Nika know about the Synestryn?"

Andra gave a shaky nod. "They attacked us when we were kids."

Logan pulled in a deep breath, sniffing the air. "Nika's right. Synestryn are closing in. Fast."

Madoc righted himself and let the grin fill his face. Finally, something he could kill.

"We've got to get out of here," said Paul.

Andra held her sister's face against her chest. "Not without Nika."

"Right. Can you carry her?" Paul asked Andra.

She nodded and unhooked the clear bag of fluid from the stand. "Come on, Nika. You and I are going for a ride." She handed her sister the bag and lifted her into strong arms.

Andra was ripped, and Madoc took a moment to enjoy the sight before drawing his weapon. "I'll take point."

"I'll bring up the rear," said Paul. "Logan. You're going to have to shield us all from sight. Are you strong enough?"

"Yes," said Logan, though he didn't sound convincing. He was sticking close to Paul now, as if worried he might need a bodyguard.

Smart leech.

"She'll need to leave the bloody gown behind," said Logan.

"All of you turn around," ordered Andra.

Madoc did, making sure the others had as well. He heard a drawer open and close and the soft rustle of fabric. Then a sgath howl split the night, loud enough that Madoc could hear it through the thick glass. The Synestryn were close.

"We're done," said Andra. "Let's go."

Madoc rolled his shoulders and headed out the door, ready to kick ass.

Andra held Nika close as they raced out of the building. Amazingly, no one seemed to notice their passage.

It was as if they were invisible, just as Madoc had said. Not only that, but the guards had opened each door for them without having been asked. She had no idea what to think of that except that Logan must be using some weird mind-control mojo. It was best if she didn't spend too much time thinking about just what he could do with that kind of power.

Nika clung to her with weak arms, trembling and hiding her face against Andra's neck. She was covered in a clean nightgown now, but Andra had seen what had become of her sister's body when she'd helped her change. Poor Nika's body was a skeleton covered by loose, pale skin. Her belly was sunken and her ribs and hip bones protruded grotesquely, breaking Andra's heart. The only recognizable thing about her body was the ring-shaped birthmark on her left shoulder—the same one that graced Andra's calf.

It had taken every ounce of willpower Andra had to not break down into tears at the sight of her sister's wasted form. It was a wonder Nika was still alive. Why hadn't the doctors done something before now? Why had they waited until it got this bad before treating her more drastically? Was her psychosis so much worse than her physical state that they hadn't even noticed?

She had no answers, but she sure as hell was going to find some.

They hurried out into the parking lot, and out of the corner of her eye, Andra saw movement. She held Nika tighter and sped her pace. The howl of those demons got louder as they neared, and she was sure she could practically hear the sound of their claws scraping across the pavement.

"We're not going to make it," said Logan from behind her.

"Get in your truck and go," Paul ordered Andra.

She thought about telling him she wouldn't leave without him, but the truth was, she would do just about anything to get Nika out safely. He was a big boy, and she'd seen firsthand that he was capable of taking care of himself. "What are you going to do?"

"Kill the fuckers," said Madoc.

Paul's voice came from beside her, strong and steady. "Don't worry. We'll be right behind you."

He pressed one finger against her bare arm for a moment and she felt a shock of energy jump into her, like static electricity, only it didn't hurt. Instead, an odd sense of peace flittered over her skin, making her feel safe and protected.

She looked down and saw a bright bloodred mark on her skin where he'd touched her. "What was that?"

"Bloodmark. I'll be able to find you now, wherever you go," said Paul. Something about his tone, the way he spoke the words, told her that it was less a statement of fact than it was a promise. He would find her.

"They're here," whimpered Nika.

Andra didn't stop to ask her if she was sure. The trembling in her body told Andra she was. How she knew it was true was another story—one that they didn't have time for right now.

Paul took a fighting stance between her and the direction of the howls. He gave her one last look, then turned away.

Andra had to choke down the urge to go back and fight at his side. She belonged there. She knew it was true, though she had no idea how she knew. There seemed to be a lot of that going around tonight.

Andra slid Nika into her truck, jumped into the driver's seat, started the engine, and drove away. In her rearview mirror, she saw half a dozen of those furry things leap from the shadows and charge the men.

Paul's sword flashed under the lights of the parking lot as he slashed at one of the demons, his body strong and fluid as it moved across the pavement. She could watch him move like that for hours and still not be bored. He made fighting look so easy, so effortless. Almost beautiful.

Andra hit the curb and pulled her attention back to her driving. She didn't look back again. Nika was safe. That had to be enough.

But it wasn't. She felt as if she were abandoning the only people on earth who had even the slightest prayer of saving her sister from her insanity. Not to mention leaving behind a man who made her body come alive every time he touched her. As selfish as it was for her to even put that in the equation, she did. She wanted more time with him to figure out what it was about him that called to her and made her heart pound.

"They're going to die," whispered Nika. "There are too many monsters. And more are coming."

Andra glanced sideways. "You don't know that."

"I do. They're coming, Andra. I feel them." Nika looked as lucid as she ever did, not that that was saying much. "Please, we have to go back."

Andra's hand clamped hard on the steering wheel so she wouldn't do anything stupid and turn around. "I can't risk it. You're too weak."

"Please, Andra. Go back."

"You're more important."

"We need them."

Shit. Maybe she was right.

Andra's knuckles were white and her body tightened in indecision. There was so much at stake here. Nika's life hung in the balance no matter what she did. If she went back, she might be ripped apart by monsters. If Andra didn't turn around and the men were slaughtered, then Nika might spend the rest of her life screaming in fear. At least until she starved to death.

"Please, Andra. *I need him.*"

The pleading tone in her voice finally decided Andra. She hadn't been able to do much for her sister for eight years. In all that time, Nika had never asked for anything from Andra until now. This was something she could give her, and even if it was the wrong choice, it beat the hell out of starving to death. Didn't it? Heaven knew she didn't like the idea of leaving those men back there to die. Not to mention what would happen to the people in the hospital if the monsters managed to get in.

Where Nika's bloody gown was.

"Buckle up and hold on," said Andra.

They were on a long road leading out to a major street. The only traffic out here was farmers and people headed to the hospital. Andra took a hard one-eighty and hit the gas. The truck spun around with a rocking jolt and headed back up the hill.

"Hand me my shotgun. Under the seat."

The parking lot was up ahead. The fight was still raging. It looked like Paul and Madoc had taken down three or four of those things. She wasn't sure what Logan was doing, but he was working hard at it—standing totally still with his hand raised and some kind of light pouring out of it, splashing up against the nearest wall of the hospital. Freaky.

Andra took the offered shotgun and told Nika, "Get down and stay there."

Nika did, but Andra heard her frightened chanting, "They're coming, they're coming, they're coming. . . ."

Since she was out of hands to roll the window down, Andra used the butt of the weapon to break the glass out of the driver's-side window. She cleared enough of it out of the way to shove the barrel out.

Three of those roach things had shown up, and they were all in a nice, neat little clump.

Andra killed the lights on her truck and sped toward them. They didn't see her coming until it was too late. She floored it and slammed the front of her truck right into them. The things scattered like bowling pins. One of them went under her wheels and made the truck bounce with a sickening crunch as its exoskeleton collapsed under the wheel.

She executed another hard turn, nearly clipping a BMW in the parking lot, and went back for more, just in case they didn't stay down.

"You okay down there?" she asked Nika.

"Yeah," she said, but she didn't sound okay. She sounded like she was wishing for an airsick bag.

"Just hold on. We're almost done here."

From this angle, she had a great view of Paul and Madoc slicing away, their thick arms and muscular backs working almost in unison. That was a beautiful sight to behold. Pure female fantasy fuel.

She pulled her gaze away and focused on business. One of the things she'd hit got back up. It was oozing green stuff from a crack in its chest, which worked for her. Andra aimed and fired at that crack, hoping her shot might be able to bust through. The thing exploded like a watermelon filled with dynamite. It flew into a bunch of bits, making her windshield wipers a necessity. Green, fleshy bits smeared over the glass, and her stomach gave a warning heave.

Andra swallowed to keep everything down. There wasn't time to be sick now, so her stomach would just have to wait.

She scanned the area, but she was running out of targets. The men had done their job and now stood near piles of fur leaking black blood.

Nika could not see that. She was way too fragile to face a sight straight out of her mind's own horror flick.

"You stay down, baby," she told Nika. "We'll be out of here in a sec."

She drove her truck to the men just as they were cleaning off their swords. Logan looked paler and thinner than he did before, but other than that, he seemed fine. Paul was breathing hard, but unhurt. Madoc, on the other hand, had taken a nasty gash across his thigh.

"You came back," said Paul. It sounded like an accusation, but one she was willing to let slide.

"Couldn't let you have all the fun."

Madoc snarled at her, "Get the fuck out of here. It's not safe."

"He's right," said Paul. "His blood will only draw more of those things."

"They're close," whispered Nika from where she bent down.

This time, Andra believed her.

Madoc growled like some kind of wild animal, then said, "You two go with her. I'll draw them away."

Nika grabbed her head and started chanting, "No, no, no, no . . ."

"Scoot over and take care of her," offered Paul. "I'll drive."

Andra was glad to. She pulled Nika into her lap, making sure her eyes were covered and her IV stayed safely in place. Logan got in the passenger's side. He really didn't look well at all. In fact, he looked a lot like he had when Madoc had carried him into her apartment—thin and pale and shaking.

Paul drove off, leaving Madoc behind.

"Is he going to be okay?" asked Andra.

"If he gets mobile, he'll be fine." Something in his tone said it was wishful thinking. "Logan, did anyone in the hospital see us?"

"No," whispered Logan on a weary wisp of air. "I shielded them."

So that was what he was doing out there. Holy freaking cow. This was getting weirder by the moment. It was one thing to know monsters were real—she'd gotten used to that notion years ago—but magic? That was a little harder to swallow.

And made way too much sense, considering the things she'd seen over the past decade.

Her whole perception of the world shifted in that moment, and it was as if she were suddenly looking back-stage at all the mechanics happening behind the scenes. There was so much more going on than even she knew. She wasn't sure she really wanted to see any more. Her life was already complicated enough as it was.

"Where do we go now?" Andra asked.

Paul shot her a quick glance, then looked at Nika. Compassion wrinkled his brow, and he shook his head. "If you go home with us, we may be able to help her."

Nika was still chanting, "No, no, no . . ."

Andra couldn't stand to see her like this. If there were anything in her power she could do to help, she had to try. It didn't matter how much she didn't want to dig deeper into this new world of magic she'd just discovered. She was Nika's big sister, and she'd do whatever it took to make her well again.

Andra smoothed Nika's white hair back from her face, hoping to comfort her. "It's worth a shot."

Madoc made sure he left a nice, easy-to-follow trail of blood as he walked out of sight of the mental hospital. None of those whack jobs inside needed to see the kind of beating he was about to lay out. Their minds would really be fucked-up then.

The hospital was nice and isolated, which meant there was plenty of farmland out here, all of it framed by thick growths of trees. He found a dark, secluded spot with plenty of room to fight before he stopped.

His body was humming with power. It pounded against his eyes and scratched at his veins trying to get out. Hell, he felt like he was going to be shaken apart by it if he didn't do something soon, and that little skirmish hadn't even been a challenge. Thank God the night was young. He had hours of darkness before all the Synes-tryn would retreat back into the holes where they lived and he wouldn't be able to find them and kill them any longer.

Madoc ripped off his T-shirt and tied it around the wound in his thigh to slow the bleeding. He didn't want to pass out from blood loss while there was still fighting to be done. He needed every ounce of exertion he could get to stave off the fucking pain grinding at his bones. Not to mention that if he passed out, it would be the last thing he did. Literally.

Then again, maybe that wouldn't be so bad. There was no way death could hurt more than living. No fucking way.

A deep, growling rumble shook the ground. Demons were nearby. They'd found his scent and would be here any minute.

Good. He could hardly wait.

Chapter 8

Nika felt the monsters' hunger. Their excitement. She didn't want to go with them, but she had no choice. A sliver of her mind was inside them, dragging her along on their hunt.

She tried to think about something else—to turn the channel in her head so that she was back in the truck with Andra, safe and sound in her sister's lap. She liked that part of herself. Even though there were strangers in the truck with her, and one of them wanted to drink her blood, it was better than the other places she existed right now.

So many places. So many monsters. She couldn't keep track. Her mind was torn into too many pieces and she no longer felt there was any of her real self left.

Nika saw through the eyes of a pack of sgath as they hunted. She felt damp grass under her paws and the warm night air ruffle her fur. Her claws dug deep into the earth with every powerful stride of her body. Prey was close. She could smell its blood, rich with power.

Her belly rumbled with hunger and her mouth watered, dripping glowing saliva onto the ground as she passed over it. She was close. She could hear her prey's slow, steady heartbeat.

Her pack broke through the trees and she saw then what she hunted. He had a sword and wore the luminescent collar that marked him as a Theronai—a warrior who wanted to kill her and rid the earth of all of her kind.

The part of Nika that knew she was human cheered for the man—the same man who had been near her hospital bed earlier. But the part of Nika that was beast hissed at him in hatred. She was going to sink her teeth into his flesh and gulp down his blood before it could soak into the earth and be wasted.

More pieces of her huddled inside three more of the sgath as they charged the man. She saw his attack from all angles at once and her human mind had to struggle to turn the images into something she could translate. It was too much input. Too much hatred and rage coming from all sides of her. She didn't want to see the man's death, but if she stayed among the sgath, she feared that was what would happen.

The man looked into one pair of her eyes as she lunged for his throat. He didn't recognize her. He didn't know this wasn't what she wanted. She didn't want him to die.

He didn't even appear to move, but she felt the metal of his blade slide through her belly. She landed hard on the ground and her insides were oozing out of a neat opening. Her paws were clumsy and couldn't push all the organs back in. Her own blood smelled like food and she was so hungry. She knew it was futile and that she was dying, but couldn't stop herself from lapping it from the ground as she bled out.

Back inside of the real Nika, her stomach rebelled at the acid taste of the blood, the thick, rotting smell of it. She shoved out of the thing's mind, only to find herself trapped inside another. It was hiding from the man, waiting to strike as soon as he turned his back.

Only years of practice allowed her to pull back into her real body.

God, she was so weak. She could barely lift her head. "He's in trouble," she managed to get out.

"Who?" asked Andra.

"The Theronai who was with you tonight."

"I don't know any Theronai, baby," said Andra in that patient, gentle voice she always used with her crazy sister.

Nika wanted to scream at her that she wasn't crazy—her mind was just shattered into a thousand fragments that lived inside others—but she knew from experience that it never worked. When she shouted, the orderlies came with needles and put her real mind to sleep so that she had no place to retreat to. No place to hide.

Dreaming was a horrible collage of blood and hunger and war, with her mind trapped inside so many monsters. But that wasn't the worst. She could hardly stand being with Tori anymore. The things they had done to her were hideous. Inhuman. She wasn't even really Tori anymore—she was something dark and twisted the Synestryn intended to use as a weapon.

But Nika had promised Tori she wouldn't leave her, so she hadn't. Not once in all these long, painful years.

"You have to warn him," said Nika. "There's a sgath hiding nearby. Behind him."

"What the hell is she talking about?" asked Paul. "How does she know about Theronai and sgath?"

"I have no idea," said Andra. "But what I do know is that she's been dead-on accurate all night. I suggest you listen to her."

The truck slowed and then stopped. Nika forced her eyes open, though the effort was nearly more than she could stand. She felt like a deflated balloon, empty and limp. Useless.

"Who are you talking about, baby?" asked Andra.

"The man. With you."

"Madoc?"

The name sounded right in her mind, like the wind roaring inside her had suddenly died down and she could hear herself think again. "Yes. Madoc. He's in trouble."

"How do you know, child?" asked a new voice. She turned her head toward him and saw a faint silvery light coming from within his eyes.

She knew that light. That hunger. Panic gave her strength and she scrambled away from the monster. "He wants my blood. Don't let him have it."

"I won't hurt you," he said.

"Liar, liar, liar." Oh, God, she was losing herself again, spreading back out into the night, back into the minds of the monsters who hunted and killed and shoved their sins into her soul each time they did.

She called out to Tori to help her, but there was no answer, and she couldn't find her baby sister's mind among all the rest. They pulled at her, stretching her into a thousand thin strands that she was sure would break. She couldn't take this anymore. She had to stop fighting. Give up. Let them have her.

She didn't care anymore. She'd do anything to make it stop, even if she broke her promise to Tori.

"I'm sorry," she heard herself whisper. It was a good sound, her own real voice coming out of her own real mouth. She could take that sound with her and be at peace. "I'm sorry."

Nika went limp in Andra's arms. Her breathing was labored, and Andra could see the rapid beat of her heart in the veins along her temple.

"She's dying," said Logan.

Outrage and denial rose up in Andra, consuming her. "No!" she shouted. "She's not. She's going to be fine. Her IV bag is empty. That's all. We need to get her another." She prayed to God it was true. She couldn't lose Nika, too. If she did, she'd have no one else. No family. No friends.

Paul's hand settled on her arm, and warmth and compassion fell like a blanket over her skin. She wanted to crawl into his lap and stay there, where she felt good. Protected. Where Nika would be safe.

But that was artificial. Whatever this thing between them was, it wasn't real. Just a bit of magic, probably designed to trick her. And even if it wasn't, it didn't do a damn thing for Nika.

Andra pulled her sister close and rocked her. She tried to think of a way to soothe her, but nothing came to her, not even the faint memory of a song they used to sing. Nothing.

"We need to get her to a place she can rest, eat," said Logan. "She's too weak to travel."

"There's a Gerai house not far from here. We'll go there."

She didn't know what a Gerai house was, but she trusted Paul to know what he was doing. "What about Madoc?" asked Andra. "We should at least let him know what she said."

Paul's body shifted as he pulled out his cell phone and dialed. In the quiet of the truck's cab, she could hear the deep sound of Madoc's voice through the thin plastic. "Kinda busy," he panted.

"Nika said you're in danger."

There was a grunt and a monstrous howl of pain. "No shit. Tell me something I don't know."

"She said there's a sgath there, hiding behind you."

"How the hell would she— Hold on." A series of vicious growls filled the line, then silence.

"Madoc?" said Paul. "You there?"

No answer.

"Madoc?" He glanced over at Andra and shook his head.

A sharp yelp of pain filled the line. It sounded like someone had kicked a dog. "Yeah, I'm here. Found the fucker. Killed it."

"We're packing it in for the night. Can you catch up?"

"Still bleeding."

"Then get it stopped and come join us."

"Why?"

"Because it would be nice to have another sword around to guard the women."

Andra almost said she could guard herself, but she held in the stupid, self-indulgent lie. The more swords they had between Nika and those things out there, the better.

"I kinda had plans," said Madoc.

"Change them, will you?"

"Fuck. Whatever. I'll go clean off in the lake and meet up with you soon. Good enough?"

"Yeah. Thanks, man."

Madoc didn't bother to reply. The guy was not exactly Mr. Friendly. Andra was glad he was on their side.

Paul got the women settled in one of the bedrooms of the Gerai house. Like so many other Gerai houses, this one was isolated, far away from prying neighbors. It was a three-bedroom ranch, stocked with food, clothes and supplies—anything they might need to refuel and protect themselves and any humans who might be along for the ride. Because these places of refuge were kept up by the blooded humans known as Gerai, the term stuck.

Never before had Paul been so glad they had a safe place nearby. Nika didn't look good.

Andra slid Nika under the covers, then lay down beside her and held on tight. Nika looked so frail beside Andra, like a word spoken too harshly would shatter her thin bones.

Even if she was a Theronai like Andra, she could keep going for only so long. They needed to get some food into her, get that IV out of her arm without her bleeding everywhere. They really didn't need to draw more Synestryn.

Andra stroked her sister's hair and whispered to her in a voice too low for Paul to hear. Whatever she said, her body was tight with tense desperation.

Andra must have known how bad Nika was, even if she didn't want to admit it. Her fear gave her away. He could see it in the way her fingers trembled as she ran them over Nika's head, the way her eyes darted frantically over her sister's thin form as if looking for a way to fix her.

Paul had to grit his teeth to hold himself back from Andra. He wanted to comfort her and pull her into his arms and shield her from all the bad stuff in life. Ironic. In his line of work, that was all he had to offer. Anything else was just a temporary illusion.

He made himself step out of the room and close the door. He needed Logan to look at Nika and see if there was anything to be done for her, no matter how small. Now that she was asleep, at least he wouldn't scare her.

Logan was out in the front yard of the small house, sniffing the air. Darkness seemed to close in around him, but it suited him well. He belonged out here in the middle of the night. All the Sanguinar seemed to be most at ease in the dark.

Paul didn't understand it, but he'd come to accept it over the decades. He'd much rather be lying on some sun-drenched beach, but that wasn't in the cards for him. He could no more work during the day than a rancher could do his job in the middle of Manhattan. It just wasn't going to happen.

"Are we clear?" Paul asked.

"Yes. For now."

"You should go see what you can do for Nika while she's asleep."

Logan didn't turn. He continued to stare out into the night. "There's nothing I can do. She's dying."

Paul's eyes slid shut in grief. Poor Andra. She loved her sister so much. He could see it in every move she made. Nika was her world, and she was going to lose her.

Whatever it took, he'd help her through this. Be there for her. "Why is she dying?"

"I can't tell without taking her blood, and she's too weak for that."

"Can't you do anything? Help her hold on for a while longer so she can get stronger?"

"Why should you care what happens to one single soul?" asked Logan.

He didn't bother to remind him that Nika probably wasn't human. "Don't you?"

Logan turned and stared at Paul with those icy eyes. "No. Why should I? She was raised as a human. They care nothing for my kind. They call us vampires. Have you seen the films they've made about my people? The lies they tell their children about us, as if we were out to hunt their kind to extinction?"

"They're your food. That would make anyone feel a little uneasy, don't you think?"

"I only take their blood. I would hope that fact would put them at ease if they stopped to think about it for a single moment. Why would I kill something I need to survive? It would be like a farmer cutting down his orchard to make it simpler to harvest this year's fruit."

A sudden realization came to Paul—one he'd never even considered. "You resent them. The humans. Don't you?"

"Of course not."

"You do. You are pissed off because you need them. Or us. I have to admit, I'd be a little pissed, too, if I had to depend on someone else so heavily."

Logan snorted. "You say that as if you don't need a woman to live."

Maybe Andra.

Paul stifled a thrill of excitement and chained his needs until they quieted. He was going to have to figure out what this thing between them was, but now wasn't the time. She had more important things to think about. "I do need a woman, but I've lived on my own for a long time. You never have."

"Enough of this." Logan shoved past him. "I'm going inside."

"It all makes a lot more sense now. You Sanguinar aren't all dark and brooding. You're pouting. You don't like the rules and you can't change them, so you're pouting."

"You know nothing of what it's like to be my kind. Stop pretending you do."

"Am I wrong?"

Before Paul saw it coming, Logan had grabbed him and shoved him up against the door. Logan was weak from exertion, but even weak, he was still strong enough to make Paul take notice.

He could feel the edges of the small window pressing into his back as well as the man's bony forearm cutting off his air. "We're not pouting. We're dying. Two more of my brothers died while you slept. They starved to death because there is no food for us, and yet your people look down on us like we are vultures, resenting us for the blood we must have to live."

Paul kept his hands off his sword with an effort of will. He wasn't about to cut down the only person around who might be able to save Nika. He decided to be a bigger man than that and held up his hands in surrender.

Logan let him go, but Paul was going to be wearing a bruise across his throat for days, he was sure. "You want more blood?" croaked Paul. "Fine, take some of mine, but use it to save the girl."

Logan's eyes flared and a predatory hunger dilated his pupils. "Give me your arm."

Chapter 9

Logan came into the bedroom without knocking, making Andra jump up from the bed. She tried to cover her startle, but the slight lift at the corner of his beautiful mouth told her he knew what she was doing. And found it amusing.

His color was better and he looked as if he'd gained weight again. It had to be some kind of optical illusion, because no one's size changed that fast. It wasn't possible.

Then again, she'd seen a whole lot of impossible things in the past twenty-four hours.

"Leave us," he ordered her, nodding to Nika.

"Like hell I will. I'm staying right here where I can keep an eye on you."

"And do what? What do you think you could possibly do to stop me if you wanted to?"

He had a point. She didn't even have her shotgun. Okay, time to make nice. "I'm worried about her."

"With good reason. She's not likely to survive."

Andra locked her knees and her throat closed up for a moment as panic grabbed hold of her. A giant well of grief was building inside her, and the only thing keeping it from spilling over was hope—the hope that he was wrong. That there was something someone could do with all the magic she'd seen to put Nika back together.

"Please," she begged, not even caring about her stupid pride. "Please do something to save her."

Logan's jaw bunched and his eyes fell shut in defeat. He let out a heavy sigh. "Fine. I'll try, but there's little I can do without her blood."

"How much do you need?"

"Not much, but more than she can give."

"You can have mine," said Andra.

Logan leaned toward her until his nose was almost touching her neck. She braced herself for his bite, but it never came. Instead, he breathed in deeply, as if smelling her skin.

He straightened and shook his head. "Not today. I took too much from you before. But I will hold you to your offer and drink from you again once you are fully recovered."

"I'm fine now. Nika is the important one here."

Logan pinned her with a bright stare. "Paul would argue that point. Besides, he needs you. You should go to him."

She wanted to, but that was just more of the artificial hocus-pocus stuff. As long as it wasn't real, she could ignore it. "I will once you try to help Nika."

He stared at her for a long moment before giving her a single nod. "Go fill the bathroom sink with water, wet a towel, and bring it to me."

Andra did as he asked. When she returned a few seconds later, Logan was sitting on Nika's bed with one hand on her forehead and the other between her flat breasts. His head was bowed as if in prayer, and she could almost feel a shimmering kind of heat coming off of him.

He lifted his head. His breathing was a little labored. "Come hold the towel nearby."

Andra went to him and held it out. Drips of water slid down her hands and landed on the hardwood floor.

"I'm going to take the catheter out of her arm and

put it in the towel. I want you to wrap it up as quickly as you can and shove it in the sink. Run water over it to drown the scent. We don't want the smell of her blood getting into the air and bringing the Synestryn down on us."

"They can really smell it that well?"

He gave her a look that made her feel like an idiot for not knowing the answer. "Do you want to take the chance?"

Andra shook her head.

"Okay. Here we go." He took the tape from Nika's arm. Her thin, loose skin stretched too easily, making the job more difficult. He lifted her arm. "I'm going to lick the blood away and heal the wound with my mouth, so if you don't want to see that, don't look."

"Nika can't fight off an infection. Please tell me she's safe from the germs in your mouth. They're magic or something, right?"

He smiled then, and the beauty of it nearly made Andra drop the towel. She wondered how many women had fallen at his feet because of that smile alone. That was one serious natural weapon.

"Magic germs. I like that," he said. "Don't worry. It's perfectly safe for her."

"Safe. That's good."

"Are you ready?"

"Yeah."

The plan went just as he'd said. He pulled the IV out of her arm and plopped it down on the towel. Andra wrapped it up tight and raced it into the bathroom, where she ran water over the whole mess. She left the water running and went back to make sure Nika hadn't suffered any ill effects of being licked by a vampire.

Her arm was fine and her skin was whole, as if she'd never had the IV. "That's so cool," she told him.

But Logan wasn't listening. He was staring at the wall with wide eyes that were darting back and forth as if he were in REM sleep. Every second or two, his body would jerk like he'd been hit with a jolt of electricity.

Not good.

Andra waved her hand in front of his face. "Hey. You in there?"

His mouth started to move, but no sound came out.

"Logan."

Nothing. Andra put her hand on his shoulder and shook him. "Logan! Snap out of it."

He did. Finally. His eyes blinked slowly and stopped their Ping-Pong routine. He sucked in a deep breath as if it were the first one he'd had in a while.

"Leave us. I need time to examine her."

"I'm not leaving."

"I promise you I will not harm her. I also promise you that if you don't go drag Paul in from outside, the Synestryn will likely find him before sunrise."

Drag Paul? "What are you talking about?"

"I needed strength to attend your sister. Paul offered me his blood. Unfortunately, I needed quite a bit and he had already donated recently. He's outside. Recovering."

"Why the hell didn't you say something before?" said Andra.

"I did. You chose to ignore me."

She had to go to Paul. She couldn't leave him lying out there in the dark with all the monsters roaming around. "If you so much as muss her hair, I'm going to kill you. Are we clear?"

Logan gave her a patronizing smile. "Go to your Theronai. Nika is safe in my care."

Andra believed him, which might have made her certifiable, but there it was. Paul needed her now, and without him, Andra wasn't sure she could keep Nika safe from the monsters. Besides, she owed him. He'd given his blood to help Nika, and in her book, that made him a hero.

She had just turned to leave when he said, "Oh, by the way, that necklace he wears is yours if you choose to take it."

Andra stopped in her tracks. She'd felt that, too, but brushed it aside as one more irrational feeling. "Paul never said that."

"Because he's protecting you."

Andra frowned. "From what?"

"From the responsibility of the power you will wield if you choose to wear it."

"Power?"

He gave her a level stare. "More than you can imagine. Enough to keep your sister safe. Maybe enough to heal her as well."

It took her a couple of seconds to process what he was saying. This whole thing was so far-out, she didn't know what to think at first, but one thing was clear. If Paul could help her save Nika, she was going to make him do so. "Is that why I keep feeling weird when I touch him?"

"Yes. It's nature's way of helping you find him. I suggest you don't wait too long to make up your mind about whether or not you're going to claim what's yours. Nika is nearly out of time. She'll be lucky to survive three days at this rate."

Three days. Andra's throat tightened as she fought back tears. "I don't need any time. I know what to do."

First she was going to make sure Logan wasn't full of shit. Then she was going to do the only thing she could.

Save Nika.

Andra found Paul slumped on the porch. His big body was limp and unmoving. Panic skittered over her skin as she raced to him, looking for signs of life.

She pressed her fingers against his neck to feel for a pulse, and warmth spread up her arm. He pulled in a shuddering breath, and Andra's eyes closed in relief. His pulse was strong and he was breathing steadily.

Now all she had to do was get him inside, where there was at least a door between them and the monsters. She knew from experience that that wouldn't stop them for long, but at least it would slow them down. Out here in the open with darkness all around them, nothing would.

Andra gave his arm an experimental tug. Lord, he was heavy—easily eighty pounds heavier than she was. She could do it, but one of them was going to get their shoulder dislocated in the process.

Maybe if she pushed him over the wooden planks, it would be easier. He might get splinters in his ass, but she'd be glad to pull those out for him if they lived through it. She was pretty sure she'd enjoy getting a nice long look at his muscular backside, anyway.

She moved him just enough that his head lolled to one side. The iridescent choker he wore caught and held light from the single bulb glowing above them.

That choker was hers. It always had been. She wanted to take it back.

All this magic hoo-ha left her stumbling in the dark, but she had some strong instincts about this thing, and she wasn't afraid to follow them, especially after Logan's coaching. If Nika didn't make it, she had nothing to lose, anyway.

Andra reached out and grazed it with the tip of her finger. A happy tingling sensation swept up her arm and settled deep in her chest, giving her confidence that this was the right thing to do. The colors inside the band swirled around that contact, as if it knew she was touching it. A plume of sapphire blue spread out from under her finger, expanding in concentric rings as it moved across the necklace.

The color was so pretty, so rich and deep, she wanted to have it for her own and see it grace her throat. Just as the thought entered her head, the band split open and fell from Paul's thick neck.

Andra retrieved the slippery length from the wooden planks and let it slide over her fingers, passing it from one hand to the other. It was still warm from Paul's body and heavier than she would have expected. It looked as though it were made out of some kind of plastic, but now that she held it and felt its weight, she knew that wasn't the case.

The ends were blunt, with no clasp, but she figured that the same magic that made it come off would fasten it again. She placed the band around her throat and the ends seemed to find each other as if they were drawn together like magnets.

As soon as she felt the muted click of the band connecting to itself, Paul's eyes opened. Gold chips shone bright within the deeper brown of his eyes, making them sparkle under the porch light. His gaze moved to her throat and his hand went to his own.

"How did you . . . ?" His voice was a shocked whisper of sound, barely audible over the crickets chirping nearby.

He reached out and placed one blunt fingertip against the band and slid it over it, brushing her skin along the edge as he passed. His pupils dilated and his nostrils flared. He let out a deep, satisfied groan that made a shiver course up her spine. "So good," he told her. "You probably shouldn't have done that, but it feels so good not to hurt anymore."

"Are you okay?" she asked. "You were unconscious."

"I'm perfect now. Thanks to you." His finger moved from the choker up the side of her neck and down along her jaw. "You are one of us."

"Who's us?"

"We're Theronai."

"What's that?"

"We're one of three races of guardians. Sentinels. We stand watch over the gate to another world, protecting it from Synestryn invasion. We also protect humans from falling victim to their evil."

"Like you did with Sammy?"

He nodded. "We were put here to protect others. It's in our blood—in your blood. It's why you nearly kill yourself trying to find those lost children, why you never give up. You're like me. I had hoped you weren't human, but knowing it's true—"

"Of course I'm human." Even as she said it, she questioned the truth of her words. She'd always been different. So had her sisters. Andra had dismissed their weirdness as some kind of random genetic quirk, but now that Paul said the words, she realized she'd been wrong. She was different from all the other humans because she wasn't human herself. It made too much sense not to be true, despite her desire to deny it.

Her mom had always been secretive about their father, evading questions, lying when she did give answers. Andra had always thought she was covering for some deadbeat, but maybe there was more to it than that.

If only Mom had lived so she could ask questions and find out the truth. Now all she had to go on was the word of a man she barely knew and her gut instincts—instincts that told her she wasn't human. She was different. That was why she could find lost children.

Andra's world shifted. The colors that had painted her life's experiences changed from a distorted mass of mixed-up memories and unexplainable events to something clear and visible. That oddly shaped piece of the puzzle that had never quite fit suddenly fell into place. "How could I not have known?"

Paul stroked her cheek, his eyes bright with compassion. "You were never told. But it's okay. You're not alone."

"Maybe not, but my whole life has been a lie." She couldn't help but feel betrayed by her mother. How many times had she asked Mom about their father? How many times had Mom looked her in the eye and lied?

"That lie protected you. It probably saved your life. And it gave me time to find you."

"That doesn't excuse what she did."

"Maybe there was no lie," said Paul. "Maybe your mother didn't know."

"She knew something. I can see it now, looking back. She lied."

"But you know the truth now. You're a Theronai. You can accept that and move forward or wallow in the past. Your choice."

She didn't have time to wallow. Logan had said Nika might not even live three days. "Nika needs me to move forward."

A satisfied gleam lit his eyes. "Then we should finish this, you and I."

"Finish?"

He nodded, staring at her mouth. "And then I'll show you the truth. And my power—your power now. Let's go inside."

Andra stood and offered him her hand. He took it, but not because he was unsteady. His stance was solid and strong, just like the rest of him. "You seem to have recovered."

"I'm still a quart or two low, but I feel great." He slid his hand to the back of her neck and held her still. He was a few inches taller, and she found herself looking right at his mouth, wishing she had the guts to kiss him again. What she'd had already wasn't nearly enough. Never would be.

"Later," he said, and it sounded like a promise. "When it's safe. And we have plenty of time."

Andra's mind went foggy around the edges. Something was happening inside her—some kind of warmth was swelling up, taking over. "Time?" she asked.

Paul nodded again. "Lots of time. I'm looking forward to getting to know you. Learning what you like."

She liked him. Too much. So much it made her dizzy with the force of it and whatever was happening to her.

Andra swayed on her feet and grabbed hold of his arms to steady herself. His muscles were hard under her fingertips, sculpted so her hands fit just right against him.

"You and I, we can have forever if you want it."

Forever sounded pretty good right now, considering how she was feeling.

A sane part of herself said, "But I hardly know you."

"That'll change soon enough. I'm going to take you inside and we're going to finish what you've started."

He scooped her up in his arms and she had the sensation of flying for a split second. A laugh bubbled out of her, and she sounded almost drunk to her own ears.

She rested her heavy head on his shoulder and closed her eyes as that swelling warmth expanded inside her. "What's happening to me?"

He buried his nose in her hair and whispered low in her ear, "Shh. Just let go. You're mine now."

Chapter 10

Paul felt like a god. They weren't even completely united yet, and already she had changed his life. The pain was gone. Vanished. Strength surged through his body with every beat of his heart. Sure, he didn't have as much blood as he was supposed to, but it hardly mattered. Andra was in his arms, and he felt invincible, like he could beat down an entire nest of Synestryn single-handedly and not break a sweat.

Her body felt good against him and he didn't want to set her down. Not ever. He could feel the sleek firmness of muscles in her back and thighs, while the gentle swell of her breasts was so soft and yielding against his chest. Her short hair tickled his nose, baby fine and feather soft. And she smelled so good.

A man could lose himself in a woman like her and never feel deprived, never want for anything.

He had to stake his claim and make it final. A little twinge of guilt made him pause, but he brushed it away as inconsequential. She had no idea what she was getting into, but he couldn't let that stop him. Not anymore. She'd taken his luceria of her own free will, and he wasn't going to let that miracle pass by. Not now, and probably not ever. He needed her too much. She had to stay with him. Be his. Belong to him and only him. He'd make sure she'd never regret it.

Something about that thought process was off, but he didn't care. It was time.

Paul laid her down on the couch, knelt beside her, and pulled his shirt off over his head.

Andra smiled and leaned toward him, purring. She ran her hands over his shoulders and down across his lifemark. The branches swayed in reaction to her touch, and the single leaf he had left shivered. Her fingers were warm and curled against his flesh, kneading his muscles.

Paul's body responded predictably to a gorgeous woman's caress. His skin flushed hot and his dick hardened, making him wish he could lose the jeans, too. She was so pretty lying there, stroking him, staring at him as if he were the only man on the face of the planet. All he wanted to do was strip away her clothes and spread those long legs out so he could touch her, taste her, make her come just for him.

Oh, yeah. That was definitely a good plan.

But not until their ties were complete. Unbreakable. Not like what he'd had with Kate. Once Andra was his, he'd do all of that and more.

His sword was right at his side, ready and waiting as always. He gathered her hands and held them still so she wouldn't accidentally get cut as he drew the blade. "My life for yours," he told her as he sliced a thin cut over his heart, signifying his willingness to shed his blood for her. The promise filled him up, made him feel stronger, whole. He'd do anything to protect her, and because she had taken his luceria, he would live long enough to fulfill that purpose.

He pressed his finger against the cut and smudged a bit of blood against the luceria. It shrank to fit close to her skin, the colors once again swirling frantically. Blue. There was more blue now than any other color.

Disbelief rattled through him, freezing him in place and making him stare.

This was working. Andra really was his lady. Even

seeing it, he still could hardly believe his good fortune. He reached out, intending to hug her to him in thanks, but the world dissolved, and she along with it.

His eyesight failed for a moment before returning again, but when it did, he was no longer in the Gerai house in Nebraska. He was in a small bedroom covered in rock-band posters and bits of girlish frill. A red feather boa hung over the dresser mirror, and a purple silk scarf had been tossed over the bedside lamp. A teenage girl was lying on her stomach, propped up on her elbows, reading a magazine on the bed. Her bare legs were waving in the air behind her; her toenails were painted bubblegum pink, her feet twitching in time to music pounding out of the radio.

The girl looked up from her magazine like she'd heard a noise, and Paul could see now that it was a much younger version of Andra. She was maybe nineteen or twenty. She was thinner, less muscular, and so cute it made him grin.

This was a vision of her past—something important the luceria had chosen to show him. Paul scoured the scene, soaking it in.

She was beautiful, but in a childish sort of way. He preferred the way she looked now—confident and womanly and ready for whatever he had to give. Still, he would have given nearly anything to have known her then, when he would still have had time to be patient with her and ease her into his world carefully. Slowly.

But that wasn't possible now. He needed her too much to slow down. The only thing he could do now was learn what he could about her to help make her transition as easy as possible.

A crash of breaking glass filled the air. A high-pitched scream followed, and then ended abruptly, as if cut off. Andra jumped from her bed and raced out of the room. Paul followed, unseen. Three steps down the hall, she came to a dead stop in front of a doorway. The door was open. Fresh blood coated the bright white paint and dripped off the bottom of the door, soaking into the carpet. She took a tentative step forward, and her bare foot sank into the wet carpet. Blood oozed between her toes.

She jerked her foot back and looked like she might throw up.

"Mom?" she whispered. "Oh, God." Her hand reached out toward something on the floor just as another scream sounded from a room at the end of the hall.

Andra turned and rushed toward the scream.

Paul passed by the bloody door and saw the remains of Andra's mother lying on the floor inside the bedroom. The Synestryn had left her head and taken the rest. The woman's lifeless eyes stared up at him, her mouth frozen open in a silent scream. A heavy trail of blood marked where they'd dragged her body out the window. From the guttural sounds coming from the darkness outside, Paul was certain they were still out there, feeding on her corpse.

That had been Andra's mother. Probably the most important person in her life. And now she was dead.

Andra opened the door at the end of the short hall. Another window had been broken here, too. Only this time, the sgath's work was not yet done. One of them crawled through the opening, its eyes glowing bright green. Its black forked tongue flicked out ahead of it, and it let out a feral hiss.

Andra stood frozen in fear. He could see the fine trembling of her thin body, hear her breathing too fast and hard.

"Mom! Andra! Help!" shouted a child inside the room. "Tori, get back!"

The sgath lunged forward and grabbed a small girl around the waist. She couldn't have been more than eight. She had the same dark hair and blue eyes that

Andra did, only her hair curled in a wild mop. Her girly pink nightgown bunched up over the thing's furry arm as she struggled to get free.

Another girl, maybe twelve or thirteen years old, grabbed the sgath's paw in an effort to free her younger sister. The sgath twisted around oddly and raked its back claws across her thigh. She yelped and let go, falling back against the wall.

It was Nika. Paul was sure of it, only her hair was still dark and she was also years younger.

Nika pushed herself to her feet and looked at her wound in horror, then up again at her sister. "It's going to take Tori away."

Paul wasn't sure how Nika knew that, but she seemed to be sure. He had no idea what the sgath's plans for the child were, but it was clear it had some other purpose for her than food.

The smell of Nika's blood was in the air now. Another sgath crawled in through the broken window.

Andra snapped out of her shock and looked around frantically for a weapon. She grabbed a lamp off the nearest nightstand. With an enraged bellow, she hurled it across the room and hit the sgath holding Tori.

Of course, the lamp did nothing to the sgath. It broke against the thing's head and fell into a useless pile of pieces.

Blood pooled at Nika's feet, dripping heavily from her wound. Already, the poison from the sgath's claws was racing through her system, making her face flush with fever. Paul had no idea how she had survived that wound—sgath poison was usually fatal if not treated immediately—but he'd seen her future and knew that she had somehow pulled through.

The monster holding Tori turned to leave, and Andra jumped onto its back.

Paul screamed at her to stay away. It wasn't safe. He reached for his sword, only to find he had none. Had no body here. His voice made no sound, either—he was only an observer and could do nothing to help. Everything that was going to happen already had, and he could change nothing.

Andra clung to the sgath's back with her legs and dug her fingers into its eyes. It howled in pain and flung its head wildly to toss her off its back.

Andra held tight, clawing and digging. The sgath reared up and slammed her into a wall. Her head hit hard. Drywall crushed under the impact, and Andra let out a hoarse grunt of pain. Her grip loosened and the sgath moved away, letting her body slide to the floor in a limp heap.

Paul yelled at her to get up, but no sound came out of his mouth.

On the other side of the room, a sgath crouched at Nika's feet. She was shaking, but unable to move. The sgath's tongue flicked out, lapping up the blood as it seeped from her thigh. Her eyes were heavy-lidded and glassy, but her lips were moving and she stared at Tori, completely ignoring the sgath who fed from her.

"I won't leave you," she whispered to her sister, over and over. "I won't leave you."

Tori was screaming and fighting, but her small body was no match for the sgath. It carried her out the window and off into the night. The last thing Paul saw of her was her little arm reaching out toward her sisters for help.

Andra pushed herself to her feet. She could barely stand. Her body wobbled as she picked up a wooden desk chair and crossed to Nika. The sgath was too busy eating to notice her approach. She slammed the chair over the thing's head.

It yelped and turned around to attack.

An armed man rushed into the room. He could have been a plainclothes police officer, or maybe just a neighbor with a gun. Whoever he was, he saw the thing and opened fire. A few bullets later, the sgath decided to leave, leaped out the window, and raced away.

Andra collapsed to her knees at the window. "Tori!" she shouted. "Tori!" Her scream turned into a sob and Paul could hear her heart breaking.

There was an odd blur of movement around Nika, but Paul didn't care about that. The need to bear witness to Andra's pain was too strong. She'd lost her family that night. Her mother and sister had died, and Nika had gone insane from the poison or trauma. No wonder Andra was so protective toward Nika. She was the only family Andra had left alive.

Paul mourned for her and wished again that he had found her earlier. In time to save her.

"I'll help you keep Nika safe," said Paul. This time he heard his words and knew he'd returned back to the present. "You won't ever be alone."

But Andra didn't seem to hear him. She was lost inside her own vision—whatever the luceria had chosen for her to see.

Energy pulsed around Andra, vibrating the air. She could feel the power flowing through the necklace, but could not yet touch it. Something was missing, but she had no idea what.

That power that had been hovering there, waiting for her, erupted in a tidal wave of electricity. Her hair stood up on end and her skin heated as bright sparks arced over her limbs. Her eyes grew hot and she felt like she might explode.

Andra shut her eyes tight against the pressure, and her vision filled with scenes from Paul's life. She saw him as a boy learning to use a sword, his limbs awkward as he became accustomed to their ever-growing length. She saw him as a teenager going toe-to-toe with half a dozen demons. She saw him as a younger man standing over the graves of his mother and sister.

She heard him vow that day to do whatever it took to rid the world of the Synestryn. He'd give up his freedom, his power, his life—anything—to protect those whom the Synestryn hunted.

Then she saw a woman. Kate. She was standing on a lush hilltop, her long blond hair and billowing skirt flowing out behind her on the wind. Her deep green eyes matched the color of the surrounding forest, and when Paul approached her, she felt his resignation. His acceptance. He'd loved her, but Kate loved another. He'd tried to force her to stay with him, and she'd rejected him.

"I will never be yours," she told him.

Andra watched as she took his luceria off and placed it back around his neck. Paul fell to his knees and clutched his bare chest as she watched, her face calm and impassive. Leaves fell from the branches of his tattoo until the limbs were nearly bare, and he was sweating and writhing on the ground in pain.

Kate saw his suffering, too, but after watching for a long moment, she turned her back on him and walked away. Toward another man.

Hours later, two young men found him lying on the ground. They carried his lanky body back to a village and laid him on the dirt floor inside a rough cottage. A beautiful woman in a gray gown knelt beside him. She placed her hands on his chest and bowed her head as if in prayer.

Slowly, small buds began to form on the limbs of his tree tattoo.

The woman slumped over him and a craggy-faced man caught her up in his arms before she could fall.

The teenaged Paul opened his eyes and saw what the woman had done. Andra didn't know the language they spoke, but she understood the words all the same.

"You aren't finished growing yet, Theronai," said the woman in a weak voice. "It saved your life. That and the fact that you weren't with her for long. Fortunately, you'll recover this time."

The older man shot him a warning look. "There won't be a next time. I won't allow Gilda to do this for you again. It costs her too much. Do you understand?"

"Yes, sire."

The older man looked to one of the boys who'd brought Paul there. "Find Kate. Bring her here to answer for her actions."

The boy bowed and fled from the cottage.

"Go now, Paul, and make sure you're worth the trouble you've caused this day."

Paul pushed himself to his feet and made his way unsteadily out the door. Andra could feel his anger and embarrassment as if they were her own. She could also feel his determination to do good and make this older man proud.

Years rushed by in Andra's head. She saw tiny glimpses of his life. His struggles to live up to his expectations. His battles. He'd fought and killed thousands of monsters, saved hundreds of lives, and had surely been worth whatever trouble he'd caused.

Why, then, didn't he feel he'd done enough?

When she came back to reality, she asked, "What the hell was that?"

"What did you see?"

"You as a boy. What Kate did to you. I don't understand what happened, but it nearly killed you, didn't it?"

He looked away. "It's in the past. What matters is what we do now."

"Logan said that you might be able to make me strong enough to help Nika."

Golden shards of hope lit up within his eyes. "Is that what you want?"

"Yes."

"Then we must complete our union."

"How do we do that?" she asked.

He leaned toward her, staring at her mouth. "I've given you my promise to hold your life sacred above my own, and now, to seal us together, you must give me a promise in return."

Chapter 11

"What kind of promise?" asked Andra.

"Promise to stay with me," Paul told her. It was an open-ended vow, and one that would tie her to him for life. Part of him knew tricking her was wrong, but the rest of him didn't give a shit. He wanted to keep her. Forever. He didn't want to give her the chance to walk away like Kate had. He never wanted to go back to that life of torment again.

"I can't stay with you. Nika needs me."

Her rejection flooded him with anger and resentment. He wanted to roar at her that *he* needed her, too, but he held his tongue. Now was not the time to lose his head. He had to be careful here. Cautious. He'd been hasty when he'd bonded with Kate, and he wouldn't make the same mistake twice. He was older now. A grown man with three more centuries of maturity to keep him steady.

Three more centuries of pain screaming at him to make it work this time.

Paul took her hand in his and made his tone patient and understanding. "I would never stand in the way of you caring for your sister. I already told you I'd help you keep her safe."

She frowned at him as if trying to figure something out. "But this is a real promise, right? I can feel it." She pressed her hand to her chest. "Whatever I promise will happen, whether or not I still want to uphold my end later."

So, she did know the stakes. He tried to convince himself that was for the best, but failed. He needed her to free him. To save him.

"Then promise me whatever you can. Give me as much as you can and I will be content." Somehow.

She nodded slowly and spoke her vow with careful wording. "Okay. As long as it doesn't get in the way of Nika's safety, I promise to stay with you for three days."

Three days. A mere blink of time to a man like him who'd lived for centuries. Even Kate had stayed with him longer.

Paul's grand visions of a pain-free future at Andra's side crumbled to dust. There would be no forever for them, only a few brief days. He wanted to scream at her that it wasn't enough, that she had to take it back and give him more, but it was too late. The bond was made, the deal done, and Paul could already feel that promise becoming a part of him, albeit a small part.

Resentment rose up in his throat, leaving a bitter taste behind. He'd spent his entire life fighting and suffering through pain and loneliness so that he could keep humans safe from the Synestryn. He'd never once shirked his duties or tried to avoid the more dangerous missions so someone else would have to take his place. He'd nearly died from injury or poison more times than he could count, but every time, he went back to the front lines as soon as he was able, because they needed him. And now, to survive, he needed a partner—the only thing he'd ever wanted for himself. He'd finally found another woman who could save his life so he could keep fighting. He was willing to give her everything he had, including his life, and all she could offer him in return was three days.

How could she do this to him? How could she betray him so cruelly without even giving him a chance to prove to her how much he had to offer?

How could she be like Kate?

"You're angry," she told him, frowning at him in confusion. "What did I do wrong?"

Paul stilled his rioting thoughts. She could probably already feel his emotions leaking through the connection of the luceria—his ring and her necklace. "You didn't do anything wrong. I was just hoping for more time. That's all."

She narrowed her eyes as if she knew he wasn't telling her the whole truth. "It isn't enough?"

She didn't understand, but then how could she? She wasn't part of his world. She didn't know what her vow meant or how it affected his life. "It will be fine," he reassured her. At least it was longer than he probably would have lived without her. He should have been happy about that. But he wasn't.

"What happens then? At the end of our time?" she asked him.

"The luceria falls off and you are free." *And I go back to dying in pain.*

"That's it?"

He chose to misunderstand her question. He didn't want her knowing of his weakness—her power over him, and the guilt it would cause her if she knew the truth. She deserved better than that. "That's all you were willing to give."

"But what happens if I decide to stick with you longer than that?"

Paul had been so outraged he hadn't stopped to consider it. Hope rose up in him once again. He didn't have to die. She could still save him. All he had to do was make her love him before their time was up. Then she'd promise to stay with him forever.

He could do it. He had the ability, now that he was connected to Andra. He could use the luceria to invade

her mind and whisper to her soul that he was the only
man for her. He could convince her that she was lost
without him, and that they'd been made to love each
other. It would work.

He lifted her chin and looked into her eyes. Maybe
he should start now, while she still knew nothing of
what he could do. He'd saved her life—Nika's, too.
She trusted him more now, which was going to make
it easier for him to slip inside her natural defenses. To
slip inside her. Make her body need him as much as
her mind did. Then she'd have no choice but to stay
with him.

That part of his plan was going to be easy. She already
wanted him. All he had to do now was show her how
good it could be between them.

Paul flooded their new link with his desire for her. He
hadn't stopped wanting her since he'd met her, and it
was easy to let that feeling roam free and take over. Let
her feel what he did—that prowling need to touch her.
Taste her. Get her naked and wet beneath him, where he
could have his fill.

Her eyes fluttered shut for a moment, and she
groaned. Then she looked at his mouth and her tongue
peeked out to wet her lips. Oh, yeah, she was definitely
feeling him now.

There was nothing Paul could have done to prevent
himself from kissing her, so he just gave in. He settled
his mouth onto hers, fitting them together as if they'd
been made for this sole purpose. She let out a little gasp
of surprise, then melted into his kiss. Her mouth was
warm, soft, and pliant, and the tip of her tongue reached
out to caress his lower lip.

Paul's hands pulled her upright, clenching against her
back. He held her in place while he enjoyed her mouth,
stroking and tasting and teasing her until she returned
each thrust of his tongue with one of her own.

Somewhere in his mind warning bells were going off,

but he ignored them. Andra was in his arms, willing and eager, and nothing else mattered.

Her hands slid up over his bare shoulders and it was all he could do to keep from growling with pleasure. The spark he'd felt when he touched her before had magnified until it was a blazing, glorious fire in his gut. Her lightest touch ignited him, making him wish he could will away their clothes and sink into her supple body. She'd love it. He'd make sure she did. He'd kiss every smooth expanse of her skin, explore every tempting dip and curve with his tongue. He'd strip away any reservation she had with tender caresses of his hands and mouth. He'd spread her out and worship her body with his until there was no room left for anything between them but slippery passion.

Then she'd be his. Totally. Completely. No turning back.

She was already close, hovering on the edge of giving him everything he wanted. It wouldn't have taken much to push her over. Her mind was open, receptive, and weak right now. It would take just a small brush of power over her thoughts and she would be on her way to total devotion.

His slave.

That thought stopped him cold. He didn't want that for her. That was how the Synestryn worked. They forced their human servants—the Dorjan—to love them, worship them.

Paul pushed himself away from her, both her mind and body, before he did something irrevocable. Unforgivable.

Andra tried to pull him back against her, but she was weak and was no match for his will, even as threadbare as it was right now.

"Why did you stop?" she asked in a voice rich with arousal.

"We can't," he told her in a strained whisper. "I want to, but . . . this is just wrong. It's not real."

"That wasn't real?" she asked. Her voice shook. "It sure felt real to me."

Paul scooted a couple feet away, leaving Andra lying there, all sprawled out and breathless. He had to look away and focus on the empty fireplace in order to regain his self-control.

"Yes. It did." Because he was such a fucking bastard. He was making it feel real for her.

Paul's stomach clenched and he had to adjust his jeans in order to pull in a breath without emasculating himself. "I'm sorry."

"For what?" she asked in a husky voice. "I was right there with you, ready, willing, and eager."

The lingering effects of their kisses were still visible. Her skin had heated, and a pretty pink blush had spread up over her cheeks. Her lips were swollen and parted in invitation, and the languid sprawl of her long legs made Paul's fists tighten painfully in order to keep himself from reaching for her.

"I know. Neither one of us was thinking straight. Logan and Nika are only a doorway away."

"Nika," she breathed as if she'd forgotten she even had a sister. "What the hell was I thinking?" She covered her face with her hands and let out a frustrated growl.

The urge to comfort her tugged at him, but he managed to keep his distance.

"I'm going to go clean up this blood before it is a problem." He stood, or rather, had intended to. Instead, he kind of lurched upward, winced as his erection was pinched painfully against his fly, and limped toward the kitchen.

"Logan treated Nika's blood like it was some kind of toxic waste. He had me wrap up the IV in a wet towel so the monsters couldn't smell it, and leave everything under running water."

"I probably should have been more careful with mine, but I wasn't thinking straight."

She'd followed him into the kitchen, but kept a safe distance. A smudge of blood was on her shirt as well. He nodded toward it. "You're going to need to change. I'll have to burn that shirt, along with anything Nika bled on."

Andra saw the blood, looked at it in horror, and stripped the shirt off, leaving only her sports bra behind. It was modest enough, but not nearly as modest as it would have needed to be to keep Paul from wanting to charge her.

"Is there a clean one around here?" she asked.

"At least one of the bedroom closets will be full of clothes. Take whatever you want."

She turned to do just that when a scream ripped through the little house. Nika's scream.

Andra slammed the bedroom door open, unable to contain her fear for her sister. It was only twenty steps to the bedroom, but in that time, Andra's mind went through all the horrible things Logan could have done to her. Or maybe it wasn't Logan at all. Maybe the monsters had found them because of the blood.

When she got into the room, Nika was out of bed kicking and hitting Logan. He was standing in front of the open window, blocking the exit with his body. "She needs me!" screamed Nika. "I have to go find her."

"I'm right here," said Andra, rushing forward. "I'm fine."

Nika's eyes met Andra's, but there was little of the sister Andra remembered left inside her right now. All that was left was the panicked desperation of fear. Andra had seen it enough times before to wish they had some kind of tranquilizer with them. That was the only thing that had ever worked at the hospital to calm her down so she wouldn't hurt herself.

"Not you," screamed Nika as if in pain. "Tori. They're

hurting her." Nika clawed at Logan's body, but he did not move or even try to stop her from assaulting him.

Logan grimaced and looked at Andra. "I don't want to hurt her, and if I try to restrain her, I will. You need to calm her down."

Nika screamed in outrage and pulled a framed picture from the wall. She slammed it into Logan's face. He ducked aside, but not enough. The frame splintered, the glass shattered, and some of it hit him, opening a gash along his temple.

"Shit," said Paul from behind her, and rushed into the bathroom.

Nika pulled a jagged shard of glass from the broken frame. It was about ten inches long and she held it like a weapon she was aching to use. Her arms were shaking with the effort of holding it up, and she swayed as if she were about to fall over.

Andra stepped forward slowly. "Nika, please put the glass down. You're going to hurt yourself."

Nika's eyes were wild, but they pleaded with Andra to understand. "I have to go. Tori needs me."

"Tori is gone, baby. No one is going to ever hurt her again." Saying the words made Andra's throat tighten against the need to scream and lash out the way Nika was. Part of her envied Nika's ability to let go and rail at the world. But Andra had to be strong. Stay in control. She was the only one left to take care of Nika.

A fat tear slid down Nika's sunken cheek, breaking Andra's heart. "They're hurting her now. I can see it. *Feel* it. Please help her. Save her." Nika stared out into the night. "She's calling your name. Can't you hear it?"

Andra closed her eyes against the image of her baby sister's cries for help. She'd been eight, wearing a pink nightgown, clawing at the arm of the monster that held her. That had really happened, and even though it was years ago, it was still as horrible and devastating now as it had been then. Andra had failed her baby sister and let the monsters take her.

And now they were killing Nika, too. Slowly. Horribly.

Andra swallowed her pain, ground her teeth to fight back the tears, and stepped toward Nika. "You have to let her go. I know it's hard to accept. It took me years to do so myself, but she's gone, baby. I searched for her a long time—for years—and never found her."

"I see her."

"It's not her. It's the monsters lying to you, tricking your mind. Tori wouldn't want you to suffer like this."

Paul came out of the bathroom with a wet towel. Logan replaced the shirt he'd wadded up against the wound with the towel. "I have to leave before I draw them here," he told Paul.

Paul nodded, but kept his eyes on Nika and that make-shift weapon.

"I'll feed so I can heal, and be back as soon as possible."

"If you're not back by daybreak, I'm taking them to Dabyr."

Logan nodded and left.

"Let me have the glass," coaxed Andra.

Nika gripped the shard tighter, her paper-thin skin only a fraction of an inch from the broken edge. She couldn't stand any more physical damage. She was too weak.

"Just what the hell do you think you're doing?" barked Madoc from the doorway. "Logan dashed out of here like his ass was on fire. What did you do to him? And why the hell didn't you let me watch?"

Andra turned around to tell him she was trying to help her sister, but he wasn't talking to her. He was talking to Nika.

He strode forward, pushed Andra out of the way, and said, "Give me that fucking glass and get your ass back in bed before you fall down."

Nika craned her neck to look up at him and blinked a few times. Then, amazingly, she offered Madoc the broken glass.

He took it and tossed it onto the dresser without looking where it landed, shattering. He was too busy glowering at Nika as she moved slowly toward the bed. She crawled back onto the mattress.

Madoc yanked the blanket up until it covered her to her neck, then nodded once as if satisfied.

He turned to Paul. "You can't even keep one scrawny woman in bed?"

"It wasn't Paul's fault," said Andra. "Logan was watching her."

"Fucking leech," growled Madoc under his breath.

Andra sat on the bed and checked Nika's hands for cuts. She was paler than normal and sweating, but appeared to be unhurt. In fact, she seemed to be calm again and more herself. "Are you okay?" asked Andra.

Nika nodded. Her eyes were red from crying, but at least the tears had stopped falling.

"No, she's not okay," spat Madoc. "She's too damn skinny. Girl needs a cheeseburger."

Andra glared up at him. She didn't care how big he was; he wasn't going to talk about Nika as though he knew her. "She has trouble eating. Back the hell off."

Madoc rolled his eyes and folded his body into a chair near the window. "Feel better? I'm all the way across the room now."

Nika grabbed the strap of Andra's bra, reminding her she still hadn't put a shirt on. "You have to find her. Promise me you'll find her."

Andra gathered what was left of her patience. "I can't, baby. Tori's dead. When you feel better, I'll take you to see her grave so you'll know it's true."

"Empty hole, empty hole, empty hole." That vacant look was back, and Andra wanted to scream in frustration and anger.

Instead, she smoothed Nika's white hair away from her face and forced her voice to come out even and calm. "Try to get some sleep. We have to leave soon, and I want you to try to eat something before we go."

"No blood. I won't drink it. You can't make me." Nika was gone now—only an empty shell of insane terror remained. Andra had seen the look enough times to know it was useless to try to reason with her. Without the drugs the hospital gave her, she probably wouldn't even be able to sleep, either.

Nika was wasting away in front of Andra's eyes and there wasn't a thing she could do to stop it.

Paul's strong hand cradled her shoulder, and the touch of his bare skin on hers helped soothe her. Gave her the strength not to lose hope. "No blood. I promise."

"Chick thinks you're feeding her blood?" asked Madoc.

"Back off," warned Paul. "You don't have any idea of what's going on here."

Madoc snorted. "I know she'll die if you don't feed her."

Anger swelled up inside Andra until she had no choice but to let it out. She moved from the bed and stomped over to where Madoc sat. "You think you know what's best for Nika when not even her sister or a team of doctors can help her? Fine. You take care of her, then. Apparently, you're some kind of expert."

"You coddle her."

"She's sick. She needs to be coddled."

Madoc stood up to his full height and stared down at her with bright green eyes devoid of all mercy. "Protected. Not coddled."

"I am protecting her."

"Not from herself."

Andra couldn't take any more of his arrogance. "You're a fool if you think you know what's right for her."

"Then I'm a fool."

"Fine. You take care of her tonight, but I swear to God, if you hurt her, I'll kill you as slow as a man can die." It was a promise, and she felt the angry heaviness of it bear down on her. She stumbled and Paul caught her, holding her up.

Madoc gave her a cold, empty smile. "You shouldn't make promises you can't keep. Didn't Paul tell you that when he collared you?"

"She doesn't know the ways of our world yet," said Paul. "But it's not going to matter, because you're not going to hurt Nika, right?"

Madoc shrugged. "Guess we'll see."

"I'm not leaving him alone with her," said Andra.

"Sure you are. We have a deal. And while we're all here making promises . . ." Madoc knelt down in front of Andra. He drew his sword and cut open his chest, right through his shirt. "My life for yours."

Thank God Paul still had a hold on her arm or she would have fallen on her ass just then. Madoc's vow felt like a lead blanket covering her. Trapping her.

"What the hell?" she managed to croak.

Madoc gave her another empty smile. "You'd better get used to it. You've got a shitload more of that headed your way once we get home."

Paul ran a reassuring hand over her bare back. "Don't worry about it. Everything is going to be fine." He shot Madoc's chest a meaningful glance. "Clean yourself up."

"Sure will. Then the two of you can get the hell out. The crazy girl and I have work to do."

"She's not in any shape to work," she told Madoc as he went to the adjoining bathroom.

Andra moved to follow him, ready to pound on him until he stopped being an ass. Paul stepped in front of her and she ran into his hard body.

"Leave it alone, Andra."

"I can't. She's my sister. She's weak and she can't look out for herself."

"Madoc won't hurt her. And someone needs to be with her so she won't try to escape through the window again."

"It should be me," said Andra.

"You told him he could stay. Now you've got to live with it. Trying to stop him is only going to hurt you, and I can't let that happen."

Nika had quieted, but she was still staring at the ceiling, her lips moving over and over in a silent chant. Andra hadn't been able to do anything for her, but Madoc seemed to at least be able to get her to listen. Maybe it was best if she let him try things his way. Nothing else was working.

Except that thing Paul had helped her do earlier to get her to eat. Maybe if she could convince him to show her how to do that, she could learn to help Nika on her own. He said she had power now, and she knew exactly how she wanted to use it.

"Okay," said Andra, feeling a glimmer of hope.

"You know what she likes to eat," said Madoc as he came out of the bathroom. "Make her something and leave it outside the door. I'll get her to eat."

Andra prayed his confidence wasn't hollow. "Just be careful with her."

"Yeah, yeah. She's fragile and all that shit. I got it already. Now get the fuck out."

Chapter 12

Paul took care of burning the clothes he and Madoc had bled on during their oaths to Andra. While the cloth burned, he found her a clean shirt to cover the tempting swell of her breasts.

When he came back into the kitchen, Andra had made a mountain of food for Nika. "There's no way she'll be able to eat all of this," he told her.

"I know, but she freaks out over certain textures and colors. This way she'll have some things to choose from. Besides, I could use a meal, and I figured you all could, too."

Her movements were jerky and awkward, and he could see an angry red patch of skin where she'd burned her hand on something. Through the luceria, he felt her frustration. Her fear for Nika's life. Her determination not to fail her sister.

He didn't dare tell her it would be okay. Life had taught him that it often wasn't. People died every day. Eventually, Nika would, too.

"I want to try to reach her," said Andra. "The way you did with Sammy."

"We can try," he told her.

Hope lit her face, but he held his hand up before she could get carried away. "Don't get your hopes up too high."

"Hope is all I have right now."

"I get that. Believe me. But there's a good chance it won't work because the damage happened so long ago."

"I don't care how small the chance is. I have to try. Just tell me what to do."

"You've got to learn to control my power so you can use it."

"How do I do that?" she asked.

"Practice. We go outside where we won't blow anything up, and start trying things to see what works. Eventually, you'll get the hang of it."

"Eventually isn't good enough. I'll just have to push myself until I'm able to do whatever it takes to save Nika."

Paul wasn't about to let her hurt herself, but the idea of her needing him was a heady thought. If she needed him, she'd stay with him.

"I won't make you any promises, but we'll do what we can."

She turned and looked at him with a kind of frantic desperation. "This has to work, Paul. It just has to."

At that moment, Paul knew the truth. If Nika died, Andra would, too. She'd never be able to forgive herself or let go of the pain and move on. The two sisters' fates were tied together. If Paul wanted her to live, then he had to find a way to save Nika.

So that was what he'd do. No matter what it took.

Andra followed Paul out into the night. The house was situated along one side of a cornfield, tucked back behind a clump of tall trees and thick scrub. She couldn't see the road from here, or any other houses, but there was a faint glow in the distant sky that she guessed belonged to Omaha.

He led her away from the house and out to the edge of the corn. His hand was warm and solid, and she held on to it like a lifeline. If this failed . . .

It couldn't fail. This had to work.

"So, what do we do?" she asked.

"First, you have to get a feel for drawing on the power inside me. Think of it like a big swimming pool filled with energy and you can siphon off as much of it as you want at a time."

"How do I get to it?"

He slid one finger over the band around her throat. "The luceria connects us." He held up his hand and showed her the matching ring. "Power can flow through them, from my ring into your necklace."

Andra could almost see it happen as he explained it. It was as if she had been born with the instinctive knowledge of what to do, and that knowledge was just now waking up inside her.

"Try something simple at first." He picked a stick up off the ground. "Try to light this on fire."

"How?"

"Close your eyes and relax."

Andra did, and felt his body move until he was standing behind her. His voice was quiet in the darkness, flowing over her skin like a breeze. Crickets chirped all around them, and a soft wind whispered through the cornfield. She could smell the richness of the earth rising up from the warm ground, feel Paul's strong body pressing close against her back.

His hands stroked her arms in a slow, lazy rhythm that calmed the beating of her heart. The skin of his palms was slightly rough, totally manly.

"That's right," he said against her ear. "You're doing great. Now, I want you to focus on the luceria. Feel the weight of it against your skin, the warmth of it as it holds your body's heat close."

She did. She could feel that and so much more. It gave off a subtle vibration so faint she hadn't noticed before. It was as if the necklace were shaking—about to burst with energy.

Andra's mind reached out and touched that energy, and like a shock of static, it gave her a sharp jolt. She jumped back from it and let out a little yelp.

Paul's hands tightened on her arms and held her in place. "It's a lot, I know. I'm sorry, but there's no other way. It's probably going to hurt a little."

Like losing her virginity. Best to just grit her teeth and get it over with so she could get on to the good part.

Andra made herself reach out for that flow of energy one more time. She braced herself for the shock, and this time it wasn't so bad. She accepted the pain and let it flow over her, let it fill her up.

"Good. Now let go of it. Let the power out so it can burn the stick."

Andra wasn't exactly sure how to do that, but she figured she'd better get her aim right. She didn't want to set the house on fire or singe their toes.

She looked at the stick and imagined she was Superman, sending out a beam of heat with her eyes.

That wasn't even close to what happened. There was no beam and the stick didn't burst into flames, but it did start to smoke as she felt the power inside her dissipate, making her feel lighter.

Victory surged through her and she jumped with the thrill of it, only to find that on the way back down, her legs could no longer hold her up.

Paul's thick arms caught her and he lowered her to the ground. "Easy, now."

Andra's head spun a bit and her body felt watery, but she'd still done it. She'd tapped into a source of power that might save Nika.

Paul held her in his lap as if she were dainty enough to fit, which made her smile. She'd never met a man who made her feel as feminine as he did. She'd worked out and packed on muscle because she needed the strength to fight the monsters, not because she enjoyed it. In fact, it would be kinda nice not to have to pump iron for hours each week just to feel like she had a fighting chance at survival. With Paul and his deadly sword around, maybe she wouldn't have to.

It was just three days, she reminded herself. Nothing more. She shouldn't go getting all excited over changing her lifestyle just because a man was around today. That didn't mean anything about tomorrow.

She had to stay strong and keep pushing. Nika needed her.

"Let's go again," said Andra.

"Give yourself a minute," he said as his thumb slid over her arm.

His touch felt nice. Maybe too nice. She was almost content to sit here all night and let him touch her. Hold her.

And who was holding Nika? Sure as hell it wasn't Madoc.

"I'm good to go," she told him. "What's next?"

"How about I teach you to see in the dark?"

"I'd rather learn how to help Nika."

He shook his head. "That's complex. It's going to take time."

"I don't have time. Nika doesn't have time. She's dying."

"I know, but there's only so much you can do. You can't start slinging around the kind of power it's going to take to help her. Not yet. Our connection is too new and small. You might end up hurting her."

"Then let's stretch it out."

"It's not that simple. These things take as long as they take."

He was hiding something from her. She could feel it. "There's something you're not telling me. What is it?"

"I'm protecting you."

"I don't need you to protect *me*. I need to you protect *Nika*."

He pressed his hand to her cheek and the touch felt

good. Right. A hum of strength flowed into her and she wanted more. "You have to come first."

"Then teach me how to get enough power to help her. Without her, I have nothing."

His mouth tightened into a grim, flat line. "It's too soon. We shouldn't force it."

"Screw that. I want to force it." She couldn't sit here in his lap anymore. She had to get up and put some distance between them before she did something she'd regret, like punch him for not cooperating.

Paul followed her up. His eyes darkened to a rich, chocolate brown, as if the idea of rushing things appealed to him. "It's not smart. I won't take the chance you might do yourself harm."

"It's not your choice. I'm going to do whatever it takes to help Nika. It doesn't matter how dangerous it is. If I can't save her, nothing matters. Don't you get that?"

"I do. More than you know."

"Then help me."

Paul stepped forward. He pressed his hand flat against her chest, just below the luceria and above the swell of her breasts.

"What are you doing?" she asked.

"I'm giving you what you want. More power."

"This seems like an odd way of—"

A hot jolt of energy ripped through her, streaking from where his ring hovered near her skin with only the fabric of her shirt between them. The jolt wasn't exactly pain, but it was one hell of a close cousin.

Andra was left breathing hard, shaking. Weak. She felt like she'd just run a mile uphill after a bout of stomach flu.

"You were saying?" asked Paul with a smug grin lifting his voice.

"Was that enough?" she asked, praying it was so. "I sure don't feel stronger."

"Hardly. That was a mere spark. If you want to help

Nika, it's going to take a lot more than that. Plus, you'll have to learn to channel it."

Andra wasn't sure how much more she could take, but she knew how much more she was going to make him give her—enough to fix Nika. "Then teach me."

He stared into her eyes, his expression deadly serious. "Be sure, Andra."

"I'm sure."

Paul said, "Put your palm on the ground."

She knelt on the ground and speared her fingers through the dry grass so she could feel the dirt. He knelt beside her and his hand pinned hers in place.

"Now, close your eyes. What do you feel?"

"Weeds. It's warm. A little damp. There's a rock under my finger."

"That's just the surface. Go deeper."

"I can't touch anything deeper."

"You also can't touch Nika's mind, but you have to learn how to feel your way around inside it."

Andra got his point. She didn't tell him she'd been peeking around inside the thoughts of lost children for years. Whatever she was able to do with them didn't work with Nika—she'd tried—so she made herself concentrate. His body was hot and hard against hers. It was easier to feel his muscular thigh brushing hers than it was to feel inside the ground, but she kept trying. She thought about what it must be like in the ground, all dark and heavy, but she sensed that she still wasn't getting it right.

"Sorry. I'm not feeling anything."

"That's because you're doing it on your own. You have to use my power. Pull it from me."

"I don't know how."

"I'll help," said Paul. His hand cupped the nape of her neck and she felt his ring hit her necklace and stick like a magnet. He leaned down over her until she could feel his breath fan her cheek, and he placed his free hand next to hers on the ground. Her neck warmed beneath the band, and that warmth spread down her arm and into each fingertip. It wasn't like the jolt before. It was gentler, or maybe it just felt that way because the power was draining out of her into the ground.

"Can you feel the soil just below your fingertips?"

Andra nodded. That part was easy.

"Below that is a layer of broken rock. The roots of the plants have dug their way in through tiny cracks, soaking up the water that's trapped there each time it rains."

Andra squeezed her eyes shut and tried to see what he described.

"About thirty feet down there's a thick slab of stone. Old stone that's been here since before my grandparents were born." With every word, the power flowing into her seemed to increase. She could feel it expand to fill up her arm and it vibrated faster with each passing second.

"Can you see it?" he asked in a mere whisper.

"I can imagine it, but I can't see it."

"You're not letting me in. My power is flowing through you, but you're not using it."

"I'm sorry, but I don't know what I'm doing wrong."

"Nothing. The inadequacy is mine, but I can fix it." He pulled in a deep breath. "Don't fight me. It will be easier if you are accepting."

She didn't know what he meant until she felt a pressure inside her skull as if something were trying to bore its way in. Her instincts were to fight the invasion, but she tried to let it happen.

"Relax," she heard him grate out in a pained tone.

She let out the breath she was holding and urged her tight muscles to loosen. He wasn't going to hurt her. Paul would never hurt her.

The pressure in her head released suddenly and she

could feel a sliver of him inside her mind. "Just let me take the wheel," he said.

The words echoed in her head as well as in her ears. It was freaky, but nice, too. She felt surrounded. Safe.

Andra did as he asked, and let her mind wander.

"God, you're beautiful," he whispered over her thoughts. "Selfless. Strong. Brave. I'm humbled."

She had no idea what he was looking at, but she started to grow uncomfortable with the idea that he could see inside her.

"No. Don't fight me. I'll stop poking around, I swear."

The presence inside her mind receded, and she could feel him keep his word. Andra relaxed again and let him steer.

"Ready?" he asked her.

She was, but she didn't have to say the words. He was part of her and already knew.

"Here we go."

She felt another shocking jolt, only this one was less painful, more like a wave of pressure rushing through her. Her eyes felt like they'd be pushed from her head, but there was an odd tingling in them, too. Her lids were still closed, but she saw something huge lurking in front of her.

Rock.

"I can see it," she whispered.

"Good. Tell me what else you see."

She wasn't sure which way to go, so she went down farther, burrowing her way through the solid rock until she came out the bottom. "Water," she told him. "There's lots of water down here. And something shiny." Or at least it would be shiny if there were any light. "How can I see without light?"

"You're not really seeing; you're perceiving it as if you were seeing it, though, since visual stimulus is what your mind is used to interpreting."

"This is so cool."

She felt him grin against her ear, felt his presence

glow with warmth inside her mind. "Now, I want you to pull back until you're near the soil again, almost at the surface, but not quite."

Slowly, Andra did as he asked.

"Now, do you feel all the seeds in the soil?"

"Feel the seeds?" Andra poked around, trying to figure out what he meant, when she stumbled across one. Life. The potential for life inside the tiny speck was incredible. Powerful and determined, waiting patiently for the right time.

"That's it," he said in a low voice. "Now tell it to grow."

"What?"

"Tell the seed to sprout. Bring water up from the ground and convince it to grow."

"How do I talk to it?"

"Just try it. I'll guide you."

Andra poked around the little thing with her mind, prodding at it as if to wake it up. Nothing happened. "It's not working."

"That's because you're not using me. Draw from me the strength you need to make it listen."

She didn't know how to do that, either, but she felt like she *should* know.

A warm ring of power glowed around her neck, so she went there first. The luceria could siphon off his power. That was what he'd told her. She concentrated on that ring and imagined plugging a cord into it like she would her TV. At first, she didn't think anything had happened, but then she felt another one of those waves wash over her.

She let out a groan and thanked God she was already on the ground. It saved her some time, since that was where she would have ended up anyway. Her head spun as if someone had given her brain a good twist, but she'd connected herself to Paul's power and stayed that way.

She could feel the huge ocean of strength deep inside him, just waiting for her.

And she wanted it. Craved it. That ocean could save Nika, and if she could have found a way, she would have drained every bit of it from him.

Problem was, she couldn't seem to reach it, or at least not much of it.

"We're not close enough," he told her. "Not united the way we need to be for you to get what you want. Yet."

Whether it was a promise or a warning, she wasn't sure, but she felt him slip out of her mind, leaving her oddly alone again.

She opened her eyes to look at him and ask him what he meant, but she didn't get that far. The lush, rich carpet of grass and flowers under their bodies distracted her. Even in the dark, she could see the vibrant colors of wildflowers that had not been there moments before.

"I did that?" she asked him.

"Sure did." He pushed to his feet and put plenty of distance between them.

"So I'm ready now?" she asked. "I can help Nika?"

"Not yet, but soon."

"How soon?"

He shrugged and his eyes slid away. "It depends."

"On what?"

He shoved his hands through his mussed hair and turned away. It was an evasive maneuver and she knew it.

Andra grabbed his shoulder and spun him around. "It depends on what, Paul?"

"We're rushing things. We've got to slow down."

"No. There isn't time. I'm a fast learner. Let's just get this over with."

His mouth twisted as if he'd tasted something bad. "That's not the way it works. You can't just plow through this, or blast your way through with a shotgun. It takes time."

"We've got three days. Is that enough?"

"Probably not," he said as he turned away again, his eyes sliding to the ground.

"What are you hiding from me?"

Paul looked over his shoulder and gave her a grim, resigned stare. "I'm sorry. I won't help you do this. I won't let you hurt yourself."

Frustration rose up inside her, and she shoved it at him in anger. As childish as it was, she wanted him to suffer as much as she did—she wanted him to know what it was like to have the means to help Nika so close, but still fall short.

Andra felt her frustration and anger slide through their connection and saw his face darken as he suffered through the gnawing, helpless feeling she'd forced him to endure.

Seconds after she'd done it, she already felt bad. It wasn't his fault she couldn't do this. It was hers. It had always been her fault when she failed.

Instinctively, she reached out for his mind, wanting to apologize, hoping to soothe him. He let her in, and his eyes slid shut as if he enjoyed the feeling of having her inside him.

Andra brushed against his thoughts. There were so many—so many intense feelings she could hardly make sense of any of it. She saw his need to keep her safe glowing like a beacon, shadowing all else. Such devotion was humbling, and she had no idea why he would care so much that she survived. It had something to do with the energy pulsing within him, but she couldn't sort out the knot of thoughts and feelings enough to figure it out.

There was something else looming inside him, too. Something darker that hid behind that beacon. Andra reached for it and felt a hint of knowledge flicker through it—knowledge he was hiding from her.

Curious, Andra got closer to it and studied it. She felt Paul try to push her out of his mind, but she dug in her heels and refused to leave. She needed to learn what this thing was he was hiding and why it was so important to him to keep it from her.

"That's enough," she heard him say, but ignored it.

She shielded her eyes from the glowing light and took hold of the hidden knowledge with an unbreakable grip.

His power. She could have it all if she were close enough to him. That was what he'd been hiding.

"You're not ready," he gritted out between clenched teeth. "It's too soon."

Trust, love, intimacy. That was what she needed to have to strengthen their connection enough for her to save Nika. No wonder he said it would take time. Those things couldn't be had overnight. At least, not all of them.

Intimacy. Sex. She could share that with him.

Andra felt another strong push against her as he tried to drive her from the truth. "I don't want you whoring yourself out like that."

"It's not like I don't want you," she said, though whether it was her voice or her mind speaking, she couldn't tell. "I don't normally have sex with men I've just met, but I'll make an exception for you." For Nika.

"Sex and intimacy aren't necessarily the same thing."

"Maybe not," she said, "but there's only one way to find out if it's close enough."

Paul groaned and she felt a wave of desire rise up inside him, eclipsing that glowing beacon. "I didn't want it to be this way between us. I wanted to do it right this time."

"Right is whatever works." Whatever saved Nika.

"I don't want to have sex with you because you think it will save your sister," he said.

"Then don't. Have sex with me because I want it.

Because you want it, too." And just to be sure he did, she nestled her body against his. While locked inside his mind, she couldn't see him clearly, but she could feel the heat of his body—feel his powerful muscles trembling as he fought himself.

With an almost violent force of will, Paul pushed her from his thoughts and she landed hard back inside her body. For a brief moment, the place felt odd to her, not quite like the home it had always been. But as soon as she felt it, the sensation faded and everything went back to normal.

Paul stood before her, his hands locked around her biceps. She could feel his arms shaking as if he couldn't decide whether to pull her closer or push her away.

Andra didn't need any help deciding what she wanted. He was standing right in front of her—a heady combination of noble sacrifice and raw physical power. He was the kind of man women could only dream about, the kind who existed only in fantasy, and yet he stood before her, solid and real, and the answer to every one of her prayers.

She reached up and laced her fingers around his neck. His hands dropped to his sides and curled into fists. He was stiff and unyielding in her arms, but Andra didn't relent. She went up on her tiptoes and pressed a soft kiss at the corner of his mouth.

His lips tightened, but she felt his abdomen clench and knew he was fighting himself. He wanted her.

"All you have to do is give in. Give me what I want," she whispered.

Paul clamped his eyes shut and sucked in a quick breath.

Andra moved lower, kissing her way along his angular jawline until she reached his neck, just below his ear. Her tongue flicked out, just barely grazing his skin. "I know you want it, too."

"What I want isn't important." He was winded, and

she swore she could hear his resolve weakening with every beat of his heart.

"It is to me. I know you'll be careful with me." Andra gathered his fist in her hands and unclenched his fingers. She kissed his palm, then settled his hand over her heart so his fingers cupped the swell of her breast. "I trust you."

Those three words broke him. She felt him crumble, and his face changed from a mask of steely determination to a look of unrelenting hunger. He grabbed a fistful of her short hair and angled her head back, forcing her to look into his eyes. There was no mercy there. Not anymore.

His voice was a low rumble, almost menacing in its ferocity. "Don't say I didn't warn you."

Andra was going to get what she wanted. She only hoped she was woman enough to take it.

Chapter 13

Madoc was ready to storm out of the room and leave Nika to fend for herself.

Freaking lunatic chick nearly scalded his balls off with a bowl of soup, and now she was eyeing the spoon like she had plans for that as well.

"Not going to happen," he warned her.

Nika glared at him. "You can't make me drink your blood no matter how well you disguise it."

So far, he'd been Mr. Nice Guy—or at least nice for him—but that wasn't working, so it was time to move on to plan B.

"It's not my blood. The Sanguinar can't have it and neither can you. Now settle the fuck down and eat something."

Nika clamped her lips shut. She probably hadn't meant to dare him like that, but too bad for her. She had.

Madoc eyed her frail body. He hated to manhandle her. She looked like she'd snap in two if he brushed against her skin, which was why he'd be careful not to do that, even by accident.

But what choice did he have now? He had to get some food in her or she was going to drop dead, and that couldn't happen. She might be able to save the life of one of his brothers.

Maybe even him.

Madoc looked at his ring again for the fifty billionth time in the past ten minutes. Nothing. No swirling colors, no vibration. Not a fucking thing. All he saw was that what little color was left had faded even more since yesterday—the colors dying as his soul did.

A vicious flare of rage filled him up until he wanted to scream and break the furniture and pound his fists into the walls until there was nothing left but dust and blood. It wasn't fair. After all these centuries of loyal service, of working and sweating and bleeding to do his sworn duty, it wasn't fair that she couldn't be the one to save him. Ease *his* pain.

It was the Solarc's sick joke, no doubt. Someone needed to bust through the gate and pound the king of Athanasia's ass hard. Madoc didn't care if he was the Solarc's descendant. Fucker deserved a good, thorough beating.

A soft gasp brought his attention back to Nika. He'd mutilated the spoon he'd been holding—bent it until it was no longer usable.

Fuck. At least he hadn't been touching her at the time. He would have done the same thing to her fingers or arm.

Madoc flung the spoon across the room. Nika's blue eyes widened and she tried to move away from him across the bed.

No more. He was through playing. "Enough fucking around, Nika. You're going to eat and get strong and figure out which one of the men you can save once we get back to Dabyr. Got that? I'm not going to let you starve yourself to death."

She was still wide-eyed and shaking, and knowing he'd done it made whatever sliver of his soul was left alive shudder in disgust.

Madoc pulled in a deep breath and gathered every bit of patience he could find. What he really needed was to spend a few hours pumping iron, then a few more pumping into a woman. He didn't need to be playing nursemaid.

But he was, and he was stuck, so he reached out slowly and wrapped his hand around her wrist, which was about as big around as two of his fingers and a hell of a lot more fragile.

Nika froze inside his grasp and her eyes kinda rolled back in her head. Her whole body started shaking and she let out a jagged cry of pain.

Madoc let go as if she were on fire. "Oh, God. I'm sorry," he heard himself saying, expecting blood to start shooting out of her arm where he'd touched her. He must have broken a bone or something, but he didn't see any sign of a break. Not even a red mark.

She flopped around on the bed, sending food flying everywhere. When she started scooting off the side, Madoc rushed around the bed and kept her from falling off.

Maybe she was having some kind of seizure and it had nothing to do with him.

Yeah, right. And he was going to live happily ever after, too, surrounded by bunnies and kittens and puppies and all the cotton candy he could eat.

If he didn't do something, she was going to hurt herself, so he crawled on the bed and pinned the blankets down over her body, using his arms and legs to pull the fabric tight, being careful not to touch her again.

Slowly, the shaking stopped and her body went still. He couldn't tell if she was breathing, and panic filled him up until he was sweating it through his pores.

Madoc pressed his ear over her heart, desperate to hear a beat, feel her chest rise with her breath. Something.

Seconds passed and he thought he felt something, but he wasn't sure. Then he heard a faint pulse and her tight little nipple pressed against his cheek as she pulled in a deep breath.

Madoc's eyes closed with relief. He hadn't killed her.

She shifted against his hold on the blankets, so he sat up, still straddling her legs, but not putting any weight on her.

Her skin was pale and her eyes were glassy, but she stared at him, and for the first time tonight, she looked lucid. "Thirsty," she whispered in a dry voice. "Can I have some water?"

Madoc nodded and eased off the bed. He retrieved the spilled cup from the floor, rinsed it out, and filled it up at the bathroom sink. As he was coming back, he saw Nika try to sit up and fail. Her arms weren't strong enough to support even her meager weight.

Which meant he was going to have to touch her again. Holy fuck, he didn't want to do that. Not that what he wanted had ever really mattered in the scheme of things.

He set the cup down and slid his arm beneath her shoulders to lift her up. She was bony as hell and weighed about as much as his cheerful disposition. He held the cup for her so she wouldn't spill—not that it would matter with the mess of food the bed was already covered in. She emptied the cup and slumped as if even that small effort had drained her.

"Thanks," she told him, and still she seemed sane.

It creeped him out more than a little.

"Can I have some toast or crackers?"

"You want to eat?" asked Madoc, unable to hide his shock.

"If it's not too much trouble."

Trouble? Just what the fuck did she think was all over the bed? Looked like a whole hell of a lot of trouble to him. "You gonna throw it at me or try to chop my dick off with the edge of the cracker?"

This time she was the one looking at him as if he were crazy. "That isn't my first choice, no. I'd rather eat it."

A package of crackers had come along with all of the other food. Madoc found it under a bowl of macaroni and cheese and wiped off the majority of the mess with his shirt, adding to the mix of foods soiling it. He tore the plastic open and held out the sleeve to her.

She reached for it, but her hand was shaking so hard, Madoc pulled it away. "I'll do it," he told her, sounding disgusted.

He pulled a saltine out and held it to her mouth. She took a bite, chewed, and her eyes closed on a blissful moan. "God, that's good."

Madoc frowned at the cracker and looked at it, searching for the secret ingredient that made her so happy. Whatever it was, he'd like to cover himself with it and let her lick it—

Holy hell. He was so not going to go there with her. Not in a million years. Not if every hooker on the face of the planet keeled over and he had no one left to fuck.

Nika was clean. Precious. Breakable. And not his.

Besides, he didn't like bony chicks. At least, he didn't think he did. His dick thought different, but then it had always had a mind of its own.

"More?" she asked.

Madoc fed her another bite and watched her eat. She was pretty enough, though he imagined that with an extra twenty or thirty pounds she'd be drop-dead gorgeous. Way out of his league.

Besides, even if she were stronger, she'd probably still be too fragile for the kind of fucking he liked to give— hard and fast and often. Hell, she'd probably be the kind of woman who wanted him to stick around afterward to cuddle, too. He couldn't stand that shit. He just wanted to get off and get out.

The line of thought made his cock throb, and the remains of the cracker turned to powder in his grasp. He shifted his hips so she couldn't see his boner and grabbed another saltine.

After eating about six of the crackers, she fizzled out as if she were full.

"Do you think I could convince you to run me a bath?" she asked, looking at the food stains on her clothes. "I'm a mess."

"You sure you're up to it?"

"I know I'm not up to sleeping in this filth all night."

"Yeah, whatever."

"If you don't have time, I'm sure Andra will help me."

Like hell. This was his job tonight, and he was damn well going to do it. "She's busy."

Nika gave a little hurt frown that made him want to kiss it away.

Whoa. He really was losing it. Since when did he want to kiss anyone? He couldn't even stand to kiss the women he screwed.

A hopeful suspicion lit him up and he looked down at his ring again for some kind of sign. Nothing. Not a fucking thing.

Hope died a swift death, which was exactly as it should be.

Don't say I didn't warn you.

Andra was swiftly having second thoughts about taunting Paul—practically daring him to have sex with her. Something in him had changed the moment he'd given her that warning. She saw it in his eyes, a kind of predatory glow lighting the golden chips. Even his posture had changed. He was no longer offering her comfort. His hold on her was hot and hard. Possessive.

Andra tried to shift, but his grip tightened. His thick arm wrapped around her back and held her in place. His other hand was still clenched around her hair, holding her so tight it almost hurt. She probably could have escaped if she'd really put her mind to it, but she wasn't sure how long her escape would last. That predatory vibe coming off him was strong, warning her that if she tried to run, he'd be right behind her. And those long, powerful legs of his would have no trouble catching her.

"What are you doing?" she asked him.

His voice was quiet, so she had to strain to hear over the singing crickets. "Giving you what you want. The power to help Nika."

"Good. Okay. I can deal with that."

"Whatever it takes?" he asked, and his mouth brushed her ear, his words trickling into her like a dark seduction.

Andra's stomach tightened and her voice dried up. She nodded.

He let go of her hair and moved around her body until his fingers encircled her throat, covering the luceria. Sparks leaped from his fingertips and sank into her, sliding down her body and into the earth. She stiffened at the intensity, but Paul soothed her with small strokes of his thumb. "Shhh. I'll stop if you want, and we'll go inside. We can try another day."

Nika didn't have many days left if things didn't change. "Just get on with it. I can take it."

He chuckled and she felt the vibration all the way to her toes. This man was swiftly going to her head, and she wasn't sure how safe that was for her.

His thumb continued to stroke a lazy path over her neck. She fought the urge to squirm so he'd move lower.

"So brave on the outside. But I know how you really feel. Your heart is racing," he told her. "I'd almost think you were afraid."

Pride rose up inside her, making her spine straighten. "I'm not afraid. I just don't know what you're going to do."

"Yes, you do," he said as he lowered his head toward hers.

It was no gentle, coaxing kiss, as before. It was hot and demanding, and stole the breath from her lungs. He thrust his tongue inside and pressed his body down upon hers, forcing her legs wide to make room for him.

She probably should have shoved him away for being so forward, but she didn't want to, God help her. She wanted what he was giving her, and then some.

A moment later, another wave of energy rushed through her and left her shaking in its wake. Her body felt as if it were on fire, burning from the inside out. An achy hollowness settled low in her belly, and she needed to find a way to make it stop. Not being one for long-term relationships, Andra knew sexual frustration, but this was beyond anything she'd ever felt before. This was not a want, but a need, like breathing.

She wasn't sure she wanted to feel this desperate for anyone, but she didn't have much of a choice. Not anymore.

She ground herself against his thigh, trying to find some kind of relief, but there was none to be had that way. There were too many clothes blocking her skin. She needed more contact. More friction.

A rough moan rose up out of her, shocking her with the frantic, needy sound.

"That's right," Paul murmured against her mouth. "Now we're getting there."

She didn't know exactly what he meant by that, but she didn't really care anymore. She needed to get him naked and inside her. Right now.

Andra pulled at his shirt and heard fabric rip under the force of her desperation. The fabric fell away from his chest, revealing the tree tattoo she'd seen earlier, only now it was no longer bare. Small buds had formed all along the branches, making it look almost fuzzy.

She ran her finger over it, distracted from his body by the way it had changed. "More magic?" she asked.

"Nothing compared to what's in store for you."

Chapter 14

Paul had to pace himself or he was going to hurt her. He wanted her too much. Needed her. He thought it was bad before, but now that he'd seen inside her mind, it was much, much worse.

She was beautiful inside. So caring and generous. So afraid of being alone. So afraid of failing Nika again. That fear made all of Paul's oversize protective instincts stand up and roar. He was going to make sure she was never alone again—that her family was safe. Whatever it took, whatever it cost, Paul was going to protect her from the one thing she feared most. Losing Nika.

He had no idea how he was going to do it, but he would find a way. They'd find a way together.

And he was going to start by making sure she could use as much of his power as she could stand. It was what they both wanted. All he had to do was make sure he held back enough that she didn't end up getting hurt.

He opened his eyes and stared down at her. She was so beautiful in the moonlight he could hardly believe she was real. Her cheeks were flushed and her mouth was open, her breath coming in fast, panting bursts. He swore he could almost see the shimmer of heat rising from her skin.

Mine.

She'd taken his luceria, and that made her his. Bound her to him.

"Open your mouth," he ordered. He'd been dying to kiss her all night and hadn't had nearly enough to appease him. Not even close.

A look of concern crossed her face. "Paul, are you—"

"Open. Your. Mouth."

She did, just a little, and Paul kissed her deep and hard. She hadn't opened wide enough for him, so he urged her to give him more. Take more.

She tasted so damn good, he'd never get enough of her. He licked along her lips and tilted her head back so he could get a better, deeper angle. Her soft sigh told him she didn't mind one bit. In fact, her arms came around his neck and she held him tight, as if trying to keep him from getting away.

Like he'd stop now. Not a chance. He had warned her this might not be safe, but she hadn't listened, and now she deserved everything she got.

Heat poured off of him until he thought he'd combust. His dick strained against his jeans, begging for release. His heart pounded hard and fast, and the power inside him swelled and pulsed as if it knew what he had planned for her and couldn't wait to be let free.

Paul shoved her shirt and bra up, baring her breasts to the moonlight. She was beautiful here, too. Perfectly shaped to fill his hand, her nipples puckered and tight. It wasn't cold out here, which left only one other reason. She wanted this, too. Maybe not as much as he did, but he was going to fix that.

He covered her breast with his palm, groaning at the intoxicating feel of her naked skin against his. Her tight nipple jutted up into his hand, making him crazy. He knew his hands were rough from years of combat, but he didn't care. He had to touch her, feel her naked skin against his own. He rubbed his palm across her nipple, making her suck in a sharp breath. His mind was too fogged to figure out whether that sound was good or bad, but he knew one thing she'd like for sure—one place he wasn't too rough for her.

He pulled his mouth away from hers and eased down her body, moving all of her bunched-up clothes out of his way, over her head and arms. Paul swept his tongue across her nipple. Andra's hips bucked and she ripped the clothes from her arms and grabbed fistfuls of his hair, holding him to her.

"More," she ordered.

Paul happily complied and covered her with his mouth, pulling on her hard.

Her fingernails bit into his scalp and she let out the most beautiful sound of pleasure he'd ever heard.

Deep inside him, something was happening—something truly wonderful—but he didn't know what it was. He couldn't think straight. Not with his mouth latched onto her breast and her body writhing under his. Not with the moonlight bathing her skin and the scent of her arousal heavy in the night air.

Power flowed out of him, trickling into her everywhere their bare skin touched. It was erotic feeling her soaking it up, feeling her accept what he needed to give her.

"Oh." She breathed in and he felt her hold her breath for a moment. "That's what you meant."

Paul couldn't speak. His throat was too tight with the need to shove more power into her and force her to take it all. Only his need to protect her held him back and allowed him a precious measure of control.

The ferocious need to take her welled up inside him. If she couldn't take more power, she was damn well going to take his cock inside her as deep as it could go.

His fingers went to the waistband of her jeans, desperate to get her naked. He wanted to feel her skin against his and find out if she was as wet and ready for him as he needed her to be. He didn't think he could be gentle anymore. Not the first time. Maybe after a few rounds, after he'd ground down the rougher edges of his need.

She stiffened and moved to stop his hand, but Paul brushed off her attempt. She tried again and he growled his frustration while he captured her hands and pinned them over her head against her discarded shirt.

"Paul." She whispered his name as if she were frightened.

He didn't want to stop, but he was compelled by his vow to look around and find out what had scared her. Once he killed it, he could get back to her sweet, firm body.

When he looked around, he saw nothing. "What?" he asked her in a voice thick with need.

"You're holding me down."

So? She'd tried to stop him. What did she expect him to do?

"Let me go." Her eyes were wide and bright with banked fear.

Paul looked at where his hand shackled her wrists. His hold was tight enough to bruise. Tight enough to hurt her.

"Shit," growled Paul. He let her go and shoved himself away from her. He was going too fast in his desperation. Forcing her. That hadn't been his intention.

Had it?

His erection throbbed in time with his racing pulse and his skin was fever-hot. Inside, he was shaking with need, but he managed to lie still on the dry grass and not jump her again.

Her face came into his line of sight and she wore a tentative, worried frown. "You okay?"

Paul shut his eyes. He couldn't even look at her without fighting the need to stake his claim. And even when he closed his eyes, he could still feel her skin under his hands and her nipple against his tongue. Those were not the kinds of things a man forgot.

She touched his face, and he gritted his teeth against the urge to throw her back down and take her hard and fast, before she had a chance to stop him.

"We don't have to stop, but slower is good," she said. "Can you go slower?"

"Probably not. I don't know what you do to me, but I'm dying here. I need to be inside you." Just saying it nearly turned him inside out with lust.

Andra pulled in a shaky breath. Her breast brushed his arm, and he could feel the silky smoothness of her skin. She was still shirtless.

Paul opened his eyes to look because there was no other choice. He had to see her bare breasts.

She watched him stare and went up to her knees. "Slower, okay?"

Paul nodded, unable to speak. He wasn't sure if he could slow down, but he knew he'd try. He'd do just about anything to get her back under him where she belonged.

Before he could find the will to move, Andra straddled his hips. "It worked," she told him.

"What worked?"

"Intimacy." She took his hand and pressed it to her breast. "When you kissed me here, I felt it—felt our connection get stronger."

"Maybe I should do it again, just to be sure."

She gave him a sultry smile that made him want to feel her lips wrap around his cock while she sucked him off. His whole body shook with the effort to stay still and not force her to do just that.

"You're beautiful," she told him.

"I'm a man."

She stroked her fingers over his lifemark, trailing down toward his jeans. "You're still beautiful. All hard and muscular. It's a real turn-on."

"If you're so turned on, then you won't mind letting me feel. Are you wet, Andra?"

She held his stare as she unbuttoned her jeans and slid the zipper down so slowly it made his balls ache. Instead of letting him do the job, she eased her hand inside her panties. Her eyes went heavy and her head fell back as she moved her fingers over her own skin.

Paul couldn't take any more. Not one second. He grabbed her wrist and pulled her hand out. Her fingers glistened with her arousal in the moonlight. He'd done that to her. He'd made her wet and now he was going to taste her.

He took her fingers into his mouth and nearly came right there. She tasted of salt and woman and unsated need. But not for long. He'd satisfy her and fill her up with his seed so there'd be no more question that she was his woman. She'd smell like his. Taste like his. Be his.

Andra watched him with heavy-lidded eyes and he could feel her jeans rasping against his stomach as her hips shifted like they had a mind of their own.

"Take them off," ordered Paul. "I want you naked."

Andra lifted a brow in challenge. "You, too."

Whatever got her naked worked for him. Paul unfastened his sword belt and set it within easy reach. As soon as it left his body, the weapon became visible, displaying the intricate carvings of vines on the scabbard. He shoved his jeans and boots off just in time to watch her do the same.

She was still wearing her panties, but she tossed the rest of her clothes aside and her eyes fixed on his heavy erection. It bobbed in answer to her eager stare. "If you keep looking, I'm going to disgrace myself."

A smile of pure womanly greed curved her mouth. "Oh, yeah?" She reached out and wrapped her fingers around him, making him suck in a hard breath. "I think I'd like to see that."

"Maybe later," he told her, and pushed her back down in the soft, thick grass. "Right now, I have other plans."

She stroked him with her fist. Her fingers were just long enough to do the job right, and they felt like heaven. Paul had to clench his teeth to stop himself from coming all over her hand.

He pulled her hand away and his dick gave a throb of resentment, which he ignored.

"You're still wearing your panties," he said.

"I'm shy."

Paul let out a bark of laughter he couldn't contain. There wasn't a shy bone in her body. She was teasing him and that was fine. Two could play that game.

He kissed her mouth until she was breathless, and then moved down her neck and over her collarbone. He loved each breast with his mouth and tongue, pulling sweet moans of pleasure from her until he couldn't take any more. He trailed kisses down her ribs and over her taut belly, sliding her panties off as he descended.

Her legs were long and muscular, like the rest of her. But even with all those feminine muscles, she was still woman-soft, woman-smooth. He had to touch her and soak up the feel of her skin beneath his. He wasn't sure he was ever going to get enough of her, but he was damn well going to try.

He went back up her body, spreading her legs as he caressed them. Every inch higher he went drew a new shiver from her, another soft moan. Restraint nearly killed him. It would have been so easy to just slide right inside her. But she'd asked him to go slower, so he would.

When his finger slid over her sex, opening her slick folds, she jumped at the contact.

"Oh," she breathed on a long sigh as her body went limp.

Paul wasn't waiting for an invitation. He parted her legs wide enough to make room for his shoulders and settled between them. The grass tickled his body, but it was soft enough that he didn't worry about Andra's back. He could ride her as hard as he wanted and not fear hurting her. Which was good. He didn't trust his restraint to hold once he felt her body close around his dick.

The scent of her heated body made his head spin and his mouth water. He parted her flesh, and Andra's body tensed. He didn't know if it was because she was eager or anxious, but he pressed soft, soothing kisses along the insides of her thighs to quiet her so she'd let him do as he pleased with her.

It didn't work. She was strung tight, vibrating with tension.

His mind wanted to relax her and ease her anxiety, but his body had other ideas. He needed to taste her again, to make her come. After an orgasm or two, she'd be plenty relaxed.

The idea was too potent to resist, so he didn't. He pushed her legs high and wide and held them there while he took her with his mouth.

Andra grabbed his hair in her fists and let out a sharp cry of need. Her hips bucked beneath him and he gripped her tight to hold her still while he flicked his tongue over her sensitive little nub.

Then he felt it. She was poking at his mind frantically, trying to find her way inside.

Kate had never wanted that closeness with him. She'd always kept her distance. Cold and aloof. She'd never so much as let him kiss her.

But not Andra. She was trying to get closer to him, trying to become a part of him. Paul's soul swelled with satisfaction and he let her in, feeling a dark grin stretch his mouth. He had nothing to hide from her—not anymore—but he guided her toward what he wanted her to see most. She was going to see all of him, feel his desire for her, and it would magnify her own.

In her innocence, she didn't realize he was funneling her through his thoughts, steering her toward his vibrant, consuming need to have her and keep her forever. She went along easily and he let her feel it, let go of his control and let her feel how much he wanted her.

A raw moan escaped her lips, and she arched into

him, holding his head tight against her. As if he needed any encouragement. He could feel how close she was, how much she wanted it. Needed it. Her body was trembling on the brink, and all it would take was the slightest push to send her over.

Paul's dick throbbed as he slid a finger inside her tight, hot body. She let out an almost pained whimper, so he suckled her hard, giving her what she needed. That was all it took.

He felt her orgasm sweep over her, felt her muscles tighten as it crashed against her. She let out a loud cry of release that made Paul's world shift beneath him. The echo hadn't even died down yet and already he wanted to make her do it again. And again.

Her body relaxed beneath him, going soft and pliant. She was still hovering inside his mind, but her presence was faint and content. Her legs were splayed wide, her sex glistening in the moonlight.

If he'd been a better man, he would have moved away and let her rest. But he wasn't better. He needed her too much. Sweat beaded up on his skin and his muscles were knotted with pain. He had to have her. Now, before she had the chance to deny him.

He kissed his way back up her body, praying she'd understand his need.

"I'm sorry," he grated out as he aligned his body to fit hers.

She opened her eyes. Paul expected to see shock or maybe even revulsion, but instead, she wrapped her arms around him and pulled him toward her. His hips moved of their own accord, easing his erection inside her. She was snug, but relaxed, and so wet he slid in without hurting her. *Thank God.*

His arms shook with restraint as he braced his weight over her body. He was dying to shove deeper and rut inside her, but he held back. "You okay?" he found the strength to ask.

She purred and arched her back so he slid deeper. Paul sucked in a breath and gritted his teeth to stave off his orgasm for just a little longer. As much as he needed to come, he needed to be sure this would not be a one-time thing. It had to be good for her. He had only a few days to prove to her that she couldn't live without him, and jerking off inside her in thirty seconds flat was not the way to do that.

He stilled his body and concentrated on her face, the smooth curve of her cheek, the soft swell of her mouth, the way her eyelids fluttered when his cock twitched inside her.

"You're not moving," she whispered, and tightened her muscles around him.

Paul gasped for air. "I'm trying to hold on to a little control here. You're not helping."

"I don't want your control. I want you."

"I'd be too rough right now."

She gave him a sexy, knowing smile. "Rough is nice once in a while." She caught his bottom lip between her teeth and slid her tongue across it before letting it go. "Besides, I'm tough. I can take it."

Not only could she take it; she wanted to. He could see the desire shining in her eyes, feel it flickering through their connection.

Paul's control broke open. He slid from her body and surged back into her again, forcing her to take all of him. Andra's eyes widened and her pupils dilated as he held himself deep inside her and ground his hips against her.

"Oh, God," she breathed, and clutched at his ass. "Again."

He complied, but not because she asked. He had no choice. His instincts were raging now, his body moving hard and fast in response. Somewhere in the back of his mind, he thought he should be doing something else. Kissing her, petting her? He was no longer sure. Nothing mattered but the tight grip of her sex around his cock and the slippery heat forming between them. She was tight and slick, and her body cushioned his thrusts, accepting whatever he gave her.

The base of his spine tightened and sparks formed in his vision. He was close and he wanted her right there with him, plunging over the edge.

Paul forced his way into her mind and let her feel what he was feeling. He channeled his power into her body, stretching the boundaries of their link as hard as he could, forcing her to take more than she ever had before. Andra cried out against the pressure, but he didn't relent. This was what she wanted—what she needed to help Nika—and he was going to give it to her.

Her body bowed up off the ground, lifting his hips with her. It buried him deep inside her, and Paul was lost, reveling in the feelings of his body and mind as they filled her up. His orgasm grabbed him by the throat and choked the air from his body. He shoved her back to the ground and seated himself to the hilt while his seed shot into her.

Pulses of power filled her in time with those of his body until he could feel her straining against the sensation. It was too much for her, and she followed him, crying out as her climax rocked her hips against his. Her stomach tightened rhythmically and a shimmering light flowed up her arms and out of her fingertips, sinking into the earth.

Slowly, the light faded and silence descended over them. Even the crickets were still. A soft breeze cooled his skin while he struggled to slow his uneven breathing.

He'd had centuries of sex and it had never been like that. Either it had something to do with the connection they shared, or he'd been doing something really wrong for a really long time.

"I think you killed me," she said. Her voice was hoarse and raspy.

"Maybe, but what a way to go." Paul eased himself from her body, but didn't go far. The raw, savage need he'd felt was gone now, but when he looked at her spent, damp body lying there and saw the proof of their union shining on his cock and her thighs, he knew it wouldn't be gone long. She was his now and he wasn't going to let her forget it.

"You're just a bit possessive, huh?" she asked him without opening her eyes.

She'd felt his thoughts. Paul reveled in the knowledge that they were close enough that she could. "Absolutely. I suggest you get used to it."

A small smile lifted one side of her mouth. "A girl could get used to that kind of sex really fast."

And just like that, Paul was hard and ready to go again. "It won't ever be like that with anyone else," he told her. He sounded harsh, almost angry, but had to let her know he wasn't replaceable.

She cracked one eye open. "Down, boy. I'm not running off. You can relax."

No, he couldn't, but if he didn't back off, he was going to scare her away or piss her off so badly she'd never let him have her like that again. And that couldn't happen. He had to get a grip. Fast.

She pushed herself up and looked down between her thighs. A shocked look crossed her face, then faded to distress. "I can't believe I forgot to make you cover up."

"Cover up?" He didn't know what she meant, but she seemed so upset he needed to fix it. Whatever *it* was.

"You didn't wear a condom. Please tell me you aren't suffering from some sort of magical crotch rot."

Paul blinked, at a total loss. His body was still humming along and his mind had yet to catch up and get its share of blood supply. "Magical what?"

"STDs," she said, as if he should know what she meant. "You know, venereal diseases."

Finally, it sank in. "Oh, I get it. Human diseases. No, you don't have to worry. Our kind doesn't get sick—at least not like that."

She held up her hand. "I don't want to know any more right now. Maybe later."

"I can't give you a child, either," he told her out of obligation. He knew it might mean she left him for a man who could father her children, but he had to take that chance. It was something too big for him to ignore.

She went still and cocked her head to the side. "Are you serious, or are you just saying that so I'll let you get away without wearing a condom again? Because that ain't happening."

"I'd wear a hazmat suit and a tutu if that's what it takes to get back inside your sweet body. Whatever you want. But I am serious. Our men can't father children. Something was done to us. We don't know what, but we're all sterile now."

She frowned at that and reached for him. Maybe she'd felt his anger that he'd been robbed of that joy, or maybe something on his face had given him away. He wasn't sure. But whatever it was, she was stroking his hand as if offering condolences, which he guessed was fitting. The absence of life was nearly as desolate as the loss of it.

"I'm sorry. I mean, I'm not looking to be a mom right now, and with the crazy way my life is, probably not ever, but at least I have a choice. I'm sorry you don't."

"Me, too. But that's old news. No sense dwelling on it. I just thought you should know."

She was oddly quiet for a moment as she gathered her clothes. When she turned back around, her eyes were bright, as if she'd been staving off tears. "You know, in a way, you're lucky. You'll never have to worry that your child will be snatched away from you in the dead of night, or that they'll come back to you a drooling, terrorized shell of what they once were. You'll never have to worry whether you're good enough to keep them safe and protect them from danger. You'll never have to know the anguish of failing them."

She was talking about her sister Tori now—the one who'd been taken that night eight years ago. He knew because he'd seen it happen, and felt her guilt over not being strong enough to stop it.

Paul pulled her into his arms because he couldn't not hold her. She needed him now, and it was his duty—his honor—to give her whatever she needed. "You didn't fail your sisters," he told her.

"Yes. I did. I still am failing Nika."

"Maybe not," said Paul. "You're stronger now. *We're* stronger now. We can try again."

She let out a shuddering breath and clung to him with desperate strength. "What if I fail again?"

"Then you do, but you can't lose hope. I know people who may be able to help her even if we can't. We'll do whatever it takes, okay?"

He felt her nod against his cheek. "I'm not sure how much more hope I've got in me."

"Don't worry," he said, tightening his hold. "I'll hope enough for both of us."

Chapter 15

Prince Eron stood on the balcony overlooking the city below. Frigid wind whipped his long hair about his head and made his eyes sting. The twin moons were both waning. Tomorrow, the gate to Earth would open and he would go through to find his daughters. It would be summer there, if his calendar was correct—the eighth summer since he'd last seen his girls.

Not even a year had passed on Athanasia since the Synestryn attack on his Earth family. Certainly not long enough for him to stop grieving for Celine. To stop missing her with every breath he drew.

Heavy footsteps sounded behind him on the stone floor.

Eron didn't even need to turn around to see the look of displeasure on his older brother's face. He could hear it hanging heavy in his voice. "You're not going," said Lucien.

"Yes. I am."

"It's not safe. It could kill you."

Anger welled up inside Eron, but he tried to control it. If he were going to survive the trip through the gate, he needed to remain calm and focused. "Not knowing if my daughters are alive or dead is killing me, too."

"I'll find them for you and report back. It's safer that way."

"What if they need me?"

Lucien's broad hand settled on Eron's shoulder. His voice softened with understanding. "That's the risk we all took when we decided to walk this path. We knew our children would grow up not knowing us. It's the price we must pay."

Eron spun around, knocking his half brother's hand away. His careful control shattered to splinters, gone beyond repair. "My daughters may be dead. None of our brothers have been able to find any trace of them. I need to go back. *I need to know.*"

The yellows and golds in Lucien's eyes stirred, swirling and twisting around his pupils. Compassion stilled his features and he placed his hand on Eron's chest. "This path has become harder than any of us would have imagined, but we must continue on course."

"I only want to see my girls. I will not interfere with our plans."

"You know it is not that simple. You're still weak from your last trip—from ridding Nika of the sgath poison. You won't be able to shield your passage, and Father will feel you cross over."

"I'm strong enough."

"No. You are not. Not yet. Father will kill you, and then what will happen to your daughters?"

Eron bowed his head over Lucien's hand. He was right. They had so little time on Earth that none of the others could spare much to take care of his children.

They had their own to care for.

"I can't do this anymore," said Eron. "The cost is too great."

"As it is to all of us, but reports show our predictions were right. The Synestryn are growing more powerful, and there are not enough Sentinels left to hold the gate. We must persevere."

"So, you're going back." It wasn't a question. Eron knew Lucien was more dedicated than all of them, no matter the personal cost. But then, he had more to lose here than any of them, should their plans fail.

"I am. Alone."

Eron shook his head. "How can you continue to go back after knowing what my daughters have suffered?"

Lucien looked out at the moons, then down into the countryside, dotted with lights from the homes sprawled across it. "I go because it is the only way to save what we have here. The only way to protect my home. My family." He looked back to Eron and his eyes were swirling with the golden fire of determination. "We must not fail."

Eron sighed in resignation. Their path had seemed so glorious at first. So righteous.

But now ... Eron pulled his most prized possession from the pouch hanging over his heart. The photograph of his woman and their three daughters was worn and faded, but he hardly needed it to remember the lines of his beloved Celine's face or the sweet curve of his babies' cheeks. The image was burned into his memory, where their happy faces and the knowledge that he'd failed them would live for eternity.

With a trembling hand, he handed the page to Lucien. "Will you seek them out for me? Find out if my baby girl escaped capture?"

Lucien looked at the image and gave a solemn nod. "I will try."

"How many hours will you have there?"

"Nine. No more."

Eron prayed it would be enough. "The summer always robs us of our time with them."

Lucien shrugged. "It is how it must be."

"I know. And I suppose I shouldn't resent it so much anymore. Celine is gone and my time with her is over."

"Maybe the humans are right, and their heaven does exist."

"It is a beautiful notion—to be reunited with those we love to live in peace forever. Celine believed in it."

If anyone was deserving of such a fate, it was Eron's beloved.

The sharp click of heels rushed down the hallway and Aurora slid around the corner. Her long, pale hair was mussed from her run, and a bright pink flush stained her cheeks. Her sunset-colored eyes were wide with fear, her soft lips parted to ease her labored breathing. Of all the women in their world, she was the most beautiful, and even Eron, whose heart belonged to another, had to pause for a moment whenever she entered the room. She was a servant, but as the most treasured possession of the Solarc, she knew more freedom than most.

She was also their most powerful ally.

"The Solarc comes," she whispered.

Lucien stowed the photograph away in his jacket. "I must leave now. The gate will be aligned to open in a few more moments."

"Go, then. I will stay here and distract Father. If you find my girls, give them my love."

"I swear it." Lucien's eyes flared in the darkness, their swirling colors rioting in response to his vow. He cupped Aurora's cheek and spoke in hushed, urgent tones. "The Solarc cannot know where I've gone, or our lives as well as those of our children on Earth would be forfeit. I won't allow that to happen."

She bowed her head. "Yes, Highness. I understand."

Lucien left through a hidden doorway, and Eron turned to Aurora and held out his hand. "Come to me. We'll distract Father and cover the signs of your sprint here all at once."

Aurora went into his arms without hesitation. When Eron kissed her, she pretended to enjoy it as a good servant would, letting out a soft moan. Eron felt nothing. As beautiful as she was, she was not Celine. She didn't smell like his Celine or taste like her. But he faked his response to their embrace all the same, knowing it would distract his father as nothing else could.

The lives of Eron's children, if they still lived, depended upon it. If the Solarc knew his sons had broken his law, he would slaughter them all without regard to the fact that those children were his grandchildren as well.

Eron knew. He'd seen it happen before.

Paul was so sweet he made Andra cry, damn it. She wiped the tears away and pulled her rumpled jeans back up over her hips. She didn't have time to cry. She had a sister to save.

Power pulsed inside her, making her skin feel as though it were glowing. The intimacy she'd shared with Paul had worked the way he said, and now she wanted to see whether she had the ability to help Nika. Or if maybe she needed another go-around in the grass with Paul.

They were both appealing options.

Her body sang, satisfied and replete. Normally, she would have felt like sleeping for half a day, but this was not normal. Not even close. For a moment there at the end, she thought she might have actually been able to see through his eyes, feel through his skin.

Surely that was just an illusion—a side effect of magical sex or something.

"Do you think our connection is strong enough now?" she asked him.

Paul lounged naked in the grass, watching her dress with drowsy eyes. "It's possible, but if not, you can't rush this kind of thing. It's not safe for her."

"If I can get her to eat, that will be enough. I just have to keep her alive long enough to get stronger." Long enough for Andra to get stronger, too. The process was definitely going to be a fun one.

"What then?" asked Paul. There was an odd note in his voice—a hint of challenge, maybe? She wasn't sure.

"What do you mean?"

"Assuming you can heal Nika, what then?"

Andra pulled her shirt down over her bra. "I haven't thought that far ahead. I guess she'll come live with me. Finish school. That kind of thing. She has a lot of living to catch up on."

"I mean, what happens to us? Once you don't need me anymore?"

She smoothed her short hair back in place to give herself a moment to think. Everything was coming at her too fast. She couldn't keep up. "I don't know, Paul. I just met you last night. That's not much of an 'us' to think about. I like you, but Nika has to come first."

He looked away, but his jaw was tight with anger or frustration. She didn't know him well enough to tell the difference, which only served to prove her point.

And yet she'd slept with him and enjoyed every moment of it. Enjoyed it so much she was already wondering if she'd get a chance to do it again.

"You're using me," he said.

She couldn't deny it. After what he'd done for her, she owed him her honesty. "I am."

"At least I know where I stand. That's more than I had last time." He stood and stalked off, still naked, pausing only long enough to grab his sword.

Last time. With Kate.

A pulse of anger filtered through their connection before she felt it close off.

Andra scrubbed her hands over her face. He was such a good man. He didn't deserve to be used like this, but she had no choice. She'd been honest with him from the beginning. Nika came first. It was the only way Andra could live with herself.

Paul resisted the urge to slam the back door of the Gerai house as he entered the kitchen.

He shouldn't have been so hurt that Andra was using him. Hell, he was using her, too, in a way. It was a symbiotic relationship. She needed him to help Nika, and he needed her to survive. It was a fair trade—one he was actually benefiting from more than she was.

But if that was the case, then why did it piss him off so much?

Madoc was in the kitchen, with a stack of sandwiches in front of him. He didn't bother swallowing before saying, "What the fuck crawled up your ass?"

Paul really wished he'd remembered to grab his clothes before coming back inside. There was nothing quite as uncomfortable as talking about his ass with another man while standing in the nude. So he ignored the question. "How's Nika?"

"Sleeping."

"Good. Mind keeping an eye on Andra for me while I get dressed? I'm sure she'll be in in a sec."

"Whatever."

That was as close to a yes as Paul figured he'd get out of Madoc. "Thanks."

"The only spare clothes are in Nika's room, but if you wake her up, I'll cut off your balls."

"Yeah. Thanks for the warning, man," said Paul.

Madoc grunted in response and went back to his sandwich.

When Paul eased the door of the bedroom open, Nika didn't even shift. In fact, she was so still, he stared to detect the faint shift of the covers over her chest as she breathed. When the blanket moved, he let out a relieved breath. Thank God she was still hanging on. If she'd died while Andra and he were outside making love, she never would have forgiven herself, even if there had been nothing she could have done to prevent it.

Paul slipped silently into the walk-in closet and searched through the neatly labeled clothes for his size. Everything was new and stiff, but the outfit was clean, it fit, and it covered him up.

"You know, you could have come back out and gotten

your clothes," said Andra from the closet doorway. He hadn't heard her come into the bedroom, which made him question where his head was. Maybe she was just really quiet.

Her cheeks were flushed with color and her hair still had bits of grass in it. Her lips were red and puffy from where he'd kissed her a little too hard, and the luceria around her throat had deepened to a swirl of rich, sapphire blues. The Sapphire Lady. He liked it.

Hell, he loved it. Just thinking about keeping her made his dick swell in anticipation. No way could they be together long without a repeat performance of what happened outside.

"I don't normally storm off naked," he assured her.

She shrugged. "I didn't mind. I enjoyed watching the show. You have a great ass."

A grin tickled his mouth and he gave in to it. He loved how she could do that to him—how she could make him smile when there didn't seem to be any reason to do so. "Yours is pretty nice, too."

"So, this mad thing you've got going here. Wanna talk about it?"

How could he explain what he was feeling to her without looking like a needy bastard? He sure as hell didn't want to tell her that he'd die without her. No one should have to live with pressure like that. He didn't want to be a burden. If she was going to stay with him, he wanted it to be for a real reason. Not guilt. "Maybe later. I think we should see what we can do for Nika, first."

Andra nodded. "Okay. Rain check, then."

"Sure."

He saw her shift gears from him to Nika. That familiar look of guilty concern he'd come to recognize filled her eyes, and she glanced back over her shoulder to where Nika lay. "What do we do?" she asked him.

"I wish I knew for sure. I don't know what's wrong

with her, so we'll have to play it by ear. Go slow and easy."

"Is there a chance I could hurt her?"

He couldn't lie to her. "Yes. But at this point, what are your options? What are hers?"

"You said there were people at your home who might be able to help her, right?" Her voice shook with insecurity.

Paul ignored his own problems. He'd worry about those later. Right now, Andra needed him.

He took her hand and a subtle rush of warmth flowed between their fingers. It would be so easy to focus on the physical and ignore the problems around them, but that wasn't going to solve anything.

"The Sanguinar—the men like Logan—are our healers. They might be able to help if we can get her to the point where she can give them her blood."

"I don't know if she'll go for that, but we can try."

"They can make it painless for her. Take her blood while she sleeps and make sure she never knows."

"That's a little creepy, don't you think? How do you know it's never happened to you?"

Paul had lived with it for so long, it didn't bother him anymore. "I don't. I just choose not to worry about it. As long as we're there, she'd be safe. I'd never allow anyone to hurt her any more than you would. But that's not our only option. Even if the Sanguinar can't help her, Sibyl may know what can."

"Who's Sibyl?"

"She's a seer. She knows things that no one else does. She might be able to see what we need to do to heal Nika. There are magical artifacts roaming around the world that can do amazing things. She may know of one that could help and tell us where to find it."

"So there's hope," said Andra, grasping his hand tight.

Paul slid his finger along her cheek, reveling in the smoothness of her skin. "There's lots of hope."

"If there are all of these people who can help, maybe I shouldn't mess with her. I could make things worse. We should just take her to your home, where people know what they're doing."

"Have some faith in yourself. You know Nika. You love her. You're not going to do anything to hurt her. Besides, Logan said she was too weak to travel." He didn't want to tell her that he'd feared she was already dead when he walked into the room. There was no guarantee she'd even live through the night.

Andra looked into his eyes, silently pleading with him to help. "I don't know what to do, Paul. I don't know how to help her."

"It's okay. I'll show you."

Chapter 16

Nika didn't even move when Andra slid into bed next to her. Her skinny frame dipped with the mattress under Andra's weight, but she didn't so much as bat an eyelash. Andra pressed her hand to Nika's head. She was cool to the touch. The pulse fluttering in her neck was faint and unsteady.

"We'll do it like we did before, remember?" asked Paul. "Just open yourself up and let me guide you. We're just going to go look around first."

Andra nodded. Paul's hand slid around to the nape of her neck, his ring locking with her necklace. She felt the band around her throat warm. Her breathing sped up, and a fizzing kind of pressure built inside her. Her head started to throb and her stomach gave a queasy twist.

"You're fighting it," he said.

"I don't mean to." She tried to relax, but her jaw clenched against the pain and nausea. She wasn't going to be able to do this. It was going to be like losing Tori all over again. She was going to just stand there and watch while her sister slipped away and—

"Stop it," growled Paul. "That's not going to happen. Focus."

Andra pulled in a deep breath and tried to do as he said. The pressure built until sweat broke out over her skin and she was shaking with the force of it.

Still nothing happened.

Andra opened her eyes and looked at Nika's small body. She was so weak. Helpless. Her mind was a writhing mass of madness and images too horrible to be real. That night had destroyed her. Maybe it was the trauma, or maybe it was some kind of infection from the monster's yellow saliva. It had licked her wound, lapping up the blood. Something could have gotten into her body and infected her with this illness. Maybe she needed a magical antibiotic.

The pressure inside Andra released suddenly, as if a bubble had popped. She let out the breath she'd been holding, and when she looked up, she was no longer in the bedroom with Nika. She was somewhere dark.

She could hear the steady drip of water echoing off hard walls, smell the musty dampness in the air. It was cold here—the kind of cold that seeped into your blood and stole away your will to move.

"You shouldn't be here," said Nika. She appeared near a rock wall, her image shimmering and translucent, like some kind of hologram. She was younger, maybe sixteen, and her hair was dark and wavy, like it had been before the night Mom and Tori died. She wore a black dress, and although she was thin, she wasn't skinny.

"Where is here?" asked Andra, looking around. It was a cave of some kind, but not those pretty ones with the glistening formations. This was an oppressive black hole deep in the ground.

"Shh," whispered Nika. "They'll hear you. You have to leave."

"I can't. I need to help you."

"There's nothing you can do for me. Not anymore."

"Please, Nika. Let me help."

Nika frowned in confusion and her head tilted to one side. "You see me and yet you still don't believe."

"Believe what?"

Nika turned suddenly and her eyes grew wide.

"They're coming. You have to go. Don't try to come back. They'll find you and kill you both."

Before Andra could ask who was coming or what she meant by *both*, she was thrust out of Nika's mind and back to the bedroom.

Nika thrashed on the bed and her eyes were wild and fearful. "They're coming for her."

Andra swallowed a cry of anguish and held Nika down. "What are you talking about, baby?"

"Tori. They're coming for her. They're going to hurt her again." She grabbed onto Andra's shirt with a surprisingly strong grip. "You have to go find her. Save her."

The bedroom door slammed open hard enough to leave a dent in the wall. Madoc charged in, sword drawn. His mouth was twisted into a snarl of rage, and the veins in his neck and arms stood out in stark relief. "What the fuck did you do to her?" he demanded.

Paul stood and put his body between Madoc and the women. "We were trying to help her."

"Some help. She was sleeping a minute ago. I told you what I'd do if you woke her up."

The high chime of metal sliding on metal made the hairs on the back of Andra's neck stand up. "You could try," said Paul.

"I'm fine," said Nika, struggling to sit up.

Andra wasn't about to let these men kill each other because of a simple case of testosterone poisoning. She wasn't sure what she was doing, but she figured anything was better than doing nothing, so she pulled on Paul's power and used it to shove both men back with a hard wall of air.

The men hit the bedroom walls with a jolt and stayed there like they were glued.

Wow. She hadn't expected it to work quite so well.

"Stop it," she ordered them. "You two are going to calm down and act like rational human beings. I don't care if you are men."

Nika's voice quavered from the bed. "You should let them go, Andra. I don't think this is smart."

"I don't care how smart it is. They're not going anywhere until I'm sure they're not going to kill each other."

The rush of energy coursing through her made her limbs shake, but she held the pressure against the two men until she was sure it was safe. Paul calmed down first, his face draining of rage.

Nika slid from the bed and walked over to where Madoc was pinned and snarling. She seemed to be steadier on her feet now. Stronger.

Maybe what they'd done had helped her somehow, though Andra had no idea what she'd done to help.

Paul rubbed his shoulder like it hurt, but pride shone in his face. "That was one hell of a stunt. I didn't know you could do that."

"Neither did I," said Andra.

Nika put her hand on Madoc's chest, and his body went still, as if he were afraid he'd hurt her if he breathed. "Get back to bed," he snapped at her.

"Not until you calm down."

"I'll paddle your ass if you don't go back to bed."

"No, you won't," said Nika with total confidence. "You'd never lay a hand on me."

"I wouldn't push him," warned Paul.

Madoc's green eyes lit up with a promise of violence. "Listen to the grown-ups, honey, or you'll end up regretting it."

"I am a grown-up," said Nika.

Madoc snorted.

This was not going to end well. Andra went to her sister before she poked the stick at the caged beast one too many times. She took Nika by the shoulders and led her back to bed.

"He's right. You shouldn't be up and around yet. You're still weak."

"I'm feeling better since I ate," said Nika.

"You ate?" asked Andra. The band of fear around her chest loosened a little, giving her room to breathe. "That's great news, baby."

Nika looked to where Madoc was pinned. "He helped."

Both Paul and Andra stared at Madoc in shock. He'd been right. He did get her to eat. Who knew?

In thanks, Andra let the force holding him to the wall dissipate. He didn't try to lunge for her or attack, but he sure looked like he was aching to. His big fists clenched and released over and over, making the bones pop as they shifted. "I'm going outside now. Don't any of you follow me." He pointed a thick finger at Nika. "Especially you."

He left the room, shutting the door behind him.

Nika slumped back against the pillows. She was pale, but the wildness in her eyes had faded. For now.

Andra would take the gift without question and treasure the time she had with her sister for as long as it lasted. "Do you think you could eat some more?"

Nika shook her head. Her eyelids drooped. "Not now. Gotta sleep more. Maybe later."

Andra smoothed her white hair back and felt her body go limp as she slipped almost instantly into sleep.

"I don't know what we did, but it seems to have helped," said Andra.

Paul was still watching the way Madoc had gone, his gaze speculative. "I'm not sure we did anything," he told her. "I mean, I'd love to tell you otherwise, but I'd be lying."

Another failure, but it didn't sting nearly as badly as it would have otherwise. She didn't care how Nika got help, just so long as she did. "She seemed lucid just now."

Paul was still watching the doorway, frowning. "She sure did."

"And she ate. That's more than I'd hoped for. Do you think it's safe to move her yet?"

He nodded. "We'll see how she's feeling when she wakes up, but I think it would be safer to move her to Dabyr than to stay here another night. Besides, Sibyl is waiting. She wanted you to be there tonight, so we're already late."

"If we travel during the day, the monsters can't find us, right?"

"Right."

"We'll leave in the morning, then." She leaned down and kissed Nika's head. "Did you hear that, baby? You're going to be okay. We're going to get you help."

The sun was sinking near the horizon by the time Paul pulled Andra's truck up to the gate of the Sentinel compound he called home. Dabyr. The warriors' stronghold.

Andra and Nika had slept most of the way here, and he hated having to wake them now. Andra looked so pretty in sleep—her cheeks rosy pink, her short hair tousled around her face, her full mouth parted as if waiting for a kiss.

He smiled for the camera, knowing Nicholas would be on duty, slid his ID card into the slot, and waited for the gates to open.

Paul parked her truck in his slot in the multicar garage. The compound was an odd combination that was part ski resort and part military base. The stone walls of the main building glowed pink in the waning light of day, and at this time, Dabyr would be bustling with activity. Over five hundred souls called this place home, and among them were Theronai, Sanguinar, and some of the Gerai—the humans who served in their cause.

Paul killed the truck's engine and stroked Andra's cheek to wake her. Her skin was so warm and soft to his battle-scarred hands, and the thrill of pleasure that ran through his arm only heightened the sensation. He still couldn't believe she was his—at least for two more days.

Andra sighed and leaned her head back, offering Paul more of her smooth skin to caress. He knew better than to take advantage of the situation like this, but pride filled him up and he couldn't help but slide his finger over the luceria. In the hours it had taken them to get here, the colors had settled even more, their swirling increasingly lazy and slow.

The rap of knuckles against the glass jarred Paul out of his happy place, and he jerked his hand away as if he'd been caught doing something naughty.

Morgan Valens stood outside the driver's door, giving Paul a knowing grin. White teeth stood out in stark contrast against Morgan's brown skin. His Egyptian heritage was evident in his bold mouth and canted brown eyes. Women adored Morgan. Paul had heard them whispering about his stamina and prowess in bed, and the last thing Paul wanted was for Morgan to be the first thing Andra saw when she woke up. He didn't need that kind of competition.

Paul rolled down the window. "What do you want?" he asked a little more gruffly than his friend deserved.

Nika stirred from her sleep, letting out a soft, whimpering sound.

Morgan leaned over so he could see the women better. "Joseph is looking for you. You didn't report in yesterday and he's pissed."

"Yeah, well, he can just be pissed. I was busy."

Morgan eyed Andra's sleeping form, and Paul shifted his body to block his view. "Busy. I see. Two women will definitely do that to a man."

"They need our help. Nika was too weak to travel yesterday or we would have been here sooner." As Sibyl had asked. He wasn't looking forward to facing her disappointment.

"You'd better tell Joseph that before he puts your ass on perimeter duty during the rainy season."

"I think he'll make an exception this time."

Morgan shook his head in awe, his eyes sliding over the luceria gracing Andra's throat. "Another female Theronai. This place has already gone apeshit since Helen arrived. Once the men find out there's another ..."

"It will give them hope," said Paul.

"It will send the few who are left here scurrying to the four winds, searching for their own women."

"Does that mean you'll stick around here while all the others go out searching?"

A car door slammed, followed closely by a second. The sound echoed off the thick concrete walls of the giant garage. Madoc must have pulled in right behind them.

"Hell, no. Not unless one of them happens to show up before I'm done packing." Morgan nodded his head toward Nika. "She okay?"

"I hope so."

"Want me to carry her inside? I'll be real gentle so she won't wake up."

"Touch her and die, Romeo," said Madoc from behind Morgan.

Logan was beside him, looking a little green.

"You caught up fast," said Paul. Madoc had waited for Logan to feed before they followed Paul and the women. They had to have left at least an hour after Paul had.

"You just drive like an old man," said Madoc.

"No," argued Logan. "You drive like a maniac."

"I would have happily let you out anywhere you wanted, leech."

"In the daylight? What a gentleman you are," said Logan.

Madoc flashed him a smile full of sharp teeth.

"As much as I love your company, I'm going inside.

I have work to do." Logan stalked off toward the entrance to the main hall.

Andra shifted beside Paul, rubbing up against his thigh. She woke slowly, body first, and Paul could do nothing but watch. She stretched her long legs, then her arms, then straightened as much as the cab of the truck would allow before bothering to open her eyes. The show she unknowingly put on with that lovely stretching made every man there stare. He shifted so she wasn't on display—at least not to anyone but him.

"Where are we?" she asked on a yawn.

"Home." He didn't say whose. He was hoping too much that it would be hers as well as his very soon.

"Already? That was fast." She looked over at Nika and pressed her hand against her sister's forehead. Nika didn't stir. "Has she been asleep the whole time?"

"Yeah. She was making a few noises, though."

Madoc went around the truck, the sound of his heavy boots loud on the concrete.

"What kind of noises?" asked Andra.

"Nothing horrible," said Paul as Madoc opened the passenger-side door. The whimpers had been heartbreaking, but he didn't feel the need to share that with Andra.

"Andra, this is Morgan Valens."

"Nice to meet you," said Andra through the open window.

Morgan smiled, dipped his head in a small formal bow, and offered her his hand. "A pleasure, my lady."

She gave his hand a brief shake and Paul's eyes were fixed on Morgan's luceria, looking for even the slightest sign that they might be compatible. Nothing changed, and Paul let out a silent sigh of relief.

Morgan's smile faded as he realized the same thing. She couldn't save him.

"When is her ceremony?" asked Morgan.

"I'm not sure yet."

"What ceremony?" asked Andra, frowning.

"It's just this thing we do for women like you. Don't worry about it."

Madoc unbuckled Nika's seat belt and slid his arms under her body. "Where is she going?" he asked.

"I can get her," said Andra, scrubbing her face with her hands as if trying to wake up. "You don't have to bother."

Madoc snorted. "She doesn't weigh enough to be a bother. Which way?"

Andra let out a sigh of resignation. "Wherever your medical facilities are, I guess."

"Our doctors make house calls," said Paul. "We do have an infirmary, but I don't think she'd like it there. Too sterile and cold. She'll be more comfortable if you're close by."

"Where will I be staying?"

Paul lowered his voice. "I was hoping you'd stay in my suite." Preferably naked, but he'd take what he could get.

She blushed as if she'd caught his stray thought, which made Paul let out a bark of laughter. Maybe she did have a streak of shyness in her somewhere after all.

Andra sniffed and pulled on an air of indifference. "We're going to Paul's suite. Do you know the way?"

Madoc didn't answer, but he turned and carried Nika toward the door.

"I'll let Joseph know you've arrived," said Morgan. "But I'll walk slowly so you have a chance to . . . settle in." He winked at Andra and hurried after Madoc, opening the door for him so he wouldn't have to jostle Nika.

Andra was still blushing, which Paul decided was a good look for her. Especially when her blush spread out over her bare breasts and belly, and he was the cause of it.

The door to the main building shut behind the men, leaving the two of them alone.

Paul took her hand and ran his fingertip across the silky skin. "There are going to be a lot of people here who will want to meet you. Especially our men. They'll all want to give you their vow. That's the ceremony Morgan was talking about."

"I'll meet whoever you want, and let them all beat their chests or cut themselves or whatever it takes to get Nika help."

"I figured that's how you'd feel. I just didn't want you to be taken by surprise. A lot has happened to you in a really short time."

She turned her hand over and laced her fingers through his. Her grip was tight, almost desperate. "I'm tough. Don't worry about me."

"Sorry. It's my job. Besides, someone's got to."

She looked away, but not before he could see the sheen of tears brighten her eyes. "We should go. I don't like leaving Nika alone."

"She's not alone. Madoc's with her," said Paul, then after his words and their connotation sank in: "Right. We should go."

Chapter 17

Andra followed Paul through the underground tunnel that led from the garage to what he called the main hall. She wasn't sure *hall* was the right word for a room with a glass ceiling fifty feet overhead and enough space to fit a football field. Halls were dark and long and skinny, not huge and bright and filled with live plants in every corner.

The room was separated into sections. Half of it was set up with mismatched kitchen tables that seated anywhere from two to twelve. Every table was decorated with a vase of fresh flowers and a bright, cheery yellow tablecloth. The other half of the room was cut into two more areas—one with a huge TV and plenty of overstuffed couches, and the other with a pool table and several video game systems hooked up to more big TVs.

Several children lounged around, and a couple adults were sipping coffee, keeping watch over everything. When Andra came in, everyone stopped what they were doing and stared.

"What is this place?" she asked Paul.

"We call it Dabyr. It's home for about five hundred men, women, and children."

"You mean those kids *live* here? It's not just a vacation spot?"

"That's right."

"Why?"

"Some because their parents live here, though most of them are orphans under our care. Today was a school day, but now that the school day is over, they hang out and do kid stuff."

"But it's summer."

Paul smiled. "We like to keep them busy so they stay out of trouble."

"They don't look like they're causing any trouble to me," said Andra.

"That's usually when they're at their worst. Especially the teens. They're always planning something—fighting against the confines of this place."

"I would have loved to have a place like this to go when I was a kid."

"You say that now, but many of these kids have no choice about being here. They can stay here, or they can die when the Synestryn hunt them down for food. That kind of thing grates on the more rebellious teens."

"Do they make any other kind?" she asked.

"Not since I've been alive."

They passed through the dining area and turned right, entering a long hallway. "Where are we going?"

"I thought we could check to be sure Nika is settled in my suite before we go see Joseph Rayd."

His wide shoulders stretched the gray knit of his shirt, letting her see the yummy bulge of muscles over his back. His dark blond hair was mussed, and from her side view she could tell he was in desperate need of a shave.

Or maybe not. The soft scratch of those whiskers over her skin would be a pleasurable sort of pain—the kind a woman could definitely get used to. Paul knew what he was doing when it came to giving her pleasure.

"Who is Joseph Rayd?"

"The unlucky bastard who was elected to lead us. He keeps us all in line—as much as anyone could. He'll need to know about you and Nika."

"He's going to agree to help her, right?"

"He will. Nika is one of ours now."

Andra let out a slow breath of relief. She was sure that if anyone could help Nika, it would be these people.

Paul led her down another long hallway that reminded her of a hotel. Doors lined each side, though they were farther apart than in any hotel she'd stayed in. At a door near the end of the hall, he slid a key card in the lock and opened the door for her to enter first.

Andra was shocked to find that though it looked like a hotel room from the outside, inside it looked like a normal home. The place was neat, with only a few pieces of art on the walls—all seascapes. One wall was lined with shelves that groaned with the weight of hundreds of books. The couch and matching recliner were worn, but looked comfortable, and the flat-screen TV nearly took up one wall all by itself. A small kitchen was tucked into one corner, with a round table and two chairs crowding the space.

"Took you long enough," said Madoc in a low voice. He quietly shut the door he'd just come out of so the latch didn't even click. In his hand was an empty water glass.

"How did you get in my rooms?" asked Paul.

"Morgan had Nicholas pop the lock remotely." Madoc went to Paul's kitchen and ducked his head to peer into the refrigerator.

Andra nodded to the glass. "Did you get her to drink?"

"Yeah. She's sleeping again, though."

"Good. Where did Morgan go?" asked Andra.

Madoc pulled out a beer, opened it, and took a long pull from the bottle. "I'm sure he went to tell everyone we've found two more women. This place is going to be crawling with men within the hour."

"I've got to go see Joseph," said Paul.

"Then I'm staying here with Nika." Madoc pulled

a chair out from the small kitchen table and crammed his body into the tight space. He leaned back and got comfortable, as if he weren't planning to leave anytime soon.

Paul gave a grudging nod. "Fine. Stay." He turned to Andra. "You should stay here, too."

"I think I should talk to this leader guy with you. Just in case he needs any convincing to help Nika."

Paul's mouth tightened. "I don't think that's going to be a problem."

"Maybe not, but if I go along, then I can make sure it's not."

"Suit yourself."

Andra dropped her overnight bag and followed Paul to the door. He opened and held it for her to exit. When she hit the hotel-style hall, she was jarred again by the fact that this wasn't some suburban home. And then she was jarred even more when she collided with the chest of a man coming down the hall.

Andra bounced off the man and Paul steadied her before she could fall on her ass and humiliate herself further. Paul's hands were surprisingly strong, even for a guy as big as he was, and though she was steady on her feet, he didn't let go. He kept a loose grip on her waist and elbow, and his touch caused a surge of heat to lance through her stomach. She knew she should pull away, but it felt too good to be touched by such strong, capable hands. She'd seen what the man could do with a sword—the brutal lethality he was capable of—but right now, all she felt was gentleness and warmth and tingly spirals rioting around in her belly.

"Joseph," said Paul in greeting. "I'd like you to meet Andra Madison."

Joseph was taller than Paul, nearly six and a half feet. He had broad shoulders, but they were bent, like he bore the weight of an invisible burden. Deep worry lines etched his handsome face, and his hazel eyes were sunken and rimmed with red from lack of sleep. His short dark hair was graying at the temples, and his clothes looked like they had been slept in. Twice.

Andra automatically held out her hand in greeting and she felt Paul tense beside her. Joseph shook her hand with a firm grip. "It's wonderful to meet you, my lady."

My lady? Andra looked behind her just to make sure he wasn't talking to someone else. "Uh. Thank you."

"It's a formal term. Don't worry. You'll get used to it."

Yeah, right.

When Joseph let go of her hand, Paul relaxed, though she could see his intense gaze scrutinizing Joseph as if looking for something.

Andra ignored Paul's oddness. Maybe these two weren't on the best of terms. She really didn't care as long as he agreed to help Nika. "Do you know why we're here?"

Joseph nodded, but he was frowning at the ring on his left hand—the one that all these men seemed to wear. "I've heard your sister is ill. Morgan said she's dangerously thin."

"She's ... troubled." Andra's cheeks flamed with embarrassment, not because her sister was sick, but because Andra had let it happen. It was her failure that had nearly killed Nika.

"It's her mind that is most at risk, Joseph," said Paul. "She's lived with this for eight years."

Joseph's mouth opened in shock. "That can't be right. Eight years? And she still lives?"

"She's strong," said Andra. "She doesn't look like it now, but she's a fighter. She tries so hard to overcome the images in her head. She's been in therapy for years, but nothing seems to help."

"Of course not. Human therapy would do nothing to aid her. I'm calling in Tynan." Joseph pulled a cell phone out of his pocket.

"Logan said she's too weak to give him her blood."

"Then we'll find another way. We won't let her die. She's too valuable."

Andra wasn't sure what he meant by that, but if he thought she was valuable, and that made him act faster, then it worked for her.

"The men will all want to see her, touch her," said Paul. "I think that would only make things worse."

Andra grabbed Paul's arm. "I am not going to let a bunch of men parade through her room pawing at her."

Paul cupped Andra's cheek. "Of course not. But you have to understand how much these men are suffering. If she is compatible with one or more of them, the way you are with me, it might be another way to help her."

Andra was torn. She wanted to do whatever she could for Nika, but she'd seen what these people were like. They were aggressive, demanding. Scary. At least, they would be to Nika. "You saw the way she reacted to Logan."

"She seems to be fine with Madoc," said Paul.

Joseph's dark brows rose. "You don't think . . ."

"No. I checked. His luceria didn't react to her. In fact, the colors are faded." He said that last part like it held some kind of special meaning.

"Do you think we need to keep an eye on him?" asked Joseph.

"Yes. I know he'd never hurt her as long as his life-mark holds out, but once it's barren . . ."

"I'll have Nicholas keep an electronic eye on him. His security cameras pick up everything."

Andra looked between the men, trying to figure out what they were talking about. "Are you guys saying that Nika might be at risk with Madoc?"

"I'm sure he's fine right now. He's just . . . running out of time."

"He's *dying*?"

Paul's mouth opened and shut again as if he were deciding what to say. "Yes, but it's not contagious. We just need to be watchful for signs that he's changing. Getting . . . darker."

"The man is already about as angry as they come. I'm going back inside with my sister."

"We need to talk, Paul," said Joseph.

Paul gave Andra the key card. "I'll be back as soon as I can."

"Don't worry. I'm not going to need your help with this."

Andra went back into the suite and found Madoc standing in Nika's doorway. He filled up the space, so that she could hardly see her sister sleeping peacefully on the bed. But she was, and something inside Andra loosened and relaxed.

"What are you doing?" demanded Andra in a whisper.

Madoc spun around like he hadn't heard her come close. He scowled and pulled the door shut before pushing past her, ignoring her question.

"Don't ignore me. I asked you what you were doing."

"I was just checking on her."

"Paul says you're dying, and it sounded like before you did you were going to turn into something nasty. Is that true?"

"Close enough." He flopped down on the couch and powered on the TV.

Andra snatched the remote away and turned it off. The threatening look that crossed his face gave her pause, but she didn't back down. "I want you to stay away from her. Far away."

"Just what the hell do you think I'm going to do, lady?"

"I don't know, and that's the problem. I don't know anything about you guys or what you do or what you're capable of. What I do know is that if Paul is worried, then it must be bad, because he knows how to handle himself. Nika doesn't."

"You're fucking nuts if you think I'm going to do anything just because you say so."

"I'm her sister. She's my responsibility. I may not be
able to take you in a fair fight, but if you don't stay away,
I'll find you and kill you in your sleep. Are we clear?"

Madoc rose slowly from the couch, his powerful legs
bunching with muscles. A truly frightening light glowed
inside his feral green eyes. As angry as he was on the
outside, inside was worse. Much, much worse. There was
something dark in there. Something dangerous lurking
behind the facade he showed the world.

His voice dipped to a low, quiet threat. "Feel free to
come by and take your best shot. Room two-nineteen.
I'll leave my door unlocked. But since you want us to be
clear, if you do come by, you'll be on my turf. My rules.
I won't play fair."

"What's that supposed to mean?"

"It means that if I want to see Nika, there's not a
fucking thing you can do to stop me. And if you try,
you'll regret it."

"She's too good for you."

Madoc flinched, but covered it quickly. "She's too
good for you, too, apparently. You were there the night
this happened to her, weren't you?"

"Fuck. You."

Madoc gave her a sneering smile. "Anytime you
want."

"Stay away from her. She's too innocent to protect
herself from the likes of you."

"At least I'm able to keep her safe. Protect her. You
can't even get her to eat."

Oh, God. He was right. Andra felt like she'd been
punched, but she tried not to let it show. "I got her here,
didn't I? Paul will make sure she's safe."

Madoc snorted. "Paul is only helping her to get in
your pants. Keep you collared. If you think it's anything
else, you're full of shit."

Andra's hand went to the luceria around her throat. It was vibrating now, warming under her touch. A second later, the door to Paul's suite slammed open and Paul and Joseph came in armed with swords in hand.

"What the hell is going on?" demanded Paul.

Madoc took a step back. "I was just leaving. Seems I'm no longer wanted here."

Paul's color was high, and he looked as if he were ready to strike Madoc down. "Did he hurt you?"

Andra had to swallow to find her voice. "No. I'm fine. I just don't want him around Nika anymore."

"I heard you the first time," growled Madoc. He pushed his way past the two armed men and left the suite.

Paul came to Andra and pulled her into a hug. "Are you sure he didn't hurt you?"

"Yeah. Just pissed me off."

He kissed her temple and tightened his hold. "He's good at that."

Joseph cleared his throat. "I'm going to go check into that thing you asked me about, Paul."

"Thanks."

"We'll catch up later." Joseph left and closed the door behind him.

Paul tilted her face up to look at him. "I could feel your pain as clear as if it had been my own. What did he say to you?"

"Nothing I haven't said to myself a thousand times. Forget about it."

"Not going to happen. It kills me to see you suffer." His tone was so gentle, so loving, it was going to make her cry.

She pushed away from him before it could. "Just let it go. I want to know what we're going to do for Nika."

Paul's jaw tightened in frustration, and he pulled in a deep breath. "Tynan is on his way and Joseph is going to request an audience with Sibyl."

"Good. That's all good, right?"

"Yes. That's all good. We're going to take care of her."

"Madoc says you're only helping Nika to get to me."

"Madoc is an asshole."

"That doesn't mean he's not right," said Andra.

Paul sat down on the couch and pulled her down next to him. "If I'd never met you, I'd still be doing everything I could to save Nika."

"Because she's valuable to you?"

"Because that's what I do. That's what we all do. Every one of us has taken a vow to protect humans from the Synestryn. So even if she weren't one of our own, I'd still be right here, fighting for her. It's the reason I exist."

Andra felt the truth of his words ringing through their bond. She felt his conviction, his honesty, wrap around her and hold her tight. It felt so good not to be alone anymore. Even if it were for only a few days.

Her eyes burned, and she couldn't blink fast enough to make the tears dissipate. One slid down her cheek, and she turned around so Paul couldn't see her weakness.

"Don't," he told her. "Don't pull away from me. You don't have to be strong and in control all the time."

"Yes, I do. I have to keep it together. Please try to understand that."

He was quiet for a moment, and she could feel some of his frustration pulsing through their link. She didn't enjoy frustrating him, but she knew if she cracked now, she'd break wide-open and destroy herself. She had to stay strong.

"How about I get us some dinner? Give you a few minutes alone?"

Andra nodded. "That would be nice."

"Any requests?"

"Surprise me."

When the door to Torr's suite opened, he knew it would be her. Grace Norman. The last person on the face of this planet he wanted to have see him like this, as helpless as a babe.

If his body hadn't been a worthless pile of meat, he would have simply met her at the door and gently shooed her away. She was a timid creature, and it wouldn't have taken much to send her scurrying.

At least, she was timid with everyone else. Not with him. He was paralyzed from the neck down, unable to hurt a fly. No one feared him anymore. He couldn't even hold his sword, much less swing it.

Grace gave him a cheerful smile as she entered the room carrying a plastic box full of her torture devices. "How are you today?" she asked.

She slid over the floor on silent feet. Her name fit her, but Torr was sure that her naturally swift, graceful movements were not the product of long hours of dance class. From what he'd learned about her, she'd learned to dodge fists and flying bottles at a young age.

Never again. Her stepfather was rotting in a hole in the ground, and she was safe here.

He wished telling himself that would ease the knot of tension he felt between his eyes every time he saw her, but it didn't. Somehow bringing her here wasn't enough. He wanted to do more.

Then again, that was the story of his life these days. He couldn't even feed himself, much less protect Grace from imaginary threats.

"I'm tired. Go away," he growled at her.

She made a clicking sound with her tongue. "Not nice, Torr. I'm here to help you, whether or not you want it."

She was such a pretty thing, especially when she smiled. The smile never touched her sad brown eyes, but he'd gotten used to that over the past few weeks. She came to see him every day, and nothing he'd said or done had scared her off.

"Send someone else," he said.

The halo of curly black hair around her head made her look younger than her twenty-two years. He should have been able to see her as a child, given that he was pushing four hundred, but with her, it just didn't happen. She was a woman—one he found sexy as hell—and that was part of the problem. There were so many things in his life that he wanted now and couldn't have. He didn't appreciate her adding to the pile.

"Why?" she asked. "Don't you think I know what I'm doing?"

Of course she did. She knew just how hopeless he was. She knew he'd be paralyzed for the rest of his too-long life, and she pitied him. That was why she was here. She was too kind not to act on that pity.

"I don't have time for this," he told her.

She kept smiling and set the box down on the table next to his wheelchair. "Don't be a baby. I'm not going to hurt you."

"Of course not. I can't feel a damn thing."

"Okay, Mr. Cranky Pants. Be that way. I'm still not leaving. I've got an hour before my shift starts."

There was nothing he could do to stop her. He was weak. Helpless.

If he'd had any strength left whatsoever, he would have used it to end his miserable life as soon as he realized the Sanguinar were unable to heal him—before they wasted any more precious blood on trying to cure him.

Grace wheeled him to his bed, which was the focal point of his living room. All the equipment it took to keep his sorry ass clean and fed was too big for his bedroom, so now he lived here. All day. Every day.

He craved freedom so badly he was sure it would tear his mind apart. So far, he hadn't been that lucky.

"Have you heard the news?" she asked as she adjusted his chair until he was lying flat. She attached some straps and cranked the lever that eased him back onto his bed.

This blasted device made it easy for someone as small as Grace to move him around, but it also meant that she didn't need any help. It meant he had to be alone with her.

The longer he was alone with her, the more of himself he lost. His pride had been the first thing to go. In its place was a burning ball of shame and humiliation he could not escape.

"What news?" he asked, unable to stave off his curiosity about the world outside.

Grace slid her hands inside the waistband of his sweats and peeled them off his legs, leaving him in a pair of boxers. She stared for a bit too long, making him wonder just how ugly his body had become as his flesh wasted away with disuse.

She swallowed visibly before answering. "They found two more women like Helen. They're here."

Torr refused to think about what that meant—or at least he tried to. More women so soon after Helen? It didn't seem possible, and yet it was happening. Maybe she wasn't some genetic anomaly after all. Maybe his brothers could be saved.

The news did him no good, but he was still glad the rest of the Theronai had hope.

"Do you want to go see them?" she asked.

"No." He'd never even consider seeing if either one of them was compatible with him as long as his body was useless. And no matter what lies the Sanguinar fed him, Torr was pretty sure they had no idea how to fix his paralysis.

Grace eased the head of the bed up and wrestled with his T-shirt. His muscle mass had started to shrivel away, but with his bulk, he still had to be quite a load for her to maneuver. She wasn't very big, maybe a few inches over five feet, but she'd never once complained that he was too heavy. Maybe she was stronger than she looked on the outside, too.

Unlike many of his brothers, he still had a healthy number of leaves remaining on his lifemark. He'd always felt blessed not to be suffering like so many others, but that blessing had become a curse. He had years left before his tree was barren, which would force Joseph to end Torr's life.

She managed to get the shirt over his head, and he got a nice view of her breasts—soft, full breasts she kept hidden behind baggy clothing. He knew they were soft because she'd accidentally brushed his cheek once while she'd undressed him.

He still had dreams about that innocent accident, only in his dreams, she'd been naked and he'd been a whole man. He always woke before they got to the really good part, but he enjoyed the fantasy for as long as it lasted.

"Are you sure?" she asked.

"Yes, I'm sure. I can't even give them my vow. What possible good would it do for me to see them?"

She combed her fingers through his hair to straighten it. Torr gritted his teeth against the feel of her fingers on his skin. She'd spent hours touching him—massaging his muscles and exercising his limbs so he'd stay flexible—but he never got to feel any of that. He just got to watch her hands slide over his legs, leaving a shiny path of massage oil in their wake.

For all the good it did him, she might as well have been rubbing some other man's body.

That thought filled his head with the need for violence. He wanted to lash out and crush everything in his path. Not that what he wanted mattered anymore.

"I don't know," she replied. "I just thought that if one of them were compatible with you, maybe she could help you."

"Heal me, you mean?" he asked in a bitter, angry tone.

"Yes. The thought had crossed my mind."

"That's not the way it works. Why don't you leave the doctoring to the leeches and stick to your duties in the kitchen."

Grace flinched as if he'd hit her, and until he saw it, he didn't think he could feel any worse.

He'd been wrong. He felt like total shit for hurting her feelings like that. She was only trying to help.

Everyone was only trying to help. It wasn't her fault he was sick of needing it.

"I'm sorry," he whispered to her. "I didn't mean that."

She nodded, but didn't look him in the eye.

She poured some oil into her palm and rubbed her hands together to warm it. He couldn't feel the cold, but she still took the time to see to his comfort.

She was way too kind to be anywhere near him. He was toxic—as poisonous as the giant fanged slug that had latched itself onto his spine and taken away his life. If she stuck around, he would only end up hurting her more.

"I really wish you'd just leave me alone," he told her, trying to keep his voice calm.

Her slippery hands slid up his leg toward his crotch. He saw it, but felt nothing. His mind was thrilled by her touch, silently urging her to move up and take his dick into her slick hands, even as he knew what a useless waste of time it would be. He wouldn't feel that either. No matter how turned on his mind was, his body refused to respond.

He'd never again know the pleasure of the flesh—the intimate embrace of a woman's body, the hot slide of skin on skin.

"I know you do, but I'm not leaving. When the Sanguinar figure out how to fix you, you'll be grateful that your body hasn't curled in on itself. It will still take you some time to build your strength back, but at least your body will be able to move so you can rebuild it."

"The Sanguinar have no idea how to fix me."

"They're smart. They will figure it out."

"After the kind of life you've had—the beatings, watching your mother die a slow death—how can you still have hope?"

"I have hope *because* of the life I've had. For fifteen years I prayed every night that someone would save me and my brother from the hell our lives had become. And then you came."

"So?"

"So, it's only been a few weeks since you were paralyzed. If I can wait fifteen years for a miracle, then so can you."

Fifteen years? No way. "No. I can't. Not like this."

Grace shrugged and continued to massage his calves. "You don't have a choice. I'm not letting you give up."

"It's not your decision."

She looked up at him then and tears glittered in her sad brown eyes. "Until you can move, it's not yours, either."

Chapter 18

Paul saw Zach coming down the hall toward him like a battering ram. His leopard green eyes were red and sunken from lack of sleep, and his light brown skin had a sickly gray cast to it. Paul hadn't seen him in two weeks, and in that time he'd grown thinner, more desperate.

All the Theronai had heard the rumors that he'd possibly found his lady last month, and that she'd run from him. He'd been looking for her ever since. With no luck.

"Where are they?" demanded Zach.

"Who?"

"The women you brought here. I need to see them. Make sure they're not my Lexi."

Paul held up his hands to stop Zach from moving past him. "They're not Lexi. I promise."

Zach struggled against Paul's hold. "You might be wrong."

He wasn't, but he didn't say that. Diplomacy was a better, safer course of action here. "Andra is about five-ten with short dark hair. Nika is about five-seven and has long, white hair. They both have blue eyes. Does that sound like Lexi?"

Zach's shoulders slumped in defeat and his head fell forward. "No. She's little. Not that tall. Damn it."

"I'm sorry, man. I know this is killing you. Have there been any leads?"

"A couple. She's always gone by the time I get there."

"Is it true that the bloodmark you put on her isn't working?" Paul had heard rumors, but he hadn't believed them.

"Yeah, it's true. I don't know how she did it, but she's been able to block it somehow."

Paul laid a hand on his brother's shoulder. "I'm sure you'll find her."

"Or die trying," said Zach, and he turned around and went back the way he came.

Paul stared at his friend, watching him practically stagger away. Zach had always been so proud and strong, and now he was reduced to a desperate mess.

And he'd spent only moments with Lexi.

Paul had been with Andra for two days now. If she walked away from him, he was going to suffer much worse than Zach did before he died.

At least he still had hope. Andra might want to stick around. Zach had been rejected outright. It was a wonder he was still breathing.

If Zach didn't find Lexi soon, there was going to be another sword hung in the Hall of the Fallen before too much longer. Paul was sure of it.

Another brother lost.

Grief welled up in Paul until it threatened to choke him. They were dying too fast. All of them. Not just his brothers, but the Sanguinar, too. He'd even heard the Slayers' ranks were shrinking at an alarming rate, their thinning bloodlines no longer able to support the magic they once wielded.

If something didn't change soon, the Synestryn were going to win and overrun the earth. They'd slaughter every human alive, no matter how small a trace of powerful blood they had, and they'd use that power to open the gate to the Solarc's kingdom. There'd be no one left to stop them.

One problem at a time. That was what he needed to focus on. If he thought about his future, or lack thereof, he wouldn't be able to keep going, and that was what Andra needed him to do. Keep going.

They'd just finished eating, and Andra was back checking on Nika when Paul heard a quiet knock on his door. He opened it to find Joseph standing there with Tynan, one of the Sanguinar.

Paul hesitated to let them in. He didn't want to disturb Nika's rest, but even more than that, he didn't want one of the Sanguinar anywhere near the women. Tynan was going to want their blood. His protective instincts made that hard for him to accept, even though he knew Tynan was on their side.

"I'm sorry," said Joseph. "Sibyl has already left."

"When will she be back?"

"I don't know. She left a note saying that you should have come earlier, as she asked."

"I couldn't bring her earlier. It was too risky for Nika. She damn well should have known that."

"Maybe she did. You can ask her when she gets back. In the meantime, I brought Tynan to help."

"I need to see the women," said Tynan.

Paul let them in. "You don't need to see Andra. Nika's the sick one."

"I must catalog Andra's blood as well," said Tynan.

"No fucking way. Logan's already had enough. Get him to share."

"All that he's taken is gone. Used up to keep the hospital occupants from seeing the attack. We need more."

"Tough shit."

Tynan's too-pretty face was smooth and impassive. He was inhumanly pale and his icy blue eyes dropped to Paul's bare throat. "You've claimed her. She's one of ours now. You can't deny the need to study her blood."

Andra's blood. Just a little, but more than Paul was

willing to give them. "You don't need it now. Maybe later."

"Later might be too late," said Joseph. "You never know what might happen, and we need to be able to figure out where she came from. Another woman capable of uniting with our men just appears—with a blood sister, no less—and you're standing there telling me that it isn't important that we track her bloodline?"

"It's not important to me."

Joseph's face darkened with anger. "Of course not. You've already got your lady. What about the rest of us? We're losing ground day by day and you're standing in the way of our researching her bloodline? I didn't think you were that selfish."

Paul winced. It was selfish, but the thought of spilling Andra's blood and giving it to yet one more of the Sanguinar was more than he could stomach. "It's her choice. Not mine."

"Her life is in your keeping," said Tynan. "You've claimed her as your own. Who better to trust with the decision to spill a small portion of her blood? With you here, watching over her, how could she come to harm? You'd cut me down before I had a chance to take too much."

Paul felt his hand sliding to his sword. It wouldn't take much to reach out and grab it. He'd never liked Tynan. He was too smooth. Too emotionless. Like a reptile.

"This isn't negotiable, Paul," said Joseph. "I'm not giving you or the women a choice. We need to know where they came from and how we missed finding them until now, and the only man who can do that is Tynan. So lead us to the women or just get the hell out of our way, but this is happening."

"What's happening?" asked Andra from behind him.

Paul went to her and placed his body in front of hers in an openly protective gesture. "They want some of your blood."

"For research purposes," explained Joseph. "We hope to find out more about you, about how you're able to absorb Paul's power without harm."

"You think my blood will tell you why I'm a magic sponge?" she asked.

Tynan laughed, letting out a melodious, completely inhuman sound. "Lovely image. Fitting. I think I'm going to like you."

"Stop flirting with my woman," growled Paul.

"Your woman?" asked Andra in a tone that was part warning, part feminine curiosity.

Paul felt his face heat. He was overstepping his bounds. He had to remember that. She did not belong to him no matter how much he wished otherwise. She could do as she chose.

The idea pissed him off.

Paul stepped aside so he was no longer shielding her body from the leech. "You want him to suck on you? Fine. Be my guest."

"Uh. As in bloodsucking vampire? Like Logan? That kind of suck?"

"Yes," said Paul, feeling pleased with her appropriate disgust.

"No," said Joseph and Tynan at the same time.

Andra looked between the three men and took a half step closer to Paul. "Sorry. I gave at the office," she told the men.

Tynan shot her a fabulous, model-beautiful smile full of white teeth. "It's painless. I promise."

"That's what all the vampires say," she told him.

"Lovely creature. I do hope your sister is like you. We could use a little humor to lighten up the place. All these stodgy old Theronai are about as much fun as a funeral."

Joseph let out a low growl of warning. "Back off, leech."

"See what I mean? No fun at all. But you and I, dear,

we could have plenty of fun together." Tynan's voice dripped with promise. He took a step nearer Andra, and another. Paul unsheathed his sword and held the naked blade in front of Tynan's too-pretty neck.

"Not one step farther," he warned the Sanguinar.

Tynan held up his hands in surrender, but it wasn't his hands that were dangerous. It was his icy blue eyes—the kind that would mesmerize prey and hold them still while he fed. Those eyes were fixed firmly on Andra and she wasn't looking away.

"Apparently this is a bad time," said Tynan.

"Anytime is a bad time for you to suck my woman's blood," said Paul.

"I'll just leave and come back when she's more willing. I'm sure her sister will hold out that long."

"You can help Nika?" asked Andra.

"That is why I'm here."

"Then do it." She held out her arms as if letting him choose which one looked tastier. "Take as much as you want. Just help her."

Tynan's eyes brightened with hunger. "So generous. So selfless. Your sister is lucky to have you."

Paul tightened his grip on the sword. "He wants Nika's blood, too, Andra."

"He can't have it. She's too weak. He'll have to take mine instead."

"That's not the way it works, lovely," said Tynan. "I'll need hers, too."

"Logan said she's too weak."

"I'm not Logan. My skills are far greater than his, which is why I'm here now."

"That's enough!" shouted Joseph. "I'm in charge here. You all elected me leader and you're damn well going to accept that leadership, because I'm sure as hell not doing this job for the fun of it."

Paul stared at Joseph, stunned. This outburst wasn't like him at all.

"Now," Joseph said. "Tynan is going to take a little—and I mean a little—of Andra's blood so we can try to figure out where she came from. Paul, you're going to just sit there and take it. And, Tynan, if I sense even the slightest hint of magic coming off of you, I'm going to cut off your closest appendage with my sword—likely your head. You can get your leech buddies to reattach it, if you think they're good enough."

Paul looked at Andra, ignoring Joseph's orders. He didn't care if they cast him out for defiance. She was his to protect, and he was not going to be forsworn the day after he made the vow to do so. He stepped in front of her so that she could see only him. "Are you really going to allow Tynan to take some of your blood? We can fight them."

Andra's blue eyes widened in surprise. "You're kidding, right?"

"I'm deadly serious. Those are our only two options."

"We can't fight these guys. They're the good guys. Right?"

Paul nodded. "Though 'good' may be stretching it a bit. We are on the same side of the war, if that's what you mean."

"It is. Besides, he's the one who's going to help Nika."

"I will do whatever I can," said Tynan.

Andra pulled in a deep breath and said to Tynan, "It's okay. Take some blood from me, but there'd damn well better be juice and cookies waiting for me when you're done."

Andra was beginning to dislike the vampires almost as much as Paul and Madoc seemed to. If this kept up, she was going to be sucked dry before the week was out.

Paul stood over her, his hand on his sword, while Andra sat at the kitchen table next to Tynan. Joseph had excused himself to deal with some kind of emergency, warning Tynan to tread carefully.

"I promise this won't hurt," said Tynan as he leaned forward.

"Touch her neck and you die right here," warned Paul.

Andra looked up at him and couldn't help but stare. She'd never seen him look so fierce, not even when he'd faced down those demons who'd stolen Sammy. He looked like a warrior bent on revenge, barely in control of his anger. His broad shoulders blocked out the light from the living room behind him, casting his body into silhouette. Shadows flowed over the side of his face, throwing his masculine features into harsh relief. His jaw was clenched and his nostrils flared.

Andra touched his arm in an effort to soothe him, but succeeded only in making him flinch. "Hurry up and finish," he told Tynan.

"Your arm, my lady," said Tynan.

Andra was no one's lady, but she didn't stop to argue the point. She wasn't sure how much longer Paul could hold out. She could feel his possessiveness smoldering through their bond.

Andra extended her arm. "You promise it won't hurt?"

Tynan gave her a suave smile that would have made most women's panties melt. "Just look into my eyes and it will be over before you know it."

"No," barked Paul. "She's mine." His voice was so raw the words were hardly decipherable.

Andra wasn't sure whether she was more flattered or annoyed at Paul's possessiveness. If it hadn't been for their connection and the fear for her she felt coming off of him in waves, she might have been pissed off at his barbaric declaration. As it was, she knew that he was only trying to protect her from what he perceived as a threat. "If you don't want me to look at him, then maybe you should be the one to distract me," said Andra with what she hoped was a seductive smile.

He leaned down, fisted his hand in her short hair, eased her head back, and took possession of her mouth in a searing kiss. Andra's world tilted on one end and she sighed into his mouth. Her free hand came up and wrapped around the nape of his neck to hold him in place so he couldn't pull away this time. Somewhere beyond the floating sphere of Paul's kiss Andra was dimly aware that something was being done to her other arm. She didn't care what.

Paul's tongue teased her mouth open and she tasted his growl of approval as he slid inside. His hand tightened in her hair—a pleasurable bite of pain. He pressed her back into the chair, his lips and tongue sliding over hers in a near-frenetic need.

Andra's belly warmed and her limbs became pliant and willing. The luceria hummed happily, resonating with the purring of his ring against her throat. His hot fingers pressed against the pulse in her neck, and she was sure that the blood thrumming there had heated to near boiling.

Her breathing sped up, and she could feel the flush of desire sweeping up her chest. Everything outside the two of them faded away into meaninglessness. She'd never felt anything so consuming before, and had there been any room left inside her tingling body for fear, she would have been terrified. This was not the kind of kiss that ended with each of them going their separate ways. This was the kind of kiss that melded hearts together and changed lives. There was a kind of magic in it—a kind of power that wove them together with delicate tendrils of need. Andra was sure that there was nothing short of naked, sweaty sex that was going to quench the fire that burned in her belly.

She was all for it.

Paul's body tensed with effort; then she felt him start

to pull away. Andra tightened her grip on him, using all her strength to hold him in place. But he was stronger and he captured her hand in his and held it at bay.

Andra was left panting, needy, aching. Now that they were apart, she could feel Paul's lust—separate from her own—crashing over her in violent waves. He wanted her as much as she'd wanted him and yet he'd stopped.

Slowly, as her muddled mind cleared, she remembered they had an audience.

Andra's face was already flushed with passion, so she was sure that no one noticed her blush.

Tynan cleared his throat with a delicate cough. "I'm, ah, finished."

Andra pulled her hand away and looked at her wrist. There was nothing there but unblemished skin. "I didn't feel a thing," she admitted.

"I beg to differ," muttered Tynan. "But I'm glad I didn't hurt you."

"Go help Nika," ordered Paul. He was standing a few feet away, facing mostly toward the windows. Andra could see the pained expression on his face, and the rigid control he was trying to maintain.

Tynan's dark brows rose. "Are you unwell, Theronai?"

"I'm fine. Go help Nika."

Andra stood, needing to touch him—to soothe him. She reached for him.

Paul jerked away. "Don't come any closer or I'll have you naked on the floor under me in thirty seconds. I don't care who's watching."

Andra's body was shimmering inside with the residual effects of their kiss. It took an effort of will to gather her composure and keep herself from running her hands over Paul's taut back.

"He's right," said Andra, glancing at Tynan. "Nika needs you."

Tynan bowed his head. "As you wish."

"Are you going to be okay?" she asked Paul, starting to grow concerned.

"Yes. This is just the Sanguinar's version of a joke. I'll be there in a minute."

Andra wasn't laughing. She ached too much to find any of this funny.

She looked at Tynan's face and couldn't see a sign of any humor lurking in his eyes.

"Where is your sister?" he asked.

"I'll show you."

Andra took Tynan to the room where Nika was resting. The door opened quietly. It was dark, so Andra flipped on the lights. Nika didn't move, but she'd spent years having doctors and nurses invade her sleep, so she was probably used to it by now.

She was so thin and frail, almost skeletal. Her pale hair blended in with the stark white pillows. Blue veins spread out across her temples and over the backs of her hands. The bruises from the restraints and IVs were dark, ugly marks that hadn't yet begun to heal.

Andra's heart broke open and bled for her sister. If this didn't work . . .

"How long has she been asleep?" he asked, frowning at Nika.

"Hours. She woke up and had a little bit to eat before we left Nebraska, but she slept the rest of the way here. Madoc gave her some water when we arrived, but she went right back to sleep."

Tynan sat on the edge of the bed. He picked up her bony hand with exquisite care. His long fingers hovered over her pulse for a moment. When he looked up at Andra, his face was grim. "She's not sleeping anymore. She's unconscious."

Chapter 19

Andra locked her knees to keep from falling. "Are you sure? I thought she was getting better when Madoc managed to get her to eat. I never would have left her side if I'd thought otherwise."

Guilt ate at her, making her stomach turn. She was so swept up in Paul and his world that she hadn't even noticed her sister had gotten worse.

"She hasn't been unconscious for long, but I can feel her slipping away. Her body is getting weaker."

"What do we do?"

"I won't know until I have some of her blood."

"If she's weak, that will only make things worse."

"No. I need only a drop or two." He was looking at her for permission.

Andra had no choice. No options. "Okay, but no more."

Tynan nodded and put Nika's finger to his mouth. Andra saw him pierce the tip with his sharp fang, and just as quickly his tongue swiped over it, sealing her skin.

He froze. Nika's hand slipped from his grasp and fell back to the bed. His eyes started to dart around like crazy—just like Logan's had done—and a deep moan rose up from his throat.

Andra held back her panic. She didn't know what was going on here, but she wasn't going to leave Nika in the way if Tynan started thrashing around. She moved around the bed to gather Nika in her arms and get her out of the way just as Tynan's eyes slowed and he let out a harsh breath.

"You okay?" asked Andra.

He didn't seem to hear her. "That poor child," he whispered, and looked at Nika as if she were already dead.

"What happened?" demanded Andra.

"Her blood." He wiped his mouth like he didn't want to risk tasting any more of it. "I know why she's suffering." He looked up at Andra and his expression was that of a doctor giving a family member the worst news possible. "I'm sorry," he said. "I can get her to eat and help her body heal, but there's nothing I can do for her mind."

Andra held back her tears through sheer force of will. "What is it? What's wrong with her?"

"The Synestryn got her blood somehow."

Andra knew how. "Our family was attacked when she was twelve. One of those things ripped her leg open." She couldn't bring herself to tell him that the monster had licked Nika's blood from her wound and Andra hadn't done a thing to stop it. She'd just stood there, letting it happen.

"It's a wonder she lived. Their claws and saliva are poisonous."

"She was sick for a long time, but she got better. At least, I thought she had. It took a while before I realized that she wasn't ... herself." Those first few weeks had nearly been more than Andra could take. Her mother had been killed. Her baby sister had been missing and presumed dead, though Andra refused to believe it. Nika had been in the hospital, holding on to life by a thread. Andra was alone, making all the decisions herself. She had been nineteen, just starting college. She was barely old enough to be out on her own, much less holding the fate of two children in her hands. She was torn between hunting for Tori or staying with Nika. She tried to do both, but exhaustion put her into the hospital, too, and the choice was made for her.

She'd wanted to turn to her mom so badly, be held and told everything was going to be okay. But Mom was dead and the doctors kept looking to Andra for all the decisions. She had no choice but to suck it up. So she had.

"Your sister is psychic, isn't she?" asked Tynan.

Andra nodded slowly. She'd always written it off as creepy coincidences, but it was true. Nika had known a lot of things she shouldn't have. "Is that why she's like this? Why she thinks she sees things that aren't there?"

"The blood that was taken from her forged a connection with the sgath who took it—a kind of mental link. She could have handled that, but it got worse. Somehow, the blood of that creature was consumed by many others. Nika's presence inside of that sgath was split each time her blood was passed on. From what I can tell, this has happened more than once."

"You can tell all of that from a drop or two of blood?"

"Yes." He didn't look like it made him happy.

"So why can't you fix it?"

"I'm not skilled enough. There is a Sanguinar in Europe who may be, but even that's not likely."

Hopeless rage filled Andra up until she shook. "Why the hell not?"

"Because Nika's been cut into too many pieces. There's not enough left to put her back together, and even if we could, the scars would likely leave her mind ruined. It's best if you let her go. Let her suffering end."

"No," whispered Andra. She couldn't let Nika go, too. She couldn't be alone.

Warm, strong hands settled on her shoulders. Paul. She hadn't even seen him come in the room.

"You heard her, Tynan," said Paul. "We're not letting her go. You can have whatever blood you need, but you can't give up on her."

Tynan stood. "As you wish. I will go and research what must be done."

"How long will that take?" asked Andra.

"I shouldn't proceed without speaking to my brothers and gathering my strength."

Paul said, "I'll call on the Theronai to donate blood to the cause. Every one of the men will be hoping Nika is his lady. You should get plenty of volunteers."

"Have them meet me in our lounge after sunset tomorrow. I'll need at least that much time to prepare."

"We're going to speak to Sibyl, too, as soon as she gets back."

"Good," said Tynan. "Any advice she can give will be welcome."

"Since when do you take advice from her?" asked Paul.

"Since the life of that woman hangs in the balance." Tynan turned and left.

Andra couldn't move, couldn't speak. She'd fought so long and hard for Nika, and it still hadn't been enough. Nothing she'd ever done had been good enough when it came to her family.

She'd failed over and over, and nothing she'd heard made her believe that this time would be any different. "I'm sorry," she whispered to her sister. "I'm so sorry, baby."

Paul pulled her back against his chest and held her tight. His arms felt warm, strong, and comforting. Part of her wanted to turn in to him and hide in his strength, but the rest of her wanted to shove him away and scream at him for making her soft. She couldn't be soft right now.

"Stop it," he said. "Stop pushing me away. We're in this together."

"She's *my* sister."

"And you're *my* wife, which makes her my sister, too."

Shock froze her tongue in place for a moment. She turned around and looked up at him. "Wife? I never agreed to that."

"You're wearing my luceria. It's the closest thing my people have to marriage."

"We are not married."

He flinched and his jaw hardened. "Fine, we're not married as you know it, but I still feel like she's my family. I would do anything in my power to save her."

He was right. Andra was pushing away the only ally she had. "I'm sorry. I know you're trying to help."

"So was Madoc. But you sent him away."

"Because he's unstable. You said so yourself."

Paul smoothed her hair back from her temple. His touch was gentle, almost loving. "You can't understand how it is for us, living with pain the way we do for centuries. It makes our edges rougher. Makes us angry and desperate."

"Centuries? You live that long?"

"So will you."

Shock rippled through Andra, silencing her. It didn't seem possible, but there was a lot of that going around lately.

She gathered her wits enough to speak, but not enough to keep from blurting out the truth. "Living eight years with the guilt of letting my family die, of not being able to help Nika, is more than enough. I can't imagine several lifetimes of that kind of torture."

"No one said longevity was easy. We all carry burdens, and in the case of the male Theronai, we also can endure decades of crushing pain. That pain makes Madoc harsh, but I swear he'd never hurt Nika."

"I can't take any chances."

"She seemed to do better when he was around."

"That was a coincidence."

Paul shook his head. "What if it wasn't? Nika needs all the help she can get."

"I'll think about it."

"Okay. Fair enough." He kissed her head and moved away. "I'm going to go round up the men and get them to feed Tynan so he's strong enough to help her."

"Then I want you to come back, so we can try to help her again, too."

"Whatever you want, Andra. It's yours."

Paul had to fight himself to walk away from Andra. She needed comfort and he wanted to be right here where he could hold her. But she needed Nika more, so he forced himself to leave and do what he could to help.

He found Joseph sitting in his office even though it was well past time that he should have stopped working for the day. Through the window behind him, Paul saw several Theronai and humans in the training yard, practicing swordplay or pumping iron. Joseph should have been out there with them, blowing off some steam to ease the pain Paul knew he felt, but instead Joseph was here in his office, poring over a large map. Idly, he slid his fingers back and forth over the luceria around his throat. Even though Joseph was unbound, he had refused to visit Nika to see if she could be his mate.

Paul was going to have to do something to change his mind. More than any of the Theronai, Joseph needed to stay strong so he could lead his people. Without him, there would be chaos and people they loved would die.

Paul stepped inside the room to get a better view and recognized the map as a copy of the one they used to track Synestryn nests and sightings. Red dots littered the thing, ringing around Dabyr as if it were a bull's-eye.

They were closing in. None of the Synestryn had broken through their security here yet, but it was only a matter of time before they found a way in.

That was why the humans trained. There was no guarantee the Sentinels would live long enough to protect them from that eventuality. They had to learn to protect themselves, though how they would do that, Paul had no idea. They simply weren't physically capable of that kind of strength.

"I hate to bother you, but I need a favor," said Paul.

Joseph leaned back and rubbed his eyes. He looked like he hadn't slept in days. "Sure. What's one more?"

"I'm sorry. I know you've got a lot on your plate, but this might actually help in the long run."

Joseph motioned for Paul to sit. "I'm listening."

"Andra's sister might not make it, but Tynan is going to try to help her. I need you to issue a call for blood to all the Theronai and Gerai."

Joseph let out a heavy sigh. "Since Helen showed up last month, more and more of the men have left to go hunt for their own ladies. Now that you've found Andra, it's going to get even worse. There aren't many Theronai left here, but I'll issue the order."

"Maybe you should call the men back for this—lure them back with the hope of Nika's survival. If she lives, she may be compatible with one of them."

"Even if she is, what about those who aren't compatible? I'm going to have a pile of pissed Theronai on my hands."

"Better that than a dead woman."

Joseph held up his hand as if to ward away any more pressure. "I know, I know. I'll do it."

"Did you want to meet her first?" asked Paul. "See if she might be yours?"

Joseph kept his head down, but he couldn't hide the hopeful light that glittered in his eyes for a moment. "I can't do that. I'm still holding it together. Sixteen leaves left as of this morning. Let the others go first."

"Always the last in line, eh?"

"That's only one of the many benefits of leadership," said Joseph on a sigh. He looked tired. Worn down.

Paul felt concern tug at him. If Joseph didn't survive, they had little hope of keeping any semblance of order. "You've still got another eight years left on your term. Are you going to make it?"

The man shrugged. "Probably not, but I'll get as far through my two decades as I can."

"Come see Nika," urged Paul. Their leader needed to be strong. Having a lady at his side would ensure that like nothing else could.

"Maybe later. I've got to get some things done first. Don't worry. I'll put the blood order out within the hour. Nicholas has some way of calling all the men back automatically via text message or something."

"Thank you. This means a lot to me."

"Don't thank me yet. Once all the men show up, you're not going to get a moment's peace."

"No one but you gets near Nika until she's better."

Joseph leaned back in his chair, his hazel eyes dark with worry. "I'm going to have to post a guard then. You know how hard it's going to be for the men to stay away."

"That's not a bad idea. Maybe Angus or Drake is a good choice."

Joseph nodded. Both men were bonded Theronai. She'd be safe with them. "They're out hunting, but I'll have them report back, too. Who knows? Maybe Gilda could even help her. She has a decent amount of healing ability herself, and it doesn't cost us any blood if she does it."

"We'll take all the help we can get," said Paul.

Joseph's eyes went back to the map, and he suddenly looked older than he should have. "I hope Nika lives," he said. "We need her if we're going to hold the Synestryn back."

"Even if she does live, she's not going to be in any condition to fight."

"We'd give her time to heal, of course, but we need everyone we've got out on the front lines fighting. You and Andra will need to get out there, too."

Paul couldn't look the man in the eyes, but he had to tell Joseph of his failure. The man didn't need any more bad news, but Paul owed him the truth. "I think I made a mistake."

"Join the club," said Joseph.

"No, I mean a big one."

Joseph rubbed his temples as if they throbbed. Exasperation filled his tone. "We all make big ones. In our line of work, those are the only kind out there. What I wouldn't give to have overdue bills or a leaky toilet or, hell, even a drug-addicted teen to deal with. Instead, I get to deal with determining the fate of the freaking planet. And most of those people I'm working to save don't even know I exist. I make a mistake, the human race ends. So, tell me, just what is it you think you did that's so bad?"

"I've bonded with a woman I can't keep."

Joseph stood slowly, all signs of fatigue gone. "What do you mean, you can't keep her? Of course you're going to keep her."

Paul looked down at his ring. Three shades of blue swirled and writhed within the iridescent band. As long as the color wasn't fixed, he still had time to walk away, but he'd be back where he started with only days to live. "She only gave me three days."

Joseph's shoulders bowed under the weight of that news. "You're kidding me. Doesn't she know what's at stake?"

"Right now, all she can worry about is her sister. Give her some time."

Joseph slammed his hand down on the map covered in red. "We don't have any more time. We need her. Do whatever it takes, but bind her to you for good."

"I don't know—"

"Swear it, Paul," demanded Joseph, leadership ringing in his voice. "Swear you'll do it."

The urge to give in and make his vow was so strong it made Paul's stomach clench. "I can't. She doesn't belong in our world. If she doesn't want to be here, I won't force her to stay. After our time is up, I'm letting her go."

"The hell you are." Joseph leaned forward over the desk and gave Paul a serious frown. "Make things work out with her. We need her. It's your duty to convince her to stay and make sure she's happy once she does."

"It's not that simple."

"Damn it, Paul! You'd better be taking this seriously. We're all counting on you. All of the Theronai need you to make this work."

"I can't *make* her stay."

"Of course you can. Our men are out there every day risking their lives so that others won't even have to know about the dangers we face. We allow humans to live in the bliss of ignorance and all we ask in return is that when one of them turns up able to aid our fight, they do so. It's not much to ask."

"Except to the one who is unlucky enough to join the war."

"Fuck that," snarled Joseph. "I'm done with waging a noble war. We're fighting demons. And worse. They're closing in on us more every day. We'll all die if you don't do this."

"So, now I'm responsible for the lives of all the Theronai, too? Don't you think I have enough pressure?"

"Apparently not, or you'd find a way to tie her to you so tight she'd never be able to get away."

"She doesn't want it, Joseph."

"Fuck what she wants. *Make* her want it if you have to."

Magic. Coercion. That was what Joseph was talking

about. Paul knew, because he'd had those very same thoughts. "You don't see a problem with that?"

Joseph reached around the desk, took Paul's arm, and dragged him toward the window overlooking the training field. He pointed a thick finger at the glass. "Look out there. I see seven good men who don't have a year left to live. I have a problem with *that*."

Paul wanted to avert his eyes, but he couldn't. Those men were his friends. His family. He couldn't let them lose hope. Maybe Joseph was right. Maybe what Andra wanted wasn't as important as giving his people a reason to live—the hope that there might be more women out there like her. The hope that they might not lose this war.

"You take a good look," said Joseph. "Remember those faces when you see your woman. Every one of those men would do whatever it took to save you. I think you owe them the same thing."

He did. He owed them his life. His soul.

But it wasn't just his life at stake. It was Andra's.

If she didn't want to stay with him, he wouldn't force her. He knew how desperate things were, but if he had to force Andra's compliance, he didn't deserve her.

Paul steadied his nerve. He didn't like this any more than Joseph, but he couldn't give in. "I'm sorry, but I won't force her. It's got to be her choice."

"Then pray to God that she makes the right one." His voice sounded heavy, worried.

"What is it you're not telling me?" asked Paul.

Joseph shook his head. His shoulders seemed to bow a little farther under an invisible burden. "We can't let her go. If you won't do what's necessary, I'll find a man who will. Surely she'll be compatible with one of our men."

Rage rose up inside Paul, furious and ugly. "If you do, you'd better wait until after I draw my very last breath, because any man who tries to take her by force will have to come through me first."

"You wouldn't kill one of your brothers in arms."

Paul hated himself for realizing the truth. Maybe his feelings for Andra were intensified by the union they shared, or maybe he would have felt this way regardless of their bond. Either way, he wasn't going to let her be forced into a life of death and fear unless it was her choice.

"For her," he told Joseph, "for her, I would."

Chapter 20

Madoc felt as if his skin were going to split open. He needed sex, but he couldn't get it here—at least, not the kind he needed to take off the edge. The Gerai women—especially Thea—were willing to take what he needed to give. They just weren't able. He'd end up hurting one of them, and then there'd be hell to pay.

Violence was his second choice. There was a whole world full of Synestryn out there that needed killing, but he couldn't bring himself to leave Dabyr to do the job. He couldn't bring himself to leave Nika.

Fuck.

He shoved the loaded barbell up again, hoping that the physical exertion of weight lifting would hold him together for just a few more hours. Sweat poured off his body and his heart felt like it would explode, but he kept on pushing.

"Need a spot?" asked Neal. The Theronai's body bulged with muscle. He was more than able to give Madoc a hand.

"Back off," grunted Madoc.

"Suit yourself," said Neal. "I need to get back to training anyway. Playtime's over."

But the man didn't leave. He stood there, watching silently as Madoc shoved the bar back up.

"What the fuck are you looking at?" asked Madoc.

Neal shrugged his huge shoulders. "Nothing. Just wondering if you'd heard about the call for blood."

"Not interested." Madoc's arms shook as he brought the weight back down to his chest.

"You sure? I heard Paul found himself a female Theronai. She has a full-blooded sister who's sick."

"I was there. Know all about it."

Neal hunkered down, his eyes lighting with interest. "You've met her?"

"Yep."

"So are you going to donate blood?"

"Not my woman. Not my problem."

Neal made a sound of disgust. "Selfish bastard. Just because she's not yours doesn't mean you shouldn't help."

"Sure it does." His arms started to shake under the strain of the weight. His muscles burned and he pulled in some air to fuel them.

"She may not be compatible with me, either, but I'm going to donate."

"Good for you. Better for the leeches," said Madoc.

This blood order reminded him way too much of the way it had been with Torr. Nearly every man here had bled into Tynan, and it still hadn't been enough to save Torr. Poor bastard was still alive, but locked inside his useless body, trapped and unable to get out.

Madoc would have rather died.

What if that was what happened to Nika? What if they weren't able to save her?

Fuck.

"Better for the woman," responded Neal. "How can you live with yourself, man? Don't you care about anyone but yourself?"

"Nope."

Madoc racked the bar and pushed himself to his feet. He couldn't sit around and do nothing. He had to get out of here before he went crazy. Go find a hooker. Get laid. Maybe hunt down some nasties.

"You're an embarrassment," said Neal. "We took vows to protect others even if it cost our lives. Donating blood doesn't even hurt."

Madoc's tank top hid the fact that his lifemark was mostly bare. The Band had inked him with a couple of fake leaves that were good enough to fool anyone not looking too closely, but Madoc didn't trust Neal not to look. Nothing got by that man. If he'd known Madoc was out of time, he would have him shipped off to the Slayers before dawn. Game over.

"I'm not letting any fucking bloodsuckers in my head," said Madoc.

"Even if it means the woman dies?"

"She's not going to die." Madoc grabbed a towel and wiped the sweat from his body. He was tired of being in public, tired of pretending he was still one of them.

"You don't know that, but I hope you're right. For your sake as well as hers. That kind of guilt is a heavy load."

What if Neal was right? What if they didn't get enough blood for her? Most of the men were out hunting for their own women and hardly anyone was home. It could take days for them all to return. Days Nika didn't have.

Fuck.

He couldn't let that happen. Not to Nika.

He stomped away from Neal and called Nicholas on his cell.

Nicholas's surprised voice came over the line. "Madoc. You never call. You never write. I was starting to think you didn't care."

"Fuck the small talk. Where's Tynan?"

"Sounds serious. Hold on," said Nicholas. There was some typing in the background; then the head of security came back on the line. "He's headed from the dining hall toward the Sanguinar wing."

"Can you stop him?"

"Sure. I'll lock the doors, but why—"

Madoc hung up and broke into a jog. People looked at him funny as he sped by, but he didn't give a shit.

Tynan was pushing on the locked door when Madoc found him. The leech turned around and his icy eyes went wide with fear.

Good. That was going to make this easier.

Madoc scanned the walls for the security camera, found it, and ripped it down. Bits of plastic crumbled inside his fist and he dropped the broken mess to the tile floor.

"Madoc," said Tynan. He held his hands up in front of him. "What are you doing?"

"She's dying, isn't she?"

Tynan blinked for a moment, as if he hadn't expected the question, and it took him a second to catch up. "Nika?"

"Yes. Nika."

"I'm going to do everything for her I can."

"You didn't answer the question."

Tynan's eyes moved around as if looking for an escape. "I'm sorry. I'm afraid she is."

"Can you fix her?"

"I don't yet know. I still have to do some research and see if this kind of thing has ever happened before. And there's always an issue of having the strength to help her even if I do find out how."

Madoc prowled closer and lowered his voice so no one else could hear. "Take mine."

Tynan pressed himself harder against the door, as if trying to get away. "What?"

Madoc held out his arm. "Take my blood. Use it to save her."

The Sanguinar's eyes flared with hunger. "You've never before given your blood to any of us."

"I fucking know that. Do you want it or not?" Madoc bobbed his thick arm in front of the leech.

"Yes." It was an eerie, hissing sound that gave Madoc second thoughts for a split second. He knew he was going to regret this—he just didn't care.

"How much?" asked Tynan, licking his lips.

"Whatever you need to save her." Madoc wasn't going to last much longer anyway at this rate. He might as well do something decent with his blood.

Tentatively, Tynan wrapped his slim fingers around Madoc's arm and brought his wrist to his mouth. Madoc had expected it to hurt, but his life had been all about pain for so long, a couple of fang pricks didn't even register. All he felt was a strong tugging motion against his skin, and even that started to fade away within moments.

Slowly, a hazy kind of weakness filled Madoc's limbs. It didn't bother him or worry him, but he knew it wasn't right. His body grew heavy, and he decided it was a good idea to sit down. Tynan seemed stronger than normal and had no trouble easing him to the floor without breaking his hold on Madoc's arm.

Buzzing filled his head and his eyes grew heavy. He really needed a nap and wished to hell he could go curl himself around Nika so no one could get to her.

The odd thought was gone as quickly as it came. Madoc didn't have the strength to walk right now, anyway. Not that he cared. He didn't care about a fucking thing.

Tynan felt as if he were flying. For the first time in decades he wasn't starving. Wasn't cold. Power roared through his veins, a heady mixture of strength and invincibility. Madoc's blood was pure. No one else had ever partaken of his vast power, which had only grown over the centuries. Tynan had never tasted anything like it, and probably never would again.

What he'd drunk from Madoc was enough to fuel his body for decades if he limited the amount of magic he used. Too bad he couldn't keep all that giddy power for himself. He had to share.

Nika wasn't the only one in need. Selfishness was not an option if his kind were to survive. Threescore Sanguinar occupied the sleeping chamber in the depths of the compound, and spread out among them, the blood he could spare and still aid Nika would last for only a few months at best. But at least that was a few more months than they had now.

Tynan slammed the locked doors open with a scream of shredding metal, leaving Madoc slumped in the hall behind him. Since the security camera had been disabled, Tynan was sure that Nicholas would be coming along any moment to see what had happened to his precious technology. Madoc's brothers would see to his care.

Tynan wondered if they knew what Madoc was hiding from all of them—that his soul had begun to die.

He briefly thought about telling them, but it was none of his affair and he didn't want to let on just how much he could learn about a person when he drank from them. It would only scare off the others when their time grew short.

Besides, Tynan had plenty of his own secrets to keep, including the fact that the blood Madoc had offered could only partly be used to save the girl. He had more important plans for the rest of that power.

Tynan descended to the lowest level of the south wing, down four flights of stairs, past six layers of security that ensured that only those of his kind could pass. There was currently peace between them and the Theronai, but it had not always been so. The Sanguinar were too vulnerable when they slept. It would be too easy to wipe them out if another war broke out. Secrecy and their usefulness in healing were the only protection they had, and they used both to the best advantage possible.

He pulled open the heavy steel door that had usually wrenched at his arms, but today he needed merely a slight push to send it flying open. It hit the stone wall with a metallic boom, startling the Sanguinar who stood guard over those who slept.

Connal shot to his feet, hiding the book he'd been reading behind his back. He was fairly short for one of their kind, but more muscular. It was as if the lack of blood had not hampered his body's strength. Connal had grass green eyes set in a babyish face that even three centuries could not age. The Sanguinar looked perpetually eighteen and was typically treated with the same level of respect.

"You startled me," said Connal.

"Catching up on your reading?" asked Tynan.

"I borrowed it from Briant."

Tynan wrinkled his nose in distaste. "Tell me it's not one of his erotic vampire novels."

Connal's boyish face darkened. "He said it was one of the best. I just thought I'd try it."

Tynan shook his head. "You should stick with the classics. That stuff will rot your mind."

"Hasn't hurt Briant. That man's smarter than all of the rest of us put together." Connal marked his place in the book and set it aside. "What are you doing here, anyway?"

"I've come to feed the others."

Connal's eyes darkened with hunger and excitement. "The new girl? She's blooded?"

Tynan decided to keep the true source of his power to himself. "Very, but I suggest you keep your distance. Her Theronai is quite . . . protective."

"He can't be everywhere at once. I'll find her alone and—"

"You'll do nothing of the sort. You'll leave the girl alone." Tynan imbued his words with a hint of his newly acquired power, forcing Connal to listen and obey.

Connal gave him a quick nod.

Tynan went to the end of one long wall. Enclosed in

that wall were dozens of sleeping Sanguinar. They would stay in their magically enhanced sleep for fifty years before waking. It was the only way the dwindling food supply would hold out. Each year more Sanguinar went to sleep and fewer woke. Even in sleep, some of them died of starvation. Without more food—more powerful blood—there was little anyone could do.

Tynan pushed on a section of wall and it opened to reveal a small stone bowl. At the bottom of the bowl was a hole that led to a series of tubes that fed each of the sleeping Sanguinar. It didn't take much blood to keep them alive, but they had to have some, and it had been almost two months since their last feeding.

At least in sleep they didn't feel hunger. Tynan wished he could say the same.

He held his wrist over the bowl and willed his flesh to open. Dark red blood trickled from the small wound into the bowl. With every drop that spilled, Tynan felt his power dwindle. Before he was too weak, he willed his flesh closed and licked the remaining blood from his wrist. He couldn't waste a drop.

The high of actually being full was gone and the familiar hunger pangs were back. Not as bad as before, but not pleasant. It was easy to drown them out when he was working, and he had plenty of work to do. Not only did Nika's situation require his full attention, but he also had to figure out how such pure bloodlines had gone unnoticed. First Helen's, now Andra's and Nika's. If they could find more women like them, he might be able to save his people from starvation.

It was more hope than he'd had in decades.

"Are you going to share with me, brother?" asked Connal. He handed Tynan a jug of saline to clean out the system of tubes and make sure all the precious blood went into the Sanguinar.

Tynan regarded the young-looking man. Connal had never called him *brother* before. How odd that he would now. "When you are asleep and helpless as a babe, I will feed you. Until then, you must find your own food. There are plenty of blooded humans in the compound. Ask them to sustain you."

"None of their blood runs as pure as the blood I smelled coming from your veins. The power must feel incredible."

Connal's eyes were too bright. Too greedy. Perhaps it was time for him to sleep. Any Sanguinar who became too desperate became a liability. Their kind could not afford any more weakness than they already suffered.

"I'll send someone to relieve you of your guard duty while you find sustenance," said Tynan as he left the chamber.

He barely managed to close the heavy door, and by the time he did, he was shaking with effort.

He wasn't going to last much longer before he, too, had to sleep. Before then, he had to find out how to save his people from starvation, and these women were the key.

He'd made sure of that as he'd fed from Andra—altered her slightly to ensure his kind would be fed.

Tynan didn't particularly like manipulating people, but he'd had no choice. His people were starving and he'd been desperate to take action while he had the chance. Paul was a formidable warrior and he had plenty of time alone to taint Andra's perception of his race. The Theronai looked down on the Sanguinar—thought of them as barbaric for their need to drink blood.

Tynan had not asked to be born like he was—unable to live without the blood of others. He'd been a victim of his parents' choices the same as any other child. He could no more help his blood thirst than a deformed child could help their birth defect. It was not fair that his people should suffer, and it was his job to see that they survived.

He'd done the only thing he could while Paul was so

busily distracting Andra with his kisses. He only prayed that what he'd done to her would work. The Sanginar were running out of time, and the remaining traces of the Solarc's blood in human bloodlines were too weak to sustain his race any longer.

He'd had no choice. He'd done what he was forced to do. He hoped that one day, if she ever learned of his manipulation, Andra would see that and forgive him.

Chapter 21

Madoc woke to the sight of Nicholas's worried face and wished like hell he'd stayed asleep. His head pounded more than normal, which, combined with all that spinning, made his stomach give a dangerous heave.

He had no idea what was wrong. Maybe he'd fallen and bashed his head, or taken a hit in combat hard enough to rattle his brains. Wouldn't have been the first time.

Then it came back to him. Tynan. He'd given the leech his blood.

On the heels of that thought came an even more distressing one. "How long have I been out? How's the girl?"

Nicholas frowned in confusion. "Not long, and what girl?"

"Nika. Andra's sister."

Madoc pushed himself up to a sitting position and fought off another wave of twisting nausea. He was going to pound Tynan's pretty face in next time he saw him for taking so much.

Then again, maybe that was what it was going to take to help Nika.

"I don't know, man. I saw the camera go black and I was sure I was going to get here and find Tynan dead on the floor. Instead it was you lying there. What happened?"

"None of your fucking business," growled Madoc.

"Did you hit him? Slam him into the door?"

"No."

Nicholas rubbed a hand over his face and looked at the door leading to the Sanguinar wing. "Then what the hell happened?" he asked.

Madoc turned his head slowly so it wouldn't spin away and saw the ruins of the steel door. It looked like it had been blown open with a battering ram. The metal was deformed and torn away where the lock had once been. "Dunno," said Madoc.

Maybe Tynan had consumed some of Madoc's pain when he'd taken his blood and it had pissed him off. Served the fucker right, if that was the case.

"I wish you hadn't killed my camera. That would have been quite a show. You sure you don't know?"

Madoc ignored the question. "You got any of those cameras in Paul's suite?"

"No."

"Damn."

"Why don't you just go see the girl if you're that worried?"

"Her sister won't let me." It sounded like a lame excuse to him. Since when did he let a woman boss him around?

Probably since she was right. He had no business around Nika. If she'd been his lady, it would be different, but she wasn't.

Madoc looked at his ring for the millionth time, just to be sure he hadn't missed anything. The colors were still the same. Muted, faded, nearly motionless. Dying.

"Do you think you're compatible?" asked Nicholas in a reverent tone.

"No." Madoc pushed himself to his feet, using the wall to steady himself. The dizziness eased, but not much. He needed liquids and plenty of them if he was going to refill what Tynan had taken.

Nicholas looked at his own ring, which swirled with lots of color. He still had plenty of time, and Madoc resented him for it. "I haven't gotten to meet her yet. Joseph has ordered us all to stay away until she's better."

If she ever got better. No one seemed to be doing anything to help her, and it pissed Madoc off. "Do you have one of those master keys on you?"

Nicholas frowned, making the small scars on his face pucker. "Always. Why?"

"I need one."

"And you expect me to just hand it over?"

Madoc slammed Nicholas against the wall and held him there by his shoulders. He tried to cover up how unsteady he was—how close he was to puking all over the man's shoes. "Unless you'd prefer I take it from you."

Nicholas wasn't the least bit scared. The fucker. "What are you going to do with it?" he asked, totally unconcerned by his position.

"None of your fucking business."

"Seems a lot of things fall into that category with you." Nicholas moved quicker than Madoc's fuzzy head could follow, and a second later Madoc was against the wall face-first. Nicholas had him pinned there, his thick forearm right at the base of Madoc's skull.

"I'll ask you again," said Nicholas in a patient tone. "What are you going to do with it?"

The urge to fight rose up inside Madoc, screaming for release. The constant pressure inside him pounded at him to let go and tear into Nicholas. It would feel so good to give in and drive his fists into something. Vent some of his rage that Nika wasn't his and never would be. She couldn't save him.

"You could try it," whispered Nicholas, apparently knowing what Madoc was thinking. "Normally, I'd say you'd have even odds, but not today. You're weak. I can feel your legs shaking just holding you up. I'd have you on the ground and bleeding in seconds, and that's not going to get any of us anywhere. So why don't we pretend we're gentlemen and you tell me why you want the key?"

Madoc's teeth bit into his lip as his face was mashed harder against the wall. He couldn't even stop it from happening. Nicholas was right. He was weak. His only choice was to play nice. Not his strong suit. "I just want to be near her in case they need help."

"What the hell makes you think they'd want *your* help?"

"They don't. That's why I need the key."

"I'm not going to let you into Paul's suite where you can go causing more trouble."

"I don't want inside Paul's suite. Just the one next door. I swear."

The pressure against Madoc's neck eased as Nicholas backed away. Madoc turned in time to see him drop a plastic key card on his way down the hall.

"I'll be watching," said Nicholas without turning around. "Kill another camera and I'll make you eat it."

Andra couldn't seem to make that magic stuff work anymore. She could feel the invisible strand of power connecting her to Paul, but she couldn't seem to do anything with it. No matter how hard she tried, she couldn't find a way inside Nika's head. She wanted to help her, get her to wake up, maybe eat again, but nothing she tried worked. Maybe she was just too tired, or maybe Paul needed to be closer to her.

Maybe she just didn't have what it took to do the job.

Her eyes burned and her knees ached—a sure sign she was nearing the end of her strength. Again.

Andra laid her head on the pillow next to Nika's and prayed for her weakness to abate. Just for a while.

The room was quiet, restful. The muted blues and
greens reminded her of the ocean on a calm day. There
was no clutter in here, just the bare necessities of a bed,
bedside table, and dresser. Even though it had the feel
of disuse, nothing was dusty or stale.

Nika was safer here than she'd ever be in Andra's
home. Paul had sworn to her that no Synestryn had ever
breached their magical defenses. Even if one of the people here bled, the monsters couldn't smell it.

Andra felt the weight of despair flattening her heart,
and she tried to remind herself that there was still hope.
Tynan was researching a cure. Sibyl might be able to see
what they needed to do.

There was still hope. She just had to be patient, give
these people time to work their magic.

Andra watched the even rise and fall of Nika's chest.
She was calm and still. Peaceful. At least Nika wasn't
suffering. If she had been, patience wouldn't have been
an option.

Paul rapped his knuckles lightly on the doorframe of
the bedroom, making Andra jump. She hadn't heard him
come back, but she was so glad to see him. She wanted
to rush into his arms and let him hold her. He was the
only person who seemed to make some of her anguish go
away, and she really could use a little of that right now.

She sat up on the bed and saw that his handsome face
was lined with concern and something else. Something
deeper that worried her.

Without thinking about it, she poked around in his
thoughts, looking for the source. She wasn't very good at
this, and she could catch only bits and pieces, but she saw
Joseph's angry face at the forefront of Paul's mind.

She brushed up against a writhing mass of aching
emotion and recognized it for what it was. Guilt. She'd
felt it herself too often not to know it instantly. He felt
like he'd made some kind of mistake—one that couldn't
be erased.

A gentle pressure filled her head as he pushed her out of his mind. "None of that," he said.

"But you're suffering."

"We'll talk later. I brought help."

A young woman stepped out from behind him. She had thick, curly black hair and sad brown eyes despite the tentative smile on her face. She came up to Paul's chin, but the way she curled in on herself made her seem smaller. Younger.

She didn't raise her eyes to look at Andra, as if it would somehow be disrespectful. "My lady," she greeted her with an awkward curtsy.

Lady? There it was again. Andra looked at Paul in question.

"I promise you'll get used to it."

Not likely. "Call me Andra. Anything else just confuses me."

The woman nodded, but still didn't look up. "I'm Grace. I was told you might need some help caring for your sister."

"Thank you, but we're fine."

"No, you're not, Andra," said Paul. "You need a break, and Grace here knows what she's doing. Let her help."

Andra didn't want any help. Nika was her responsibility. "Not interested."

Grace flushed a deep, humiliated red. "I'm, uh, sorry for overstepping my bounds. I seem to be doing that a lot lately. I won't bother you again." She turned to leave, but Paul was faster and caught her arm.

Grace flinched as if she'd been slapped, and cowered, covering her head with her arms. It was a knee-jerk reaction. One she'd gotten used to making, apparently.

Someone had hurt Grace. Often.

Paul's jaw clenched as he saw Grace's reaction for what it was, but it didn't seem to surprise him. He loosened his grip and pretended Grace hadn't thought he was going to hurt her.

Grace recovered and forced her body to straighten. Her cheeks darkened further with embarrassment and she glued her eyes to the floor.

"Please stay, Grace," said Paul in a gentle, soft voice.

Seeing his long fingers wrapped around another woman made Andra's stomach turn. It didn't matter that it was just her arm. He might as well have been feeling her up, the way it made Andra burn with jealousy.

Before she realized what she was doing, Andra was off the bed, her fists clenched.

Paul's mouth curved with a knowing grin. He looked at Andra with his brows raised. "Problem?"

"No," she choked out.

"Liar."

Grace tugged against Paul's grip. "I really should go. I'm sorry to have disturbed you, my lady." The poor thing was nearly beside herself with embarrassment. It wasn't her fault Paul was fondling her.

"Let go of her, Paul."

"Not until you agree to let her help. She knows how to care for Nika. Don't you, Grace?"

Grace gave a shaky nod. "Yes, sir."

"Tell Andra how you know so she'll relax and let you help."

"My mother was comatose for two years before she died. We couldn't afford a hospital, so I cared for her." The way her voice broke, Andra was sure that the death had been recent.

All the residual jealousy burning inside Andra evaporated. Grace had lost her mother, too. That tied them together somehow. Made them sisters.

Grace would need a distraction—something to keep her occupied. Someone to talk to. "Let her go, Paul. She can stay."

Paul released her, and Grace stood still, vibrating with tension as if unsure what to do next.

Andra took pity on her. "Come here and meet my sister, Nika."

Paul slipped out of the room.

Grace stepped forward tentatively. She looked down at Nika, and the look of compassion that filled her eyes with tears told Andra that her sister would be safe with this woman. Grace would not allow her to come to harm. "How long has she been like this?"

"Not long. She's always been too thin, but it got worse this week."

"Does she have a feeding tube?"

"No. She didn't want one."

Grace nodded. "We'll have to get some fluids in her. When was the last time she was changed?"

"Changed?"

"Isn't she wearing a diaper?"

Andra hadn't even thought about that. She shook her head.

"That's okay. I can take care of it. I brought some absorbent pads along, as well as extra sheets. Just in case."

Paul came back toting a large box. He set it on the dresser. "Are you going to need anything else?"

"I'll have to put in an order for some diapers, but Torr's supplies will work until then."

Paul's jaw tightened. "How is he?"

Grace patted Nika's hand as if telling her everything would be okay. It was such a natural, unconscious gesture for her, Andra didn't even think she knew she was doing it. Maybe that was how she'd been with her mother.

"He's the same," said Grace.

"I should go see him." Paul's voice was heavy with grief, making Andra wonder who Torr was.

"Please don't." Grace blushed and looked at the floor. "I mean, I think it would be better if you didn't. I'm not sure he could stand seeing you ... like that." She motioned to her neck and pointed at the pale band of skin around his throat—where his luceria had hung before Andra had taken it from him.

"I understand. Will you give him my best when you see him again?"

"Yes, sir. I will. Thank you."

"We're glad you're with us, Grace. You've taken such good care of him."

"I'm not sure he'd agree."

Paul gave her a sad smile. "He's a proud man."

Andra peered into the box and saw sheets, some extra pillows, and cans of hospital-grade meal-replacement shakes. Maybe Grace did know what she was doing. She'd certainly thought this through better than Andra had.

"He's a good man. I pray the Sanguinar will find a way to help him," said Grace.

"I'm sure they will," said Paul, but he didn't look convinced.

Grace's face lit with hope.

Paul came up behind Andra. She could feel the heat of his body reaching out to her, drawing her in. "It's time for your ceremony, Andra."

"I need to stay and help."

Grace shook her head, keeping her eyes down. "It's best if you don't, my lady. When she's better, she'll be glad it was a stranger caring for her needs rather than you. It's less embarrassing that way."

Andra didn't care about that. She'd do whatever needed to be done to take care of Nika.

"Grace is right," said Paul. "And all the men are waiting. It won't take long."

Andra looked at Grace's sweet face. She was already sorting through the things in the box, her movements confident and sure. She knew what she was doing better than Andra did.

Paul looped his arm around her shoulders. "It will be fine. I promise."

Andra gave in. Taking a few minutes away, where she could think straight, was probably going to do Nika more good than if Andra stayed and made a mess of things. Besides, ceremonies were boring. She'd have plenty of time to think while they droned on about whatever formal garbage interested them. Maybe she'd even catch a quick nap.

As soon as they reached the large auditorium-like room and Andra stood face-to-face with dozens of large, intense-looking men, she knew napping wasn't in her immediate future. Every pair of eyes was on her—or more accurately, on her neck.

Her hand went to her throat in a nervous gesture. "Are these guys vampires?" she asked.

"No. Theronai. Like us."

"Why are they looking at me like they're really hungry and I'm a filet mignon?"

He lowered his voice and leaned close to her ear. "You're certainly edible, but they're staring because they're all hoping that you might be compatible with them the way you are with me."

"Can I bond with more than one of you?"

Paul hesitated and she felt a surge of fear clog their connection. "One at a time," he said, sounding like uttering the words had cost him dearly.

Andra slanted him a sideways glance, but his face was a stoic mask. He led her up to a raised platform, and one by one the men started taking off their shirts and lining up at the stairs.

"You know," she whispered to Paul, hoping to lighten his odd mood, "I've had some dreams that started out just like this."

He lifted a brow and nodded to the first man in line. "Yeah? I bet none of them have ended like this will, though."

The first man had a not-so-handsome face that was crisscrossed with thin scars, but she hardly noticed past his laser blue eyes. He walked up to her, knelt at her feet, sliced his chest open with his sword, and in a deep, solemn voice, said, "My life for yours, my lady."

A warmth curled around her, then solidified into a heaviness that bore down on her shoulders. Paul's strong arm held her around the waist and kept her steady.

"That's Nicholas Laith," said Paul.

The man rose, gave her a smile and a wink, and hopped off the platform to make room for the next man.

Each one of them went through the same routine, and each time, that invisible weight grew heavier. By the time the ceremony was over, Andra could hardly stand. Sweat had formed along her hairline and between her breasts, and she was shaking from head to toe.

"It's almost over," said Paul.

The last man came up to her. He'd hung at the back of the room the whole time, watching silently, standing apart from the rest. He had short brown hair and watchful black eyes. When he got close, Andra caught the faint scent of a forest in winter coming off of him—clean and cold. He didn't remove his shirt, which caused a stirring of whispers among the other men. Instead, he cut through the fabric, cutting deeper than the rest of the men, by the amount of blood he spilled.

"My life for yours," he vowed, refusing to bow his head, but instead looking into her eyes as he gave the words.

Andra stumbled under the weight, but Paul held her up. The man held out his hand, and the ring he wore was nearly white. Only the faintest trace of sapphire blue swirled beneath the surface.

Andra felt Paul's body tense around hers. The man said nothing, but there was a silent air of challenge in his stance.

"I won't give her up, Iain," said Paul. His voice was rough, almost a feral growl of sound.

Iain was silent, but he lifted Andra's hand and pressed

a hot kiss into her palm. She felt his tongue flick over her skin and quickly pulled her hand from his grasp.

In the center of her palm was a dark red mark, like the one Paul had placed on her before.

"How dare you put a bloodmark on my lady?" demanded Paul. Some primal, instinctive need to kill rose up in Paul, clogging their link with its power. Andra didn't understand the cause, but she knew what it meant.

He reached for his sword, but Iain's was already unsheathed. If she didn't stop this, it was going to end in bloodshed. Lots of it.

Andra stepped between the men, praying that Iain kept that lethal blade off her skin. "It's not going to happen, big boy," she told Paul. She forced him to look down at her, distracting him from the need to hurt Iain.

He stared at Iain, breathing hard, his color high. He still wasn't listening.

Andra pressed her hands to Paul's chest, digging her fingers in just enough to get him to listen. "I'm tired. Take me back to your place."

That got his attention. He blinked a couple of times and gave her a tight nod.

"Stay away from my woman," warned Paul.

"As long as she's yours, I will," said Iain.

Andra ignored the possessive comment in favor of averting disaster. She'd talk to Paul later about the fact that she was her own woman, but now, she needed to get him out of here. "Please, Paul," she said, letting her fatigue come through in her tone. "I need to lie down."

She tugged on him and finally he started to leave. Andra peeked over her shoulder as they exited the room and those watchful black eyes were locked right onto her. There was no warmth inside that man. None at all. If she hadn't seen his blood for herself, she would have sworn he had ice flowing inside his veins.

Chapter 22

Paul needed to stake his claim—make sure Andra knew that he wasn't letting her go to another man. Not while he drew breath.

It wasn't going to end with her the way it had with Kate.

Paul led Andra by the hand, pulling her down the hall faster than was comfortable for her. He forced himself to slow down and take her fatigue into account. It wasn't her fault that Iain was compatible with her.

He could feel fine tremors of worry and weariness cascading down her arm. The Theronai inside him demanded that he take action and force her to relax, but the man understood there was little he could do to make that happen, short of making Nika whole again.

"What was that all about?" she asked him. "Why did that guy leave a mark on my hand?"

"So he could find you later."

"Why would he need to find me?"

The last thing he wanted to do was tell her the truth, but he owed her at least that much. "Once our time together is up, you'll be free to bond with another man if you want. Iain wants to make sure that he's able to find you when that happens."

"What if I don't want to be attached to anyone for a while?"

"I'd like to be able to tell you that it's your choice, but times are desperate. Iain will do anything in his power to convince you to be with him." He paused, debating whether or not to tell her the rest. In the end, he couldn't hold back. "So will I."

"We still have some time before I have to think about that. Right now, I've got enough to deal with."

"First, you need to get some rest. You're exhausted, and that ceremony couldn't have been easy on you."

"Can we go outside and get some fresh air first? I just want to feel normal again for a few minutes."

"Sure. Whatever you want."

Andra nodded and followed behind him through his suite and out the sliding glass door. It was already hot, and the air was warm and heavy with humidity. The grounds were well tended, and flowers bloomed nearby, making the air smell sweet. There were no unnatural noises—no traffic, no flight patterns above to ruin the solitude of their home.

Paul pulled in a deep breath and tried to convey a sense of peace to Andra through their link.

She clutched at his hand and wrapped her free hand around his wrist, as if worried he'd try to pull away. He could feel the soft press of her breasts above his elbow, feel the rapid beat of her heart, subtle but strong against his skin.

"It's nice out here," she said. "Private."

He'd never enjoyed it so much as he did now, with her. "You'll always be welcome at Dabyr. No matter what happens."

"I think Nika will like it here when she wakes up."

Not *if*, but *when*. At least Andra hadn't lost her sense of hope. That was good.

"I'm sure she will."

She leaned against his shoulder and Paul wanted to shout with joy. Not only was she touching him, but she was looking to him for comfort. Needing him, if only a little.

He couldn't let her down, so he looped his arm around her and hugged her close. He stroked her arm and let out a deep, satisfied breath, letting her feel his sense of satisfaction and utter rightness. If he never got anything more from her, this gift of trust she offered would always be with him to ease him in his final days.

"There's a kind of peace about this place, isn't there?" she asked.

"There is. The Gerai make it a beautiful home for us. And it's safe here. Nothing can harm you here with so many Sentinels around."

She looked up at him. Her eyes were bloodshot. It was a sure sign she'd been using his power, straining herself. He hadn't felt the tug of energy leave his body, so she must not have been using very much. Then again, their conduit was still too new, so she could get only a trickle out of him.

Maybe the trust she was showing him now by letting him see her weak would help that change. He could hope.

"When Nika is better, you'll let her stay here, won't you?" she asked.

"Of course. We want both of you to stay."

She looked away then, but didn't pull away. She stayed pressed up against his body, letting him hold her. "I'll come visit, but I can't live here."

"Why not?"

"I need to work. I can't let any more children end up like my sisters."

"So, we'll work together. We got Sammy back, didn't we?"

He felt something rising up inside her—something that scared her and had done so for so long she didn't even notice it anymore. He tried to figure it out, but she blocked him, shutting him out. Paul didn't even think she realized what she was doing. It was like she was so used to hiding this facet of herself that she didn't even need to try.

"Are you poking around up there again?" she asked. Her fingers slid up his chest and toyed with the collar of his shirt.

"Maybe a little."

"See anything interesting?"

"Always. Everything about you intrigues me."

He felt her soften against him a little, lean a little harder against him, trusting him to hold her steady. Paul closed his eyes and reveled in her trust, as small as it was.

"Who is Torr?" she asked. "The man Grace was talking about?"

"He's a Theronai. One of our strongest, most capable fighters."

"What's wrong with him?"

Paul's chest tightened with grief. "He was injured the night we found Grace and her brother and rescued them from the Synestryn."

Andra patted his arm, soothing him. "What happened?"

"He was poisoned by a Synestryn we've never seen before. None of the Sanguinar know how to cure him, and he's been paralyzed from the neck down ever since."

"Poor man," breathed Andra. "I wish there was something we could do to help."

"Me, too."

"Why didn't Grace want you to go see him?" she asked.

Paul's arms tightened around Andra. She was more precious than she realized in so many ways. "I've found you. Seeing that is only going to make things harder for him."

"Why?"

"Because he's trapped. He can't go out and look for a

woman like you for himself. Unless the Sanguinar find a way to heal him, he's going to be stuck here, dependent on the care of others until he dies. He's a proud man. That must be a kind of living hell."

"Maybe the Sanguinar will figure out how to help him like they will with Nika."

"Maybe." Hope was a powerful thing, but it was in damn short supply right now.

She turned in his embrace until she was facing him. "You don't think they can help him, do you?"

Paul sighed. "They've been trying for weeks now with no success. Even with all the blood donations they've been getting, they just aren't powerful enough to fix everything."

"Once they fix Nika, I'll give Tynan my blood for him."

She was so generous, so strong, so beautiful. He couldn't help but love her.

Paul wasn't sure she could handle any heartfelt confessions right now, so he kept his feelings to himself. If she bothered to look, she'd see how he felt about her.

He cupped her cheek, reveling in the smoothness of her skin. "That would be good. Thank you."

"It's the least I can do."

Paul watched her mouth move and wished like hell he was kissing her.

"Your job is dangerous," she said. Her fingers slid up into his hair and she tugged his head down close to hers. "If anything . . . bad ever happened to you, I'd want someone to call me so I could come back and help you, too."

She was already talking about leaving as if it were a foregone conclusion. She wasn't even thinking about staying.

Make her stay. . . . Tie her to you.

It was Joseph's order and exactly what Paul wanted.

He wanted her tied to him so tightly she wouldn't be able to tell where she stopped and he started.

But what about what she wanted?

Make her want it.

He could do it. He just wasn't sure he should. His people needed her, but it wasn't his right to force her to do anything. Was it?

Paul closed his eyes to block out the sight of her. She was too tempting to his senses. Even with his eyes closed he could still smell her skin, warmed by the night air. His own body heated in response and he felt a fine sweat bead up along his brow.

He'd never do anything to hurt her. Not even for his brothers. But what was the harm in using his abilities to convince her she wanted to stay? Nika would be here, so she could be close to her sister. She'd be safer here than she would back in Omaha. He had plenty of money at his disposal, so he could give her material things, too. Not that those seemed to be important to her, but she might enjoy them. She'd be surrounded by friends, always cared for. Always loved.

"Paul? You okay?"

She sounded worried, but Paul couldn't bring himself to speak. This decision was too important and he was hovering on the edge.

Her fingers settled against his jaw. He hadn't shaved today and he was probably poking her skin with his beard. She didn't seem to mind.

He wondered if she'd mind his beard rasping against her breasts and belly as he kissed her. Maybe the inside of her thighs.

She shivered in his arms and let out a little moan of need.

He realized then that she'd slid into his thoughts, trying to figure out what was wrong when he didn't answer her. She'd seen the images that danced in his head—

images of her laid out naked before him, flushed and
rosy from his mouth.

Paul stood as still as a Sentinel stone. If he so much
as flinched, she might run the other way. He wanted her
too much, and in a way she could hardly begin to understand, based on her human upbringing.

She snuggled her hips against his and he was sure she
was able to feel what she did to him. How hard he was
for her.

"I'm not running," she told him.

"You should."

"Maybe. But I'm not. At least not yet." She kissed
the corner of his mouth and Paul had to hold himself
back from taking control and kissing her like he really
wanted.

"What if it's now or never? What if I don't let you
go?" he asked.

She let out a sweet, feminine laugh. "I suppose we'll
just have to see how that works for you. For now, I'm
yours." She ran her hands down his back until she was
cupping his ass. "And you're mine."

"Yes, I am." He lifted her face and kissed her, trying
to tell her without words how much she meant to him
and his people. How precious she was. How much he
loved her.

His ring buzzed happily, warming his finger.

Andra melted into him and opened her mouth under
his. Her wicked little tongue dancing against his sent a
shock of pleasure down his spine. He groaned into her
mouth and tilted her head back so he could kiss her
deeper.

All that lust that Tynan had planted in him as a joke
came roaring back to life. His blood felt as if it were on
fire and his heart pounded hard enough that he was sure
they could hear it all the way in the dining hall. Paul
tried to stay in control, but it was a futile effort—a battle
lost before it even began.

He picked her up and carried her inside to his bedroom before he lost his mind and took her out here, where anyone could pass by. For now, she was his and only his, and he didn't want anyone else seeing her naked.

And she was definitely going to be naked as soon as he could manage it.

Andra pulled her mouth away from his just as he cleared the bedroom door. "Not here. Grace will hear us."

"I don't care."

"I do."

"Then block the sound. Put up a barrier to keep it from leaving the room."

"I can do that?"

Paul didn't want to talk or teach her anything right now. He wanted to take her and make her come so hard so many times she'd never be able to live without him. "Yes," he said between clenched teeth.

Paul set her on the bed and felt a tug of power as it left his body. The air around them shifted and his ears popped as she put the barrier in place.

He pushed her back onto the mattress and covered her with his body so she couldn't get away. A dark grin pulled at his mouth. "Now you can be as loud as you like."

"Think you can make me scream?" It was a challenge. One Paul was more than ready to accept.

Actions spoke louder than words, so instead of answering her, he simply bundled up all the searing lust writhing inside him and shoved it through their link. The conduit connecting them trembled at the force of his need for her.

So did Andra.

She arched up off the bed and sucked in a gasping breath. Her eyes widened in shock and her fingernails dug into his arms hard enough to leave marks.

"Oh. My. God." Her voice was rough with unsated lust, but not for long.

Paul couldn't take his eyes off her. He loved seeing her this way, nearly helpless in her need, knowing he was the only man who could ease her and give her what she wanted.

"No one else can ever make you feel like this," he growled at her. "Only me."

"Don't stop. Please."

Paul straddled her hips and slipped his fingers under the hem of her shirt, rubbing his knuckles across her stomach. She was soft and smooth and he'd never get enough of touching her, not if he lived forever. "You like that?"

Her low groan was his only response.

"Stay still and I'll give you what you want."

She looked up at him in question. Her blue eyes were dark with desire. Her mouth was already puffy from his kisses. By the time he was finished, it would be a lot more so.

Andra reached for him, but he captured her hand and placed it on the pillow by her head. "Don't move or I'll stop."

She nodded her understanding and Paul slid another wave of lust through their link. It flowed easier this time, hardly taking him any effort at all to make her gasp and writhe beneath him.

Beautiful.

Paul unbuckled his sword belt and propped it against the nightstand so it was still within easy reach. Now that it was out of the way, he could move more easily without fear of scratching her. He scooted down her legs enough that he could unbutton her jeans. He slid the zipper down and peeled back the denim. Her dainty pink panties made his stomach clench with desire.

Andra whimpered as if she'd felt it, too. Maybe she had. She wasn't blocking him out. She was open and receptive to him, soaking up everything he gave her.

She reached for him, but Paul said, "No, you don't. I'm not finished yet."

Her arm fell back to her side, but her fist was clenched in frustration. Her eyes warned him of retribution, but he didn't care. He could hardly wait to see what she'd come up with.

Paul bent down and blew a puff of air over her belly button. Andra sighed and her stomach tightened, showing off the muscles in her abs. So pretty. His fingers barely brushed her skin, just stirring the fine hair.

She shuddered and her breathing sped up. A warm flush spread down her body, and Paul had to strip her bare and see just how far it went.

He took his time getting her undressed, kissing each new patch of skin as it was revealed. By the time he was through, they were both sweating and shaking with arousal. He could smell the scent of her need and it served only to heighten his own. He wasn't sure how much more he could stand.

As much as he'd wanted to tease her, going so slowly had done the same for him. He enjoyed every kiss, every swipe of his tongue over her flesh, but it wasn't enough. Not nearly. He wanted to be inside her sweet body as deeply as he was inside her mind. Filling her up so there was no room for any other man but him.

He stripped himself while she watched.

His ring was hot with the demands he was putting on the luceria. Their connection was still too new and fragile for the amount of power flowing between them, and yet he couldn't stop. He needed to push her more—tie them together more tightly with his power.

Make her stay.

The skin beneath her necklace was bright red. He ran his finger across the slippery band and it was hot and seething with rich plumes of sapphire blue.

"You're killing me," she breathed, clenching the sheets in her fist.

Paul covered her body with his and nudged her thighs wide so there was room for him between them. She arched up, trying to merge them together, but he evaded her and pinned her to the bed, holding her there with his weight. His erection throbbed with need, spilling liquid drops against her inner thigh.

"Tell me you want it," he demanded.

His fierce little warrior glared at him in frustration, which only made him that much harder. "You know I do, damn you."

"No other man could ever make you feel this way—make you want it the way I do. You know that, don't you?" He sent an image into her, along with his words. He showed her how pretty she looked when she came around his cock, reminded her how good it felt when she did.

"God, yes. More."

In the end, he could deny her nothing. Whatever he had to give, it was hers. So he slid inside her, relishing the slick heat of her body yielding to his. "Look at me."

She opened her eyes, which had darkened with passion until they were the same sapphire blue as the luceria. When she reached for him this time, he didn't stop her. Her fingers brushed over his brow and down his cheeks until they settled as light as butterflies on his jaw.

Her body tightened around his erection, making him suck in a hissing breath. At the same time, he felt her use their link to push back some of the desire she was feeling for him, the way he'd done to her.

Her need was softer, less jagged and harsh than his own, but no less demanding. He let it fill him up and swell inside him, warming all the dark places that had stood empty and cold for so long. He'd never really known how lonely he'd been until now—until she'd swept it all away and made him whole.

"I get it now," she whispered.

"Get what?"

"Intimacy. The two of us together, like this, sharing the same space. It has a kind of magic to it."

That made him smile. "It does. Want to see another trick?"

"Mmm. I can hardly wait."

He didn't make her. He lowered his mouth and fit it perfectly to hers. She tasted of hope and silent wishes, and he couldn't get enough of her.

His hand glided along her flank, soaking up her heat while he slid inside her mind and let it merge completely with his own. She didn't resist. In fact, she welcomed him with a soft sigh of surrender.

Instantly, Paul's perceptions shifted until he could see what she saw, feel what she felt.

Through her mind, he saw himself as he hovered above her. His face was rigid with the strain of self-control. Muscles in his chest and arms bulged and the veins throbbed with his lust-heated blood. His lifemark was in full bloom, bright green with the merest hint of baby leaves just beginning to form. His hair was a mess, but she found it charming. Her skin was hot and so sensitive to his touch she could feel the minute ridges of his fingerprints rasping against her flesh. Her breasts ached for the wet heat of his mouth and the slippery glide of his tongue. The walls of her sex stretched to accept him, and yet she hadn't once complained.

"Wow," she breathed. "That is . . . Wow."

So she was feeling him as well, which meant she could feel that there was nothing gentle about his need. It clawed at him to thrust hard and deep, to take her and come inside her.

Her tone was high and desperate. "You really need to move now."

Paul moved. He slid out of her and back, letting his body move to please her most. He bent so he could kiss her breasts and love her nipples with his tongue and teeth. Andra clenched around him, and he could already feel her drawing near a climax. She responded to him so fast it humbled him. He'd never had a lover as responsive as she was.

"Don't you dare think about another woman right now," she warned him. Jealousy surged through her, making her words come out in a fierce snarl. Her nails dug into his scalp and sent streamers of sensation rioting along his spine.

At this rate, he wasn't going to last long, either. Not that he minded. She was right there with him, showing him what she needed, and he was more than willing to give it to her. Whatever she wanted.

He pushed her to the edge and held her hovering there, driving deep inside her with each powerful thrust of his hips. He knew just when to pull back to keep her on the brink, quieting her with soft strokes of his hand. Finally, after the third time he'd done it, she grabbed his shoulders and used a surge of magically enhanced power to flip him over until she was straddling him.

Her head fell back on a sigh of pleasure as she sank down on his erection. Her breasts were red from his stubble, and her nipples were puckered and distended from his mouth. Her ribs expanded with every heavy breath she took, and sweat gleamed on her flushed skin.

Andra braced her hands on his chest and rocked her hips. The branches of his lifemark swayed in response to her touch, arching toward her splayed fingers.

Paul felt a zing of sensation every time she ground herself against him just the right way. Whether it was hers or his, he couldn't tell. It didn't matter anymore. All the sensations they felt, they shared, and he could no longer separate them. She squeezed him tight and now he was the one on the edge, gritting his teeth to hold back his climax just a little longer.

It didn't work. She sped her pace and it sent her flying into her orgasm headfirst. Paul was right there with her. His body tensed and he let out a rough shout of completion as the first wave of release crashed against him. Andra's voice rose along with his, echoing off the barrier she'd created around the two of them.

Paul pulled her close and kissed her open mouth as he came inside her. His vision faded, but he didn't care. He had the feel of her against his body and in his mind, the sound of her voice singing in his ears, the taste of her on his tongue, and the scent of her in his lungs. And still, it wasn't enough to sate him. He'd never get enough of her.

Their bodies quieted until only small quivers of their climax remained. She was draped limply over his chest, breathing hard. Paul gathered her limbs and rolled her over, but couldn't bring himself to leave her body. Not yet.

He arranged her arms until she looked comfortable. By the time he was finished, she was pulling away from him, seeping out of his mind so that the space felt empty and darker somehow.

"You're leaving me?"

"I thought you'd want your space now that we're done," she said.

She still didn't get it. "This is the way it's supposed to be between us. Not just during sex, either."

"I don't think I can handle having you in my head all the time. It's a little crowded up there."

The comment hurt his feelings, but he tried not to let it show. "It didn't feel crowded to me."

"You're used to all of this." She pushed against his chest and he took the not-so-subtle hint that she wanted him to move away.

Paul didn't budge. He liked being inside her too much. In fact, he could probably go another couple of rounds before he wore himself out enough to stop. Just looking at her, knowing that flush over her skin was his doing, made him hard. "You'd get used to it, too, if you'd let yourself."

"I'm giving you almost a week. What more do you want?"

"A lifetime," he shot back at her. "Several, actually."

She frowned as if she hadn't understood what he said, but then he saw her eyes widen in shock as she realized he was speaking literally. She prodded at his mind, seeking the truth; then she pulled out completely and a thick wall slammed down between them.

Shit. He'd lost her. Scared her off.

"You can't mean that."

"I do. You're mine, and I'm keeping you." To emphasize his point, he ground his hips against hers, making her feel every inch of him still hot and hard within her.

Her eyes fluttered shut and she bit her lip to hold back a soft sound of pleasure. He heard it anyway.

"Stop. Please. This is too much."

It wasn't nearly enough. The need to possess her was raging inside of him. He had to find a way to keep her forever. Three days were never going to be enough. Hell, forever might not be, either.

Make her stay.

It was an order, given to him by their chosen leader. Defying that was the same thing as betraying his people. He had to make her stay.

That brilliant, glowing pool of power inside him swelled in response. He'd never been able to access it before Andra, but now that he was connected to her, he could use their link to draw upon that power and channel it through her for short periods of time. He could use it to do his will. To make Andra do the same.

"What are you doing?" she asked in a weak, frightened voice.

Paul didn't answer. Instead, he called to his power and felt the seething waves of it rise to do his bidding. He channeled a thick column of it toward their link.

"Paul," she whispered. "You can't. I can't take that much."

"You can. You will." That didn't sound like him. There was a dark, discordant note in his words, as if there were another voice speaking along with him, harsh and out of harmony.

The closer the column of glowing energy got to their link, the more it looked as though he were trying to channel a waterfall through a drinking straw. Maybe she was right. Maybe it was too much.

But it felt so good. He was close to something important—some kind of breakthrough that would change his life.

"Please." Andra's voice sounded faint and far away.

"Just relax," he said in that jumbled voice. "It will be easier on you."

The first drops of energy hit their link. Power slingshot from him, through her, back into him. The feeling was amazing. Sparks dribbled from his fingertips and slid over Andra's skin, leaving angry red streaks behind.

He'd heal her later, when it was over and she belonged to him forever.

"You're hurting me."

He paused. Something here wasn't right. He just couldn't figure out what it was.

"Paul!" His name was a shout of pain.

He was hurting Andra. Killing her with his need for her to stay by his side. He loved her and he was killing her.

He couldn't do it. He had to stop.

That massive column of power plummeted back into the glowing ocean inside him. Searing agony streaked out through his limbs, but he gritted his teeth and took it. His body locked up against the pain.

"You need to breathe, damn it," he heard Andra say. She was so far away.

His lungs were crushed under a wave of pressure. There was no room to breathe.

Then her mouth was on his, kissing him, filling him up

with air. He wished he could see her. She was so beautiful. He wanted to see her again before he died.

"You're not going to die unless I'm the one doing the killing." Another breath filled him.

Andra pulled at his power, though he had no idea what she was doing with it. Whatever it was, it felt good. Cool. Clean. Just like her.

Mine.

That thought ricocheted around in his head so loudly he was sure she'd heard it. He was just as sure she wasn't going to like it.

Chapter 23

Andra pulled back in shock at the possessiveness inside him. He wasn't just playing at the caveman attitude. He really meant it. As in forever, which for him was a really long time.

She had no idea why he would want to be stuck with one person for so long, much less someone who failed as often as she did. He had to have suffered some kind of brain damage at some point. That was the only explanation she could think of.

He'd seen inside her. He knew how horribly she'd failed her family when it meant the most that she succeed. He'd seen the repercussions of her failure in every one of Nika's terrified delusions.

Nika was dying because Andra had failed, and yet Paul still wanted her. Didn't he know she would only end up getting him killed, too?

He was sleeping now. She could feel the restful waves drifting out of him. They calmed her frantic need to run away enough to allow her to stay by his side.

Andra smoothed his messy hair away from his face. He was such a sexy man, so handsome in a rough sort of way, with just enough bad boy in him to make her panties perpetually wet. He was a walking fantasy. His thick, demanding erection was just an added bonus.

He'd come, but was still hard. For her. She'd seen that

clearly enough to know the truth. He wasn't closing his eyes and thinking of someone else when he took her. He wanted only her.

Part of her glowed with the knowledge, but the rest of her was wondering how he could feel that way when he knew just how flawed she really was.

Maybe it didn't matter what a coward she could be so long as he liked her body. Yeah, that was probably it. Made perfect sense.

And hurt like hell.

Andra scrubbed her face with her hands. She'd been so confused since she'd met him. Everything had been turned upside down and she was always one step behind, frantically trying to catch up and figure out what was going on.

If it helped Nika, it would all be worth it. She'd go on her way, and maybe when she came back to visit her sister, she could see Paul, too.

That would be nice. She didn't want to belong to him or tie him down, but she didn't want to never see him again, either. They could date when things weren't so crazy and maybe get to know each other like normal people. Or, at least as normal as people like them could ever be.

She would enjoy getting used to having a big, sexy, sword-wielding warrior with a nonstop erection around. What girl wouldn't?

It could work. They might even end up close enough that she'd be willing to give that forever thing a shot—once she was sure he knew she wasn't the dependable sort. As long as he got rid of his delusions about her, she'd be willing to try. Chances were it wouldn't work, but they sure would have fun giving it a try.

Madoc pressed his cheek to the bare wall, wishing he could slide through the faded paint. He knew the walls of the suites at Dabyr were insulated against noise, and there was no way he could hear Nika's heart beating. But he could feel it. Just on the other side of the wall. Faint, but steady. She was still alive.

Pain racked his body, but even so, some of the brittleness in his bones bled away as he pressed himself as close as he could get to her.

The suite next to Paul's—the one Madoc was in—was empty. No one would be coming by. Nicholas's electronic eyes couldn't see him in here. It was just him and the steady beat of Nika's heart. Alone together.

He didn't know why he was here. He had no business being here. He needed to be out there, fighting. Fucking. Blowing off some pressure so he could keep going for just a little longer. Just long enough to know she was going to be okay.

It shouldn't have mattered to him, but apparently enough of his soul was left that it did. He wasn't sure anymore how much of a good thing that was, but he accepted it—like he accepted the pain pounding through him with every breath.

As soon as she woke up, he promised himself he'd leave. He'd go and never come back. He wasn't sure how much longer he could trust himself to stay away from her.

And if she bonded to one of the men here, he was pretty sure he'd go lethal. It was best to leave before that happened. But not until she was better. Not until she was safe.

Zach wheeled Torr outside where he could watch the sunset. They both needed some fresh air and Zach really needed a sanity check. All of his friends were slipping away. Kevin and Thomas were dead, both in the past few weeks. Drake had Helen now. They were still spending every second together, and as much as he was happy for his buddy, he was so jealous it made his stomach burn. He could hardly stand to look at Drake anymore without wishing for that same kind of happiness so hard he ached down to his bones.

Lexi was gone. He couldn't feel her today, though every once in a while—every few days—his bloodmark would suddenly start doing its job again and he'd get a hint as to her direction. It never lasted long enough for him to track her, and every time he got that little ping, it was from a different location.

She was always moving. Always running.

He didn't even know why she was so afraid of him. She'd never stopped long enough for him to find out.

Zach parked the wheelchair near a bench along the sidewalk. The grounds here were parklike—perfectly trimmed grass interspersed with beds of flowers and huge, towering trees covered the land. Their new head gardener apparently had a knack for his job. The place had never looked nicer.

Torr stared straight ahead, not bothering to turn toward Zach even though he could still move his head. The rest of him was paralyzed, and already, the heavy muscles that had powered his body were shrinking and fading away, leaving only a hint of what he once had been. The decay had been so fast, Zach was sure the man wasn't going to last much longer.

"How you holding up, man?" asked Zach.

Torr's amber eyes glowed with anger. "How do you think? How well would you be holding up if your body was a useless pile of bones and you had a tube up your dick so you didn't wet yourself?"

Zach wanted to offer Torr peace, but he had none to spare. "I'm sorry."

"Yeah, we're all fucking sorry. All of us except Joseph. He denied my request again." Rage vibrated in his tone, and a hint of something else. Something helpless and desperate.

"He's not going to let you die yet. You haven't given the Sanguinar enough time."

"If you were sitting here, you'd know that was a lie. Every day in this body is an eternity. It's time to let it end."

Zach clasped Torr's arm, even though he knew the other man couldn't feel it. "We can't give up on you yet."

"So instead, you torture me? How kind."

"How would you feel if it was me sitting there? Would you give up on me?"

Torr turned his head then. Torr glared at Zach with so much fury lurking in his eyes that Zach almost had to look away. But he didn't. He owed his friend more than cheap denial and avoidance.

"If you were sitting in this chair, I'd love you enough to slit your throat and watch you die."

"No, you wouldn't. You'd be out there searching for that thing that bit you. You'd be bleeding into the mouth of a leech every other day. You'd be fighting to save my life."

Torr looked away and his voice dropped to a quiet, solemn tone. "You're wrong, but I forgive you."

It sounded as if he were saying good-bye, and Zach felt a stab of worry. "You're not going to die, Torr. We're going to fix this thing."

"You'd better hurry, then."

"Why? Because you're going to give up?"

"I already have. If Joseph won't kill me, I'll do the damn job myself."

"How are you going to do that? No one is going to help you."

"I heard about the women Paul brought here. Grace told me she had to go help because one of them was dying because she couldn't eat."

Zach put the pieces together. "No fucking way."

"I've stopped eating. Don't know why I didn't think of it before. Guess I just wasn't thinking clearly."

"Joseph won't let it happen."

"I'm not giving him a choice. I'm done. Four hundred years is enough for any man."

Zach couldn't let his friend give up like this. He knew Torr was suffering, but if he just held out a little longer, the Sanguinar would figure out something. "Don't do it. Come with me to find Lexi."

Torr gave a humorless laugh. "Sure. Why the hell not? Just strap me to the roof of your car and we'll go on a road trip."

"I mean it. Let's get you out of here for a while. The change of scenery might do you some good."

Torr's jaw clenched. "The only thing that's going to do me some good is a sword through my heart."

"No. We've started finding our women again. What if yours is out there, too?"

"What if she is? It's not going to make a difference now. I'm not going to tie down a female when she might be able to save a man who can actually do some good."

"I can't believe you're giving up."

"No? Try sitting here for a while and you'll believe it. I'm done, Zach. I've had a good run. It's time to let go. I have."

"I'm not giving up on you yet."

"Fine. Waste your time. I just don't care anymore."

"I do. I want to help you get through this."

Torr stared out into the night, but he was seeing something else. "There is one thing you can do for me."

"I'm not going to kill you."

His mouth flattened in frustration. "No. This is something else."

"Name it."

"I don't want Grace taking care of me anymore."

"Why not? Isn't she treating you well? I thought she was—"

"That's the problem. She's too nice. Too innocent. She shouldn't have to see what I'm going to do to myself."

"Then don't do it."

"I've already made up my mind," said Torr.

"Sorry. I'm not going to make this easier on you. As far as I'm concerned, Grace is staying."

Torr's face darkened with humiliation. "I don't want her around, damn it."

Zach was beginning to suspect there was more to it than Torr's concern for her. "You like her."

"I'm protecting her, as my vow demands. She's too soft for her own good."

Torr felt something for the woman. Zach was almost sure of it. Almost. "I like 'em soft. I could take her off your hands for a while, I guess. Hunting for Lexi has kept me so busy it's been a long time since I got laid."

Torr's nostrils flared in anger and his voice whipped out like a lash. "Don't you fucking touch her."

Zach grinned. "I knew it. You do like her."

"You are such a bastard," growled Torr. "You'd better pray I never walk again, because the first thing I'd do is kick your ass."

Zach crossed his arms over his chest and gave Torr a taunting grin. He hadn't gotten that sanity check he needed, but he'd found Torr's reason to live. It was good enough for him.

Andra was gone when Paul woke up. He reached for her before he remembered what had happened. By the time his hand hit the cool, vacant sheets, he remembered everything he'd done and already knew she wouldn't be there.

He got out of bed, wrapped the sheet around his hips, and sought her out. He couldn't face her right now, not after what he'd almost done, but he had to know she was safe and close by.

He found Andra in Nika's room, lying next to her with her back to the door, stroking Nika's white hair. Soft, comforting words rose from her, but Paul couldn't hear what they were. Grace was sitting in the corner of the room, knitting or crocheting or something else involving lots of yarn. She hummed to herself as her fingers moved so fast they blurred.

Grace looked up at him, finally noticing him, and her body tightened as if she were about to jump up. He didn't know why she was nervous around him, but he held his free hand up and shook his head, telling her to stay where she was.

He needed a shower and some time to pull himself together and figure out how to fix what he'd done.

Disgust left a bitter taste at the back of his throat that wouldn't go away. He'd showered and dressed and still had no clue how to approach Andra with his apology for his lapse in judgment.

He wasn't even sure she really knew what he'd been trying to do to her. She knew it hurt, but she might not know why.

He'd been ready to enslave her. Even the thought made him sick.

A knock at his door pulled him from his angst. He finished strapping his sword around his hips and went to answer it.

Cain stood there, filling the doorway with his bulk. His moss green eyes were dull and red, as if he hadn't slept in days. The scent of combat clung to his skin, and dust coated his clothing. Wherever he'd been, it hadn't been fun.

"Sibyl sent me," he said without preamble.

"Did she accept our request?"

Cain nodded, but didn't look pleased. "She said she'd see you first thing in the morning."

"Why not now? The night's still young."

"We just got back from hunting and we're exhausted. The child needs her rest."

"What happened?"

Cain rubbed his temples. Weariness hung heavily

on his frame, weighing him down. "Ask Angus, but you probably don't want to know. I'm going to crash."

"Thanks," said Paul. "Andra will be relieved to know there's still hope."

Cain looked as if he were going to say something else, but settled on, "Don't expect any miracles. Sibyl's been acting a little strange lately."

"Sibyl always acts strange." She was perpetually eight years old and could see the future. That was weird on any scale.

"More than normal, I mean. Just cut her some slack, okay?"

"We need her."

Cain sighed. "I know. Everyone does. That's the problem."

"I swear this has got to be harder on you than it is on her."

"She's like a daughter to me," said Cain.

Paul wondered what that must be like—to have a child he could call his own. "That sounds nice."

"Some days, yeah."

But not today, apparently.

Cain shoved away from the doorframe. "I'm going to sleep. See you around eight tomorrow morning, okay?"

"We'll be there."

Chapter 24

Gilda couldn't stop shaking. Every ounce of strength had been wrung from her when she opened that portal. She couldn't even hold on to Angus as he carried her back to their suite. Not that he needed the help. His arms were strong and solid around her, holding her easily against his chest as if he hadn't also spent the last few hours fighting nonstop.

His gait was a little unsteady from the wound in his left thigh. It wasn't life threatening, but the urge to mend him was nearly overwhelming.

"Later," he told her, knowing her thoughts. "I'll be fine for a few hours. You need to rest."

The idea of sleeping made a scream bubble up in her throat. Every time she closed her eyes she saw that . . . abomination. She still wasn't sure if it was real or if she'd imagined it.

"It was real," growled Angus. His arms tightened a bit around her as if trying to protect her from it even now.

"I need to get clean."

"A bath can wait. You need rest."

She could still smell the stench of that thing burning—hear the screams ripping from its tiny lungs.

God, what had they done? It was just a child.

"Not a child—a demon. It tried to kill Sibyl. We did what we had to."

It had looked so ... human. How was that possible? Gilda swallowed hard, trying to stave off her tears.

She'd killed a child tonight. And tomorrow, she was going to have to hunt for more and kill them, too.

"Don't think about it right now. Later, after you've rested, you'll see things more clearly."

They neared their suite and the lock opened for Angus. He nodded to the camera outside their door—a silent thanks to Nicholas, who was undoubtedly the one on the other end.

"None of this makes sense," she told her husband as he set her down on their bed.

"Of course not. We're all too tired to make any sense of it. Let it go tonight. Tomorrow we'll figure out what needs to be done."

"I need a bath." She sounded desperate, but she had to wash the smell of that child's burning flesh from her hair.

"Okay, love. I'll run one for you. Stay put."

Gilda couldn't support her weight enough to stay upright. She slumped onto the pillows and felt tears slide over her temple, soaking into the covers. Her eyes stung and she knew they were probably bloodshot from the amount of power she'd channeled tonight.

At least Angus wouldn't know she'd cried. She loved him too much to make him suffer through her tears.

The fall of water splashing into the tub filled the quiet and helped block out the echoes of those small screams.

She couldn't do that again. Not ever. She'd lost too many of her own babies over the centuries to take another from some other mother. Even she was not that cruel.

The Synestryn had finally won. They'd found a way to protect their progeny from the Sentinels by giving them human faces.

If she hadn't seen it for herself, she never would have believed it.

"The bath is ready," said Angus. His strong body was outlined by the light from the bathroom. Even after all these centuries, he was still as strong and steady as he'd been when she first met him.

She still didn't understand why he loved her. She'd done so many horrible things. Tonight was just one more.

"Stop it," said Angus in the tone he used to command the Theronai. "We did the right thing tonight. I won't have you killing yourself with guilt."

Despite his harsh tone, his fingers were gentle as they undid the row of buttons down the front of her gown. She'd have to burn the gray silk. She'd never be able to wear it again without thinking of what she'd done wearing it tonight.

Angus stripped her naked, then did the same for himself. His lean body was roped with muscles, and even though he had more gray hair now, more scars, he was still beautiful to her.

He picked her up again and headed for the bathroom. "That's right," he whispered. "You just think about the good things for now. We're together. We love each other. We're safe and healthy and surrounded by friends."

"How can you do that? How can you always see the good in things?"

He settled them into the big tub together, holding her close so her weak body wouldn't slip under the water. "Because I have you. All the rest of the world could fall away and as long as I still had you, I'd count myself lucky."

He was too good for her, but she'd always known that. It was only one of her many secrets.

Maybe it was time to tell him about her betrayal. If anyone was capable of forgiving her, it was Angus.

If.

That was the problem. Without him, she'd be lost. As

selfish as it was, she couldn't risk that. She needed him too much. She'd driven everyone else she loved away.

Gilda reinforced the door on that secret part of her mind, making sure it was tightly locked and barred so he'd never see—never even suspect it was there. She'd do anything to take back what she'd done, but it was too late for that. She was going to have to live with it—one more mistake to add to the list of unforgivable ones she'd made. There were so many, she wished she'd lose count, but she never did. She remembered every one of them.

"Good news," said Paul from the doorway. "Sibyl has agreed to see you."

Andra closed her eyes and gave a quick prayer of thanks. She kissed Nika's head and eased off the bed.

Paul was shirtless, and the sight of all those masculine ridges made her heart pound. It didn't matter that she'd had him only a few hours ago. She wanted more. She probably always would.

"Do you think she can help?" asked Andra.

"It's possible."

Grace had been knitting in the corner of the room for hours, but her needles stopped then. She kept her eyes lowered when she spoke. "I've heard about some of the things Sibyl knows. She's amazing, my lady. I'm sure she'll be able to help Nika."

Andra wanted to hug Grace for being so sweet. She might be timid and shy, but she wasn't going to let it get in the way of lending someone else comfort. "Thank you, Grace."

She blushed and her needles started moving again, though not as smoothly as before.

"Let's take a walk," said Paul, obviously wanting to talk to her. "Grace can hold down the fort, right?"

"Yes, sir."

Andra nodded and followed him outside. Dawn was

just starting to make the faintest glow against the eastern horizon. The rest of the sky was filled with stars.

Paul was oddly quiet, almost somber. And he wasn't touching her, which wasn't like him at all.

"Is something wrong?" she asked.

He looked like he didn't want to talk. His jaw was bunched, but he finally gave up the fight. "Yeah. I shouldn't have done what I did to you last night. It was inexcusable."

Andra frowned at him, at a total loss. She even tried to peek into his mind to figure out what he meant, but all she met was a solid wall. He wasn't letting her in and it made her feel . . . lonely. She'd gotten used to sharing thoughts with him and realized how much she was going to miss that when she left. "We shouldn't have had sex?"

"No. Of course not that. I'm talking about what happened after."

When he'd hurt her. "Forget about it," she said. "I have."

"How can you say that? I tried to take away your free will last night. *I tried to enslave you.*"

"And it hurt like hell, so don't ever try it again or I'll have to kick your ass."

He pulled her to a stop under a huge maple tree. The feel of his hand on her arm warmed her from the inside out. She liked him touching her way too much for her own good.

"You still don't get it, do you?" said Paul. "I violated you. I tried to do to you the very thing that I kill others for doing."

He really was making a bigger deal out of this than it was. "Listen, I knew you wouldn't do it. You're not like that. You don't have it in you."

"How do you know?"

"I've been poking around in your head for a couple of days now. You're a good guy. You just lost your head for a minute. No big deal."

His mouth was hanging open in shock. Andra smiled and gave him a quick kiss.

At least, she'd intended it to be quick. Instead, he grabbed her arms and held on to her, kissing her back with a desperation so strong it startled her.

When he finally let her come back up for air, she was dizzy and clung to his wide shoulders. "What was that for?"

"For being the perfect woman."

Andra snorted. "I think you need some more sleep. You're not thinking straight."

He knelt at her feet and clasped her hands tightly in his. She could feel the calluses his sword had worn into his skin and they were oddly comforting to her. He was a warrior, capable of keeping her and Nika safe.

If she stayed.

Her resolve to leave wavered. She didn't have much out there waiting for her. He was right that she could do her job from wherever she was. And he would help her. She was sure of it. He'd never leave a child alone and afraid.

Paul pressed his palm flat on the earth and she felt that same kind of humming she'd felt earlier tonight. Only this time it didn't hurt. The power flowed through her easily in a gentle trickle that warmed her skin.

The ground beneath them trembled. Paul lifted his fist to her, and when he opened his hand, a gold band shone against his palm.

"I thought you might feel more comfortable being with me in the way of the humans, since you were raised as one."

Andra blinked, unsure her eyes were working. Paul stood and slid the gold ring onto her left hand. "Marry me, Andra. Stay with me."

Shock froze her in place and stole the breath from her lungs. She looked down at the ring on her finger. It fit perfectly, glowing without a blemish or scratch. She had no idea how he'd done it.

She had no idea why he'd want her.

"I can't," she whispered. She wanted to say yes, but she couldn't do that to him. Or herself. He wanted a partner—someone who could stand by his side and fight the Synestryn, someone he could count on. Andra wasn't that person. She failed when it mattered most, and she didn't want that for Paul.

She couldn't be what he wanted. If she loved him, she had to free him to find another woman who could. And she did love him. She knew she did because her heart broke open and bled that she had to let him go.

"I'm sorry, Paul. I just can't."

His expression hardened, hiding the rejection she knew he had to be feeling. He opened his mouth to say something, but before he could, sirens screamed an alarm into the night.

"Nika." Andra turned and ran back to Paul's suite, hearing his pounding footsteps right behind her.

When they got to the room, Grace was standing in the doorway and Andra could see Nika behind her. There was no blood, no monsters. She was safe.

Paul picked up the phone and dialed.

"What's going on?" asked Grace.

"I don't know."

Paul dropped the phone and went to the closet by the front door. He pulled out a heavy leather jacket and zipped it up, pulled some clear safety glasses from the pocket, and slid those on as well. "The compound has been breached," he said. "I need to go help fight off the attack."

"I'm coming with you," said Andra.

His face was stone cold when he looked at her. "Whatever. But I'm not waiting." He pulled another jacket from the closet and tossed it to her. "Don't come out without some protective gear on."

Andra nodded and asked Grace, "Can you keep Nika safe?"

"Yes, my lady. I'll have her moved to one of the safe rooms."

Andra slid the jacket on and fumbled for the safety glasses in the pocket. "Do you need help?"

Paul left and didn't look back.

Grace shook her head, making her curls bob. "No. I can get one of the human men to help me move her. You'd better go. They're going to need you."

Andra nodded once and ran after Paul.

Chapter 25

Andra didn't see Paul, but she found the fight easily enough. It was raging in an open field at the rear of the compound near the dining hall. Unearthly howls rose up from the fray, clashing with the sickening thuds of steel striking bone. Swords flashed in the predawn light as nearly two dozen men fought off the attack.

The field was littered with Synestryn bodies, but more of the monsters slithered out of the trees to the west. Some she'd seen before; others she hadn't. Each of them was scary enough to make her wish for a bed to hide under. That and her shotgun.

Andra had been in combat before, but never like this. There were so many of them. Dozens. Maybe hundreds. She couldn't tell with all the thrashing bodies. It wasn't light out yet, and although the security lights helped, there were still too many shadows. Too many places for more of these things to hide.

Fear slid under her skin, making it cold and clammy. She stood inside, watching all of this through the glass, trying to absorb it enough to get herself moving.

She had to do something. People were going to die.

Along the far side of the field stood a woman who wouldn't have even reached Andra's shoulder. She was dressed in a flowing robe of gray silk with her long dark hair hanging nearly to her hips. She had that delicate bone structure that made Andra feel like an elephant, but there was nothing weak about her. Four monsters built like wolves, with unnatural height and muscle, ran toward her. She stood calmly, lifting only her hand as they charged.

The first demon to come near her went flying backward and collided with a second one behind it. They both rolled off toward a thick growth of trees as easily as if they'd been tumbleweed. The next one to get near her hit some invisible wall and bounced off with an audible thud. The third used the distraction to sweep around behind the woman and lifted his claws to strike.

Andra tried to call out a warning, but her breath was stuck in her chest, so she did the only thing she could do. She sprinted out the door and across the training yard, dodging men and monsters in a frantic attempt to reach the unarmed woman before she was slain.

She made it only a few yards when the little woman jumped over ten feet in the air and landed on a thick branch of a nearby tree.

The monster that had been trying to kill her raked the air where she'd been a second ago, its own momentum tripping it up so that it landed on the ground. A man she hadn't even seen a moment ago stepped out from behind a heap of dead monsters and sliced through the thing from its skull to its pelvis.

Andra skidded to a stop and realized she was standing in the middle of the battlefield. Something grabbed her arm and shoved her aside just as another of those wolves landed where she'd been standing a split second earlier.

"What the hell are you doing?" growled Paul. He didn't look at her, but kept her shoved behind him and backed up toward the thick trunk of a nearby tree—the only cover available.

"Coming to help."

"Then help, but don't you dare get yourself killed."

"Good plan. What do I do?"

Something with more legs than Andra could count slithered down out of the tree. Paul saw it and sliced its head off. It didn't stop moving.

He stabbed it with his sword and flung the long body away from them. "Blast something."

Right. She could do that. Andra found the power waiting for her, only this time, it was seething with anticipation, as if needing to be used. It leaped to her call and filled her with a glowing kind of pressure. Her body vibrated with strength as she chose her first target.

One of the monsters was a few yards off, closing in on Morgan's flank. Andra squeezed a stream of power into a tight ball and flung it out of her body at the thing. A boom shook the earth and a wave of air washed back over them. When she could see again, all that was left of the monster was a cloud of vaporized bits settling slowly to the earth.

Paul shot her a quick glance over his shoulder. "I meant fire, but that works, too. Good job."

His praise made her smile, and she decided she could really get into this whole magical-combat thing. Made her shotgun look like a squirt gun.

No time to revel in her victory, though. There were monsters to kill.

Paul kept the Synestryn away from Andra, allowing her room to work. The woman had a gift for destruction. She was laughing as she wielded his power, blowing demon after demon into piles of slurry.

Angus made his way across the field to Paul's side. The Gray Lady, Gilda, wasn't looking so good. In fact, if it weren't for Angus's thick arm around her waist, Paul didn't think she'd be able to stay standing.

He set Gilda on the ground behind Paul and Andra, and took up a defensive position behind her.

"Gilda can't do any more," said Angus, slashing at a demon as it charged.

"More for me," shouted Andra. Another cluster of sgath exploded into a cloud of black blood and chunks of fur.

"I just saw Logan leave the field," said Paul. "The sun will be rising any second now."

As if his words had summoned dawn, the first direct rays of light peeked over the wall. Thirty feet in front of them, one Synestryn started to smoke. A brief second later, it burst into flames and sprinted for the trees.

"The lake!" shouted Angus, loud enough to be heard over the sounds of combat. "Drive them into the lake!"

Andra looked at Paul. She was breathing hard, sweating and shaking, and her eyes were an angry, bloody red. "Which way?"

Paul pointed to the east. "On the other side of those trees."

Gilda grabbed Andra's ankle before she could run off. "The smoke," she panted. "It will hurt the human children."

Andra nodded. "I'll take care of it."

Paul felt her pull on his power, but she was weakening. She'd used so much already and she was still so new at this.

Instinctively, Paul cupped his left hand around the back of her neck, locking the two parts of the luceria together. Energy streamed along his arm and slid into her.

A breeze stirred around them, then started swirling faster. Smoke from several burning Synestryn spiraled up and away from the compound.

"Can you keep this up if we walk?" he asked.

She apparently didn't hear him. Her face was a mask of concentration and she held her bottom lip between her teeth.

"Carry her," said Angus, bending to the ground to

do the same for Gilda. "We need to follow the men and help them."

Paul had to break contact with her necklace, but there was no help for it. He scooped her up and realized that carrying a woman while wielding a naked blade was a learned talent. Angus did it effortlessly, looking like he'd been born to it, but Paul was awkward. His sword bobbed around and he was sure he was going to cut one of them.

The air continued to spiral around them as they ran, carrying with it the stench of burning demon. By the time they reached the lake, there were only a handful of Synestryn left, and all of them were burning, writhing around in the water in a futile effort to put out the sunlight flames.

When the last demon fell beneath the water, Paul whispered, "Okay. You can stop now."

Andra let out a long breath and her head fell limply against his shoulder. "Air is heavy," she panted.

Paul grinned and kissed her temple. "You did great."

"Get the wounded inside," bellowed Angus.

Joseph was yards away, but his deep voice rang out, easy to hear. "Sanguinar are setting up cots in the dining hall. Any man who isn't wounded, come with me. We're going to see how the Synestryn got in."

Fortunately, there were only a handful of injured men, and those wounds all seemed to be superficial. Morgan had a nasty cut across his brow, but he wiped away the blood and lined up near Joseph.

Paul told Andra, "I'm taking you back inside so you can rest for a few minutes."

"Are you sure you don't need me?"

"If I do, you'll know."

Angus's phone rang. He set Gilda down and slid it out of his rumpled jeans. After a moment, his craggy face twisted with a snarl. "Is there any sign of where they took her?"

"No," said Gilda, her black eyes going wide with shock.

Angus laid his hand on her head, offering comfort. "Is he going to live?" he asked in a thick, barely controlled voice. "Do what you can. We're on our way."

"What is it?" asked Paul.

Gilda pushed herself to her feet and tried to run toward the building. She made it only a few steps before her weakened legs gave out and she fell.

Angus hurried to her side and helped her up. She fought against him as if trying to get away, but Angus held her tight. "It's too late," he told her. "You're too weak to do anything right now."

Gilda stopped fighting and clung to her husband. Gilda's shoulders shook with silent sobs. Paul had never seen her cry before, and something inside him broke open at the sight. She'd always been so strong and stoic, no matter what had been thrown at her.

Angus cradled her in his arms, but his face was anything but comforting. He looked ready to kill.

"What's happened?" asked Paul.

Angus's eyes closed in remorse, and his mouth twisted into a scowl of self-loathing. "The fight was just a distraction. They got what they really wanted."

"What?"

"Sibyl."

It took Paul a moment for the words to sink in. "Sibyl is gone?"

"Yes," Angus bit out. "And there's no sign of where they've taken her." Paul thought he saw a sheen of tears in the older man's eyes. "Logan smelled Cain's blood and found him half-dead. He said there was no scent trail to follow."

Even if there had been one, it probably would have burned off at sunrise. "Was there anything left behind? Did Cain draw blood from one of them?"

"No. None."

"We have to find her," said Gilda. Her voice was high and desperate against Angus's shoulder. She looked up at him and Paul could see tears streaming down her smooth cheeks. "We can't let them have Sibyl, too."

The vague memory of a rumor Paul had once heard tickled his mind, but he couldn't remember what it was.

"We'll find her, love." It was a vow, and Paul felt the power of it coming off Angus in waves.

"How?" demanded Gilda. "The same way we found Maura?"

Maura? He'd heard that name before when he was a child, but couldn't recall who she was.

Angus's body tightened like he'd been punched in the gut. "That won't happen again."

Joseph had apparently seen the commotion and came over to them. "What's going on?" he asked.

"Sibyl was taken during the fight," said Paul to save Angus from having to say the words again.

"I'll get the men on it right now. We'll find her before sunset."

"There's no trail," said Angus.

"Says who?" demanded Joseph.

"Logan."

Joseph's face fell, draining of all hope. His shoulders drooped a little more, and Paul wondered again just how much longer he was going to be able to hold out as leader of their people.

Andra had been silently watching this exchange, keeping her focus on Gilda and Angus. She pushed against Paul, signaling she wanted to stand on her own. Grudgingly, Paul put her down, but he kept her body tight against his side.

She reached out and put her hand on Gilda's shoulder. Her voice was soft, but rang with confidence. "I can find your daughter," she told them.

"Daughter? Sibyl isn't their daughter," said Paul.

No one paid attention to him. All eyes were on Andra. Especially Gilda's. "How?"

Andra shrugged. "Finding the lost is what I do."

Gilda pushed away from Angus and took Andra's hand in her dainty grip. Tears streamed down her face. "I can't lose her, too," whispered Gilda. "Please find my baby. Bring her back to me."

Andra closed her eyes as if trying to block out the sight of the anguish on Gilda's face. Paul could feel her struggling against herself, her heart and mind warring against each other. Finally, she pulled in a deep, resigned breath. "I promise."

Andra crumpled to the ground, helpless under the weight of her vow to a grieving mother.

"You shouldn't have done that," said Paul. He knelt beside her, running his hands over her face and arms as if worried she'd been hurt.

"What choice did I have? I've always been a sucker for a grieving parent. You'd think I would have learned my lesson by now." She pulled herself together and gathered what little strength she had left. "Besides, if Sibyl can help Nika, then I need her back, too."

"Thank you," said Angus. "For whatever you're able to do."

"I need to go see where she was taken from. The longer I wait to do this, the harder it will get."

"Do what?"

She waved him off. She still wasn't comfortable talking about her talent. "Can you show me where her room is?"

"You need to rest first."

"No time. I wouldn't say no to a big cup of coffee, though."

Angus said, "There's another way. Paul, you can pull strength from the earth and feed it into her. It's not safe to do for long, but it will keep her going for a while more."

"Do it," said Andra.

Paul looked as though he might argue, but then nodded his head. "As you wish, my lady."

Chapter 26

Paul took Andra to Sibyl's room and stood unobtrusively in the corner while she looked around. Nothing had been moved since they'd discovered Sibyl gone, and the room was perfectly neat, with everything in its place. Even the frilly, ruffled curtains were undisturbed above the gaping window. The only sign that a child had been in this room was the rumpled pink bedding that had been half pulled out the window. Apparently, Sibyl had been ripped from beneath her blankets while she slept.

The second bedroom in Sibyl's suite, the one where her bodyguard, Cain, slept, was a different story. That room was a total wreck. Furniture was shattered where Cain or the Synestryn he'd fought had slammed into it. His red blood was splattered across the walls and carpet, but no oily black blood had been found. The Sanguinar still weren't sure whether Cain was going to live or not.

Paul prayed they wouldn't lose him. Of all the men here, he was the one who had resisted the decay of time the best. Maybe it was his role as protector of a child that had kept his soul young and kept his lifemark healthy and strong. If so, then what was going to happen to him now that he'd failed in that role?

Maybe it would be kinder if he did die. At least then he wouldn't have to suffer through the guilt of knowing he'd let Sibyl down.

Paul sighed. There was too much darkness in their world right now. They all needed Andra to succeed and bring back their only remaining child.

Andra glided through the room, picking up random objects here and there. She picked up Sibyl's favorite doll, which had fallen to the floor next to the bed. Its glassy black eyes stared up at her. She stroked the doll's ringlet curls, and Paul was certain he'd seen the glitter of tears in Andra's eyes for just a moment before she blinked them away.

Paul ached to go to her and comfort her, but he didn't dare interfere. Sibyl had to be found.

"How did you know?" he asked her.

"Know what?"

"That Sibyl was Gilda's daughter."

"I've seen that look too many times before to mistake it for anything else. There's no other look quite as helpless and desperate as that of a parent who has lost their child."

It made sense, but it also made Paul question why he hadn't known who Sibyl really was. Why wouldn't that have been common knowledge?

"I really wish you'd leave me alone for a while," she told Paul.

"Sorry. Not going to happen." He couldn't have walked away from her now if she'd put a sword to his throat. She needed him, whether or not she wanted to admit it.

Andra sighed. "You're not going to make fun of me?" There was a flash of insecurity across her face that surprised Paul. He'd never seen her be anything but confident, and that little show of insecurity had him wishing he could pull her into his arms and comfort her.

"Never. How could I when you're here helping me?"

"I have to pretend I'm her. Sleep in her bed. Relive what she saw that night. It feels silly doing it, but it's what works." She swallowed hard, and the only sign of her fear was the fine trembling of her fingers around the doll.

So, she didn't just have a knack for finding the lost children. She had a gift—one that had to be grounded in magic, if what she was saying were true. Paul made a mental note to pass that information along. It might help the other men find more women like her.

"How does it work?" he asked.

"I connect with them. I go to the place where their fear began and I follow that fear."

Paul had known Sibyl all his life and had never seen her afraid. She wasn't like normal children. She hadn't aged a day in several hundred years, and she could see the future. "What if they don't feel fear?" asked Paul.

Andra lifted one smooth shoulder. "How could a child not feel fear when she's forcibly taken from her home?"

If she's not truly a child, thought Paul, but he didn't voice his worry. She needed her confidence right now. "I suppose that's true. You'll just have to give it a try."

Andra nodded and sat on the edge of the bed. "Do you know what she was wearing last night?"

"Not exactly, but she loved frilly things. All soft pastels with little bits of lace at the neck."

"And this doll. Did she sleep with it?"

"Probably. It was always with her."

Andra lay down on the bed and pulled the covers up over her. She cradled the doll to her chest and closed her eyes. "Give me some time in silence, okay?"

Paul leaned against the door and let himself stare. He loved watching her. She was beautiful. So precious. The childish things sitting about the room kept a lid on his ever-present lust, but it did little to stop a tightness in his chest from forming as he watched her.

He loved her so much. He had to figure out a way to convince her to stay here and be with him. She'd refused his proposal, but she still hadn't taken off the ring he'd given her. The gold band gleamed around her finger, giving Paul a deep sense of satisfaction. No wonder so many human men liked to adorn their women in that fashion, telling all other men they were taken.

If only she'd agreed to wear it forever rather than rejecting him. Not that he blamed her. After what he'd tried to do to her last night, it was a wonder she hadn't thrown the ring back at him, or made him choke on it.

Minutes ticked by and Paul stayed silent, not daring to move for fear of ruining her concentration. After a while, he wondered if she'd just fallen asleep. He knew how tired she was—how thinly stretched she must be after the battle.

He was just about to go to her when he saw her body stiffen. Her breathing sped up and her grip tightened on the doll. Paul was halfway across the room before he stopped himself. What if this was supposed to happen?

"I see her," said Andra in a voice that sounded faint and distant. "The monsters have her."

"What kind of monsters?" Paul asked before he could stop himself.

Andra didn't answer his question, but he wasn't sure if it was because she didn't hear him or because she didn't know how to answer. She hadn't been raised among his kind and she might not know the names for various types of Synestryn.

"She's alive. Thirsty. She's not scared. How can she not be scared?" Andra's tone was full of wonder before it turned frightened. "Oh, God! They see me. They *know* me."

Paul felt panic clog his throat, making it hard to breathe. She'd made some sort of connection with the Synestryn, and that could not be a good thing.

He knelt at Andra's side and shook her. "Come back, honey," he urged. He pulled her limp body into his arms and kept shaking her, hoping to bring her out of whatever trance or dream she was in. "Wake up."

"How can they know me?" She gasped and her body jerked. "They want my blood. My family's blood. They've had Tori's and Nika's, and now they want mine."

"Wake up!" shouted Paul, and he forced a spike of power into his words, compelling her to obey.

Andra's eyes opened and fear bleached the color from her face.

Paul pulled her close and rocked her body like a child. "You're okay now," he soothed. "You're going to be okay."

"No. I'm not," she said. "I can't do this."

"Why not? What went wrong?"

"The monsters took Sibyl to the same place where they killed my baby sister."

"Are you sure?"

"Yes. I . . . sensed that she'd been there." She shook her head as if trying to make sense out of it. "I've looked for years to find her body so I could bury her next to Mom. Even though I can feel it, I've never been able to find that place, no matter how hard I try. It's too well hidden." Her fingers dug into his back and she whispered against his neck, "I've already failed, Paul. Sibyl was taken to the same place Tori was, and I'll never be able to find it."

Andra took deep breaths, trying to calm herself enough to think straight. The weight of failure bore down on her, driving all hope away.

"I'm sure that's not true," said Paul. His big hands were stroking over her back, trying to ease away some of her tension. "We'll find Sibyl together."

Even if she did know where to go, how could she go there? How could she face that place knowing she'd already let it kill Tori? "What if we can't?"

Andra could feel the force of her vow to Gilda pulling at her, demanding she try again. The place she'd been was so dark and filled with evil, she didn't want

312 Shannon K. Butcher

to go back. She didn't want to face what had happened to Tori. What she'd let happen to the little girl who'd trusted Andra to keep her safe.

"We can," said Paul, complete confidence strengthening his tone. "You may not have been able to succeed before, but you've got me now. You've got all my strength, too."

She had no choice but to try. Even if she hadn't given her vow to Gilda, she still had Nika to think about. If there was even a slight chance Sibyl could help, she had to find her, no matter how horrible the place was.

She pushed away from Paul. Leaning on him felt good, but it didn't make her feel strong, and she really needed that right now. "I need to figure out how to get there. I'm going to try again."

Paul cupped her face and slid his thumb along her cheek. His brown eyes were filled with love and compassion, even though she'd refused to marry him less than an hour ago. She had no idea how he could look at her like that after knowing the things she'd done.

"I'll be right here," he told her, and pressed a soft kiss to her mouth. "I know you can do this."

His faith in her was humbling, and she didn't want to let him down.

She lay back on the bed, closed her eyes again, and took a few deep breaths. The pleasant warmth of Paul's hand on hers distracted her for a few minutes until she got used to his touch. Slowly, their skin warmed to the same temperature and his hand became a part of her.

She pushed out all unnecessary thoughts and focused solely on Sibyl. She imagined the little girl lying asleep in her bed, hugging her favorite doll, completely unaware that she was in danger. It was easy to see her sleeping peacefully with her cheeks flushed pink and her hair mussed around her face.

Now that Andra had that image, she tried to imagine what happened next. Had Sibyl heard a sound and woken, or had she been asleep until the moment that she was dragged from her bed? Andra went through each possibility until one felt right and it sucked her in, taking over her mind, drawing her into the image until it surrounded her.

Sibyl had been awake when the thing came for her. It was dark, both inside and out. She'd heard its claws on the window as it slid the glass up. She'd lain there, frozen in place, but not by terror. By acceptance. She'd known it was going to happen—that there was nothing she could have done to stop it.

Or rather, there was nothing she was *going* to do to stop it, which was somehow worse.

Either way, Sibyl had felt no fear, which was what Andra had always used as a trail to follow the path a stolen child had taken. Without that trail, she had no way of figuring out where Sibyl had gone.

Andra searched for something to grasp on to. Something she could use. She struggled to stay relaxed and open her mind up to the possibilities. Maybe the monster had left a trail she could follow.

She felt around for a sense of satisfaction that she imagined the thing might feel at having won its prize. There was nothing there she could connect with. The thing was too inhuman—almost mindless except for the throbbing presence of hunger that controlled it, and that was too scattered to latch onto.

Dimly, Andra was aware that her already fatigued body was wearing down under the strain of staying in this trancelike state too long. She had to hurry.

What had she grasped on to before when she'd found Sibyl the first time? She'd been in Sibyl's head, if only for a moment. There had to have been something that she used as a trail. What was it?

The vision she'd created in her mind started to fade as her body gave out; then she remembered she wasn't alone. Paul was here. She could use his power.

Andra reached inside herself to that warm glowing spot where Paul's skin touched hers. The luceria around her neck vibrated with energy. All she had to do was figure out how to use it for something as delicate as this. Combat was easy; she'd always had a knack for blowing things up. This stuff was much harder.

Nothing changed, and her strength was dwindling fast. She could feel her physical body shaking under the stress and tried to ignore it.

Desperate to find Sibyl, Andra focused on the exact spot where the luceria touched his matching ring. She could feel a tiny spark there, like static electricity arcing between two points. She reached for that spot, grasped hold of it with all her desperation and hope. Power flared inside her, filling her chest with heat. She was no longer tired. No longer weak. She felt invincible.

Instincts screamed at her to hurry, that she had no time to waste, so she lifted her hand and focused all that power so that it formed a sphere around her body. She willed the sphere to show her where to look for the trail—to highlight it so she could follow it.

One side of the globe flared to life and Andra knew that was her trail. She examined it. Poked at it until she felt what it was.

Acceptance.

Sibyl had accepted her fate, and the force of that emotion was so strong that it had left a trail—not as strong as fear, but strong enough that Andra could follow it.

Andra latched onto that acceptance, memorized it until she would know the feeling anywhere—be able to follow it wherever it led.

She followed the path south, her mind racing along it until she collided with a hard barrier. She found herself in a dark room with a single bare lightbulb overhead. The edges of the room were hidden in shadows, but somehow still pulsed with colors. Swirls of blue and green bloomed along the edges of the shapeless

-oom. It reminded her of the sea swirling about rocks
as the water was sucked back into the ocean by the
tide.

Andra had been here before, if only for a brief moment. This was Sibyl's mind.

From the shadows of those billowing clouds of color
came a little girl. Sibyl.

She wore a frilly white dress and lacy ankle socks
with shiny leather shoes. Her hair was a cascade of perfect blond ringlets tied back with a pink satin bow. In
her arms, she held a doll that looked like her miniature
twin, but instead of Sibyl's pale blue eyes, the doll had
glassy, dead black eyes like those of a shark. It was the
doll Andra's body was holding now.

"You didn't come to me soon enough," said Sibyl.
"It's too late now."

"I'm sorry I didn't come sooner. We just found out
you were missing."

"No. I mean that I told Paul to bring you to me the
night he found you. He failed to do so and now it's too
late."

"I don't understand," said Andra.

"Of course not. No one ever does." The colors behind
her darkened to a deep, desolate purple. "You shouldn't
have come here. She's looking for you."

"Who is 'she'?"

Sibyl looked over her shoulder, as if expecting someone to pop out from behind her. "Stay away. It's not safe
here."

"I know. That's why I am coming to take you home,"
explained Andra.

"If you come here, you'll be sorry," warned the child
in a singsong voice.

"I'd never regret helping you get home to your
family."

Her chubby cheeks fell into a blank mask and that
familiar sense of acceptance that Andra had memorized

flooded her senses. "If you must come, at least wait unti
it's safer. Until she is gone."

"She? Who?"

Sibyl hesitated for a moment, as if weighing a decision. "The one who brought me here."

"Has she hurt you?"

"No more than most."

Andra had no clue what to make of that, so she ignored it for the sake of time. She didn't know how long
she'd be able to hold her connection with Sibyl, as weak
as her body was. "Tell me where you are so we can come
find you."

"You will find me on your own or not at all. I will not
help you suffer."

"I'm not going to suffer unless I fail to bring you
home safe. Please help me."

"I must remain neutral," said Sibyl.

"Neutral? What do you mean?"

"I cannot choose sides. It would give her the freedom
to act. I cannot allow that. Not now, when so much hangs
in the balance."

"What are you talking about, baby? You're not making any sense. Have you hit your head?"

Sibyl's blue eyes blazed until they glowed bright yellow. Her mouth tightened in anger, and Andra had the
impression that she'd grown a few inches. The walls behind her pulsed with furious orange plumes among the
bruised colors. "I am in my right mind, Theronai. Do not
question my sanity. There can be no good end here. I
seek only to prevent your suffering."

"You don't need to worry about me."

"Someone must. The Sentinels need you more than
I."

"You're the one I want to help," said Andra.

Her tiny shoulders straightened in a pose of false
confidence Andra knew only too well. "I am . . . expend-
able," said Sibyl.

"No. You're not. No child is."

Sibyl smiled, but it wasn't the smile of a child. It was too cunning and condescending for that. "What if I were to tell you that more than one child will die if you perish trying to save me?"

"You can't possibly know that."

"Ask Paul about what I *cannot* know," said Sibyl, mocking Andra for her ignorance. "How many impossible things have you seen in your short time with Paul, young Theronai?"

The creepy little girl had a point, but that wasn't going to change Andra's mind. "I made a promise to bring you home, and that's what I intend to do."

"Ah, Gilda. Cunning wench," she said with a note of approval in her tone. "She seeks only to protect her kind, but she has always made blind decisions. I wish I were so blessed with blindness."

"She's only trying to help you."

"I need no more *help* from her."

Okay, apparently there was some bad blood there. "Then let me help you," said Andra.

"If you do, Paul will be by your side. But be warned that he views his life as no more important than a single grain of sand on the beach. There are many more just like him and the absence of one will go unnoticed. He will not hesitate to end his life so that yours may continue."

My life for yours, he had vowed. She believed he meant it, but Andra wouldn't let him die to save her.

"We'll be careful," said Andra.

"You should stay with your sister. My captors do not seek to harm me."

"Then why take you?"

"Why indeed? Perhaps you should ask yourself that until you come to the same conclusion I have."

"Which is?"

"Something you'll have to figure out for yourself."

The child smiled, gave a negligent wave of her hand, and Andra was thrown from Sibyl's mind without any option but to go. She flew through blackness until she landed with a thud inside her own head.

Slowly, she reconnected with her body and wished she hadn't bothered. Fatigue swamped her, and her muscles were sore from prolonged shivering. She felt cold. Weak. Too tired to even bother opening her eyes.

"You okay?" asked Paul. His voice was harsh with controlled panic.

Andra made an affirmative grunting noise, but could do no more.

"You were out for way too long. I'm taking you to bed," he told her, and she felt herself being lifted in his arms. Had she been able to open her mouth, she would have scolded him for treating her like a child, but as it was, she just didn't have the strength to care. He was holding her and that was enough.

She had a little girl to save, and she was going to need every bit of help she could get.

Chapter 27

Paul was worried. Andra hadn't resisted when he tucked her into bed, which meant she was a lot worse off than he'd hoped. She'd told him that they had to leave as soon as she could find the trail again, and asked him to gather as many men as he could.

He'd gone to do just that when he saw Angus turn the corner at the end of the hall. The older man wasn't moving with his normal fluid grace. Instead, his movements were jerky and rigid, as if he were injured.

Then again, his daughter was missing. That was more than enough pain for any man to bear.

"Can she help?" he asked Paul without greeting.

Paul nodded. "She's going to try. She said she made contact with Sibyl and that she's still alive and unharmed."

Angus covered his face and let out a deep breath of relief.

"She also said that Sibyl doesn't want her to come."

"My poor baby girl," whispered Angus. "She probably thinks Andra is more important to us than she is. She's always felt that, because she never reached maturity and can't bond with any of our men, she was somehow flawed and unimportant."

"That's ridiculous. How many times has she saved our lives with her predictions?"

"That's what I've always told her, but I guess a father's opinion doesn't count."

"I didn't know she was your daughter. How could I not have known?"

Angus shrugged. "Sibyl and Gilda don't get along. There aren't many men left alive who were there when Sibyl was born, and somewhere along the line, she just stopped claiming us. Even though she has a child's body, she's been a grown woman for a long time. It seemed the least we could do was respect her wishes."

"Why has she never grown?"

Angus's blue eyes clouded with a mixture of anger and sadness. "I won't answer that. Ask her if you want to know, though I doubt she'd tell you."

That meant it was officially none of his business. "We're going to find her, Angus. I know Andra can do this."

"Then why haven't you already left?"

"She nearly killed herself making contact with Sibyl. She needs a few minutes to rest before she finds the path. Besides, we're going to need to gather the men who are able to come with us."

"I want to go."

Paul put his hand on Angus's shoulder. "Of course you're going. I wouldn't have it any other way."

"How many men do we need?"

"I was just going to see Joseph about that. I don't know how many we can spare with the wall breached. We can't leave the place unguarded."

"Let me talk to Joseph," said Angus. "You go pick your men and I'll see to it that they're ours."

"He won't leave the humans unguarded."

"I won't ask him to, but he owes me some favors and I'm calling them in. She's my daughter."

Paul nodded. "Meet me back at my suite in an hour. We'll be ready to go."

*   *   *

They'd been driving southeast for most of the day when Andra lost the trail. Frustration bubbled up inside her, making her want to scream.

"Stop," she told Madoc, who was driving the giant SUV they'd been given. The thing held eight normal-size people, but only five Theronai and herself. It was packed shoulder-to-massive-shoulder with warriors, all of whom were now looking at her.

"Is this the place?" asked Morgan from the front seat. His brown skin and feral expression made his eyes look like they were glowing. There was something predatory about him—graceful, quiet movements ruled him, as if he were hunting for something no matter where he went.

"No," said Andra, hearing the sound of defeat in her voice. "I've lost the path."

Madoc checked the clock on the dashboard. "It'll be dark in another two hours."

"Do you want to try again, or call it a night?" asked Paul. He hadn't stopped touching her since they'd left Dabyr. His arm was around her shoulders, holding her close to his side.

Even with the heat of his body, Andra was cold, and so tired she could barely keep her eyes open.

"I can't leave her to spend the night with those things. I have to try again."

Paul nodded his understanding. "Everyone out," he ordered. "Give us a few minutes. Madoc, go tell Angus and the others what's going on."

Madoc gave an affirmative grunt and all four men got out of the vehicle.

"Lie down on the seat," he told her.

Andra didn't need a second offer. Her body was so heavy and numb with weariness, she felt like her skin had turned to lead. Paul had shoved his big body in the space between the two front seats and the back-seat where she lay. He looked almost comical crouched there in the small space, and for some reason, it made her heart give a little flop in her chest.

She realized at that moment that this man would do anything for her. He was commitment and loyalty personified. So long as he drew breath, he would do whatever it took to make her safe and happy. Including forfeit his life.

She couldn't let that happen. She needed to give him his ring back and separate herself from him before she no longer could. The idea of staying with him was becoming more temptation than she could stand. If she didn't walk away soon, she never would, and that scared the hell out of her, because she knew how it would end—the same way it had for Mom and Tori and Nika. She'd do something wrong and she'd have to watch another person she loved suffer or die.

The realization that she loved him stunned her stupid for a moment, and she hadn't heard what he'd said.

"What?" she asked.

"Are you comfortable?"

Hardly, but she nodded anyway.

"What's going on in that head of yours?" he asked, his eyes narrowed with suspicion.

"I'm just worried about Sibyl," she lied.

Paul smoothed her hair away from her face and gave her an encouraging smile. "Don't worry. We'll find her."

Such faith. She had no idea where he found it after all he'd been through, all he'd seen of her past, but if he could have faith, then she would, too.

Andra took his left hand and kissed his palm before she settled it around her throat. The two parts of the luceria locked together and she was flooded with a heady rush of power that never ceased to amaze her.

She was going to miss that almost as much as she was going to miss Paul.

"I'm not going to let you go," he told her as if reading her thoughts. "Fair warning."

She couldn't think about that right now. She had to concentrate.

Andra closed her eyes and searched for that trail of acceptance. It was nowhere to be found.

"Hand me the doll," she said.

Paul pulled it out of a duffel bag and gave it to her. The cool weight of the doll's porcelain head rested over her heart. She smelled the faint scent of sunshine and roses clinging to it. Sibyl's scent. This doll was somehow part of her, vibrating with its own kind of energy that Andra didn't understand.

Maybe this was what psychics felt when they connected with an object. It wasn't painful, but neither was it completely comfortable. The doll had a jumbled, chaotic feeling about it—a shadow or blemish that Andra couldn't see, but could feel.

As her body fell away, she was flung across the sky and plunged down into the earth. Her head spun and she felt nauseated even though she was no longer inside her body.

A single bare lightbulb hung from the ceiling of a room with no walls, only swirling plumes of color. Andra recognized it as Sibyl's mind, even though the colors were darker now. There were no hopeful pastel hues, only deep, muted browns and grays.

Sibyl stepped out from one of the plumes. This time she was wearing a frilly black gown covered in artistically shredded tatters of lace. Her eyes were rimmed with liner and her lips covered in a garish red gloss. Her fingernails were long and painted black.

"Trying out a new look?" asked Andra, unable to keep the parental dismay from her tone.

Sibyl frowned for a moment; then a satisfied smile stretched her painted lips. Her appearance changed back to the more appropriately girlish attire, complete with ankle socks and pink bows. No more baby hooker. "Better?" she asked.

"Much."

"I'm so glad you came," she said.

"I thought you wanted me to stay away."

Her smile widened. "I've changed my mind. This place is horrible."

"Do you know where you are?" asked Andra.

"I think so." She waved her hand and a map that looked similar to a satellite image, but recorded from a lower angle, appeared. She pointed at one spot while Andra frantically tried to memorize the nearby highways and streets. It was in northern Alabama, only two or three hours from where they were.

"Can you find me?" asked Sibyl in a voice that shook with a mere hint of fear. She hadn't been afraid before, but maybe things had gotten worse where she was.

Andra filled her voice with confidence to help soothe the child. "I can now. Don't worry. We're coming."

"We? Who's with you?"

"There are ten men with me, Gilda, and Helen." She hadn't had time to do more than meet Helen, but Paul said she was powerful. "We'll get you out."

Sibyl's eyes gleamed with a flash of anger at the mention of her mother's name. It was then that Andra noticed that her eyes were no longer blue. They'd gone completely black.

Something wasn't right here.

"What's wrong with your eyes?" she asked.

Sibyl shrugged a dainty shoulder. "It's the darkness. All of the Theronai's eyes turn black after they've been out of the light for a while."

Poor thing. All that darkness had to be hard to tolerate, even if she wasn't easily scared.

"I'll be there as soon as I can. You just hold on, baby."

Her voice was faint and tinted with sorrow. "I'll try. Please hurry. I don't know how much longer I can stand this. They have me locked up in a cage with the skeleton of another little girl. I know they're going to leave me here to die."

Andra's throat closed off, choking her with anguish. "What?"

"She's wearing a pink nightgown just like me. They let her die in this cage all alone."

Oh, God. Tori. She'd been wearing a pink nightgown the night she was taken. Her body was still there.

Andra felt her heart rip open all over again. Anguish bled from her, but it didn't lessen. She could still feel every sharp stab of guilt, every grinding wave of grief, as if Tori had been taken just last night.

Before she realized what had happened, she was back inside her body, sobbing.

"Shhh." Paul held her, rocking her against his solid chest. "I've got you."

"I found her," said Andra.

"That's good, right? Now we can go get her back."

"No. I mean I found Tori. Her body is there with Sibyl." Tori had died alone in a cage, trapped in the darkness.

Paul's presence slid into her mind, cool and calming. She felt him trying to comfort her, whispering soothing words directly to her soul.

She soaked them up and let them give her the strength to pull in her next breath. She didn't know how she would have lived through this without him. Even now, her heart was struggling to beat against the pressure of her grief. Her baby sister had died alone in some cave, and Andra hadn't been able to stop it.

"We'll recover her body," whispered Paul. "We'll bring her home."

Andra tried to control her breathing and quiet the sobs that shook her. She wanted to give up, to curl in on herself and cry until nothing mattered anymore and all the pain was gone. But Sibyl needed her. She owed it to Tori not to let another little girl die alone in the dark.

She pushed away from Paul, already missing the animal comfort of his warm body. "We need to get moving. We're not far away now, and night is coming."

Paul grudgingly let her go. He gently wiped her tears away and kissed her forehead. "Sibyl is lucky to have someone as brave and strong as you on her side. So am I."

She was going to miss him. Their time together was up in only a few more hours.

His kind brown eyes swept over her face as if soaking her in. "Don't think about that now. You've got enough to deal with to also be thinking about our future."

They didn't have a future. Not really. And as hard as it would be to walk away from him now that she loved him, she would have done it all again in a heartbeat. She now had proof that real courage and honor existed to fight back the ugly things in the world.

"We should go," she said.

He looked like he wanted to say something more to her, but instead he nodded. "Sibyl needs us."

Three hours later, they found the cave where Sibyl was being held. The strain on Andra was nearly too much for Paul to bear. She was pushing herself, and if he hadn't felt her desperate need to see this through—if he hadn't known that failing would kill something inside her—he would have demanded she stay behind in the SUV.

Not that he had any real right to demand anything from her. Less than an hour remained on the clock before his luceria fell from her neck and he was once again alone.

Paul looked at his ring. The colors had solidified completely, which meant their bond was complete. Breaking it would kill him. Unless she changed her mind about leaving him, he wasn't going to live to see sunrise. If he tried to hold out, Andra would end up paying the price. He'd already tried to force her to stay with him once. As soon as his soul started to die off, there would be nothing to stop him from finishing what he'd started. The only way to keep her safe was to walk away for good.

The saddest part of knowing that wasn't that his life was ending—he'd had a long, full life. The saddest part was going to be leaving Andra alone. She didn't deserve that. She deserved to be happy. To be loved.

Maybe Iain could give her what she really needed once Paul was out of the way.

It was full dark now, and based on the trampled dirt and vegetation near the cave entrance, most of the Synestryn had already gone out to hunt.

"Where is she?" asked Gilda, the Gray Lady. The woman looked like she was barely holding herself together. Angus's arm was supporting her, keeping Gilda from swaying with weakness.

"Inside," said Andra. "About a quarter mile from here."

Nicholas surveyed the surrounding land. "This whole area is low. We're bound to run into some water."

Shit. That made this whole rescue effort a lot more dangerous. They weren't just going to be fighting demons; they also had to make sure they didn't drown.

"The tracks they left behind aren't muddy, so maybe we'll get lucky," said Paul.

"Yeah." Madoc snorted. " 'Cause that happens all the fucking time."

"Enough," ordered Angus. "We're going in, regardless. Paul, Andra, Madoc, Nicholas, Gilda, and I are going in. The rest of you guard our exit. Don't let anything come back in and sneak up behind us."

Everyone nodded. Helen pushed her braids behind her shoulders, lifted her hands, and a ring of fire erupted around the vehicles and the entrance. "They'll have to come through that first," she said.

"Good," said Angus. "That'll help. Andra, you stay behind me and Gilda."

Andra stepped forward. "I need to go in first so I can see the way. Besides, Gilda looks like she's about to fall over."

The Gray Lady straightened her shoulders. "I'm fine, stronger than a child like you on your best day."

Angus stepped in front of his wife and lifted her chin. "That's enough. We do it her way. She's gotten us this far, hasn't she?"

Gilda gave a slight nod and looked away. "Fine. Let her go first."

Andra was already at the mouth of the cave when Paul caught up to her. "You need to be in constant contact with my power. Something nasty could pop up, and you won't have time to react if you're not ready."

"Okay. I can do that." He felt her reach out to him and open herself up. Their conduit was larger now than it had been only hours ago. Power flowed easily out of him, making his body sing.

"Tell her about the seeing-in-the-dark thing," called Helen. "She's going to need that."

"Right. If you funnel some power to your eyes, you can see in the dark. Just be careful not to do too much, though. You could hurt yourself."

"Got it. I can see everything. Thanks."

The tunnel went down steeply for twenty feet before it leveled off. This wasn't a nice, well-planned mine. It was a natural cave with plenty of twists and turns and no nice, flat surface to walk on. At one point, they had to squeeze one at a time through an opening no wider than his shoulders.

The smell of damp earth and decay clung to the air. A steady drip from a hundred places echoed off the walls. Boots scraped behind them, and Madoc grunted as he tried to fit his big body through the hole.

Andra and Paul waited on the far side of the small opening for everyone to catch up. Gilda slid through easily, but Angus wasn't so lucky. Nicholas had just as much trouble and ended up losing a chunk of his shirt in the process.

Paul could feel Andra's nerves jumping around anxiously. She wanted to get moving, and he couldn't blame her. Every second Sibyl was with the Synestryn, she was in danger.

As soon as Nicholas was through, Andra and Paul moved into another tunnel that led down deeper into the earth. They had to crawl on their hands and knees here, and Paul's shoulders brushed the walls of the tunnel.

The tunnel widened until Andra was able to stand up. Paul had to keep his head down, but at least he was giving his knees a break.

"So," she said, breaking the bleak silence. "How long do I have to be in the dark before my eyes turn black?"

Paul had no idea what she was talking about. "Why would your eyes turn black?"

The tunnel ended and at the mouth of it was a large cavern with room enough to breathe. They all filed out and Andra pressed on, crossing to an opening on the left.

"That's what Sibyl told me. Her eyes were black the last time I saw her, and she said it was because she'd been in the dark so long."

From behind them, he heard Gilda, and her tone was so odd, so full of shock and fear, it stopped everyone dead in their tracks. "You saw a girl who looked like Sibyl with black eyes?"

"Yes."

Angus drew his sword.

All the color drained from Gilda's face. "What else did she tell you?"

"She gave me the map so I could find her," said Andra.

Gilda clutched Angus's arm. "That wasn't Sibyl. That was Maura. We're walking right into a trap."

Chapter 28

A deep rumble shook the ground around Andra's body. Dust spilled from the ceiling, then small rocks. She looked up in shock and saw a crack had formed overhead. And it was getting wider.

Paul pulled Andra out of the way and shoved her into the tunnel for cover just as large rocks started dropping from above.

Shouts rose up on the opposite side of the cavern. Gilda screamed. Then Andra could hear nothing but the sound of rocks grating against one another as they filled the room.

"Down the tunnel," shouted Paul, pushing her to get her moving.

Andra moved. Adrenaline made her arms and legs move as fast as her pounding heart. She scurried down the tunnel until it let out into a shallow pit. She slid out of the opening and down until she was standing on a shelf of rock. She moved over so there was room for Paul beside her.

Dust coated his body, and there was an ugly scratch on his cheek. "You okay?" he asked around a cough.

"Yeah. You?"

He nodded absently, but he was looking the way they came, as if hoping to see the rest of their group.

"They were trapped on the other side, right? Not caught under all that rock?" She prayed it was true.

Paul's grim expression didn't give her much comfort. His jaw was tight with anger, and his eyes promised retribution. "We're on our own now. We can either go back or move forward into the trap. What do you want to do?"

"Even if it is a trap, we can't leave Tori here. Or Sibyl. At least now we know it's coming."

"If we do rescue her, we're not going to have any fun trying to find a way out."

"I'll blast one open if I need to."

Just then, the luceria fell from her throat. Andra caught it before it could hit the ground.

Paul sucked in a pained breath. "Our time is up."

"We need more," said Andra.

"That's your call. Not mine."

"What do I do?"

"Put it on. Give me a new vow." He looked as if he were about to say something else, then clamped his lips shut.

Andra locked the luceria back in place. Paul's eyes went to it and the look of longing on his face nearly made her weep. He fell to his knees and scored a line in his skin, through his shirt. "My life for yours, Andra. Always."

She hesitated. She needed time to think. What would happen to Paul if she died while wearing this thing? What if she didn't make it back out alive? It was a trap. She had to remember that.

He wanted forever. She couldn't let herself want that, too. At least not until she was sure she wouldn't be a liability to him—until his people figured out whether there were more women out there like her who could be a better match for him.

He thought he wanted forever now, but what would happen if they found more women next week? She didn't want to trap him. She didn't want him to die along with her if she messed this up and failed to get everyone out alive.

"An hour," she whispered. "That should be enough to get us out of here, right? If not, we can go for another hour."

Paul's mouth tightened and his jaw bunched with anger. "An hour. I understand now."

Andra wasn't sure what he understood, but he wasn't letting her inside his mind so she could figure it out. He was cold and stiff beside her.

The band tightened around her throat, nestling close to her skin. No vision appeared, but she really didn't need one to know what he was feeling. He was pissed.

"We'd better get moving."

Andra yearned to explain herself to him, but there wasn't time. "It's not much farther."

They moved the rest of the way carefully. Paul kept his eyes on the ceiling of rock above them, looking for more signs of danger.

The better part of that hour had passed by the time they neared a corner and Andra felt a wave of malicious intent sweep out over her. It stole the warmth from her body until her bones ached with cold. She stopped dead in her tracks, unable to take another step.

A deep groan from Paul told her he'd felt it, too. "This isn't good."

"Tell me about it."

"No. I mean we can't stay here long. It'll kill us."

Part of her didn't mind the idea.

"That's not you. That's the fog talking. Ignore it. Think of something happy and get moving."

Something happy. Tori's face popped into her head. Her crooked smile showing off her two missing front teeth. The smell of her hair when they'd lain on the couch together and watched cartoons. The sound of her giggles when Andra would swing her around by her arms.

She would have been sixteen if she'd lived—too big to swing around anymore.

The empty duffel bag over her shoulder felt like it weighed a ton. It wasn't big, but Paul had promised her it would be large enough to hold her bones.

"That's not happy," said Paul.

Andra tried to refocus her thoughts, but it wasn't easy. She had way too much stuff dancing around in her brain for her to concentrate. "Let's just get this over with."

Paul drew his sword and they stepped out around the corner together. A metal cage about ten feet on each side sat in the far corner of the cavern. The floor was littered with trash, bones, and bits of fur. Inside the cage, Sibyl sat hugging her legs. Beside her was a pile of bones and the tattered remains of clothing. A pink nightgown. The color of the gown on the skeleton had faded out over time, and was covered in dust, but she knew it was pink because she recognized it. It had been Tori's favorite—one she begged Andra to wash so she could wear it again every night.

Andra reached for Paul's arm to steady herself. She could barely breathe. Seeing her sister's body after all these years was more than she could stand. The grief nearly crushed her and ripped at her heart until she no longer cared whether she drew in her next breath. If death eased this pain, then she would welcome it. She would wrap herself around her sister and let it come take her.

"Stop that," growled Paul. "You're letting the fog in."

At the sound of his voice, Sibyl lifted her head. Andra expected to see tears, but her blue eyes were dry and her face was calm. Only her voice gave away her disappointment. "You shouldn't have come. My sister is going to kill us all now."

Another Sibyl floated down from a ledge above them. Her black skirt billowed out as she settled to the ground. This Sibyl had black eyes and a vicious smile tilting her painted mouth. "I'm not going to kill all of you," said the girl. "I need you, sister, and your pretty, shiny soul."

Suddenly, things started to fall into place for Andra. All the small differences made sense. There were two of them. Andra had somehow ended up in this girl's head when she went seeking out Sibyl. She'd found Sibyl when she'd been in her bed, but once all she had to connect her was the doll—the one with glassy black eyes—she'd somehow reached the other girl instead.

Paul stepped in front of her. "Who the hell are you?"

"Maura. Sibyl's sister. I thought the resemblance was a dead giveaway."

"Stay away from her," warned Sibyl. "She's dangerous."

"Too late for that. You should have listened when you had the chance," said Maura. She lifted her tiny hand and monsters flowed in like water, dribbling out of tunnels high up the walls. They landed like heavy raindrops or crawled down the cave walls, sticking like spiders.

Fear took a firm hold of Andra and locked her feet to the earth. There were too many of them. She and Paul were never going to live through this.

"No time for that," said Paul. "Pull it together." He grabbed her arm and dragged her toward the cage holding Sibyl. "Come on, Andra. I need you here with me."

Right. Sibyl needed her, too.

Andra gave herself a mental slap and tried to think what she could do to save them. There was no way she could fight them all. What she really needed was to find a way to keep the monsters from hurting them.

Not knowing what else to do, Andra formed a bubble around them to hold back the slavering monsters. It took an enormous amount of power—more than she'd ever used before. Her nerve endings screamed at the force of that much energy traveling through her, but she managed to suffer through the pain.

Furry, clawed things bounced off of it as they charged, making it ripple like waves over a pond.

"That'll work," said Paul, pride ringing in his voice. "How long can you hold it?"

Already sweat started beading up on her skin from the effort. "Don't know."

"I'll hurry."

The strap of the bag over her shoulder disappeared. She couldn't let herself become distracted by thinking about what that meant, so she didn't. She heard the screech of metal bending too fast and a soft word of thanks from Sibyl.

The monsters pounded the shield, and Andra felt every one of the impacts like a sledgehammer blow to her brain. Sweat slid down her temples and her legs started to shake. Paul's power flowed into her, but she used every bit of it for the shield as it came to her, leaving her none to strengthen herself. She felt hollowed out—a thin shell of brittle skin was all that was left of her, and that was threatening to crumble.

The dry rattle of bones filled her ears and she had to cover them and block out the sound. Paul was gathering up what was left of her sister. Poor, sweet Tori.

I'm sorry, baby.

Tears joined the sweat running down her face.

The shield faltered and one of the things with glowing green eyes broke through. "Paul!" she shouted, and lifted her hands to channel more power toward the breach. She wasn't sure if the hand motion did any good, but it was worth a shot.

Paul's sword came into her field of vision. It slashed through the air between her and the charging monster, lopping off one of the beast's paws. The thing howled and black blood spewed over the rocks.

He finished it off with a quick series of slices that sent its head rolling away. He kicked the body as far as

the shield would allow, where it twitched as the blood
drained from it.

Andra re-formed the shield to get the thing away
from all of them before the blood could burn them. She
felt the luceria heat as she forced yet more power into
her body. Sweat evaporated from her skin in small tendrils of steam. Her head throbbed in time with the crash
of monsters against the shield.

She wasn't going to be able to hold it much longer.

A small, cool hand slipped into hers. "You can do
this," Sibyl said, her child's voice steady and trusting, as
if she hadn't spent the day locked in a cage with the remains of the sister Andra hadn't been able to save.

"Time to go," shouted Paul.

"Go where?" Andra gasped. They were surrounded.
Only the bubble she'd built held the demons away. Already the monsters were covering it, scratching and
clawing as they tried to find a way inside.

"How do you feel about flying?" asked Paul.

"It's great if I'm inside a nice metal shell."

"The way we came in is blocked. I'm not seeing any
options here."

Neither was Andra. *Shit.* She so didn't want to do this.
"Up it is. Hold on."

Paul slid his hand around her nape, locking them
together, freeing more of his power to flow into her.
Sibyl clung to her waist and Andra held on to Paul's
shoulders.

"I can't believe I'm doing this," she muttered before
she put all her focus into the task at hand.

Energy poured out of Paul, leaping to her command.
She let the bubble shrink until they were nose to nose
with hungry monsters. She had to close her eyes to block
them out so she could concentrate, but she somehow
figured out how to use a burst of strength to push the
bubble off the ground. She didn't make it far, and they
kind of rolled around inside the bottom of the sphere,

but it lifted, giving her the confidence that this might actually work.

She pushed harder, and one by one, the monsters started sliding off the smooth shield, making it lighter and easier to move. A few still clung to it with insectoid legs, but she couldn't help that.

The ceiling was coming at them fast now, and she couldn't figure out how to slow down.

"You're going to have to break through," said Paul. "There's too much rock overhead."

"No," said Sibyl. "We're only a few feet down."

A few feet. She could do that if that was what it took to get Sibyl and Paul to safety. To get her sister's body into the empty grave next to her mother's.

Andra looked up at the rock, searching for a weak spot. A single crevice ran the length of the room across one corner, so she aimed for that. She formed a wedge out of air, much like the shield bubble, hardened it with her mind, and shoved the thing into the crack.

Her body vibrated under the strain, and her eyes felt like they were going to evaporate under the heat pouring out of her. At some point she'd stopped sweating, or maybe it was just drying faster than her body could form it. Whatever the case, she figured she had another few seconds before she passed out completely and they all landed in the writhing mass of teeth and claws below.

She was not going to let it end like that.

White spots formed in her vision, making it hard to see, but she could feel Paul's breath at her ear as he spoke to her. "You're doing great. Just a little more."

He was pushing energy into her now, helping her as much as he could. She gathered it, holding on to it until the pressure was too much for her to take. She could hardly see now, just barely enough to make out the spot where she'd shoved the wedge.

Andra let loose, hammering that spot with the force of a battering ram. Rocks rained down on them, and beneath the rumble of stone, she could hear the painful screams of the monsters below as they were crushed. The bubble held, protecting them from the big chunks, but grains of sand started making it through. The shield was getting weaker, and it wasn't going to hold for much longer.

"One more time," panted Paul. He sounded winded.

She couldn't see him now. She couldn't see anything. She let instinct guide her as she gathered her strength and hammered at the wedge again. Another fall of rock cascaded down. This time chunks the size of gravel were making it through.

"I see stars!" shouted Sibyl.

Andra couldn't, but she believed the girl's excited voice, and guided the bubble up so they could get the hell out of there.

"To the left," said Paul. "There."

Her ears started to ring and she couldn't hear anything now, either. She wasn't sure if she was out of the hole in the cave or not until she felt Paul's triumph singing through their link.

She drove the bubble sideways, making sure they didn't fall back down into the hole once the bubble popped.

We're safe. You can let go now.

It was Paul's voice in her head—his comforting presence—so she let go. They landed with a thump. Andra sucked in huge gulps of air and lay in the cool grass. Her heart hammered inside her, slowing with each beat. She could feel Paul's fingers lace through hers and reveled in the pride radiating out from him. She'd done it. She'd gotten them all out alive.

And then his presence was gone as if someone had flipped a switch. She reached out for him in her mind, but slammed into a wall. He wasn't there. She was alone again.

The luceria opened and slid from her neck into the

grass. She tried to reach for it, but her arms didn't work. Nothing worked. Everything was broken now, and Paul was gone.

The world faded away and there wasn't a thing she could do to stop it.

Chapter 29

Paul had expected there to be pain. He saw the luceria fall. He'd braced himself for the agony he knew was coming, but nothing happened. Andra had used so much of his power that it no longer pounded at his insides, trying to tear him apart.

He was going to die, but at least he wouldn't be in quite so much pain. He was thankful for that.

Paul gathered her in his arms and held her while her body recovered. The other Theronai had found them and were running this way. He saw Gilda, along with the others who had gone down there with him. They were safe. A little dusty, but safe.

Paul bowed his head in relief. Everyone had made it out alive. They had rescued Sibyl, and the remains of Andra's sister were safely stowed in his duffel bag. All in all, it was a total success. Too bad he didn't feel like celebrating.

Helen bent down and checked Andra's pulse. "Is she okay?"

"I think so. Just overload."

Out of the corner of his eye, he saw Angus crushing his daughter in a desperate hug. Gilda hung back, watching, wringing her hands as if she were itching to join in. She didn't.

"I know what that's like," said Helen. She reached

into the grass and picked up the luceria. "Looks like she lost this."

Paul's hand shook when he took it from her. Colors swirled inside the band, still more blue than anything, but not completely.

She couldn't even stand to give him another week. Only one hour. As much as he'd hoped for more, he understood. He'd made mistakes with her—unforgivable ones. He didn't deserve another week and he knew it. So did she.

He fastened the luceria around his neck and felt the first leaf fall from his lifemark. It fluttered down over his ribs, and before it had stopped falling, another joined it. Then another.

Living until sunrise might have been an optimistic estimate. At this rate, he'd have only a few hours at most.

He wanted to spend them with Andra, as selfish as that was. He swore to himself he wouldn't let her watch him die, but he ached to be with her just a little longer.

He had only a few moments before his soul would begin to fade and he'd have to leave her. He couldn't trust himself not to force her to take his luceria again. He couldn't trust himself not to hurt her or try to enslave her as he had before. He wanted forever with her too much to risk it. She'd be safer if he went to meet his fate as he'd been planning to do for decades.

He picked her up and followed the men to the vehicles. Even smudged with dirt and pale from exertion, she was still beautiful in the moonlight. He was a lucky man to have known her, even if it had been for only a few days.

A few days with Andra was worth more to him than a lifetime with any other woman.

Andra felt hungover. Her head pounded, her throat was sore, and she was pretty sure she was going to puke.

That was the thought that got her moving enough to sit up. She didn't want to get sick in her bed.

As she sat up, she quickly realized that she wasn't in her bed. She was in a car outside of that nasty cave. The doors were open and a warm summer breeze slid over her skin. Morgan and Madoc stood guard not far away, scanning the area, speaking too low for her to hear.

The whole night came flooding back to her. She'd done it. She'd gotten them out safely.

She'd found her baby sister, too. After eight years, she could finally lay Tori to rest.

Tears stung her eyes as she leaned down and unzipped the duffel bag. The tattered pink nightgown was no more than shreds now. The bones inside it were dusty, and she couldn't bring herself to touch them. This was Tori's body, but it wasn't all that she left behind. She'd brought joy to everyone around her. She'd given Andra more good memories than one person deserved to have. She hadn't lived long, but the years she'd had had been good ones, and she'd used them to spill more love out into the world than anyone else Andra had ever known.

Andra's tears dripped onto the red bag, leaving behind dark spots. "Love you, baby," she whispered. "You can rest now."

With that, Andra zipped the bag closed and put the past behind her. Tori wouldn't have wanted her to be sad. She would have wanted her to live and laugh and love.

Paul.

He was nowhere around, but when she stepped over the bag to get out and find him, she saw the glint of metal. His sword was sheathed, lying under Tori's bones on the floorboards of the SUV.

He never went anywhere without it. Why would he have left it behind?

Unless he wasn't coming back.

Andra started to panic and reached out for him so

she could find him, but there was nothing there. Her hand flew to her throat and only bare skin greeted her. The luceria was gone. Their time was over.

He'd left her. But why?

She scrambled from the vehicle and her legs gave out on her. She fell to the concrete and her palms burned from the impact. Madoc rushed to her and helped her up.

"Are you hurt?" he asked.

"Where's Paul?"

"He was here just a few minutes ago."

Andra pointed at the sword. "He left it behind. Where is he?"

Madoc watched her, his face expressionless. "He went to die."

Morgan elbowed him in the ribs. "You're not supposed to talk about it. Where the hell is your honor?"

"Fuck honor," growled Madoc. "She deserves to know the score."

"If he hid it from her," said Morgan, "it was because that was his choice. He didn't want her to know what he was doing."

She was stunned silent for a long second, then looked at Madoc. "What exactly is he doing?"

"He went to go take out a bunch of Synestryn on their way back into the cave."

"He what? Why the hell would he . . . ?" She didn't have time for that. She'd beat it out of Paul when she found him. "Which way did he go?"

Madoc knew. She could see it in his eyes.

Andra grabbed him by the shirt and gave him a shake. He was too big for her to rock him much, but he got the point. "Where did he go?"

Madoc's green eyes flicked to the right, toward a thick growth of trees. "Sun's almost up and he's been gone long enough to do the job. You won't find him in time."

The hell she wouldn't. She grabbed Madoc's cell

phone off his belt and ran as she scrolled through his phone book. Her legs were wobbly, but they held because this was important.

The phone rang, but he didn't pick up. She didn't bother leaving a voice mail. She just dialed again. Finally, on the fourth try, he picked up.

"Leave me alone, man," growled Paul.

"No," she said. "I won't."

He clearly hadn't expected it to be her on the line. "They told you, didn't they?"

"Yes, and I'm not going to let you do it." She was panting, barely able to make the words come out.

"This isn't a choice, Andra. I'm not going to let myself live long enough for my soul to die. I want you so much, I'd hurt you." He sucked in a hissing breath.

"I already lost Mom and Tori. I can't lose you, too." The mere thought was tearing her apart. She'd already lost too much. She deserved to have a little happiness for a change.

She plunged into the woods, using instinct to guide her. She wished she still had that connection to him—that she could hunt him down with her mind.

"I won't have you tied to me out of obligation," he said. His voice was growing weaker.

She had no idea what he meant. "What obligation? Love is never an obligation."

Brush and low limbs slashed at her face, but she pushed forward.

"You love me?" he asked, his voice lifting with hope.

Normally, she would have pulled back and put some distance between them. This was all way too fast, and she still had responsibilities that had to come first. Loving anyone was going to be a huge complication, not to mention the fact that if she admitted it, there would be no more hiding. No more lying to herself.

If she loved him, he could hurt her. If she loved him and he died, she'd never recover.

"Yeah," she whispered, though whether it was because she was out of breath or because she feared saying it too loud, she wasn't sure. "I love you."

"I wish I'd known. Too late now."

He let out a deep groan of pain. She could hear it nearby, and a split second later, it echoed over the phone. He was close.

"Can you hear me?" she yelled.

"Love ... you ... too." The words were so faint she could hardly hear them.

She saw a glimpse of blue that didn't belong in the forest. She wished like hell she had magic eyes again to help her see. The pink light of impending dawn was barely enough to guide her.

As she got nearer, she saw that the blue was his jeans. She'd found him.

Andra tumbled through the trees and fell at his side. He was leaning against a thick trunk, slumped and unmoving. Synestryn corpses littered the ground a few feet away. Dozens of them. Several deep gashes in Paul's flesh leaked red blood. His skin was growing paler by the second. His chest was bare, his shirt slit open along the right side where claws had torn it apart, along with his skin.

The tattoo over his chest was bare. All the leaves were dead, lying in a heap along his waist.

The luceria swirled with color, but that was fading fast.

Praying it wasn't too late, she yanked the thing off his neck and fastened it around her own. The ends locked together, but nothing else happened. She still couldn't feel him.

He wasn't breathing.

Panic made her tremble. She pressed her fingers to the side of his neck, trying to feel a pulse. It was faint and she wasn't totally sure that it hadn't been her own, but it gave her hope.

She laid his body flat, heedless of the bloody leaves and sticks littering the ground, and breathed into his mouth. His chest expanded. She did it again and again.

Then she felt it. A spark of power arcing between their mouths. He was still with her. She could feel him fighting his way back.

"Don't you dare leave me," she told him. "I need you."

The pool of power inside him was weak, but she siphoned off what she could and used it to knit his skin back together. She didn't know what she was doing, but she had to try something to keep him from bleeding out.

She covered his mouth with hers to breathe for him again, but this time he didn't need any help. He pulled the air from her lungs and kissed her in return.

His tongue slid over her lips and a low moan of pleasure vibrated in his chest. He tasted so good. So alive. Her heart overflowed with relief and gratitude.

His arms wrapped around her and he sat them both up. His mouth left hers and she could see his eyes blazing with emotion. "Tell me again," he ordered.

She knew what he wanted to hear. She could feel the hint of insecurity still lingering inside of him, and she loved him so much, she couldn't deny him. "I love you."

His eyes fluttered closed in pleasure. "God, that sounds good."

He grabbed his borrowed sword from where it had landed in the leaves, knelt in front of her, and sliced a shallow cut over his heart. "My life for yours, Andra. Forever and always."

Blood dripped down his chest, making her already twisty stomach twist harder. "I really wish you would stop doing that. I just patched you up."

He ignored her complaint and looked at her with such intensity she wanted to look away. "Give me your vow. I need it."

He needed *her*. Forever. That was what he wanted, and it scared the hell out of her.

Even so, even though she was afraid to tie him to a woman who made so many mistakes, she was more afraid of letting him go. He'd seen all her failures. He knew she'd let a lot of people she loved down. He knew she'd let them die. And still he wanted her. Trusted her.

It humbled her and yet also gave her the strength to trust herself. She wasn't perfect, but she didn't have to be. He would always be there for her when she was weak. He would always be there for her, period.

"I need you, too. So, as long as you don't get sick of me, I'll be right there by your side."

As the warmth of her promise settled over her, a smile of masculine satisfaction curled his mouth. "You're mine now, Andra, because I'm never going to get sick of you."

"Maybe I should rephrase my vow, then," she teased.

"Oh, no, you don't. I've got you right where I want you. Forever." He pulled her close and bent his head to kiss her just as the first rays of sunrise broke through the trees.

Chapter 30

Andra held her breath. Sibyl stood by Nika's bed. Tynan had used all the power he'd collected to heal those injured in the attack on Dabyr and had none left to help Nika, at least not for another week, so Sibyl was Nika's best chance right now.

Paul was at her side, his strong arm around her. His thumb caressed her waist, soothing some of the tension that had been growing in her since they'd arrived home.

And Dabyr *was* home now, as strange a place as it was.

Sibyl frowned and pressed her little hand to Nika's forehead. A moment later, she pulled back as if burned.

"Poor child," said Sibyl. "If she is to recover, it will not be by your hand."

Andra leaned against Paul, weak with disappointment. He held her up, solid and unyielding. "What do you mean? Isn't there anything I can do?"

"I'm afraid not."

Frustration burned bright inside her. She felt helpless. Even with all the power she possessed now, she still couldn't help Nika.

"There is hope, though," said Sibyl. "You rescued me, so I will offer you this boon."

"What? Any hope you can give me is more than welcome."

"There is one here who can heal her. I cannot see who he is, but I feel that he's already begun the process."

"He? So, not Grace?"

"No. Not Grace. She is a healing soul, and gives Nika great comfort, but that is all."

"So what do I do?" asked Andra.

Sibyl gave her a smile full of more wisdom than any eight-year-old should possess. "Nothing."

"Nothing?"

"You've done all you can. You brought her here. That will either be enough or it won't."

"And you can't tell?"

"No, I *won't* tell. It is no longer my turn."

Andra was trying to figure out what she meant, but she was having a hard time keeping up with all the cryptic stuff. "What do you mean, it's not your turn?"

Sibyl tilted her head, making her curls bob. "You are a sister. You know what it is like to have to share. Didn't you ever learn to take turns?"

Paul's body tensed beside her. "Are you saying that Maura can see things the way you can?"

"I said nothing of the sort. That would be against the rules." She turned and left, but stopped at the door. Without turning around, she said, "You're going to be happy together. I don't have to break any rules to tell you that."

After she was gone, the room seemed oddly empty. "O-kay," said Paul. "There are clearly some things I still don't know around here."

"Join the club. Holy cow, that girl is freaky."

"You'll get used to her," said Paul.

"I suppose I'm going to have to, aren't I?"

He bent and kissed the side of her neck, making her skin heat. His arms felt good around her. She didn't know how she'd ever survived without him. He was so much a part of her that she could hardly tell the difference between his presence inside her mind and her own.

His tongue slid down until it touched the edge of her luceria. As soon as it did, it wasn't just her skin that was hot. She was melting inside, only for him.

His wicked smile told her he knew it, too. "Yes, you are, because I'm never going to let you go."

Nika woke up suddenly, as if someone had shouted her name. The woman in the corner of her room had fallen asleep with a half-knitted sweater in her lap. Nika didn't recognize her, but she wasn't afraid.

For the first time in eight years, she wasn't afraid.

The feeling made her giddy, and even though her body was weak, she rose from her bed and left all that weak flesh behind. She had to go now.

It took her a moment to get used to the buoyant feeling of being outside her body. She was so used to the gnawing hunger and deep aches that the loss of both unnerved her, almost made her lonely for their constant companionship. Nika looked back at the bed where her shell lay. She didn't recognize that person. That skeleton.

Once again she felt a shock of recognition, as if someone had called her name.

She had to go to him. He needed her.

Nika slipped out of the room, through the front door, and into a long hallway. She didn't know where she was, but she knew where she was going. Instincts guided her like an arrow, and she raced along the dark, deserted hallways, floating above the floor.

She was close now. She could feel him—feel his power. She'd found her home, though she had no idea how she knew that was the case.

The door looked like all the others, but to her, it seethed with power. She pressed her hands against it and they slipped through the wood easily. He was in there. Sleeping.

She didn't want to wake him. He needed his rest; it

was the only time he escaped his pain. She didn't want him to hurt. That was why she needed to be near him. To soothe him. To take away his pain.

Nika glided through the door into a suite that looked much like the one she'd just left, but only on the surface. This place was a house of pain and torment. It was a house of sorrow and desperation. Even so, it was the most comforting place she'd ever been because *he* was here.

When she floated into his room and drifted onto his bed, he didn't wake. She wasn't even sure whether he could feel her or not, but she snuggled close to his side and draped her body over his. Warmth from his naked skin rose up to her, driving away the constant chill in her limbs.

As if sensing her need for warmth, he shifted in his sleep. He wrapped a thick arm around her body, pinning her in place with a heavy thigh. He didn't pass through her. It was as if he were the only real thing within this ethereal world.

Her spirit was surrounded by his heat, his scent.

This was what she needed. *He* was what she needed. He scared away the terror that haunted her. Even the vilest of creatures trembled before him. As long as she was with him, they couldn't hurt her.

Not anymore.

Chapter 31

Lexi was here. Zach felt her appear as if she'd walked through a portal into Dabyr.

He sprang from the weight bench and raced through the halls toward her. He wasn't going to lose her this time. Not again.

He turned a corner and threw himself at Drake's door, slamming into it. The thing shook, but didn't go down. She was in there. He had to get to her before she disappeared again.

Zach had just lifted his foot to kick the door down when it opened. Drake stared at him like he'd lost his mind, filling the doorway so none of Zach's craziness could spill over onto his beloved Helen.

"Where is she?" he demanded.

"Helen's on the phone. What the hell do you want?"

"Not Helen. Lexi. She's in there. You're hiding her." Zach shoved his way inside, but Drake kept his body between him and Helen.

She came out of the kitchen with her cell phone to her ear. When she saw him, her face drained of all color. She put her finger to her lips for silence and said into the phone, "No, Lexi, it's fine. No one's hurting me."

Lexi wasn't here. She was on the phone.

Shit.

It took Zach a long moment to recover from the

crushing disappointment. She wasn't here. He couldn't see her. Touch her. He couldn't take care of her.

He couldn't paddle her ass for running away from him.

"Of course I'm sure," said Helen. "You're wrong about these people. I don't know what your mother told you, but she was wrong, too. They're the good guys."

Zach glared at Drake for standing in his way. "Let me talk to her," he told Helen.

Helen's eyes widened and she shook her head, making her braids sway. "At least let me meet you somewhere and talk to you. I swear I'll come alone."

"Like hell you will," said both Drake and Zach at the same time.

Zach used the momentary distraction to reach past Drake and take the phone out of Helen's hand.

"Hello, honey," he said, struggling to keep his voice calm when all he really wanted to do was scream at Lexi for abandoning him.

"Zach." Fear filled her voice, but it couldn't disguise the fatigue that flowed through that single word.

"Where are you?"

"Phoenix. Or maybe it's Madison. I get the two confused."

"Enough with the smart-ass routine. Where are you?"

"Somewhere safe. Somewhere you and your monsters will never find me."

He clutched the plastic so hard it creaked in his grip. Anger pumped through him along with something else— something needy and desperate and afraid. "Where are you, honey? I need to come find you."

"No." The word wasn't as forceful as she'd probably meant it to be.

"Please, Lexi. I need you." His voice was so full of pleading that Drake looked at him funny, but he didn't give a shit. He was beyond pride.

"No. You're trying to trick me again. It won't happen. And I swear to God that if you harm a hair on Helen's head, I'll hunt you down myself and choke you with your own balls."

"We'd never hurt Helen. She's one of us now."

A choking sob filled the line. "Oh, God. What have you done to her?"

"We've given her a home. A family. We protect her and keep her safe. And we want to do the same for you, honey."

"Liar! Mom said you all lied as well as Satan himself. Now I know she was right. About all of it."

"I don't know what she told you, but none of us would ever hurt you. Just let me meet you. Talk to you."

"You'll try to abduct me again."

"I won't," he lied.

Another soft sob filtered through their connection, breaking his heart. She was in pain. Suffering. Tired. Everything inside him screamed for him to go to her, but he didn't know where to go. "Please, Lexi. Give me a chance. I want to help you."

"I wish that were true, Zach. God, do I wish that were true. I'm in so much trouble. I—"

There was a loud banging sound on her end of the line. Panic raced through Zach, making him reach for his sword. "Lexi? What's going on?"

She lowered her voice to a whisper. "I gotta go. They're here."

"Who is there? And where the fuck are you?"

"Not who. What. The monsters have found me again."

Monsters? She meant Synestryn.

Another loud boom filled the line.

Zach raced out of the suite toward the garage. "Lexi. Tell me where you are. I'm coming to help."

"You already know where I am. You sent them."

His heart was pounding so hard, he could barely speak. "No, honey. I didn't. Where are you?"

She hesitated. Another loud boom was followed by a crashing sound, like glass breaking. "Texas," she whispered. "Denton, Texas."

The line went dead.

"Lexi!" screamed Zach into the phone, but it did no good. She was already gone.

He heard Drake's heavy steps behind him as he raced out of the suite and down the hall, but he didn't slow. He jumped into his SUV and screeched out of the compound garage, down the long driveway. If the gate wasn't open by the time he got there, he was going to blow through it.

ALSO AVAILABLE

FROM

Shannon K. Butcher

BURNING ALIVE
The Sentinel Wars

Three races descended from ancient guardians of
mankind, each possessing unique abilities in their battle
to protect humanity against their eternal foes—
the Synestryn. Now, one warrior must fight his own
desire if he is to discover the power that lies within
his one true love...

Helen Day is haunted by visions of herself surrounded
by flames, as a dark-haired man watches her burn. So
when she sees the man of her nightmares staring at her
from across a diner, she attempts to flee—but instead
ends up in the man's arms. There, she awakens a force
more powerful and enticing than she could ever
imagine. For the man is actually Theronai warrior Drake,
whose own pain is driven away by Helen's presence.

Together, they may become more than lovers—they may
become a weapon of light that could tip the balance of
the war and save Drake's people...

**Available wherever books are sold or at
penguin.com**

THE
DRESDEN FILES
The #1 *New York Times*
bestselling series
by Jim Butcher

"Think *Buffy the Vampire Slayer* starring
Philip Marlowe." —*Entertainment Weekly*